W9-BYN-452

NO LONGER THE PROPERTY OF
BALDWIN PUBLIC LIBRARY

Eight for Eternity

Books by Mary Reed and Eric Mayer

One for Sorrow
Two for Joy
Three for a Letter
Four for a Boy
Five for Silver
Six for Gold
Seven for a Secret
Eight for Eternity

Eight for Eternity

Mary Reed & Eric Mayer

BALDWIN PUBLIC LIBRARY

Poisoned Pen Press

Poisoned
Pen
Press

Copyright © 2010 by Mary Reed & Eric Mayer

First Edition 2010

10 9 8 7 6 5 4 3 2 1

Library of Congress Catalog Card Number: 2009931421
ISBN: 9781590587027   Hardcover
      9781590587188   Trade Paperback

All rights reserved. No part of this publication may be reproduced, stored in, or introduced into a retrieval system, or transmitted in any form, or by any means (electronic, mechanical, photocopying, recording, or otherwise) without the prior written permission of both the copyright owner and the publisher of this book.

Poisoned Pen Press
6962 E. First Ave., Ste. 103
Scottsdale, AZ 85251
www.poisonedpenpress.com
info@poisonedpenpress.com

Printed in the United States of America

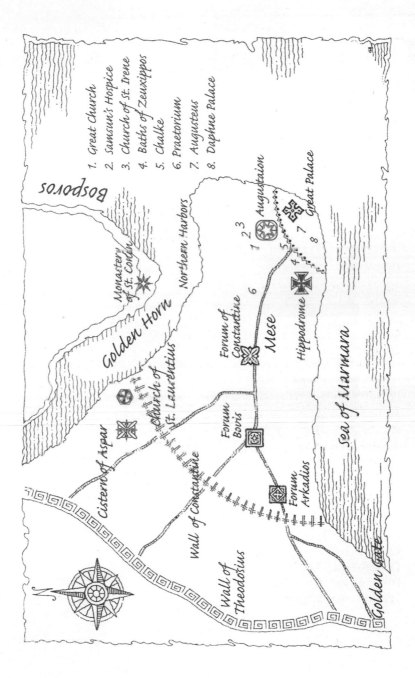

Bosporos

Golden Horn

Monastery of St. Conon

Northern Harbors

1. Great Church
2. Samson's Hospice
3. Church of St. Irene
4. Baths of Zeuxippos
5. Chalke
6. Praetorium
7. Augusteus
8. Daphne Palace

Augustaion

Great Palace

Mese

Forum of Constantine

Cistern of Aspar

Church of St. Laurentius

Forum Bovis

Wall of Constantine

Forum Arkadios

Hippodrome

Sea of Marmara

Wall of Theodosius

Golden Gate

Prologue

January 10, 532

The condemned man narrowed his eyes against the January sun, a brilliant translucent disk suspended in the early morning mist.

He would have shielded his gaze but his hands were bound behind him. He could no longer feel his feet. They had become dead things during the short voyage across the Golden Horn to the place of execution. Sandals offered no protection from the cold radiating up through the bottom of the boat.

The Urban Prefect's men had dragged him from his room just as he was finishing a plate of olives. They hadn't even given him time to change into his boots. The boots were left by the bed. They would sit there for a long time, or until one of the servants thought they could be stolen with impunity.

When he was born the ancient mid-wife who fancied herself an oracle told his mother that her son would die in his boots.

Apparently she was mistaken.

He moved forward as slowly as the guards would allow. Perhaps he was still asleep at home suffering through a dream brought on by a tainted olive. The fog drifting off the nearby water lent a dream-like appearance to the surroundings.

The Prefect had ordered a scaffold to be hastily erected on a stretch of waste ground across the Golden Horn from the city. Workers had been hammering timbers together even as the condemned man was being found guilty in the Prefect's private chambers.

Despite the hasty preparations, word of the executions had spread. From all around came the murmur of a restive crowd. Some were there to gawk, others to revel, still others to protest. The fog reduced them to shadowy ghosts moving through a distant underworld.

The prisoner paid no attention to the phantoms. He struggled to conceal the panic he felt.

His captors had taken away his bright green dalmatic decorated with roundels depicting horses and chariots, and dressed him an undyed tunic that hung straight from shoulders to knees, the clothing of the lowliest laborer.

Even so, they could not take away his dignity. They would have to content themselves with taking his life.

Broken chariots and other rubbish had been dumped along this stretch of foreshore. A bearded face peered up from between the broken spokes of a wheel. A marble hand lying nearby held a rein. The shattered statue of a once-revered driver consigned to oblivion, perhaps to make room in the Hippodrome for new heroes, or for yet another likeness of the charioteer Porphyrius.

The thought of oblivion returned to nip at the condemned man's consciousness for the hundredth time. A void opened up inside him, a sensation of falling. A bitter wind from the direction of the scaffold seemed to bring to his nostrils the faint reek of death. He was not alone this morning in dying.

And for what? For instigating a minor commotion to call attention to injustices being visited upon the population.

By what right did Justinian take the life of someone who only sought decency and fairness for his fellows? The emperor was nothing more than a man. Why should he live and others die at his whim? No, the emperor was not a man. He was a demon.

It was time to depose him.

The point of a spear prodded the young man in the back so hard he winced.

"Hurry up," came a voice from behind. "You'll be late for your appointment. My fingers are freezing. I don't want to be shivering out here all morning."

"Show some respect," said the guard walking beside the young man. "We all have to make the final journey sooner or later."

"Not with a rope around our necks we won't," grunted the other and blew on his hands noisily. The dim cloud from his breath drifted out in front of them in the cold air.

The prisoner had witnessed executions. He had always wondered about that instant before oblivion, when the noose snapped tight around the neck, before the head lolled lifelessly to the side.

During the night, in his cell at the Praetorium, he drew back to that final breath. What could it be like? To die, instantly? Or would it be so quickly done? No, even his most terrible imaginings could not encompass anything other than a quick death.

Do we know anything except by reflection? Even as we taste the wine, we are noting an experience already receding into the past. Would a hanged man recall crossing from life to death? What can such a passage be like? Would it be experienced and immediately forgotten? Or never experienced at all?

He had argued the question with himself and concluded he would never be aware of his ending. He would simply cease. And then a terrible horror blossomed in his chest.

He was going to die.

It was impossible. Yet inevitable.

Although he considered himself a good Christian, he did not pray. The words from the Gospels moved him profoundly when he heard them in the Great Church but he realized now that they had failed to instill in him any belief strong enough to call upon in his dark cell. He could not recall clearly the god of love. What came to mind were fiery pits, judgment, and eternal torments.

He decided to seek refuge in his own memories. But which? The thrill of his favorite team winning a chariot race seemed trivial, the pleasure of fine dishes served at a banquet a mockery. He thought of women he had known. One in particular. But what comfort was there in contemplating eternal separation? Instead, he settled on a recollection of himself as a child, playing with a small, carved, brightly painted horse, while seated in the sun beside the fountain in the garden of his father's house under the watchful gaze of an old servant.

One of his escorts took hold of his arm. The condemned man realized with a shock they had reached the wooden steps leading up to the platform from which he would step into eternity. He placed his dead foot on the first of the steps.

As he mounted the stairs the noise from the spectators increased. The guards looked around nervously. Their hands tightened on their spears.

Then he finally stood in the place he had envisioned so many times in the hours after his sentencing. He had seen it all clearly, in the future. A few hours hence. A long time ahead. Not now. His heart leapt. His throat tightened. He couldn't breathe. He struggled to force himself awake, to break through the black membrane of sleep.

He could not.

He was dimly aware another prisoner now stood beside him. He didn't want to look, didn't want to see the final preparations being made. It would be too much like looking into a mirror. He felt the platform tremble under heavy footsteps. Guards? The man who would carry out the Prefect's orders?

No, he would not look. He directed his gaze away into the distance, avoided looking down into the square hole on whose edge he stood or up to the stout wooden timber crossing the empty space.

Hadn't they been given enough time to even construct a trapdoor? Was it so urgent that he be deprived of life?

There was a monstrous roar of voices. The fog swirled away, revealing a sea of faces gaping upwards. A sparse line of guards edged backwards toward the scaffolds, pressed relentlessly by the assembly. Shouts and imprecations against the emperor filled the air.

He heard a thump and looking down saw the noose lying on the planks at his feet where the executioner had dropped it. Someone cursed the executioner's clumsiness. The crowd jeered.

Then he felt the rope go over his head. It was heavier than he had expected. It rasped his neck as it was pulled into place.

He looked across the Golden Horn. Mist ascending from the black water entwined the hills of the narrow promontory upon which Constantinople sat, shrouding its forums and streets in a luminous cloud. Here and there the top of a building emerged. In many places crosses made of wood and stone jutted into view, simple and elaborate, erected on churches and residences.

A vision of heaven, or of the site of numerous crucifixions.

He felt the executioner's warm breath, stinking of garlic and cheap wine, on his cheek as he leaned forward to adjust the rope with shaking hands.

The spectators surged forward. It seemed almost that they might overwhelm the guards and carry the condemned to safety. The Prefect's men managed to establish a cordon at the very base of the scaffolds.

"Hurry up!" one of the guards yelled. "What's taking so long?"

I am still alive, the young man told himself. There is still time. Death has not arrived. Not yet. Something glinted above the mists across the water. He recognized the statue of Constantine atop its high column. The emperor, crowned with a halo of seven rays, gazed toward the rising sun.

A hand hit him between his shoulder blades. He stumbled forward, toward the hole, unable to balance himself. He could see the ground below. The abyss opened.

Then he was lying on his back.

He blinked. Confused, paralyzed. Why could he not move his hands?

He remembered nothing. Where was he? In his bed?

No. On the ground. It was cold. There was a fiery pain in his side. He could not cry out. Something was wrapped round his throat.

Now he remembered.

He lay there looking up, past the dangling rope, at a square of lightening sky where a gull circled.

He was engulfed in a deafening rush of voices.

"Still alive," he heard someone say. "We'll have to do it again."

Chapter One

"The prisoners have escaped, excellency. My men are searching for them."

The lamp light trembling in the corners of the vestibule of the Church of Saint Laurentius made the speaker look old, accentuating his white hair and deepening the shadows in the furrows in his long, doleful face. He still held the parchments John had presented. One identified John as an imperial official. The other was a direct order from the emperor. An order that had become impossible for him to carry out. Sebastian's finger nervously traced and retraced the embossed lead of the imperial seal that had secured a cord around the parchments.

"As you can plainly see, I was sent here to take custody of the prisoners on behalf of the emperor," John said. "The guards here were supposed to assist me in returning them to the palace. But you tell me the two men are gone! You are…?"

"Sebastian. Commander of this detachment of the urban watch, excellency. I am under orders from the Urban Prefect Eudaemon."

"And I am a member of Justinian's privy council. From your stare I see you are doubtful. You are welcome to argue the point with my superior, Narses, provided the imperial treasurer will speak with you. How did two half-dead men manage to escape from your custody? The emperor will doubtless also wish to interview you about it."

The tall, slender man in the long, dark blue cloak towered over the stooped commander who looked up with a horrified expression. It was no secret that interviews with Justinian could end in painful visits to certain cramped rooms beneath the Great Palace, well equipped with arcane devices and sharp-edged instruments. "I cannot say how it was accomplished. Certainly the prisoners were far from dead...they may have come close to death on the gallows...but to have raced off like they did. The young fellow with the imperial seal said the two were wanted at the palace immediately and my men were to escort them."

"Imperial seal?"

"Yes, excellency. I looked at it closely. It was genuine. It was the same as this one." He nodded at the oval of stamped lead in his shaking hand. "That's why I'm confused. It isn't often one receives imperial orders and rarely twice in the same evening." His voice trailed off. He didn't have to add that it was even less often that such orders turned out to be conflicting.

"A young fellow, you say?"

"Even younger than you."

"Did anyone see them escape?"

"No, excellency, I—"

"Then how do you know they raced off?"

"They must have, to have got away, to have eluded my guards... so far. If they had still been in the vicinity of the church—"

"Is there any indication which direction they went?"

Sebastian shook his head. "I sent the young man down the stairs and remained here at my post. Someone raised the alarm when the guards discovered the vault was empty. I sent them out immediately in pursuit."

"This was when?"

"Not long ago. I'm not certain. Events have been happening so fast...."

John studied his surroundings. Even at this late hour worshipers streamed in and out of the church. Perhaps they had all come to pray to Saint Laurentius for safety from the unrest breaking out across the capital. As a Mithran, John found it strange how Christians despised those who refused to worship the one true god, while constantly imploring the aid of their own lesser deities which they termed saints.

"I will need to speak to your guards when they return, Sebastian. Let us hope they bring those prisoners back with them. Wait here."

John pushed open the heavy church door and went out into the dark street. He needed to organize his thoughts.

The odor of burning hung heavily on the air. The church sat halfway up the side of one of Constantinople's seven hills. Smoke coiled upwards from the foot of the slope where darting tongues of flame illuminated an irregular pile of ruins. Figures moved about, attempting to extinguish the remains of the blaze.

Two prisoners whom the emperor needed very badly were now at large in the troubled city. One was a Blue, the other a Green, members of the two main factions who supported the opposing chariot teams at the races in the Hippodrome. The factions loved mayhem as much as racing. Bound together by nothing more than the color of their charioteers' tunics, they ran in packs like wild dogs, fighting, robbing, and killing for the sheer joy of it.

They hated each other and frequently turned whole streets into battlefields because a charioteer's whip had strayed to his opponent's horses during a race or a supporter of the wrong team had joked about the poor embroidery in a colleague's cloak. But their anger was readily turned on any target that caught their attention—magistrates, Jews, Isaurians.

At present their target was the emperor.

Certain unspecified injustices perpetrated by Justinian had been the excuse for a public disturbance. Several of the participants were ordered executed but two survived their hangings, were rescued, and brought to the Church of Saint Laurentius.

Justinian wanted those two men. That they were beyond his reach would be a vexation to the emperor and even more of a problem for John, his chamberlain.

John took a deep breath of the cold air.

How long could he afford to wait for Sebastian's guards to return?

He remembered something. He walked a few paces to a stairway leading up an alley alongside the church. Streets with stairs were not uncommon given the city's terrain.

A beggar huddled in the dark at the foot of the stairs, barely visible.

John smelled his presence before he could see him, the sort of odor that emananted from the cages in the menagerie Empress Theodora kept on the place grounds.

"You were sitting here when I arrived," John addressed the man. "Did you see anyone running away before that?"

The beggar lifted a bristly face. His eyes were faint patches of fog.

"I am blind, good sir."

"Your name?"

"Maxentius, good sir."

"Is this your usual place?"

"On cold nights the good priest allows me to sleep inside the church, but tonight my way was barred by guards. They'd as soon see a poor creature freeze to death as let him inside. I live on charity…" A hopeful note entered his quavering voice. "Charity, yes. Those who attend this church are always generous. Perhaps…."

John ignored his entreaty. "Despite your lack of sight, can you observe much?"

"Indeed, I am aware of all the comings and goings from the church, which is why I sit here. Also, I am safe from those fools who dash about knocking down innocent passersby in their hurry to get to the wine shop or brothel. It is a good place to ask for charity, being so near the church. Charity, good sir, is all too often overlooked by busy citizens and—"

"Have there been any Blues or Greens around tonight? A group of them, perhaps? Or just one or two?"

"None, thank the Lord. When the factions roam the streets nobody's safe! When they come out to play and start wielding their blades, I go into the church. So far at least." Maxentius raised his head slightly, as if listening. "I hope the guards have left the church before those ruffians arrive here again."

"You are able to identify faction members?"

"Usually. Always when they are in groups, because of the way they talk. Both their manner and their words."

"I will instruct Sebastian you are to be allowed inside if the Blues and Greens turn up."

"You are interested in the Blues and the Greens, good sir? Have they wronged you? As they wronged me? If not for them I would not be sitting here in the cold begging."

"Is that so?"

"I swear to it. I worked as a lamplighter in the Great Church. I came across some of those ruffians carving blasphemies into a wall. They grabbed the burning lamp I carried and threw the oil into my face. And that is why I am reduced to depending on the charity of good people like yourself."

John had not noticed any sign that the man had ever been burned, but the shadows on the stairs were so deep he could hardly make out the bristly face. He handed Maxentius a coin. "I realize you couldn't have seen anything," he said, cutting off the beggar's profuse thanks. "But did you hear anyone run by within the past hour or so?"

"Yes, good sir. I heard the church doors burst open and people raced out, heading in every direction, screaming and shouting."

That must have been after the alarm was raised and the search for the missing men began, John thought. "Did you hear anyone running earlier?"

"Many people passed by. None were running."

Sebastian had insisted the prisoners had raced away, but since no one had seen them go that was only supposition. They might have left stealthily, but how could you ask a blind man whether anyone had crept by him quietly?

"Did you hear anything unusual?" John asked.

"Some military men went by."

"Military men? What made you think that?"

"The sound. Heavy boots on the cobbles."

"Anyone can wear heavy boots."

"The noise a soldier's boots make is unmistakable. And there's the creak of the leather armor, the rattle of swords in scabbards. Even the smell of them." Maxentius paused. He wrinkled his forehead and his eyelids closed briefly over his foggy eyes. "Ah. How can I describe it to a man fortunate to be sighted? I'm sure they were military men of some sort. When I heard them coming I scrambled into that doorway over there and hid. Just as well because they went up these stairs."

"And you say they weren't running?"

"No, excellency."

"Why did you think them unusual?"

"Because they were grunting and cursing. 'Hold on,' they were saying. 'Careful. I've got it.' They must have been carrying something heavy."

Or two things, John thought. He was not hearing a description of two prisoners who had been freed and fled but rather of men who had been carted away. The stairs were steep and narrow enough that it would have been awkward carrying two bodies up them. Corpses were more difficult to handle than sacks of wheat.

"How many of these men were there?"

"At least two."

"At least? You think perhaps there were more?"

"Yes, sir. There could have been three. Or four."

Enough to carry two murdered men, John thought to himself. "Where do the stairs go?" he asked.

"To the cistern."

John muttered a curse. "Mithra!"

◇◇◇

John ran up the steeply ascending, staired alley, guiding himself with one hand on the brick walls of the buildings on his left.

The darkness of the alley rendered him nearly as blind as the beggar he had left. Here and there an ill-fitting shutter high up in a wall revealed a thin orange line that did nothing to light the Stygian gloom.

He was ready to draw his blade instantly if necessary. And it might well be needed. There were still roving bands of the factions to be met, particularly in darker reaches of the city such as this, and increasingly in public squares. As the marauders grew bolder there were more reports of them breaking into houses. In this quarter the residents had long since barred their splintered doors and closed the shutters of the mean houses leaning toward each other over the narrow byways, as if in confidential conversation.

John was breathing hard by the time he reached the top of the incline. The long, heavy wool cloak he had worn over his usual light dalmatic for the chilly journey from the Great Palace to the Church of Saint Laurentius impeded his running. He cut across a packed dirt area, went past a tethered donkey, ducked under an archway, crossed a squalid courtyard, and stepped into a wider thoroughfare lit by a burning cart. Moving through the open area beyond, he became acutely aware of the immense starry dome that suddenly opened overhead. Glowing flecks of ash drifted into the sky.

Abruptly he stopped. The empty space he had been about to traverse was in fact a black sheet of water. He could see reflections of firelight in the surface.

John forced himself to approach the edge of the cistern. He did not like deep water. A long time ago, he had seen a military colleague drown.

The water might have been polished black marble, reminding him of the floor of a palace reception hall. It beckoned him to step forward and test its illusionary surface. John's lips tightened. He consciously slowed his rapid breathing, only the result of running, he told himself.

He scanned the surface of the cistern.

Something floated near the edge. He walked carefully along the verge until he could make out a lumpy half-submerged shape, then knelt down.

The water's surface was less than an arm's length below ground level. He lay down and reached forward tentatively. The floating object remained beyond his reach. Bubbles began to escape from beneath it. Whatever the object was, it sank deeper.

Gritting his teeth, John pushed the upper half of his body over the water. The black surface tilted up toward him as he stretched his arm out again. The tips of his fingers brushed cloth. He strained until his shoulder felt on fire. He tried to wriggle further forward, began to overbalance, and stopped.

More bubbles gurgled up and the object begin to vanish into blackness.

With a quick prayer to Mithra John grasped the edge of the cistern with one hand and let himself drop.

The water was freezing. He gasped and fought back panic.

Too late. The floating shape was gone.

John plunged a hand into the water at the place he had last seen it. His fingers touched and tightened around what felt like a thick, slippery cord.

He pulled himself clumsily out of the cistern with one hand, keeping his other gripped around the cord. He managed to get to his knees and tugged. Whatever the cord was attached to must have been heavy, judging from the resistance.

He put his other hand on the cord as well and saw that he held a long braid of hair, the Hunnish style adopted by many of the Blue faction.

The body finally bobbed to the surface. As John hauled it up onto the ground a brick fell out of its garments and hit the water with a splash.

John turned away. He stayed on his knees, shaking and dizzy. He had managed to keep himself from thinking as he plunged into the cistern, concentrating only on his duty. Now he could feel the black water clutching at him.

After what seemed a long time he composed himself enough to examine the corpse. The dead man's neck showed marks of strangulation and one wrist still had a loop of rope around it. At least he had not drowned. To John that seemed like a mercy.

The dead man was obviously one of the two prisoners. And since he was the Blue, then the other, a Green supporter, was still in the cistern.

John surveyed the rippling water and shuddered. Perhaps the Green had been weighted more carefully. He must be lying on the bottom, staring up into the dark.

Someone else would have to drag him out.

Chapter Two

"How could they have been murdered? It's not possible, excellency. I stationed men at every exit from the vault in case the factions decided to attack and managed to get by the sentries outside the church." Sebastian's voice shook.

The white-haired commander led the soaked John down a stone stairway from the vestibule and through a pillared vault to a heavy, nail studded door.

"I had two guards right here," Sebastian said.

The room beyond served for storage. Stacks of oil-filled amphorae sat in the corners. A row of silver lamps occupied a shelf below which an icon, paint peeling, stared out from between piled crates.

"You say that this young man with the sealed orders came down here and then it was discovered the two prisoners had gone?"

Sebastian's long face seemed to grow even longer and more mournful. "Yes. I sent him down the stairs after I saw his official seal. Before long someone shouted that the prisoners were gone and then all was chaos. Murderers were on the loose! Women started screaming they would be ravished and ran out. I asked the priest to help restore calm."

"The guards who were stationed at the door were sent out in pursuit?"

"I sent all my men out to apprehend the criminals. I thought they had escaped you see. I didn't realize they had been killed." The man's voice shook. John could see the growing panic in his face. Sebastian had barely been coming to terms with the disastrous possibility that he had allowed the escape of two men the emperor valued. Now he had to face the even more horrific fact that he had let them be murdered. "You can't think my guards were involved? Maxentius is blind," he said, voice shaking. "There are many military men in the city aside from those under my command. There are practically as many soldiers on the streets as beggars! Clearly the killers who dragged the bodies away weren't from the urban watch."

"Were the prisoners already gone when the young man who had come for them went down into the vault?"

"Yes, excellency."

"The guards down here confirmed that?"

"Someone yelled that the prisoners had escaped. Other guards came in a rush. I was calling out orders, of course."

"Was it discovered that the prisoners were gone when the door to this room was opened, or was it open when the young man arrived at it?"

"But...why would it be open, when my guards were posted right—"

"What did the guards say?"

"I didn't have time to question the guards, excellency. When they return—"

"And what about this man with the imperial seal? What did he tell you?"

"I...I...well...I never saw him again. He must have gone after the two prisoners, or gone back to report to the emperor." The thought of the emperor, whom he had failed so miserably, drained the blood from the old man's face. "All was confusion," he muttered. "All confusion."

John could believe it. The confusion in the commander's head alone was apparently enough to confound a philospher.

John looked around the small storeroom. Nothing seemed to be disturbed. It was ironic that two men should be saved from execution only to be murdered. And murdered and taken away just before the stranger with the seal arrived for them. If Sebastian were to be believed.

"I would not have permitted anyone to enter the church but the priest insisted the faithful should never be barred from prayer, especially in these unsettled times," Sebastian went on. "That's why the entrance at the top of the stairs and storeroom door were guarded rather than the main doors to the church."

The vaults at the bottom of the stairs, from which the storeroom opened, surely stretched underneath the whole of the church. There were almost certainly exits other than the stairs they had just taken. Tradesmen and laborers would hardly be encouraged to be coming and going through the vestibule. It would have been easy to get two bodies out of the church without anyone noticing.

A competent commander might have managed to see that every possible exit was guarded but he suspected Sebastian was not such a commander.

John turned to leave but paused. He had the uneasy sensation he was being watched.

He swung around. The damaged icon stared at him. The bearded face was lean and ascetic, his mouth set in a line. His great, black eyes reminded John of the eyes of a snake. Clearly the grim holy man did not approve of what he saw. Or was the icon's anger directed at whatever had transpired in front of the painted eyes earlier that night?

If only John could see what the icon had seen.

◇◇◇

"Please, excellency, warm yourself while we talk."

Leonardis, the priest in charge of the Church of Saint Laurentius, was a short, stout man with a voice so deep and resonant it might have been issuing from the vault beneath the church. He prodded coals in the brazier with an iron poker until flames leapt up.

The tiny room at the back of the church contained a plain wooden desk and stool. Scrolls and codices were heaped in niches in the white-washed plaster walls. The brazier, which appeared big enough to heat the stables underneath the Hippodrome, occupied the space in front of the wall on which hung an equally oversized silver cross. John wondered if the finely wrought metal were too hot to touch. He felt sorry for the gentle Christian god doomed to suffer the searing heat as well as a tortured death.

Even so he was glad of the heat beginning to dry his wet garments. Steam rose from his cloak and the odor of wet wool filled the air.

"We often read of monks who prefer unheated cells for their devotions," said Leonardis. "But Laurentius was broiled to death on an iron frame, as you doubtless know from your reading of the Holy Book. So it is only appropriate for his priest to mediate with the very means of the saint's torment always before his eyes." He wiped his perspiring forehead.

"What do you know about the Green and the Blue who were brought here?"

"Their rescue was a miracle. Or perhaps I should not call it a miracle, given they were common criminals. A sign from the Almighty. Twice they were hung and twice the ropes broke." Leonardis rubbed his hands together briskly, though they could hardly have been cold. "And then notice too one from each faction was spared. What if they had been chosen for behead ing like their companions in evil doing? A razor-sharp blade not so likely to break, is it? Yet they did not escape judgmen The Lord has meted out justice before the emperor had th opportunity."

"Who were they?"

"No names were mentioned. The Urban Prefect must kno He condemned them." Leonardis paused and stared at the co pulsing with heat. "It is not for us to question God's will," continued, "but doubtless much could have been learnt fr them. The emperor's servants are said to be most persuasive. could any dreadful suffering his torturers inflict be compare

the agony undergone by the blessed martyr Laurentius, broiled
to death—broiled! Imagine! Broiled like a swordfish! The faithful
call those fires that streak every year through the midsummer
skies the tears of Laurentius, but can all the tears of the blessed
cool those condemned to the fires of Hell, the endless pain? The
unendurable, never ending pain...." The priest's eyes glistened
as he spoke.

"Indeed," John said, noting the relish with which Leonardis
had posed his questions. Here was a man who enjoyed agony,
provided it was kept at a safe distance. John had met a number
of men with the same trait since his arrival in Constantinople,
and it was notable none of them had seen military combat. Yet
to hear a priest speak in the same way, with brightened eyes
and quickened speech, was repugnant. To kill was sometimes
necessary. As a youthful mercenary John had killed, but he
never inflicted extended agony. Was Leonardis a man who was
capable of violence?

"It was early when they were brought here. The fog was still
fairly heavy when the monks of Saint Conon appeared and
demanded entry," Leonardis went on. "As I understand it, they
observed what happened, decided to rescue the pair, and then
rowed them across the Golden Horn to this church. Christian
charity is all very well but I have wondered...were they bribed to
save these men or threatened that if they did not their monastery
would be set ablaze?"

Yes, thought John, either or both were possible.

Leonardis laughed. "You from the palace are so familiar with
such intrigues. How could the monks have known the ropes
would break? And not once but twice. No, perhaps it is more
simply explained, that those in the monastery saw the hand
of the Lord in the incident and felt called upon to intervene.
Remember, the monks had already seen others hung, dangling
there, not to mention still others losing their heads. They must
have felt the disgust we all feel when confronted with such dreadful reminders of mortality and human suffering."

John wondered if the priest would take so long to say so little under the ministrations of the emperor's torturers. "This church has no affiliation with the monastery?"

"No, but it possesses the privilege of sanctuary." Leonardis stirred the coals violently again. "I wish they had not been brought here. Those who attend my church have had countless miseries heaped upon them by the factions to which these men belong. I cannot tell you how many of my flock, men and women both, have come to me wounded and sobbing about robberies, violence, vile acts perpetrated on the defenseless, yes, even murder. And guards were posted to keep those criminals safe! Where are they when these men and their like roam the streets?"

John realized the priest would have been more than happy to light fires under iron frames for any Blue or Green captured. "At the time of the escape you were here in the church?"

"Yes, yes, I was, but I only heard about it when somebody shouted they had gone and guards rushed in. Armed men in a holy space! It was an outrage! And they entered while I was leading a service. A very large service it was too. In times such as these many seek the comfort that only the teachings of the church can give."

John thanked the priest and departed. The nave felt bitterly cold compared to the stifling room he had just left. The church was dimly lit and shadows were thick in the corners. The windows piercing the pale walls formed grey silhouettes giving no hint of what lay outside, but given the narrowness of the surrounding streets even on the brightest days the church must be dark without the aid of its hanging lamps.

The place seemed almost alive, menacing. The quiet space around him appeared ominous, the eyes of an icon hanging a few paces away seeming to examine John, in the fashion of the one he had seen earlier in the storeroom. This icon dismissed him with a sneer as one not of the faith.

John paused in the vestibule. He had recruited three lamp lighters he had found at work to bring the body of the Blue from the cistern but they had not returned yet. He supposed he would need to escort Sebastian back to the palace with him.

A cold wind was rising. Gusts swirled dust and straws through the half open door. He shivered. There was nothing else to be learnt here. He could see that many would believe that a supernatural hand had reached down into these surroundings to allow the missing men to escape without being seen.

If he worshipped the Christian god he might, perhaps, pray for guidance.

But he served another. And the emperor was not going to be pleased.

Chapter Three

A voice spoke from on high.

"These servants have failed us."

John lay alongside Sebastian, face down in front of a number of courtiers and guards gathered in the imperial reception hall, his forehead pressed against a pattern of peacocks with their tails spread wide. The elaborate tiling was not as cold as the water in the cistern. It wasn't his still damp clothes or the floor that made him shiver, but rather the measured words dropping onto his head.

The voice did not belong to the emperor. It was a woman's voice, feminine only in the sense of being pitched higher than a man's. It made John think of a knife being drawn across a whetstone.

Several advisors, clustered at the base of the platform supporting the double throne stirred uneasily, as if the breath of death had passed through them.

It had been known to happen.

From the corner of his eye John could see Narses, the emperor's chamberlain and imperial treasurer, John's superior at the palace. The slight, balding eunuch was eyeing John with ill-concealed rage.

"Caesar—" began Sebastian.

"Silence, you old fool, or we shall make certain you cannot talk again." Empress Theodora's voice was now chillingly sweet. "We shall deal with John shortly. But first...."

A pair of jeweled scarlet shoes entered the periphery of John's limited vision and the musky perfume favored by Theodora announced her approaching presence. The empress had descended from the ivory throne and now stood close to the two men prostrated before Justinian.

A low chuckle escaped her as she tapped Sebastian's back with the toe of her shoe. "You come here stinking of smoke and fear. Can we wonder at it? Both of you have failed. You say you know nothing beyond the ludicrous story you have just related. You expect us to believe that an unknown person bearing an imperial seal arrived at the church just after several other unknown persons had murdered the prisoners and dragged them out of the church without you or your guards noticing? You must be forgetting some of the details, old man. Perhaps the urgent persuasion of needles will help restore your memory. Take him away!"

Three guards stepped forward and dragged the unresisting Sebastian out of John's line of sight. The scarlet shoes receded, and Theodora resumed her place next to Justinian.

"Approach!" the emperor demanded. "You may stand. Report."

John did as he was ordered.

As always, the emperor's face was a cipher. Apart from a slight tightening about his lips he appeared as if he were about to welcome an ambassador or perhaps watch a performance by palace musicians. It was the worst possible expression he could have worn. It meant he was angry and when Justinian was angry, Theodora was not pleased. And if Theodora was not pleased, inevitably blood flowed.

John glanced at the empress. A venomous smile curved her painted mouth into a ruby scimitar and her hooded, dark eyes were cold.

"Caesar." He bowed toward Justinian. "As ordered, I went to the Church of Saint Laurentius to bring back the two men who escaped hanging. Sebastian has reported on what happened before I arrived. I subsequently located one of the missing men in the cistern of Aspar. The body of the other can doubtless be recovered. At that point I returned to the palace with commander Sebastian."

"And where is the body you mention?"

"Outside, Caesar."

Justinian glanced at Theodora. Was he pretending to consider her feelings for the benefit of those present? She nodded, as the emperor must have known she would.

"Bring it in!" he ordered a silentiary.

Theodora smiled from her perch as the dead Blue was dragged in by his rope of hair and deposited beside John.

"If only the dead could talk," she remarked, "what interesting conversations we might have!"

Justinian glanced down at the sodden form. "More importantly, I can't offer the masses in the Hippodrome a corpse. They are not likely to be placated by having their colleague returned to them in such a state. The body of the Green is of no more use to me than this one. It can stay in the cistern. Narses!"

The man summoned stepped forward. "Caesar?"

"What is your opinion on this sorry affair?"

"If the crowds discover the prisoners from Saint Laurentius were murdered they are likely to believe you are responsible. Which is exactly what the culprits intended. These murderous outbursts which have offended our great city lately are not mere spontaneous demonstrations of vast ingratitude from a populace who are ruled with mercy and kindness." Narses paused to judge the effect of his flattery and then continued. "Disloyal persons are organizing these outbreaks. I suspect a plot by certain parties to depose you, Caesar."

Justinian's bland countenance did not change. "Your thoughts march in step with mine, Narses. I have made it my policy to treat the factions even-handedly. I have required both to obey the law. No fair-minded person could dispute it."

"That is so, Caesar. The populace well remembers the unruly days of Anastasius when the factions rioted every other month. People are being misled."

Justinian turned to John. "I have hopes your undoubted intelligence will save you yet, since up to now you have been a good servant. Because of that I shall permit you an opportunity to redeem yourself. Find out what is happening so that appropriate measures can be taken against the ringleaders."

"And don't leave half your task undone this time," Theodora remarked. The toe of her red slipper prodded the corpse John had recovered.

John bowed and began walking backwards to leave the imperial presence.

The massive double doors at the far end of the hall opened behind him. As he backed through they swung shut, blotting out Theodora's smile. For a heartbeat her image continued to float before John's eyes, superimposed over the ornate wooden inlays and embossed metal of the closed doors like an image of the sun when it has been stared at for too long. The thought reminded John too much of certain specialities exercised by several of Justinian's servants whose role it was to persuade those with information to part with it. Swift on the heels of the thought came another: Sebastian would soon suffer their ministrations.

John turned, walked past the silentiaries standing guard, and went out through a second set of doors into a long, broad corridor whose walls were covered with hunting scenes. The suffocating presence of the imperial couple began to fall away.

Justinian had reigned over five years, long enough to have acquired more enemies than John could possibly track though he had served the emperor, at first in a less elevated capacity, since the beginning of his reign. Though he knew the emperor well, he did not know him well enough not to fear him. No one did, except perhaps Theodora, who had been his wife before he ascended the throne.

Even as John formulated plans to undertake his investigation he smelled the cloying fragrance with which Narses customarily scented his garments. In a moment the eunuch overtook him.

Narses' bald pate barely reached John's shoulder. Except for the jewels in the cape around his narrow shoulders and the elaborate embroidery covering his dalmatic, he might have been one of the acrobatic dwarfs that so amused Theodora. The embroidery depicted scenes of some sort. John did not care to examine Narses closely enough to determine what they were.

"I may be able to assist you in this matter." Narse's voice was high pitched, with a mere hint of an Armenian accent.

It vexed John to take orders issued in such tones and he avoided doing so as much as possible. It had caused the two to clash frequently in the course of their duties. "Justinian instructed me to investigate, Narses."

"Which is not to say he has forbidden you to enlist any aid. I can see by the state of your clothes you have already encountered difficulties. Appearance counts for much at court, but then I need not tell you that."

It was true, a heavy, much worn cloak thrown over a plain tunic was not typical dress for an imperial audience. Immersion in a cistern had not rendered the attire any more appropriate.

"Sometimes," Narses continued, "sensitive matters are best handled by persuasion." His smile did not reach his gray eyes; their almond shape had encouraged idle court gossip on his parentage being more eastern than officially admitted.

"I don't indulge in bribery."

"Why? Why should people give away information for free? They are far more likely to part with it for a fair price. It is simply human nature."

John stared resolutely down the corridor. On the mural beside the door leading out into the gardens a brightly costumed hunter—an emperor perhaps—impaled a fawn on his spear. If the artist had ventured to present a truer depiction of life at the palace, he would have substituted a skewered courtier.

The guards at the door stood aside for the two high ranking domestics to pass. Outside, a covered walkway lit by torches led past a line of tall cedars, above which towered the dead black bulk of the Hippodrome.

The palace walls muted the sounds of the city. John could distinguish drunken laughter and raised voices, a reminder that life and death went on its usual round. The wind carried the smell of smoke, temporarily overpowering the familiar raw odor of the overcrowded capital. As he strode along at a pace suitable for a forced march he passed one after another the life-sized bronze emperors who maintained a vigil along the walkway.

Narses kept up with him. The older man—he had reached his fifties although his smooth features were of a man years younger—occupied a higher position than John among the emperor's staff. Among other duties he served as Justinian's treasurer, with the access to the resources to conduct an investigation in ways that John could not.

"It concerns me that you might not have time to delve into this important affair," Narses continued in his soft voice. "Aren't you making preparations for a banquet honoring that Persian emissary?"

"There will be plenty of time for that."

"It must be vexing, trying to arrange the seating so as to ensure certain guests feel themselves to be specially favored without anyone suspecting they have been disfavored. Isn't that what you do?" Narses gave a girlish giggle. "Justinian uses you most capriciously, doesn't he?"

"The seating is a minor part of the task, Narses. I arrange it because I do not necessarily trust the judgment of my subordinates."

"Very wise. This Persian takes offense easily. I have met him, during private negotiations over the treaty Justinian has offered."

"The Eternal Peace, you mean?"

"Yes. Everyone knows about it."

"As treasurer aren't you concerned about paying out eleven thousand pounds of gold to the Persians?"

"If the peace lasts for eternity that comes to very little per year."

"But it probably won't last ten years. These treaties never do."

"I wouldn't be so sure. The Persians only fight us for the gold. They aren't looking for territory. Put a city under siege and demand a ransom. Carry out a slaughter and ask for a bribe not to do it again. It's all about gold with them. As it is with most people. I have learned a great deal during my many years of service. You would be wise to accept my offer of assistance."

John had not served Justinian long but he had been given an increasing number of confidential tasks and the emperor frequently asked his advice, including him in the same sensitive discussions to which Narses had long been privy. Which greatly irritated Narses. John did not consider himself the older man's rival. Narses was ambitious. John was not, but lack of ambition was a weakness one did not admit at court.

"If I find myself needing help, Narses, I may avail myself of your offer."

"What makes you suppose you don't need my help right now? You may not be in a position to have noticed, but the grumbling from the senate can be heard halfway to the Golden Gate. There are even whisperings now inside the palace walls. In the streets and squares, men are setting words aside in favor of stones, torches, and knives."

"Everyone in the city realizes that."

"But some of us appreciate it more than others. Those of us who lived through the anarchy of Anastasius' reign do not want the factions to return to the prominence they had then. Do you remember how they stoned Anasatasius at the Hippodrome? How they sided with the usurper heretic Vitalian? How Anastasius went to the factions without his crown, and humiliated himself to keep the peace? You do not, because you were not in Constantinople that many years ago."

"If you will excuse me, I must return home, Narses. It is late."

They had reached the end of the walkway, presided over by a bronze of Emperor Constantine, the founder of the city. Clearly, the man had been a soldier. A square featured face with a cleft chin sat upon a bull-like neck. The statue presented a sad contrast to the shrunken figure of the treasurer who wielded so much power in the present empire.

John turned away to cross the courtyard leading to his residence.

Narses raised his hand, gesturing John to stop. His volumi-
nous sleeve slipped down, revealing a preternaturally thin wrist,
the wrist of a skeleton or a starving beggar. Rings decorating his
fingers flashed in the torch light. "Justinian intended to present
the Green and the Blue to the masses at the Hippodrome. A
surprising and magnanimous gesture which would surely have
pacified all but the most hardened troublemakers."

"They were not murdered on my watch."

"I know that, my young colleague, but does Justinian appreciate it? What do you suppose Theodora is telling him? I am glad
she does not display such enmity toward me as she does to you.
Perhaps you do not realize the extent of your danger. Otherwise
you would not risk failing in your assignment by refusing to
employ every means at your disposal. And mine."

"The means at your disposal?"

"Why should we not assist one another? After all, we are
much alike, are we not? And consider. The credit would belong
to both of us. Your failure will belong to you alone."

"I would prefer to do the job myself and take credit for my
success."

Narses lowered his hand, his gaunt face as expressionless as
that of a snake. "You are a naive young man, John. You may find
such success to be as unhealthy for you as failure."

Chapter Four

January 11, 532

The full-bearded excubitor loitering near the Chalke gate to the palace took another bite from a wrinkled apple and pulled his cloak tighter around his broad shoulders. He looked toward the mouth of the wide thoroughfare of the Mese, past the beggars and hawkers of soiled goods both animate and inanimate who clustered in the courtyard near the massive bronze doors from which the gate took its name, not so close as to attract unwanted attention from the guards on either side but near enough to catch the attention of those passing in and out of the grounds.

On many mornings Felix stood guard here but today he was on watch for his own reasons. They did not include buying the half dead chicken thrust toward his face by a beggar, who had probably just stolen the pitiful fowl from a vendor. He swore and waved the man away.

Felix's colleague Bato laughed. "A bird like that's enough to make a man stick to apples and turnips like our emperor." Having finished his own apple, Bato tossed the gnawed core to the ground. It hardly had time to collect filth before it was snatched up and devoured by a thin boy.

"Here they come!" Felix exclaimed.

An eddy disturbed the crowd, which began to part, making way for a contingent of soldiers.

"That's not Belisarius," Bato replied. "It's Mundus."

The tall man at their head strode along with an easy swing born of countless days of foot marching. His men wore no armor or helmets, revealing hair bleached of color by the strong sunlight under which they had served in hotter climates. Each man was armed either with a spear over a shoulder or a long sword. The regular thudding of heavy boots echoed against the walls of the surrounding buildings.

Felix grunted. "Belisarius wouldn't be walking, I wager."

"Your Belisarius seems to spend most of his time consulting Justinian. Now, Mundus, there's a real commander. His Heruli are disciplined fighters, not the usual rabble who wave blunt spears at some old village women for the glory of Justinian and expect a fat purse at the end of it!"

"Mundus didn't force the Persians to beg for peace!"

"You don't suppose Belisarius did, do you? From what I hear, he had his men hiding in ditches. He was afraid to fight until his officers shamed him into it. Then he was forced to turn tail and run—from a gang of peasants armed mostly with shields. He probably would've bought that sick chicken just now to avoid a confrontation. If it hadn't been for Cabades dying and Chosroes taking the throne, the Persians would be at the walls of Constantinople right now and we'd have Justinian's eternal peace all right, being as we'd all be dead!"

Felix glared at Bato, who broke into a grin.

"You shouldn't take everything so seriously, Felix! Now I'm off to the Inn of the Centaurs to get a skin full of wine!"

"Don't wager on that racing game that was set up in front of the place the other day." Felix advised. "You may think only Fortuna influences those colored balls rolling down chutes and tunnels and popping out of archways here and there, but it's my belief the proprietor's found some way to fix the results. I lost half a month's wages!"

Mundus and his soldiers had tramped through the gate into the palace grounds and Bato went up the Mese in the direction from which they had come.

Felix wondered what, exactly, the soldiers had been doing out in the city on foot. Unrest in various quarters signalled the factions' way of demanding the release of the condemned men held at the Church of Saint Laurentius. The Urban Prefect had sent men to guard the church. Perhaps Mundus had been needed to quell violence elsewhere while Belisarius had been sent into the streets to make a show of force, to let the disgruntled factions see what they would come against if they were, in fact, looking for a fight.

Despite what Bato said, Justinian seemed well pleased by Belisarius' efforts on the Persian front. If the Persians hadn't been able to defeat him, a mob certainly couldn't.

Felix stamped his boots, trying to warm cold feet. There was a promise of frost in the crisp air. If snow fell, as it did occasionally, it would take its toll on the homeless who spent their nights huddled under porticoes. The boy who had eaten the remains of Bato's apple had stationed himself nearby, hand extended in a mute appeal for charity, the rags covering his feet fluttering in the icy wind. Felix tossed his core toward the urchin who deftly caught it on the downward arc.

Might have been me, Felix thought. The lad has a keen eye and looks sturdy despite being half starved. He might make a good recruit if—but at that point his speculation ended as he spotted the flash of sunlight on the Mese where the gathered people were scattering again.

"Belisarius," Felix breathed.

Led by their general, the mounted force clattered toward the Chalke, horses steaming in the chilly air. Felix caught a glimpse of Belisarius' face beneath the polished helmet—high cheekbones, straight nose, a black, closely trimmed beard. He presented the appearance of a patrician more than a warrior, looking too young to have seen combat, let alone to serve Justinian as a general.

As he drew even with the spot where Felix stood, Belisarius reined in his horse. For an instant Felix had the irrational idea that the great general had paused to speak to him. Instead, he turned his head in the other direction and Felix had the impression he was exchanging a few words with someone.

"An inspiring sight, Felix," came a voice from behind him. "It's enough to make a man want to leave the excubitors and sign on with him!"

The voice belonged to Gallio, captain of the excubitors.

Felix detected sarcasm in his superior officer's tone. He suspected Gallio hadn't fought with anything but his tongue for years. Reluctantly, he turned his attention away from the procession. "I'd certainly see more military action than I do keeping an eye on drunken courtiers."

The old captain gazed dourly at the horsemen streaming by. "Asking for trouble in my opinion, having two generals in one city. It's like having two women in one kitchen."

Judging from the size of his gut, Gallio knew more about kitchens than battlefields. Felix kept the thought to himself. "Considering what we've been hearing about the mood of the factions, Justinian is fortunate to have two generals close to hand if trouble breaks out."

"Fortunate? Perhaps. If they really are here by chance. Some whisper it is not the case. New orders for you, Felix. Choose several men you can trust. You'll be keeping watch on certain parties at the palace, though officially of course you are on duty guarding them from harm. Apparently Justinian has his suspicions."

Felix immediately forgot the show put on by Belisarius. Dealing with dangerous turncoats was a task that appealed to him. "You mean there are traitors in the palace? Who does the emperor suspect?"

Gallio shook his head. "You will hear when you report back." He looked after the armed force vanishing from sight on the heels of Mundus and his men. "Justinian's young commander has many admirers. But he has been sparring with armies in the deserts. The great Belisarius may find that battling angry gangs in narrow streets is a different proposition."

Chapter Five

John stood impatiently outside the Chalke gate and waited for General Belisarius to pass. He had already been stopped on his way out of the palace by the arrival of Mundus. The previous day, including his mission to the church, had been a long one. Then he barely slept. As soon as he dozed, the darkness closed in over him like inky water. Finally he lit a lamp and was able to drift off, only to come awake coughing up imaginary water, drenched in real sweat. Now the two boiled eggs hurriedly gulped down for breakfast sat in his stomach like stones at the bottom of a cistern.

He did not look forward to investigating the murders of the Blue and the Green. He didn't know where to start, except at the Hippodrome, the center of everything to do with the factions. And the Hippodrome was a very big place.

As John debated whether he should try to push through the crush which had cleared the street to make way for the mounted force, he saw Belisarius pause. His eye was drawn to a stocky, dark haired man, with whom the general exchanged a few words before continuing on into the palace grounds.

John knew the man. He had grown a slight paunch in the fifteen years since John had last seen him, but aside from that he looked no different than when they had served together as mercenaries outside Antioch.

"Haik," John called, as he strode through the crowd.

The man turned at the sound of his name. His face was long and sun browned, his hair and eyes glistening black. He had a great, triangular beak of a nose. More than once, his companions had remarked in coarse jest that if Haik were slain on the battlefield the vultures might be reluctant to feast on one of their own.

"Is it John?" Haik flashed the wide grin John recalled well. The teeth were large and even, but half of a front tooth was missing. Haik looked John up and down and his dark eyebrows rose. "Imagine running into you in the capital. And you're not dressed like a soldier either."

"Neither are you, my old friend. That cloak you're wearing is worth several months of a mercenary's pay. But you seem to have an acquaintance with at least one prominent soldier."

"Yes. Only in passing. Belisarius allowed me to travel from Antioch with his troops. I have business here."

The two men stood facing each other. They did not embrace as colleagues often do upon meeting. It was not John's way.

"Business, you say? Then you are no longer a military man?"

"No. I'm a pistachio farmer. I own a small estate."

"And what are you doing in Constantinople?"

"Right now, I'm looking for lodgings. I've been staying with Belisarius' retinue this past week and I don't want to strain his generosity."

"Stay with me, Haik. I have a big house all to myself. It isn't in the most salubrious part of the palace grounds, but right behind the stables."

"You have a house in the palace grounds? You are no longer a soldier yourself then?"

"We'll talk later. I have an urgent assignment. Ask anyone at the stables. They'll direct you to my house. I'll see you this evening."

◇◇◇

The narrow and hilly peninsula where Emperor Constantine built his new Rome two hundred years earlier had not offered an area of flat land large enough for a race track close to the palace grounds. At the Hippodrome's southern extremity, where the land sloped abruptly down toward the Sea of Marmara, a series of massive vaults supported the curved end of the track. From the base of the towering back wall, higher than most of the city's buildings, a series of archways opened directly into a vast substructure.

John stepped through one of the archways out of sunlight and into subterranean gloom. He waited until his eyes had adjusted, glanced around, then proceeded across an empty chamber to a wide corridor. Lit by torches even in daytime, the corridor mirrored the curve of the track above. It gave access to store-rooms for chariots and other racing equipment, stables, offices, supplies for the maintenance of the Hippodrome, temporary barracks for guards, makeshift jail cells, tiny chapels—all the appurtenances of a small city. When filled with 80,000 specta-tors the Hippodrome's population rivalled that of most of the empire's cities.

The secluded environs also served the needs of both trysting lovers and street women. Down here, during racing season, a prostitute could earn in a single day as much as she could make in a week in a dark alley, and while staying in out of the rain.

It was a place where criminals could work in private. More than one corpse had been found in the shadowy maze. John used caution upon entering.

A few paces down the corridor he met a man carrying a looped pile of reins. The chubby, dirty faced fellow glared at John with obvious suspicion. "You don't belong here. What are you up to, lurking about?"

"Looking for advice. I hear the Blues have a new charioteer."

"Word gets round faster than our best team. How did you hear about him?"

John waved a hand. "It's the talk of the taverns."

The other shifted his grip on his burden, and dropped several reins. "Can't keep anything quiet in this city," he grumbled. "But let them Greens try anything and they'll be sorry. Just so you know, we've men guarding the horses day and night and if anyone can sneak past our grooms to bury a curse tablet in the track they'll be demons indeed." He spat on the ground.

"I wouldn't put my money on a few lines of gibberish scratched on a piece of rolled-up lead. I'll wager on a driver with skill and brains. I was going to wager on this new man to win next time out but I hear he had an accident?"

"That's right. A bad accident. Some Greens caught him a couple of nights ago and broke his legs. Those kinds of accidents are happening all the time. Last week someone tried to poison Porphyrius."

"I'd like to meet one of your charioteers."

The chubby worker looked dubious. "It might be arranged...." His dirty fingers closed over the coins John handed him. "Yes, you'll want to talk to Junius. He's checking chariots to make certain nobody has tampered with them. If you hurry, you'll just catch him. You never know but what some Green has managed to bribe someone to do a little damage."

John found Junius, a tall, lean man with sinewy arms, in a cavernous storage room filled with chariots. He and a short companion were examining the underside of a quadriga propped up against one of the many pillars supporting the vaulted ceiling. John paused for a moment, half concealed by another pillar.

"Axle and pins in place, pole well seated," Junius said. "Perhaps that shadowy figure Porphyrius saw last night was a shade of the wine jug rather than the human sort."

"And perhaps not." The shorter man spun the left wheel. "Three spokes are partly sawn through from the inside. How long do you think the wheel would stay on once the race began?"

Junius uttered an oath. "Have it repaired and don't let it out of your sight while you do. Isn't there anything Porphyrius doesn't see?"

The other shook his head. "He's not human. Imagine anyone needing to sabotage the chariot of a graybeard like Porphyrius. He's too old to be driving chariots, let alone winning."

John stepped forward. "Junius?"

The charioteer didn't appear surprised by the interruption, just annoyed. "What of it?"

"I wish to talk to you. In private."

Junius laughed. "And a blade in the ribs in private too? You Greens must be desperate to think I'd fall for that."

"I'm not from either faction. I'm here on behalf of the emperor."

The wheel examiner guffawed. "A nomisma says otherwise, if I had a nomisma to wager!"

Junius stared at John for a heartbeat. "I'll talk with this man," he told his companion. "Leave us alone."

"You look familiar," Junius said, when his assistant had departed. "Haven't I seen you in the imperial box at the races?"

"You have a keen eye. There are always a lot of people in the kathisma."

"Few as tall. And you have the bearing of a military man. Very noticeable among all those perfumed flowers trying to brush up against Justinian's robes. What do you want to know?"

"First, one of those perfumed flowers is a prominent courtier who owns horses in which the Blues may be interested. I can put you in touch with him. If the races continue. Justinian is considering closing them down forever." He paused to let the statement sink in. "The emperor is not pleased with the factions. He's been told that there's talk of replacing him with one of Anastasius' heirs."

Junius pulled a rag from his belt and wiped grime off his hands. "You've been sent to deliver a warning."

"No. I'm looking for information. What about this seditious talk?"

"Nothing specific. There's always some malcontent ready to stir up the factions. Even a one-eyed fool can see the riots aren't always connected with who won the latest race. Some fight for the love of fighting. Some skulk round the edges looking for a chance to loot. Others brawl to defend the honor of their team."

"Indeed. I didn't need to venture into the depths of the Hippodrome to learn that. Tell me about those two who escaped execution."

"Nobody seems to know where they are. It's being whispered if they are not brought forward and pardoned there will be another riot. But then you must be aware of that too."

"So the rumors are true. What are the men's names?"

"I have no idea. I don't know every member of the factions personally. Everyone who attends the races is a faction member."

"Yes, but few of them are singled out for execution by the emperor. I would have expected word to spread quickly. Someone must know their names."

"No one around here knows the names of the emperor's enemies."

"No one would want to risk seeming connected to such men, you mean. How serious is all this talk? The usual grumbling or something more?"

Junius tossed the rag he had been using to the concrete floor. "I'm a charioteer, not a politician. I concern myself with chariots and horses, not plots. If you want to know more, ask Porphyrius. He's a palace favorite and I've noticed lately he seems uneasy."

"What makes you think so?"

"He's got a mansion in the city but the past few weeks he's been sleeping at the Hippodrome, on a bed of straw. Says there's evil abroad and he's staying here to help guard against it. I don't believe him. He can afford any number of watchmen and he's always boasted he's not superstitious."

"What is your explanation?"

Junius did not hesitate before replying. "I've thought about that. Of course the Greens are just as alert and have their own men here day and night. But consider, there are plenty of unused, out-of-the-way rooms and passageways down here. It's a perfect place to meet people unobserved, isn't it? Yes, I would certainly interview Porphyrius, but don't expect him to be as straightforward with you as I've been."

Chapter Six

John found himself wandering through the Hippodrome stables, undecided about whether he should seek out Porphyrius. The great charioteer knew the factions as well as he knew the turning posts of the racetrack. After all, he had raced for both the Greens and Blues during his long career and both had erected monuments to him on the narrow raised platform of the spina forming a barrier between the two arms of the U-shaped racetrack. If the factions were plotting together, Porphyrius would know. But if he had such knowledge why hadn't he brought it to the emperor's attention? Did John want to alert Porphyrius to his investigation? How long before he found out that John had been asking questions?

Besides, how did one interrogate a man who was immortalized in bronze? Although John's duties brought him increasingly into contact with the rich and powerful of the capital, he was still not entirely used to it.

The sound of John's name interrupted his debate with himself. He saw the grinning, beaked face of his old friend Haik.

"John! What are you up to here? Never mind. My business is done. It's getting late. Time for a cup of wine, I'd say."

"Perhaps it is," John replied without hesitation, happy to have his decision made for him. "There's a tavern I know not far from the Baths of Zeuxippus, on the way to my house. It's usually quiet."

"Quiet? Compared to your house?"

"You can't believe the number of servants that came with the house."

"Yes. I think I see what you mean. The last time we spoke we were probably sitting outside a tent, or maybe inside a tavern."

They made their way out of the Hippodrome. The colonnades along the street funneled a biting wind. Bits of straw swirled around their ankles. John recalled the fire he had seen near the Church of Saint Laurentius. One did not wish for wind when the factions became restive.

As they went by the entrance to the baths shrill shouts from a group of street urchins caught their attention. The urchins stood in the middle of the square in front of the baths and at first John thought they were playing. Then one of the boys charged at the other three with such ferocity, and was caught, thrown to the ground, and pummeled so unmercifully that it was apparent no game was involved.

The attacker rolled away and scrambled to his feet. Rather than taking to his heels he stood with clenched fists and shouted imprecations. He was a short, well-built child. His face looked fiery red, whether from the beating he'd taken or simply from fury, John couldn't tell. The other three replied in kind. They looked older than the lone boy, more gangly, but a head taller.

"Constantinople is a violent place," Haik remarked. "No one even takes notice."

It was true, the few passersby simply skirted the area around the dispute.

"I got in more than a few scrapes when I was a youngster," John remarked.

"And when you weren't so young too. Remember when we had the dispute with that—"

Haik's reminiscence was cut short as the younger boy gave a blood curdling shriek and flung himself at the others again, flailing his fists madly. The three stepped back, dodging the blows. One kneed the attacker. Another belted the back of his head with a fist. The attacker continued to lash out. Blood sprayed from the nose of the tallest boy.

Then John was sprinting toward the group.

He caught the tall boy's thin wrist before he could make use of the glistening blade he had suddenly produced.

John twisted until the blade clattered onto the pavement. He kicked it away.

He addressed the three older combatants. "All of you, return to your homes. Immediately."

When he let go of the wrist the boy sneered at him but backed away. The three walked off slowly, shuffling their feet, casting dark looks back over their shoulders.

Haik had retrieved the knife and squatted in front of the boy John had saved. "Such valor deserves a reward."

The boy took the proffered knife with one hand, while wiping blood off his face with the other.

"What was that all about?" Haik asked.

"They was Blues." The boy ran a short finger along the knife blade. "I'll cut their throats when they're asleep. They won't be able to sleep any more. I know where they live. They'll go to sleep and not wake up."

"The emperor hangs murderers," John said.

The boy didn't look at John. His eyes narrowed. "They deserve to be killed. I'll cut their throats."

"Because they're Blues?" Haik wondered. "You hate them so much because they're Blues?"

The boy gave Haik the same dead-eyed, uncomprehending expression he might have got if he'd asked a buzzard why it was ripping the entrails from a rotting dog.

"This boy is a Green," John explained.

"And my brother, too," the boy said. "That yellow bellied bastard who pulled the knife on me…his brother said something to my brother."

"It must have been very bad," Haik remarked.

"Something you daren't let anyone say and keep living," the boy said solemnly, "if he's a Blue."

"But why do you hate Blues so much?" Haik persisted.

"Well, they're just bad, is all. Just plain bad. Everyone knows that. My father told me so." The boy glanced at John and his eyes widened slightly. Had he noticed the dark blue tones of John's cloak? He quickly tucked the knife away inside his tunic.

"Go home," John told him sternly. "Don't murder anyone on the way." He added under his breath.

The boy whirled and ran off.

Haik straightened up. "The factions seem to be even worse here than in Antioch."

"Yes, and Justinian has been trying to keep order ever since I arrived in the city. He's passed laws against street violence and tried to mete justice out evenly. The Greens still claim he favors the Blues and the Blues insist he's abandoned them for the Greens."

"Does he favor one side or the other?"

"If you're a faction member, it depends on your point of view. There's no satisfying them."

Haik looked puzzled. "It can't be sheer hatred, can it? I've heard it said that the Blues support the wealthy and the Greens see themselves as champions of the masses."

"If that were the case there would be incomparably more Greens than Blues. Do you think any of those boys we saw fighting came from wealthy families?"

"But it is true that the Blues are orthodox, whereas the Greens are heretics, monophysites?"

"When it suits them. Which is to say when it makes a pretext for a good fight. They'll support any cause that gives them an excuse to wreck havoc. Remember, we were going to have a drink."

The tavern was nearly deserted. Recently, residents went about their business and then hurried to the safety of their homes. They could feel the great beast of the city stirring within its brick and marble carapace. The hard-eyed youths who usually loitered in groups of three or four now congregated half a dozen together. Their stares lingered on passersby for longer than usual. The beggar who always sat beside the baker's doorway was not in his accustomed place. A line of guards had rushed through the Forum Constantine for no apparent reason. The air smelled faintly of smoke. The fights between the street urchins had become more ferocious.

John and Haik went past the waist-high counter at the front of the tavern. Large pots were sunk into the mortar, some filled with wine, others with porridge and lentils, steaming fragrantly. Only after they sat down at the round wooden table in the back of the room did John notice that the wall mosaic at his shoulder depicted a race in the Hippodrome and a charioteer holding a trophy. It might well have been a portrait of Porphyrius. He couldn't help smiling ruefully to himself.

Haik raised an eyebrow.

"It's nothing," John said.

The tavern keeper rushed over, wiping his big red hands on the greasy tunic billowing over his belly. "Good day to you, sirs. How can I help you, sirs?"

He bowed and beamed when he addressed them and returned speedily with what they had ordered.

John and Haik were dressed too well for a place like this. Provincials with mud on their boots gaped at them while a couple of laborers in leather breeches glanced in their direction and whispered to each other. A young man in filthy clothing embroidered in gold thread sat hunched with his head in his hands. A long braid of hair dangled down into the puddle of wine on his able. He took furtive looks at John and Haik.

John saw Haik's gaze move to the drunken Blue, then away. "I hope none of our young combatants end up like him." Haik pushed a lank strand of black hair off his forehead. "You'll have to direct me to a tonsor, John. I'll be mistaken for a ruffian or a chickpea."

He had always been vain, John thought. "There is a fellow at the baths who won't nick your skin with a razor or nick your ears with too much gossip."

"It's lucky I met you." Haik stuck his knife into one of the sausages on his plate. "Imagine us running into one another in a city this size."

"If you had stayed around the palace for long we would surely have seen one another. I am surprised I didn't see you earlier since you arrived with Belisarius. You have been here a week already."

"Yes. But I have been very busy. It doesn't seem that long." Haik chewed thoughtfully. "Imagine you, my old military friend, with a house next door to the emperor."

"You told me you owned an estate, Haik. That's a large step up." John took a sip of his wine. He had not ordered anything to eat. He had no appetite. When he found himself engaged in a project he did not like to eat. Food was a distraction.

"My holdings aren't enormous. I grow pistachios mostly. Do your remember we camped for a few weeks near Telanissos?"

"Northeast of Antioch."

"That's right. That's where my land is. You can see my orchards from Saint Simeon's Church on the hill overlooking the town. The column Simeon lived on for decades is located inside the church."

"We have a lot of saints here. Some whole saints, and parts of others."

His companion's frown reminded John that, unlike many soldiers John had known, Haik was not a Mithran but a Christian. A heretic, John seemed to recall, a monophysite. Speaking to a friend from his youth had made his tongue as hasty as it had been in those days. But what did John really know about the man who sat across from him now?

"I didn't mean to offend you, Haik. The city is full of relics."

Haik waved his knife. "I am not a very religious man. But I've seen the spot where Simeon stood many times. It amazed me, to think how a man could spend his life confined to a pillar, exposed to the elements, never lying down."

"You're not here on a pilgrimage though. You said you had business."

"A minor matter."

"It's a long journey for a minor matter."

"Blame that on Justinian's Prefect of the East, the Cappadocian. He's been bleeding us dry, and demanding we bleed in gold."

"I understand John the Cappadocian has been extremely efficient in collecting revenues. If you're here to petition the emperor about it I doubt you'll get far. Half of the provinces are already here." He glanced around at the farmers who had been staring at them. "Not that they'll get to speak to anyone closer to the throne than the guards at the Chalke."

Haik shook his head. "That's not why I'm here. The Cappadocian has destroyed the postal system. They're using asses instead of horses now. Cheaper. And so much slower I decided I might as well come myself rather than send a letter, particularly when I heard that Belisarius had been recalled. If another earthquake hits Antioch the emperor won't find out until grass is growing over the ruins.

"He might not find out until too late if the Persians suddenly arrive at the walls, either."

"Very true, but the Persians aren't likely to be attacking again soon after the beating Belisarius gave them."

"There are those who say that it is Belisarius who took most of the beating. That he was lucky to escape back across the Euphrates to Callinicum. They consider him a better politician than soldier."

Haik knifed another sausage. The blade hit the metal plate with a click. "As a hot-blooded young soldier I might have felt differently, but these days I agree with what Belisarius says, that the best general is one who is able to bring about peace from war. Whoever won the battle, the fact remains that the Persians no longer threaten Roman territory. And now that Chosroes has succeeded Cabades as king and agreed to sign an eternal peace, the emperor must be well pleased.

"It can be difficult to discern what the emperor thinks about anything. You said you don't know General Belisarius well?"

"Not at all, actually. I have a good reputation in the area. I'm a respected landowner so he was happy to let me accompany him."

A couple of the provincials who had been staring got up and left, trailing a vague odor of livestock. The Blue who had drunk too much wobbled to his feet at the same time. One of the provincials paused at the bar to hand the tavern keeper two tiny copper nummi. He stared into the age blackened pouch from which the coins had come, grunted in disgust, and tossed it away. Funds had run out as they soon did in the city.

The Blue staggered off toward the door leading to the lavatory. John wondered if he had intended to follow the unsuspecting visitors into the street and rob them. If so, they were fortunate to be destitute.

John sipped his wine and watched Haik devour another sausage. Hadn't he stopped to eat after arriving in the city? He shifted his weight. The hard bench dug into his thighs. He could practically feel the glass-eyed Porphyrius in the wall mosaic looking over his shoulder. It made him uncomfortable even though he knew it was only his imagination.

"It's quite a leap, from mercenary to estate owner," John said. "What made you think of growing pistachios?"

Haik swallowed, then grinned. He tapped the half-tooth that left a gap in his smile. "Don't you remember when I broke this on a shell?"

John chuckled. "Now that you have reminded me. The way you howled, half of us in the camp grabbed our weapons before we realized we weren't under attack. We thought you'd taken an arrow in a tender spot."

"I spent five years fighting and that was the worst injury I suffered. The pistachio family has compensated me many times over for my pain. Unfortunately, I will never have my smile back. There are things that can't be fixed. But tell me, John, how did you come to live at the Great Palace in Constantinople? The last I knew you were going to Egypt."

A haughty looking youth in a bright green cloak strode in from the street and demanded a jug of wine. He set his drink on a table and headed for the lavatory.

John's gaze settled on the newcomer with automatic wariness. His thoughts were elsewhere. "Haik, there's something I should probably tell you. If you stay at the palace, before long, you will hear me referred to by another name."

"I'm not surprised. There are too many Johns around to keep track. What exactly do—"

"Behind my back I'm called John the Eunuch."

"How dare they insult you!"

"It's not an insult."

Haik simply stared at John. Then seemed to realize he was staring and looked away. "My old friend, I'm sorry."

"It happened a long time ago. I was captured by some of those Persians we are at peace with now."

Haik began to speak. An enraged shout cut him short. The Blue they had seen seated at a table earlier stumbled backwards out of the lavatory followed by the Green who had recently come in. Vomit stains down the front of the Blue's tunic revealed the reason for his lengthy stay.

"You set them on my brother, didn't you?" bellowed the Green. "Three against one, and all older too. That's what a Blue considers a fair fight!"

The Green swung his sword and caught the Blue on the side of the head.

No, John realized. It wasn't a sword but the sponge on a stick that lavatory patrons used to clean themselves when they visited the room for a major need.

The noisome weapon did no damage to the Blue but sent a spray of filth over John's head, spattering the famous charioteer in the mosaic.

The tavern keeper came out from behind the counter as the Green struck again. The Green strode forward. His foot hit some of the filth sprayed by his weapon. He slipped, fell and rolled into John's legs. The Green lay there senseless.

The reeling Blue stumbled backwards, placed his hand on the table in front of Haik, balancing himself as he pulled a long blade from his belt.

He looked down at the prostrate Green, started to lift the blade, then screamed. He lurched awkwardly to the side and shrieked again. The blade fell from his hand. The Blue looked around dumbly, confused, flecks of vomit dripping down his chin.

John saw what it was. Haik's dinner knife protruded from the back of the young man's hand, pinning it to the table.

The tavern keeper loomed over them. He brandished an enormous meat cleaver. "Sirs, please, please accept my apologies. And accept your refreshment for free. And please, come back tomorrow. I shall be happy to serve you my best wine, for free. And sausages. One can hardly enjoy a meal under such disgraceful circumstances."

The man's bald pate had turned as red as his big hands. He looked as if he'd be wringing his hands if it weren't for the heavy cleaver he carried.

Haik yanked the knife out of the Blue's hand. The ruffian squealed like a dying rat and crumpled onto the straw-covered floor in a faint.

He glanced down at the two unconscious faction members and then at John. "There's a Green family in the city who owes you more than they realize, my friend." He set the knife beside his plate, wiped his fingers on his cloak, and picked up the remaining sausage. "Excellent sausage. I will be sure to recommend your establishment to all my friends at the palace," he told the tavern keeper.

He popped the sausage into his mouth.

By now the spicy odor of the food was mixing with the coppery smell of blood.

"You are too kind, sir. Too kind. But I fear I will have to close early. The friends of these two are likely to pay me a visit." He half turned and peered out through the doorway leading to the street as if he expected the villains to come bursting through. "There's something out there, sirs. It's not just the likes of these two." He kicked at the Blue and the Green who lay together peacefully.

"There's evil abroad in the city. Evil."

Chapter Seven

"Evil! Demons!"

Sunburnt faces glistening with sweat turned toward the ragged man limping across the docks, shouting. The hoarse shouts—nearly screams—could be heard above the creak of cart wheels, the yells of sailors and laborers, the thump of sacks, and the crash of crates.

"Demons! That's what lives in the palace, you poor fools!" He shook a splintered piece of wood in the face of a hulking dock worker, who stepped back quickly, despite the fact that he towered over the mad man. "And not only there!" the man thundered. "They're everywhere! Evil has fallen on the city. Evil! The only way to root it out is to pull it up stem and branch!"

Those interrupted in their labors and not directly in the man's path greeted this pronouncement with a selection of ripe oaths, mingled with shouts of derision.

An emaciated boy had been about to steal a fish for supper out of one of the baskets lined up at the edge of the dock as a fishing boat's crew unloaded its cargo. The boat's captain turned toward the shouting, spotted the boy, and glared.

"What you saying what's new?" the boy cried, voice cracking with frustration. "You're the one who's a demon!"

The ragged man looked around the curious congregation which was keeping a distance. "Wisdom from a stripling." He laughed.

The captain of the fishing boat leapt ashore. "You and that dirty little urchin are working together, aren't you?" He grabbed the speaker's shoulder, but the wretch shook it off with a convulsive movement and lurched away. He clambered up a pile of marble blocks, destined perhaps for an imperial residence or a church. Once atop he stood with his arms spread out, face turned to the glowering sky. Many of the onlookers began to drift back to their labors. A fellow in filthy clothes preaching incoherently from on high was too common a sight to maintain their interest.

A beggar who had observed the scene from a doorway at the base of the sea wall which towered above the docks stepped out and craned his neck to see the man standing above.

"What's that about demons?" he asked. "Any 'round here? Where'd you see them?"

The man he addressed peered down. "If you cannot see them, you are fortunate. They swarm everywhere. There are several down there on the dock disguised as men…but if you have vision you can see through their fleshly disguise."

The beggar shivered in exaggerated fashion. "Which ones do you mean?"

The man pointed to the captain, now busy kicking the emaciated boy away from the baskets, helping him along with a invitation to bring his sister back and he would give her something for nothing all right, and then put his finger to his lips to enjoin silence.

"What, him?"

"See his dark face behind that sly smile? Teeth sharp as a tonsor's razor? Oh yes, my friend, he'll be waiting to take you for your final journey when the time comes! And any wind he sails on takes his passengers straight to the devil's kingdom! Because there is only one wind in all the world and that's its destination. Just take a look at him. You can see right away he's one who sails the hellish wind."

"I've heard he's had bad fortune with his crews. It explains a lot. If he's a demon...."

"He is, and the king who rules them here is Justinian. Haven't you heard he prowls the palace at night without his face? Of course! He doesn't want anyone to see his real face for fear the sight will kill them! But I intend to confront and banish him! Then will evil be gone from the city!"

"Wouldn't mind that." The beggar winked at the captain who stood listening, having banished the boy.

"I only wish I was in league with the emperor," remarked the captain. "Think how rich I would be!"

"Not much charity to be had lately," said the beggar. "Now there's evil for you. And it's dangerous being out when them Blues and Greens are having their bit of fun. But how do you expect to get in the palace? You can't just stroll in and ask to talk to the emperor, can you?"

The ragged man stared down and smiled. "Those at the palace know their own when they see them. I'll have no trouble coming and going as I please. Besides, I have in my possession a magickal charm." He shook the broken stick he carried. "It will gain me entry to the imperial audience hall quicker than you can steal a loaf!"

Chapter Eight

January 12, 532

The walkway echoed to the thud of Felix's boots. When the heat haze of summer formed shimmering visions over the sea visible between carefully clipped topiary depicting fabulous beasts, the high, airy way would offer a shady retreat behind its curtain of honeysuckle. Now at the deadest time of year, where the dense mat of vines kept out sunlight, traces of frost lingered.

The broad shouldered young excubitor frowned and tugged at his beard as he strode along. Why had Captain Gallio been so mysterious about this assignment? Why had he left the explanation to Narses? Felix would have preferred not to be anywhere within hailing distance of the emperor's chamberlain and treasurer.

That perfumed fool. His scowl deepened. A military man being ordered about by a eunuch! If he were captain he'd never—

A woman screamed.

Felix drew his sword and broke into a run, alert for ambush. Even deep in the palace grounds to drop his guard for a heart-beat could be fatal.

He reached the end of the colonnade and burst out into a walled terrace. An attractive, fair-haired woman sat on a semi-circular marble bench overlooking the sea. Her robes were dark green, decorated simply with pale yellow embroidery at the hem and neckline. A servant to one of the court ladies, who had borrowed some of her mistress' plainer clothing and would get a sound thrashing for it when she ventured back to her work, Felix thought.

She looked up as he approached. Loose curls framed her features. The red lips and rosy cheeks showed she had been at her mistress' makeup too. "Oh, what a big strong fellow. You frightened that ruffian so much he ran away...."

Felix glanced around. He saw nobody on the brick pathway that extended several yards along the terrace in each direction. Edged with naked flower beds there was no cover for anything bigger than a rabbit.

The woman laughed. "Yes, you are right, there was nobody here but myself. Life at the palace can be so boring. Sometimes I could just scream."

"A habit that might liven things up more than one might wish." Felix put his sword back in his belt.

"You belong to the palace guard, don't you? Such fine young men." She sounded as if she were out of breath from some exertion, even though she was simply sitting still. "Do you have a wife?"

The abrupt change of subject startled Felix. He shook his head. "Don't stay out in the grounds after dark," he advised. "It isn't wise, especially with all the unrest in the city."

"You don't think troublemakers can get into the palace? Surely that's your job? To keep them out?"

"No one can get into the imperial chambers. The gardens are another matter. Armies of bureaucrats, clerks, merchants, and petty officials have business on the palace grounds every day. We keep track of them as best we can. Then too, the whole complex is surrounded by buildings of all sorts, and who knows what passages run underneath our feet or whether someone can get over a wall somewhere?"

"So you really might have saved my life by showing up when you did! Would you care to escort me around the sights of the city? Better yet, why don't we meet later. After dark. The Hall of the Nineteen Couches is deserted between banquets." She giggled at Felix's dumbfounded expression.

"I am—that is—won't your mistress object to your absence?"

She waved a hand. "Not at all. I have a great deal of freedom."

"I would be pleased to show you around the city, but the chamberlain Narses is waiting to see me."

"Do you know Narses? They say he is fabulously wealthy. Of course, he is not the sort of man I prefer." Her gaze caressed Felix from head to toe. Her eyes, Felix saw, were as blue as a summer sky over the sea.

"Oh, we are old comrades," Felix heard himself say. He couldn't look away from those brilliant blue eyes and while he stared into them he couldn't control his words. "Narses relies on me for advice and often consults me on certain delicate matters."

He finally managed to turn away. Or had she lowered her gaze and released him?

He stammered out a farewell and set off down the path, accompanied by an uncomfortable feeling she was laughing at him behind his back. Why had he been so foolish as to claim friendship with a man he despised? He hadn't wanted to disappoint her, he told himself. It was what she'd wanted to hear.

Felix had nearly escaped when she called out. "You're going the wrong way! Narses is at his office now. Let's walk there together!"

She was beside him before he could protest. Felix glanced at his companion from time to time. She was as familiar with their geography as he, and he wondered if her knowledge had come from assignations in less frequented areas of the gardens. She was not so much beautiful as striking, with pale hair and plump hands. Nor was she as young as he had first supposed and the angle of her jaw suggested stubbornness and a strong will. He wondered which mistress she served and if her employer was a guest of the imperial couple.

Whoever she was, she seemed in high humor. Now and then a chuckle escaped her ruby painted lips and at one point she hummed to herself.

Felix couldn't hide his surprise. He recognized a popular though obscene song sung by military men to the glory of Theodora and her prowess in the arena of Venus.

By then they had reached a long, blocky administrative building. The woman led Felix down a corridor decorated with frescoes depicting country life and rapped on a polished paneled door decorated with ivory scrollwork. A pale silentiary answered the summons.

Felix felt it was time to assert his authority. "I am Felix, sent by Captain Gallio of the excubitors for an audience with Narses." As he spoke he was acutely conscious of the perfume of the woman beside him.

"You are expected." replied the guardian of the door. "As for your companion…."

"I am not expected," she said. "And being a female I have no doubt I would be unwelcome. Don't forget our little matter, Felix." She caught him again in her gaze, released him, and went back down the corridor. He realized she had not actually touched him once yet he felt as if she had her hands all over his body.

The room into which a thoroughly flustered Felix was ushered boasted a large desk, an ebony-armed chair, and a large iron-bound box. The only nod to decoration was a row of silver bowls of hyacinths against one wall. The bell-shaped flowers exuded a sweet, overpowering scent that filled the austere room.

The dwarfish, bald chamberlain dismissed the silentiary. He noticed Felix looking at the flowers. "Homer stated in a passage describing Juno's treachery that her bed was formed of crocus, lotus, and hyacinth. I keep these blossoms by me as a reminder that women cannot be trusted—and few men, for that matter."

Felix blinked in surprise but remained silent.

"I recognized that strumpet's voice," Narses continued. "I strongly advise you not to engage in the little matter mentioned, whatever it is, although I can certainly guess its nature. Avoid that woman or should I say viper in women's clothing. She is a demon's snare. A friend of the empress. A close friend. You grasp my meaning? Besides which, I know how men are. I will not have her interfering in what you will be instructed to carry out."

"I don't know the woman, excellency. I ran into her in the gardens."

The other's unlined face broke into a smile that closely resembled a leer. "You really don't know who she is?"

"No, excellency."

"That's Antonina. Unchaste to say the least and a practitioner of magick of the worst sort. However, as I said, a confidante of our empress." Narses giggled. "But now to business."

Chapter Nine

John ignored the first knock at the chapel door. At the second his lips tightened into a thin line and he set down the crust of bread he had been eating. "Yes?"

"It's Haik."

"Come in."

A shaft of light from the doorway fell across the gloom in the semi-circular chamber. The candles on the polished wood altar guttered, their reflections trembling on the silver cross sitting between them. Before it was half opened, the edge of the door hit John's stool. Haik squeezed into the cell-sized enclosure.

"Please close the door." John shifted his stool to make room. A plain, wooden desk sat jammed up against the altar. Documents were shoved aside to make room for John's breakfast.

"The servants told me I'd find you here. I didn't realize you'd become a man of faith."

"I haven't. It's the only place in the house I can be alone. The servants won't disturb a man at his devotions. Otherwise it's master this and master that. It's impossible to gather one's thoughts."

"You always liked having the night watch on your own, didn't you?" Haik looked around the chapel. A gilt cross curved across the domed ceiling. On the walls, painted saints suffered horrible martyrdoms. "I'd have a hard time thinking in here, myself. It's worse than a battlefield."

"I'm not having much luck myself this morning."

"Pondering some palace intrigue?"

John ignored Haik's grin. "I hope that's not what it turns out to be." He stood, retrieved his bread, stuffed the remains into his mouth, and gestured toward the door. He left the chapel and led his visitor down a short corridor into the atrium where a life-sized Aphrodite served as a graceful fountain.

Haik glanced back in the direction of the chapel. "Old gods and new no further from each other than you could spit an olive pit. I wonder who the original owner of this house favored?"

"I am sure he worshipped the emperor's god. In public. Have a seat. There's more room here and you won't sink up to your neck in cushions."

Haik sat down with a sigh on one of the benches projecting from the marble walls while John took another. "Considering the time I've spent on horseback lately, I wouldn't refuse a cushion or two. You should allow yourself a little luxury. You've earned it. You weren't born to it."

"Which is why I can't get used to being waited on."

"The servants might not vex you so much if you gave them enough to do. I found the kitchen staff throwing knucklebones. But then how long does it take to set out a loaf of bread for the master's breakfast?"

"I often have boiled eggs."

"Give them some employment. A few fancy dishes will keep them busy all day."

"I have no taste for fancy dishes. I'm happy with grilled fish from a street vendor."

"Have your cook prepare grilled fish then."

"I'd have to sit and eat off a silver plate. I'd prefer to have it from a skewer while walking the streets."

Haik laughed. "I suppose the emperor wouldn't allow you to pitch a tent in the gardens?"

"It would reflect badly on Justinian if his chamberlains did not appear to be well compensated."

Haik ran a hand absently through his long, black hair. "So you're a chamberlain. From what little I know, that's an office with a lot of power."

John shook his head. "The office has no power of its own. All power flows down from the emperor, like the water from Aphrodite's shell."

The white marble statue held an oversized clam shell in one upraised hand. Water bubbled out of the shell and splashed into the basin at the bare feet of the goddess. The tiles near the fountain glistened with moisture. Occasionally John could feel a droplet against his face. Given the chill in the air on this January day, it was not a pleasant sensation.

"There are numerous chamberlains with varied duties," John added. "Everything depends on Justinian's whim. Narses is a chamberlain but also the imperial treasurer. Which makes him my superior. And it is obvious that he intends to make certain that he remains my superior."

"I'll stick to my orchards. It's less complicated than the imperial court and a pistachio tree isn't likely to stab you in the back."

"But it might conspire to break your teeth."

The gap in Haik's grin proved the truth of the statement. He was silent for a time. His gaze remained fixed on John.

"You've been staring at me. You're wondering about me, aren't you? Do I look different? Has my voice changed? Am I the same man? Perhaps I have become treacherous and deceitful."

"I would never believe that of you."

"But that's what they say about eunuchs. They are sly creatures. Always plotting."

Haik looked down at the tiles. "No, John. Truly...I...I've been staring at you because...I can't believe my eyes, seeing you in these surroundings. Can this be the young soldier in muddy boots with whom I drank a ration of sour wine after a day's march? How did he come to be at the Great Palace?"

"After I left for Egypt I traveled for a while with a troupe of entertainers. They employed me as a guard. I didn't guard myself very well. I accidentally wandered into an area controlled by the Persians. Luckily I had learned to read and write before I ran away to become a fighting man so I had some value, especially as a eunuch."

"But at least since you no longer…well…you can't suffer from any urges…."

John looked at the slender, naked Aphrodite, one hand holding the overflowing shell, the other laid demurely between her legs. "I only wish that were so. I can remember what it is like to be with a woman in every detail. I am hardly the only soldier to be maimed."

"Yet your misfortune brought you good fortune. God works in strange ways."

"Does he? As far as I recall, I was the one who did all the work, Haik. My first glimpse of Constantinople was the bottom of the sea wall as I was dragged across a dock in chains. The Keeper of the Plate eventually employed me. If I had not worked to better myself I would have remained just another face in the administrative horde. But I distinguished myself. So when the emperor needed someone who was discreet—but disposable— for a confidential assignment, I had my chance. I made the best of it."

"You don't seem to enjoy the fruits of your labors."

"I wouldn't say that, my friend. Every morning when I open my eyes I take satisfaction in the fact that I have survived to see another day."

Chapter Ten

"They should both be dead now," said the executioner. "They would be too if I'd had time to prepare the scaffold correctly and the ropes were of better quality. I trust that the Prefect realizes it was not my fault."

"Eudaemon wasn't at the Praetorium," John said. "An assistant told me you were in charge of the execution."

"In charge but without the proper resources."

Considering the number of condemned the executioner had launched into eternity he was an unremarkable figure, noticeable only for one shoulder being slightly higher than the other. It made him look vaguely awkward and uncomfortable.

"I'm a craftsman," he said. His mild features belied the anger in his voice. "I take pride in my profession. A quick, clean death, that's what I aim for. I once met a fellow who extracted money from the condemned man's family on condition he'd make sure the fellow had an easy exit. Had no idea what he was doing. Botched the job so badly the victim's head was ripped off. He never collected his fee. Whether the family got their bribe back, I can't say."

Two boys, perhaps six and seven, whom John took to be part of the man's family, sat in a corner and goggled up at their visitor.

"I'm not here to quibble over your payment," John said. "I wish to interview you about the hanging. Kindly ask your children to leave us. It isn't the sort of thing they should hear."

The man looked surprised. "They're always asking to hear that story about the poor fellow's head again. But if you insist." He shooed them into the other room.

The rooms were part of a stolid apartment building north of the Mese, halfway down the steep hill which descended toward the long finger of water known as the Golden Horn. Furnishings were the usual wooden tables and chairs and a brazier for heat and cooking. One of the ubiquitous Christian crosses hung from the wall. The confined space smelled strongly of garlic from a recent meal.

"I understand you are called Kosmas."

"That is correct, excellency."

"From your speech I can tell you are not from the city. What brought you to Constantinople?"

Kosmas' mild expression darkened. "Taxes. We owned a farm in Anatolia. Raised livestock. Pigs mostly. A few mules and horses. For four generations we were landowners, until, finally, we couldn't pay. So I brought my wife and children to the city and looked for work. That was three years ago."

"You found employment as an executioner?"

"Most of the time I work for a butcher. I'm paid a decent wage and can bring home some meat as well. Executions aren't steady work. They bring in extra money. One day I might be able to own a small farm again. I miss the open fields. The noise the beggars make in the alley keeps us awake most nights."

"How does a farmer and a butcher come to hang criminals?"

"I performed executions in Anatolia. Even in the countryside there's occasionally someone who needs hanging and not many with the required expertise. Once a village witnesses a condemned man slowly strangled because the knot wasn't placed right....well...I took it up as a civic service. I was well known in the area."

"You may have spared a lot of curious children nightmares," John observed, with a stern glance toward the doorway to the other room. He glimpsed two heads vanishing from sight. "You were summoned on short notice to carry out the executions by Prefect Eudaemon?"

"Yes. He is familiar with my work. There have been quite a number of calls on my service of late. As a good Christian I can only deplore that, but as a family man with children and a wife to feed...you understand, I am certain."

John responded with a thin smile. In fact, he did not understand Christians at all. Was Kosmas attracted to Christianity because it was the official religion or because its most sacred symbol was a man being executed? "Describe what happened," he ordered.

Kosmas paused in concentration. In his memory he must have been seeing a picture of that cold morning. "The prisoners were ferried over from the city. Seven of them. Four were beheaded. A quick death, excellency. Much kinder than hanging. Not a task I like to carry out. But duties must be met however distasteful. Think of how those in charge of crucifixions must have felt! It's one thing to give a quick downstroke of a sharp axe and deprive a man of his life, but quite another to hammer nails into living flesh. I have never been ordered to crucify a man, but if I was I would make it less painful. Even when I slaughtered livestock I tried to be quick about it. We should never have been given so little time to prepare."

"Indeed. Continue with your account."

"Oh...yes...." Kosmas lifted a hand nervously, and John thought he intended to touch his neck in recollected sympathy with the condemned men, but instead he rubbed the shoulder that was lower than the other. "I apologize, excellency. It is a strange thing. I tend not to recall executions. I think it is a blessing the Lord has granted me."

Was that true or a convenient excuse, John wondered. "Tell me as much as you can, Kosmas."

"The first hanging succeeded. I'm not sure what faction he belonged to, but that left a Blue and a Green. Both factions, you see. The emperor wished to show even handed justice. Or so I was told. We had managed to erect two gallows on the platform and cut a pair of openings in the planks. The prisoners arrived before we could complete the trapdoors, though, so I had to push the men into the openings." Kosmas shook his head. "I hope never to have to do that again. It feels too much like murder. There are accepted procedures. That isn't one of them."

"You gave both men a shove before you realized anything had gone wrong?"

"That's right. I wasn't looking toward the ground. The first I knew about the mishap was when I heard the spectators' reaction. There are always a few screams from gawkers who expected death to be prettier, but this time it was an uproar."

"Is it true that both ropes broke? Not once but twice?"

"Yes. The fibers partially tore and stretched. Both men ended up on the ground, half strangled and dazed. But not so dazed that they didn't understand what was happening when the guards carted them back up to the platform."

"Did you recognize either of the men?"

"No. I have seldom needed to execute a man I know, thank the Lord."

"You were alone on the platform, aside from the guards?"

Kosmas nodded.

"So it was a defect in the ropes which saved the men's lives?"

"It was definitely the ropes. Everything else was in order. The gallows were strong enough. The height of the platform was correct. Neither man had an abnormal physique. Sometimes I need to make special adjustments. A man as lean as you would need to fall further than most, if you'll excuse my saying so."

"A longer journey but without any better destination. Didn't you notice the ropes were unsuitable before you used them?"

"Of course. But there was no time to find anything better. Even a poor rope is almost always good enough."

"Could they have been cut part way through?"

Panic flickered across Kosmas' features. "You don't think I had anything—"

"Where did they come from?"

"I'm not sure. Some men from the Prefect's office, or maybe men hired by him, delivered everything we needed. All the construction material, the axes and ropes. I don't supply the rope, excellency."

"Would you have noticed if the rope had been cut?"

"I should think so. I inspect them, to make certain they're strong enough."

"Are you positive no one else had access to the ropes after they came into your possession?"

"Yes. I took charge of all the equipment at once. The ropes were simply rotten, excellency. No more than that. The second set was as bad as the first. I directed a couple of workmen to attach new ropes to the gallows while the Blue and the Green lay on the platform, crying for mercy. Or so it seemed. Their throats were too swollen for them to speak comprehensibly. They couldn't stand. The guards had to haul them to their feet to let me loop the nooses around their necks. I never want to witness such a thing again. One of the guards found it all amusing. He asked why the condemned were whimpering since they'd already been hung once and it hadn't been so bad. I only recalled that just now." Kosmas shook his head. "As I adjusted the nooses I whispered a few words of comfort. Christ is with you, I told them. You may not see Him, but soon you will. The guards had to shove them forward, to their deaths, except, as you know, the ropes failed a second time. This time, just as the men were about to be dragged back up on the platform, monks from Saint Conon's monastery appeared and claimed them. Because clearly they had been spared by the Lord, the monks said."

"What do you think?"

"None of us can know the ways of the Lord. Maybe it was a miracle. If I was a gambling man I would have wagered against two hangings both failing twice."

John thought that more than a few disgruntled Christians might consider it a divine comment on Justinian's justice. "No one tried to stop the monks from rescuing the condemned men? How did they manage to reach the scaffold?"

"The crowd was getting unruly. People had pushed their way forward. There was some confusion."

"So much confusion that the guards couldn't do their job?"

"Guards are Christians too, excellency. They were not sent to slaughter monks."

"Do you suppose someone could have been bribed to insure that the execution went wrong?"

"In this city, bribery is always a possibility. We hung the first man without incident."

"Why didn't you use his rope to hang the other two? His didn't break."

"I admit, it never occurred to me, with all the commotion. I suggest you talk to Rusticus the physician. He may have noticed something I have forgotten. He examined the ropes after they broke, too. He's old—some say decrepit—but then he's the Prefect's uncle. He was there to certify the men as dead. There have been cases of men who were hung, who appeared dead to casual observers, but when examined an hour later were still alive."

"That must be even rarer than ropes breaking."

"That is so, excellency, but I speak from personal knowledge. As a child I was playing in the stables. I liked to crawl around the rafters and dive into piles of hay. I got tangled up with some reins that were dangling from the rafters on a hook. I don't know how long I hung there. When my father found me I was nearly dead. Luckily, I hadn't got myself suspended entirely by my neck. I broke my shoulder too, as you can see. I'm told they got me breathing again by dosing me with vinegar and mustard seed. It's been said that those who survive near strangulation often have strange visions. They have set one foot over the threshold to Heaven, you see. But I've never had that benefit, only pain in my shoulder."

John couldn't help thinking that each time Kosmas picked up a cup of wine, or reached down to pat the head of one of his children, whenever the weather turned damp, every time the shoulder pained him, he would be reminded of his own hanging. He asked a few more questions, until he was satisfied the executioner had told him everything he remembered, or everything he was going to reveal.

As he stepped out into the hall there was a shriek. The two boys barreled out of the room to which they had been banished and started rolling around by their father's legs. Both had belts fastened around their necks.

John closed the door.

Chapter Eleven

As John approached the Hippodrome on his way back to the palace he pondered what to do next. Should he walk up the Mese to the Praetorium in case Urban Prefect Eudaemon had returned? Or should he, after all, risk revealing his investigation to the charioteer Porphyrius who might also be able to tell him who the dead men were?

The towering wall of the stadium which dominated this part of the city had been visible to him above the roof tops and through gaps in the buildings for a long time as he came down the side street. When he arrived at the Mese he saw people clustered near the Hippodrome's entrance. There were a number of faction members, judging by the elaborate clothes and hair styles, but also a few young men who had the look of charioteers or soldiers, along with a handful of clerks.

John crossed the Mese to take a closer look. A ragged cheer ran through the small crowd.

He accosted a fellow whose tunic boasted enormous billowing sleeves with tight cuffs. "What is this gathering about?"

"We're wagering on the races."

"The race track is inside," John said. "And I don't see any horses."

"There's a wagering machine." The man flapped a wing-like sleeve in the direction of a cart on which sat what at first glance looked like an elaborately carved plinth.

When John reached the cart he saw that the peculiar object was only a solid block on three sides, which were covered with bas reliefs depicting a race. A charioteer whipped his team around the turning posts and accepted a palm after his victory while a lady looked on from a window. The back of the device—or perhaps it was intended as the front, the thing being turned sideways on the cart—consisted of a complicated series of crisscrossing, descending ramps, punctuated by holes.

A man distinguished by a huge potbelly and a cloak striped with blue, green, white, and red, stood beside the machine, exhorting the spectators. "Who'll be next to pit his skill against the demon driver Fortuna? Better than the races! All the thrills, none of the manure!"

A young fellow with the leg wrappings and muscular arms of a charioteer stepped up onto the back of the cart. He exchanged words with the hawker beside the machine, handed him a coin and received four balls colored blue, green, red, and white respectively. The colors of the traditional factions.

He grinned and raised his fist. Several men in front—friends no doubt—shouted encouragement. Then he dropped the balls into a hole at the top corner of the machine.

Sunlight flashed on them as they began to roll down the first of the inclined ramps. The green ball vanished into one hole, the white into another. The green emerged on a lower ramp. So did the red, which John had not been following. It was impossible to track the progression of the balls as they dropped, reappeared, traded places. The red ball shot out of the hole in the bottom corner of the device, into the hand of the hawker.

"Your green team has been passed at the finish line, my friend." The hawker shoved the coin he had been holding into the pouch hanging from his belt. "A good effort though. I liked the way you cut off Porphyrius at the second turn."

The men in front laughed. The loser did his best to smile. He probably felt like having the drink which he no longer could afford.

"Red again," came a voice from beside John. He turned his head. Shock washed over him. He was looking into the face of the Blue he had pulled from the cistern.

No, it was simply another Blue, with the same partly shaved head and braid of hair.

"The Reds seem to be winning most of time," the Blue said. "I think things are rigged in their favor."

"Maybe it's just time they made a comeback," put in a stocky fellow with sawdust on his tunic.

A short, slight man with the pale skin of a clerk from one of the imperial offices, shook his head. "Can't you see it's rigged? Why do you suppose the villain has a whole tray of those colored balls? Whichever team's wagered on, he selects the balls accordingly. Some are heavier or lighter. Some are misshapen."

The Blue rubbed his chin thoughtfully. "It could be. Nothing's fair in this city, is it?"

"No one would wager on finding fairness in Constantinople," agreed the stocky man. "Look at those two poor fellows the emperor's imprisoned at Saint Laurentius. I'm told he had them hung—and twice—because someone in their group made a disparaging comment about that actress he's married to."

"Justinian wouldn't do such a thing," said the Blue.

"I thought everyone was demanding the release of those unfortunates," John said. "Particularly the factions. Don't tell me you support Justinian, after what he's done to us all?"

"We're not all against the emperor," the Blue replied. "Why would we be? He's supported us for years. I'm sure he'll be setting those men free."

"You don't think those two are still alive, do you?" sneered the clerk. "People can demand that Justinian release them but even the emperor can't release anyone from the afterlife. I have it on good authority that he had their throats slit the moment they arrived at the church."

"Sounds like something Theodora would order, behind the emperor's back," remarked the Blue.

A cheer went up from the spectators as another race of colored balls concluded.

When the noise died down John said, "I'm told one of the man was Gaius." He picked the name out of the air.

The Blue seemed to actually see him for the first time and his gaze grew cold. "I have no idea who the prisoners are. Not friends of mine, certainly." He quickly moved away.

Turning, John saw that the clerk had vanished when he wasn't looking. He regretted now having worn the heavy, luxurious cloak that probably identified him as someone closely associated with the palace, someone to whom it might not be wise to say too much.

Nevertheless he wandered through the assembly, listening, trying to strike up conversations, turning the subject always to the condemned men. He learned nothing. Even a laborer in a threadbare tunic, exultant over having just won three week's wages, turned sober when John tried to question him. Whatever their profession or station in life, all residents of the capital were highly suspicious and skilled at self-preservation.

Someone laughed. John saw it was Junius, the young charioteer he had spoken with inside the Hippodrome.

"I warned you that no one knows the emperor's enemies, even if they do sympathize with them," said Junius.

"You seem to have been prophetic," John admitted. "Maybe you should try your luck at the game."

"It doesn't take a prophet to realize no one is going to risk being suspected of having any connection to men the emperor has seen fit to hang. You might have better success questioning beggars. Charioteers will never tell you anything. Not even if you pay them."

"Why do you think that?"

"Suppose you offer me a bit of gold in return for information. Not that I have any information. If I take it I'm wagering that the emperor won't have me dragged to the dungeons. Now if I were a beggar living on the street, with no future and no hope, it might be different. I might take the chance. But as it is, it would be stupid. Look at Porphyrius. He's grown rich from racing. Most charioteers won't, but still, we might. We wager we'll win a prize every time we take to the track. That's dangerous too, but not as dangerous as wagering on Justinian's actions."

John had to acknowledge the truth of what Junius said, though he didn't do so aloud.

The audience seemed to be thinning.

The hawker in the multi-colored robes noticed. "What, no one else wants to test their skill? Fortuna drives too ruthlessly today, does she?"

"Do you hand our coins over to Fortuna?" someone yelled.

The hawker ignored the jibe. "Wait. I have an idea."

He scrambled off the cart and reached behind one of the wheels. "Look! This explains it!" He pulled out a scroll, as long as his arm. From a distance it resembled lead but must have been dyed parchment because he could never have brandished such a weight over his head as he proceeded to do.

"Now you see why you have been losing all afternoon. Have you ever seen a bigger curse tablet?"

He let the scroll unroll. It reached to his feet. "There's not a demon left in hell. Every last one's been called up here to hobble your horses and steal your coins!"

Junius chuckled. "I don't doubt it. I hear a demon was spotted on the docks. And in other places too."

"They don't seem to have confined themselves to interfering with the races," John remarked.

The hawker made a show of pouring what he claimed was holy water over the scroll. By the time he climbed back onto the cart the crowd was laughing and interested again. "Now, who has the courage to race?"

"Why don't you try?" Junius said to John. "See if Fortuna is on your side or not?"

"I'd rather not put Fortuna to the test for matters of no consequence."

He noticed that the Blue he had spoken to earlier was standing on the cart.

"And which team do you support?" the hawker asked.

"The Blues. The emperor's team!"

There was general muttering.

"And who amongst us would disagree with that," the hawker said loudly, handing the Blue four colored balls.

"Fortuna!" someone yelled in answer.

"The demons," suggested another.

The Blue dropped the balls into the top hole. They flashed down through the maze-like track, popping in and out of sight. When the winner burst out of the machine the hawker looked startled. The ball skidded out of his hand, hit the bottom of the cart, and bounced away.

Several shouts joined each other. "Red again!"

Chapter Twelve

When John stepped into the atrium of his house, four excubitors were clustered around the central fountain, struggling to drag a body out of the basin at the feet of the marble Aphrodite. John's foot slipped. Looking down he saw a pink trickle running back across the black and white tiles from the fountain.

The excubitors cursed. "Grab the arm. Heave now. Harder. Harder."

They had hold of an enormously fat man. The body was in a sitting position. The head with its pasty white face lolled on the multiple chins hiding the neck. The man looked vaguely familiar, John thought.

The excubitors pulled, the man slid. Water sloshed over the rim of the basin and washed away the pink trickle at John's feet. John noticed fragments from a broken wine jug scattered on the tiles.

The body in the basin groaned. Its tiny eyes blinked.

"Pull now. Pull," ordered a broad backed excubitor. "All together. On the count of three. One. Two…."

The fat man came up out of the water and toppled forward, nearly pushing two of the excubitors to the floor. They staggered backwards like over-laden brick carriers, and dragged him out of the basin. Not dead, but still a dead weight. One yellow slipper caught on the rim. The other foot was bare.

Then the man was upright, supported by two of the excubitors. A swaying, shivering, mountain of sodden, tangled robes. The atrium was cold in January.

"Mithra!" growled the biggest of the excubitors.

John recognized the voice. "Felix."

The bear-like man turned around. "My apologies, John. Our esteemed guest Pompeius was contemplating the goddess, sat down in the water by mistake, and couldn't get up. Or so he says."

One of the excubitors snickered. "He was wrapped around her like she was a whore in an alley."

Pompeius' thick and now decidedly bluish lips moved and finally words spluttered out. "I was merely attempting to get to my...my...feet."

"Had a good hand hold," the excubitor remarked.

"Trying to pull myself up...." His words slurred together. The little eyes were noticeably red in the colorless face.

Felix glared. "Get him back to his room. See he doesn't injure himself further."

The excubitors assisted Pompeius out of the atrium, half carrying him into the hall leading past the chapel and to the back of the house. The man's swollen feet—one slippered, one bare—moved, but hardly touched the tiles.

John walked over to the basin and looked in. He expected to see the missing slipper. It had apparently been lost somewhere else. He didn't much like the thought of the fat man's yellow slipper at large in his house waiting to surprise him. Aphrodite, undisturbed, continued to spill water serenely from the shell in her upraised hand.

"That was Pompeius, wasn't it?" John said. "One of the nephews of old emperor Anastasius. I've seen him around the palace occasionally. What did you mean by calling him 'our guest'? And what are you doing here, my friend?"

Felix tugged at his beard. "Emperor's orders. I got them straight from Narses, unfortunately."

Before he could explain further another man whom John knew by sight edged slowly into the atrium. The man looked around nervously. Had he been standing near the entrance to the hall, watching, the whole time?

"Is it all right then? At first I was afraid rioters had got in." Hypatius presented a stark contrast to Pompeius. An older man but without even a middle age paunch, immaculately dressed, his face would not have looked out of place on a gold coin. Only on close examination might one notice that the deep-set eyes had pouches beneath them, the square chin was rather weak, and the aquiline nose overly large. "My family and I appreciate your hospitality, John. Even if my brother has made himself a bit too comfortable already."

"Your family?"

Hypatius glanced around again. "Pompeius and myself and my daughter, Julianna. The emperor suggested we stay with you, until the danger of rioting has passed."

"And your wife? You are married I believe?"

"Oh, yes, of course. Mary's well guarded at the house. I'd prefer to be home. But Julianna's safer here. She's an impetuous girl. She'd be out fighting in the streets. For Justinian. Caution is always the best policy."

"That's why my excubitors and I are here," Felix put in. "To guard the guests, just in case."

Hypatius nodded gravely. "Exactly. You never know. The factions might have designs on us. If you don't object, I had better go and look after my brother."

John didn't speak until Hypatius had vanished down the hall. Then he sighed. "So my house is to be a prison? Why my house, I wonder?"

"Justinian knows you barely use it. I wouldn't say Justinian is imprisoning them, though. They came to the palace as soon as the factions got restless and refused to leave."

"Since they are the closest relatives of the late Emperor Anastasius, they must be less worried about rioters than about appearing disloyal to Justinian."

"That's right. They want to stick by his side so he doesn't get the idea they're plotting against him. Not that they've allayed his suspicions entirely. I was told to keep an eye on them, and make sure they don't leave."

John could hear the disgust in his friend's voice. He knew it wasn't the kind of job Felix would enjoy. For his part, John wasn't unhappy to host the excubitor. The two men had worked together in the past but lately their official duties had kept their paths from crossing very often. Between Felix's increasing responsibilities in the imperial guards and John's attendance on the emperor there was barely spare time for the occasional brief conversation at a tavern.

"As far as I can tell, Hypatius isn't the sort to venture out into the streets until he considers them perfectly safe," John observed. "And Pompeius is lucky if he can stand up."

"I can't say I blame him resorting to the grape. He must feel like a grape being crushed between the emperor and the factions. The third nephew, Probus, abandoned his mansion and fled the city. Talk has it that some in the factions want to replace Justinian with one of the Anastasius line. But then, I'm sure you know more about it all than I do. The family suspects they'd be more likely to end wearing a noose than a diadem."

"Very perceptive of them."

John scanned the atrium. He still didn't see the yellow slipper. What he did see were puddles of wine and water on the floor and shards from the jug. He also saw two of his female servants peering in from the hall leading to the back of the house. Another servant, an older man, stood in the opposite doorway, staring uncertainly, a bucket in one hand and a rag in the other.

"Shall we clean up, master?" asked the man.

"Yes. Certainly."

One of the women spoke. "And you will want dinner. For you and your guests." She helped out in the kitchen, John thought. Perhaps she was the cook.

"Fine. Prepare something special."

"Immediately, master." The young woman kept glancing toward Felix. She and her companion went off down the hall. John thought he heard them giggling.

The remaining servant set his bucket down in a far corner and began cleaning vigorously.

"I always feel I'm out-numbered," John muttered. "Now, in addition to an army of servants, I also have three patricians and several excubitors as guests."

Felix grinned. "Don't worry, John. There's plenty of room. You should get out and explore your house some time. You'd see."

"Have the servant's been talking out of turn?"

"Not at all. It's easy to tell when rooms are never used."

"You looked around?"

"Pompeius wandered off. He was fairly inebriated when we arrived and…well, you've seen."

"Unfortunately. I'm not used to having servants creeping up on me all the time, Felix. I spent too many years sleeping in a tent with my sword at my side."

As he spoke yet another young woman entered the atrium. He couldn't recall her name, but her face, like the faces of all his army of servants, was slightly familiar. She looked toward him expectantly. Wanting something to do, no doubt. "The floor is to be cleaned," he told her.

The young woman's expression hardened. "That would hardly be appropriate. I am Julianna. The daughter of Hypatius."

◇◇◇

"I don't want to go back to that nasty little monk's cell they've stuck me in. Let's talk in the garden." Julianna darted away, into the dining room John seldom used. The wooden screens were shut against the winter chill. She pushed them open far enough to squeeze through. She moved so quickly and unexpectedly, John could only follow, once again lamenting the size of the house. Yet he could hardly have refused the generosity of the emperor.

The mansions of patricians were to be found all over Constantinople, especially in spots offering a view of the sea. A great many senators lived near the Marmara on the southern side of the city where the land sloped down from the Hippodrome. Certain imperial functionaries lived closer to the imperial couple they served. As a chamberlain to the emperor, John had been given an appropriate residence. Located behind the stables, close to the Chalke, the rambling, single story structure sat within the palace grounds but outside the palace complex itself—the enclosure which included the magnificent Augusteus throne room and the Daphne Palace surmounted by the emperor's private bed chambers, the Octagon.

John's house, with its unprepossessing brick front, was squeezed in amongst a jumble of taller residences. He had heard it said that the atrium had been added onto a couple of abandoned stables and it was easy enough to believe. An unusually large number of cramped rooms opened off the halls running from either side of the atrium. Some were used for servants' quarters, others for storage. Most remained empty. John slept in a room near the front of the house. He worked in the office between the atrium and the inner garden and generally took his meals there. For solitude he retreated to the chapel near the atrium. The suites of rooms at the rear of the house intended for living quarters—were mostly unexplored territory. He sometimes passed through them on his infrequent visits to the kitchen and workshops

The garden he stepped out into was best concealed by winter screens. Brown weeds and straggling, untrimmed shrubs choked the area. A couple of yew trees had grown up to almost twice the height of the house. Vines entangled the columns of the surrounding colonnades and bushes reached toward the covered walkways. He couldn't see Julianna but he heard her.

"If the rioters get into the palace grounds we can simply hide here," she was saying. "They'll never find—" Her sentence broke off, replaced by a series of oaths that would have made a charioteer blush.

He turned toward the direction of her voice and plunged through a tangle of evergreens. He found her bent over, tunic hitched up too high, rubbing her knee. Her calves appeared exceedingly brown and muscular for a lady of the court.

"Banged into a horse!" Straightening up, Julianna indicated a statue, about waist high, half concealed by brambles. Though eroded and partially covered by bluish lichens, it appeared to be a stone horse. "Look. There's another one."

She broke off handfuls of dry weeds to reveal a better preserved steed, this one with a carved blanket draped across its back.

"I understand the previous owner liked horses," John said.

In fact, he had been told that the official worshipped the Christians' god and horses, but not necessarily in that order. The unfortunate man would have done better to confine himself to religion. He might not have disgraced himself with gambling debts.

"I would have liked that owner." Julianna wrinkled her nose at John.

"You like horses?" That explained the muscular calves, John thought.

"I adore horses. My family has more than I can count. At our country estates." Her expression brightened abruptly. Like the sun emerging from behind one of the clouds he could see in the rectangle of blue overhead. John noticed she was little more than a girl. Her simple green robes hung loosely on her slim figure. Her black hair was drawn up, out of the way, and coiled tightly on either side of her head. There was a firm set to her jaw.

He realized why he had thought her familiar. She reminded him of Cornelia.

Cornelia whom he had met in Egypt, so many years ago after he had left Haik and the rest of the mercenaries outside Antioch. Cornelia had possessed the same dark hair, lithe figure, and strong calves, the latter a result of her bull leaping. She was part of a troupe. One of their acts recreated the ancient Cretan art of performing acrobatics with bulls. Julianna might be almost the same age as Cornelia had been back then.

Not more than half his own age now, John reminded himself. Nor was he the same then as now. He was aware of a chilly breeze rattling dead leaves. The tall yews swayed slightly, sending their shadows flickering across the garden.

"I enjoy the chariot races myself," John said. "I did a lot of riding when I was in the military."

Julianna looked at him quizzically. "You? In the military? I wouldn't have thought you were the sort." Her tone hardened again. Her mouth tightened in the same pronounced way Cornelia's used to when she got angry. Had John been so obviously staring at her?

"I spent quite a few years with a sword at my side. Judging people too quickly can be dangerous."

The girl did not quite roll her eyes. "Why do you want to talk to me?"

"I like to get some idea of who I have in my home."

"But you never have anybody in this dusty old place."

"How would you know?"

She shrugged. "You can tell the rooms haven't been lived in. There are cobwebs in all the corners. I wanted to stay at our house, with mother, but father insisted I come to the palace."

"You'll be safer here, if there's more trouble in the streets. Your mother should have come as well."

"She told me not to worry. They aren't interested in her. Just in father, and maybe Uncle Pompeius. As if anyone would be interested in uncle."

"Interested?"

Julianna laid a hand, delicate like Cornelia's, on the back of the miniature horse and absently petted the narrow back. "Oh, they say the factions want father to be emperor or some foolish thing. It's just silly. You know all that though. It's why we're here."

John nodded. "You don't take the idea seriously?"

"Certainly not! Father doesn't want to be emperor any more than this little horse does. I think it would kill him!" She spoke lightly but immediately bit her lower lip.

"You understand that you are here so that no one can force your father to change his mind?"

"I don't know why we couldn't stay in apartments at the Daphne Palace. Wouldn't we be safer there? We weren't spying on the emperor."

"Did anyone say he suspected you?"

Julianna looked down at the stone horse. When she spoke it was to change the subject. "At least at the Daphne I had some friends to talk to. Do you suppose Justinian would mind if Antonina visited me?"

"You know Antonina?"

"Oh yes. Very well."

"She's hardly your age. She's a friend of Theodora, isn't she? And older than the empress."

Julianna looked back at John. "Antonina and I have a lot in common. She's as fond of horses as I am. Her father was a charioteer. She's taught me a lot." She scowled. "You're just like father. You think I'm a child."

"We had better get out of the garden," John said. "It's getting cold." The truth was he needed to think of Julianna as a child because when he didn't she reminded him too much of the past. "I'll ask Justinian if Antonina can visit," he added.

Julianna followed him back into the dining room. He pulled the screen shut against the rising wind.

"Thank you," Julianna said. She brushed a burr off the front of her tunic. "And please accept my thanks for your hospitality toward my family."

Chapter Thirteen

Felix began to lose his nerve when he reached the top of the low marble tiers encircling the terrace outside the Hall of the Nineteen Couches. He stopped and took a deep breath. Why would a woman like Antonina invite him here?

Because she was the same sort of woman as her friend Theodora? A woman who shared the empress' malicious and often sanguinary sense of humor?

It was time for the assignation. The last pale rose of sunset had darkened to imperial purple and then black over the wall of the Hippodrome. All around the dark, blocky masses of palace buildings loomed up toward the starry sky. They reminded him of long ago scouting expeditions amongst the crags of the Isaurian mountains. More exhilarating than guarding the emperor and probably less dangerous.

Felix was not in the habit of turning down invitations from attractive women. Besides, he argued to himself, it might be dangerous to refuse the whim of a powerful patrician.

He exhaled and started down the tiers. The tramp of his newly cleaned boots echoed loudly.

In the dimness, the Hall of the Nineteen Couches was a long, black escarpment. The limited portion of the palace grounds Felix could see was mostly dark. A torch flared beneath a colonnade. There was a light behind the latticed window of the Octagon atop the Daphne. Another light shone from a window at the far end of the hall.

Was Antonina waiting there? Or someone else?

He crossed the terrace. At first he thought the covered passageway leading into the hall had been left unguarded. A soldier stepped out into his path.

He drew his sword. Then realized it was only the statue of a former emperor, emerging from the shadows as his eyes accustomed themselves to the gloom.

The interior of the hall felt colder than the gardens outside. The curtains separating the reception area from the dining space were open, allowing him to look down the entire length of the building. He might have been in a high, narrow subterranean chamber. A gargantuan mithraeum. He could barely make out the shadowy shape of the imperial table in the center. Other tables sat near the walls, each surrounded by couches where diners could recline in the ancient Roman manner seldom followed these days.

The only illumination came from several candles on a table in the far corner of the hall. Felix walked warily toward the trembling lights, keeping to the middle of the room. As he drew near he saw that Antonina had kept their appointment.

She reclined on a red upholstered couch which perched on gilded gryphon's feet. Her own feet pulled up under the lavender billows of her silk robes were bare, judging from the dainty black slippers sitting on the mosaic floor beside a taloned paw. A gold circlet encrusted with pearls held her unruly blonde hair lightly in check. Strands of larger pearls encircled her neck and fell across her bodice. The delicate pearl cascades of her earrings swung lazily as she turned her face toward him.

"Felix! You have come after all. You are a courageous man."

"Should I be afraid to meet you?" His voice had a hollow ring in the dark, empty space.

"Of course not. But I can tell from the way you approach that Narses told you who I am. That nasty little eunuch has spoiled

my surprise. Put your sword away. Do you always approach
ladies with your weapon drawn?"

Felix had forgotten he was holding his sword. He slipped it
back into its scabbard. "A common soldier shouldn't be meeting a lady of the court alone like this," he muttered, glancing
around. He couldn't see any guards or servants but surely they
were observing from somewhere nearby, from a doorway concealed in shadows or from behind one of the hall's silver columns.
Antonina said nothing nor did her expression reveal anything.
"Then again a common soldier cannot very well disobey a lady's
command," Felix added.

"You call yourself a common soldier? I thought you were
great friends with Narses."

"Does one such as Narses have true friends?"

Antonina laughed. "Well said, Felix. Sit down now."

A bare arm emerged from the loose silken garments as she
reached out to pat the couch that had been pulled up, head to
head with her own.

Felix followed orders. As he moved toward the couch the air
turned warm. For an irrational moment he imagined the heat
was radiating from the silk clad woman, then he spotted a tripod
brazier filled with embers.

He was not sure how to arrange himself on a couch. More
often than not he ate while seated on a stool. Propped up awkwardly on one elbow he felt like a fool and exceedingly uncomfortable. The sheathed sword dug into his side.

At Antonina's behest he willingly filled his goblet from one
of the two golden carafes on the table, emptied it, and filled
it again. His gaze wandered to an enormous bowl filled with
delicacies. He took another gulp of wine.

"Do you know, Felix, the first time I saw you I knew we must
meet in a more intimate setting. How has this magnificent bear
got into the gardens, I said to myself. I was afraid if I were not
careful he might devour me. Yet I was not entirely displeased
by the prospect."

She giggled.

For a long time neither spoke. Felix did not know what to say and Antonina did not offer assistance. She seemed content to stare at him, disconcertingly. Her eyes, which Felix remembered as being blue, glittered like pools of fire in the candle light. They looked enormous. He drank mechanically. The wine helped a little. It made everything feel like a dream. The flickering light accentuated the crows feet around Antonina's eyes. She was older than Felix, in addition to being far above his station.

"My father was a charioteer," Antonina finally said, as if reading his thought. "My mother was an actress. How thrilled they would have been to see their daughter dining at the palace with a member of the imperial guards."

"But you are a lady now and a friend of the empress." What could that mean for him, Felix found himself wondering. The lover of a confidante of the empress could hardly remain a lowly excubitor, could he? And the husband of such a woman would certainly be a general.

"Theodora and I share humble backgrounds," Antonina said. "Her father worked at the Hippodrome the same as mine did. He was a bear keeper."

Felix lowered the goblet from his face. "And the empress was an actress, like your mother." His words came out slurred. "The two of you must have a lot to talk about. When most court ladies were lying about being pampered, the two of you were working your way up." Felix stared numbly into his goblet. He frowned. Had he actually said that?

Antonina laughed again. "I admire a man who says what's on his mind. How tired I am of all the fops at court, lisping around in circles, in mortal fear they might utter a few words that actually mean something and thus might offend someone who must not be offended. You are not from the court, are you?"

"My forbears were German. I am a citizen of Rome." He said thickly. "This is excellent wine, but very strong."

Antonina shifted on her couch. He felt her fingers touch his shoulder, then her warm breath fell against his neck as she whispered in his ear. "Don't worry, Felix. This wine is special. It will not prevent you from doing whatever I desire. Quite the contrary."

What did she desire? This time, he had not spoken the thought aloud. Had he? As a young soldier he had lain with women in many places—on the thin mat of an Egyptian brothel, the mossy bank of a stream, the sand drifting against the weathered altar of a ruined temple. But to lie with a lady of the court, a personal friend of the empress, in the Hall of the Nineteen Couches....

"What is the matter?" Antonina asked softly. ""Why does your hand shake? Let me pour you some more of this fine wine."

◇◇◇

After what seemed like several nights had passed and the sun still hadn't risen, John gave up on sleep. He pushed aside his cover and swung his feet over the edge of the thin mattress, making the bed frame squeak. A walk in the gardens would refresh him. He could sleep some other night.

The servants had laid out his clothes the previous evening. They would have dressed him in the mornings if he were to allow it. He pulled the dalmatic over his linen tunica. The over-garment was wool with dark blue trim at the sleeves and hem, slit at the sides for ease in walking. He despised the stiff, heavy, embroidered costumes required for formal events at the imperial court. He felt imprisoned in them, paralyzed, weighed down.

He fastened his belt, ensured his short blade was in its scabbard, and then put on his well worn calf-length boots. He reached for his long, woolen cloak, then decided a brisk pace would keep him warm enough.

Outside the cool air smelled of manure and straw. John could hear whickering from the horses stabled nearby. He went on into the gardens. An excubitor, on his rounds, nodded to him. A man who spoke in private with the emperor could go where he liked, unchallenged, at any time—and John's unusually tall, lean figure was easily recognized by everyone.

He went along a mosaic pathway between shrubbery. He thought best while walking. The physical act seemed to propel him toward the solution to his problem.

Tonight he considered the murders he had been ordered to solve.

Who would have wanted the two imprisoned faction members dead? Someone who needed to insure that Justinian would not be able to placate the factions by making a display of pardoning them at the Hippodrome as he said he had planned to do.

Could that same person, or persons, have arranged for the Blue and the Green to survive their hangings, so that they could be killed afterwards, after the possibility of pardons had inflamed passions? Most of the city probably believed that the emperor had murdered the captives. They were more furious about that than they had been about the executions, which were, after all, commonplace.

Or was that too complicated?

The executioner Kosmas said the ropes had not been tampered with. Wasn't it more likely that the botched executions were a chance occurrence, and that the murderer or murderers simply took advantage of the situation?

John emerged from the path into a clearing at the edge of one of the series of terraces which descended in steps toward the Marmara. He saw the lights of ships strewn like orange sparks across the black water.

Lost in his own thoughts, he hardly noted the scene. Who was the man who had arrived at the Church of Saint Laurentius to see the captives, bearing an imperial seal, he wondered.

Was it possible that Justinian himself wished to foment a crisis to enable him to crush opposition to his unpopular policies at a time of his own choosing rather than risk some unexpected attack in the future?

If so, what was John's real role in investigating the matter?

He had risen to a lofty height but he was far more disposable than a high official—Narses, for example, who would be pleased to have him out of the way. He did not believe for an instant that the treasurer's offer to assist him in his investigation was genuine. More likely he was hoping to find a way to implicate John in the trouble. He was best avoided.

A man shouted.

In the silent darkness of the gardens the sudden noise startled him.

More shouts followed.

John came out of his musings as if from a dream. He ran in the direction of the commotion, blade in hand.

A figure barreled around the edge of a mass of bushes and practically collided with him. An excubitor.

"What's happening?" John demanded.

"A mad man's loose on the grounds."

As John sprinted around the bushes his foot caught on something. He sprawled forward. His knees hit paving stones. Looking down he saw he had tripped over a hand. The hand was attached to an arm which ended jaggedly below where the elbow should have been.

"I see you found the rest of him," came a voice.

John climbed to his feet. The excubitor who had spoken leaned over and picked up the marble arm.

"Knocked the emperor's left foot off too," said the excubitor. "Fellow doesn't like statuary, it seems. Been hacking away at statues all over the palace grounds. He's bound to start after real people before long."

John noted the group of guards gathered around a marble figure of Constantine which stood on a pedestal where two paths met.

"What does the culprit look like? Has anyone seen him?" John asked.

"A cook, out gathering herbs in the middle of the night—or so she claimed—said it was a monster, like a rampaging bear. I doubt that. Whatever she saw made her scream. That's what alerted us."

"I am sure you'll apprehend the man soon enough. I won't interfere with your work."

John started to walk away and the excubitor shouted after him. "Excellency, do you think it's wise to be here by yourself?"

John kept walking. When he judged he was shielded from sight by shrubbery he broke into a run.

His lungs burned with effort by the time he had reached the end of the walkway at the edge of grounds, in the shadow of the Hippodrome's wall. He heard a dull clanking noise before he could see anything. Then he made out the bronze statue of Constantine he so often passed on his way home from meetings with the current emperor. When he saw the broad backed soldier swinging his sword at the bronze he thanked Mithra that no excubitors had arrived before him.

"Felix!"

His friend spun around.

"What are you doing, Felix?"

The big man stared at John without comprehension. Then he looked down at his sword. "John? What...?"

"Why are you out here attacking statues?"

"What? I'm doing what?"

"Do you have a particular grudge against Constantine, my friend?"

"I...I don't understand."

"You're drunk."

Felix blinked and ran a hand through his beard. "Yes. Very drunk. That's all I remember. Drinking too much. Until you called my name...I...I...."

"You're lucky I happened to go out for a walk tonight," John said. He saw that Felix's gaze was unfocussed. "As soon as I heard about a monster like a bear rampaging through the gardens, I guessed it might be you. Let's get back to the house. Hurry up. Before the excubitors find you."

"Excubitors? Looking for me?"

"You don't remember what you have been up to?"

Felix shook his head. "I'm not even sure where I am."

John's mouth tightened. "Your good comrade Bacchus is going to get you into real trouble one of these days."

Chapter Fourteen

January 13, 532

Late in the afternoon the twentieth chariot race began. Or was it the twenty-first? Or twenty-second? John had lost count. It wasn't surprising. He hadn't slept the previous night. Justinian, seated on the throne in the kathisma, looked bored. He fiddled with the purple embroidered hem of his light wool cloak. The imperial box was cold. Located at the highest level of the Hippodrome it was easy prey for the winds that swirled around the vast stadium.

The emperor would probably be happier in his private apartments, John thought, and not just because of the weather. No matter which teams won, these races were not going to end as the emperor had planned when he sent John to Saint Laurentius for the prisoners.

The sky was leaden, glowering as if in disapproval of the events unfolding below. The thousands occupying the tiers of wooden seats seemed in ill humor as well.

There was an ominous note in the factions' chants of "Mercy for the hanged men!" that had accompanied the races already run, rolling out like thunder over the sound of chariot wheels and hooves beating a fierce tattoo on the track around the spina.

It was a sound that warned John, even exhausted as he was, that the usual rivalry of the factions was rapidly brewing into something worse.

John moved through the courtiers flanking the emperor to the back of the kathisma where Felix stood guard. "There's more than a sprinkling of blue clothing in that mass of Greens opposite."

Felix nodded. "I thought you'd notice that. It's unnatural for the factions to mingle without blood being spilled. It can only mean trouble." Except for the dark bags beneath his eyes, Felix showed no effects of his nocturnal campaign against Constantine. In fact, his expression suggested he might enjoy being called upon to act in his official capacity against a less than imperial rabble composed of flesh and blood rather than bronze and marble.

Cheers briefly submerged the continual rumble of demands as a chariot for the Greens careened around the turning posts in a shower of sand behind its four straining horses, remained upright by some miracle, and sped across the chalk finish line.

The driver just behind was not so fortunate or skilled. His chariot slewed to one side and crashed into the wall of the spina. Workers rushed onto the track to pull the wreckage out of the path of the trailing chariots. The horses rushed on, encumbered only by their yoke, while the driver staggered to safety.

The crowd cheered this mishap more loudly than the finish.

"A victory satisfies only half the partisans," John remarked. "Everyone loves an accident."

After a time the cheers, catcalls, and oaths ringing round the stadium subsided. A sudden stillness descended. It was as if the entire population of the city held its breath.

Then the rumble of discontent began once more. "Mercy for the hanged men!"

Justinian fidgeted on his throne. Below the imperial box dust rose as men raked the earth and sand smooth for the next race. "Narses!" Justinian commanded. "Step forth!"

The dwarfish eunuch rustled to the emperor's side, and bent forward to hear a whispered question.

From where he stood, John could not hear what it was Justinian had asked. He was able to make out Narses's answer. "It would be a grave mistake to accede to the demands of the unwashed horde. Where would it end? Offer them nothing."

Justinian smiled faintly. His merriment did not reach his eyes. He motioned to the guards on either side of this throne and they unsheathed their swords.

"Won't do them any good if the crowd swarms up here," Felix muttered.

Narses glanced around with a sneer. It was common rumor he had supernaturally keen hearing and it was a wise man who said nothing incriminating within sight of him, though others claimed that his knowledge of who had said what and when was gained by a vast network of spies inside and outside the palace grounds.

He addressed the emperor again, more loudly than was necessary, loudly enough to be heard by half the dignitaries in the imperial box. His reedy voice sounded shrill. "Caesar, it is in fact impossible to agree to mercy for the hanged men given they have been murdered. You cannot even produce their murderers thanks to John's bungling of his task. Yet if you attempt to explain this to those fools howling down there, there is no doubt some will seize upon the news and declare that it was you who ordered them executed in the very church itself."

Justinian frowned. It was obvious that Narses was reiterating a conversation they had already engaged in for the benefit of those within earshot. "It is as you say, Narses," he replied, his tone bland.

Felix swore quietly. "Did you hear, John? That bastard Narses is blaming you. As if you could have prevented those guards failing in their duty," he said in an outraged undertone. "And by what I hear their commander should have been pensioned off years ago. Completely useless and paying for it in a dark cell right now. In fact, there are those who whisper he was chosen specially for the task so that...." He lowered his voice even further "... certain parties could get to those prisoners and murder them."

John recalled the elderly commander, Sebastian, being dragged out of the emperor's reception hall to the dungeons. He preferred not to think about the poor fellow's current situation. Sebastian had struck John as a frightened and confused old man. Not fit to command, but even less fit to be a conspirator. "What about the guards themselves?" John whispered. "Do you suppose they were bribed to ignore orders and allow the assassin to carry out his task?"

Before Felix could answer the angry rumble of the assembly swelled into a deafening roar. John could feel the noise vibrating up through the soles of his boots. It was just as well the imperial box jutted out from the stands in such a way as to be inaccessible to the spectators. And even more fortunate that the doorway in back led to a suite of rooms, and a stairway that ended inside the palace grounds not far from the Daphne Palace.

Felix leaned forward to peer past the emperor's throne. "It's Porphyrius," he said. "Porphyrius is racing."

From the back of the kathisma the track was all but obscured by a multitude of patricians and officials. Usually they milled about, talking and laughing, more interested in each other than the spectacle below. Now they were all standing in rapt attention.

"He hasn't got the lead," Felix said.

Thanks to his height, John could see over most of the heads in front of him. Even from a distance, through clouds of dust raised by flashing hooves, he recognized the driver with the cropped grey hair. Whipping his horses furiously, Porphyrius passed the bronze statue of himself erected on the spina by the Greens and then the gold likeness placed there by the Blues.

Felix shook his head. "He must have broken from the gate very badly. There are two chariots between him and the spina. He can't win from out there."

John knew Felix was right. No matter how strong the horses, they could never cover the extra distance around the outside of the track quickly enough to overtake the two teams on the inside.

Porphyrius was usually a fury in the melee coming out of the gates as the drivers fought to be first to reach the spina.

As the chariots reached the far turning posts the driver who had gained the inside erred. John wasn't surprised. It must be unnerving to have to spend a race endlessly passing monuments to your opponent's greatness.

A wheel clipped the track's inner barrier. The chariot bounced off into the path of those following. Both drivers reined in their horses and swerved to the outside to avoid a collision. An errant wheel, snapped from an axle, spun wildly down the track along the side of the spina.

The wrecked chariot flipped over, dragging two of the horses to the ground with it. Any sounds of agony were drowned out by the crowd's clamor.

Porphyrius and his opponent were practically underneath the kathisma. Several dignitaries in splendid robes leaned over the side of the emperor's box, shaking their fists and screaming encouragement as enthusiastically as the lowliest laborers in the stands.

John glanced at Justinian. The emperor wasn't looking at the track. His gaze appeared to be directed toward the masses opposite, or the grey sky, or, to judge by the look in his eyes, nowhere at all.

The trailing chariots were just appearing around the turn. Porphyrius reared back and lashed savagely at his steeds. Almost instantaneously his opponent did the same.

Felix, seemingly as carried away as everyone else save the emperor, shouted in John's ear. "Whoever claims the inside wins!"

John looked down the track. One of the workers employed to clear wreckage had jumped onto the track and caught up with the run-away wheel. He bent to grab hold of it. He was a boy. When he straightened up four horses and a chariot were coming straight at him.

Porphyrius had time to slow his team or turn aside to avoid the boy. Instead he bought his whip down again.

The boy stood frozen. At the last possible instant he threw himself to one side.

Then Porphyrius was racing alongside the spina in the favored position.

With only two laps left he could not be caught. When he crossed the finish line the crowd screamed and stamped until it felt as if an earthquake was about to bring the Hippodrome down.

Justinian remained lost in thought to all appearances. John wondered if he was contemplating the awesome power of this mass of humanity. If directed rightly, they surely could bring down the palace walls.

Porphyrius was making his slow victory lap. He did not wave to the spectators, or look to either side.

Felix's voice rasped in John's ear again. "Can you see what color he's wearing? Isn't he supposed to race for the Blues?"

John peered toward the track. "I can't make it out. He's covered with dust."

He saw Narses saying something to the emperor who nodded. Justinian beckoned to a large man wearing a toga of the ancient style and holding a jeweled scepter. John recognized the man as an imperial herald. Justinian spoke, gesturing as he did, apparently giving instructions.

As Porphyrius completed his circuit of the track and came even with the kathisma, the herald stepped up onto the low platform at the front of the box and raised the scepter. The masses, focussed on Porphyrius noticed the movement in the imperial box. Silence fell. Was the emperor about to make an offering to them? But what did he have to offer to cool their anger?

Accompanied by several guards Justinian, Narses at his heels, brushed past John and Felix.

"Romans, your emperor greets you." The herald's trained voice rang out, audible to every ear in the eerily quiet stadium. "Now, as we all rejoice in this great hour of victory, know that our beloved emperor Justinian, merciful and just, has heard your plea. Content yourselves that in his benevolence and wisdom, he chooses to serve his people and his God. To protect the empire and its citizens from those who would do it harm the emperor decrees that the two faction members be kept in safety until they can be released without danger. Now let us offer our praise to both the emperor and our glorious champion, Porphyrius."

John thought the herald rushed the final sentence a bit. The big man practically fell over his dragging toga as he hastened off the speaking platform and out of the imperial box.

The dignitaries looked at each other and the suddenly empty throne in confusion. The throng remained silent. Stunned. They had expected their demands to be met or, perhaps, rejected. Justinian had done neither.

Standing in his chariot on the track, facing away from the kathisma toward the stands where the Greens were seated, Porphyrius raised both arms high above his head.

The Greens exploded. If the previous uproar had been the low rumble of an earthquake this one was a thunderclap. A thunderclap that went on and on.

As Porphyrius pivoted to face the Blues, John saw the reason. The great charioteer wore no colors. He was dressed in dull brown. But his upraised palms had been painted—one blue, the other green.

◇◇◇

The outcry carried to the seashore where the ragged man who had claimed he would walk into the palace and take the demon emperor to task sat with his feet in the seawater, devouring a raw fish. He looked up at the wheeling cloud of gulls overhead and smiled.

"Doves of the sea, it will not be long...."

And then on the malodorous wind came an even louder cry, torn from thousands of angry throats: "Long live the Blues and Greens! Long live the mercy of the Greens and Blues!"

The man eating a fish smiled again. "Old enemies are uniting, my feathered friends," he said, throwing fish bones into the water. "Soon they will receive good tidings...."

Chapter Fifteen

"You'll appreciate that I don't have time to spare. We've had more reports of trouble in the streets." The Urban Prefect Eudaemon did not move as if he were in a hurry as he led John slowly down a corridor at the Praetorium. He was a big, soft, wide-hipped man with dull eyes and a thick lipped mouth. Dressed like a soldier in a cuirass, his tunic cinched at the middle with a wide leather belt, leather boots reaching to his knees, he reminded John of the cow that had originally worn the leather.

The prefect would not have needed reports of unrest had he glanced out the Praetorium's entrance. A noisy gang surrounded the building, flooding the Mese back to the archway into the Forum Constantine.

The sounds did not penetrate to Eudaemon's office. The standard cross on the wall was accompanied by a bust of Justinian on a table. Codices were strewn across a marble-topped desk.

Eudaemon stood by the desk. "When I was informed you were here to see me I was inclined to refuse. Then I was told you are on the emperor's business. Even so…." He sighed. He was dressed for battle but gave the impression that fighting was the last thing he wanted to do.

"The Green and the Blue who survived their hangings. Who were they?"

"As to the Blue, I can't say. No one came forward to identify him. The Green, I learned after the hearing, was named Hippolytus. An unfortunate name for a patron of the racing teams. Charioteers are such a superstitious lot you'd think they would want nothing to do with a man whose name meant undone by horses. Still, gold smooths many a rough patch and stills fears in a remarkable fashion."

"You hang men without knowing who they are?"

"Why do I need to know a man's name when I know his crime? Under the laws of our great emperor we hang men for their crimes not for their names. Hippolytus was a wealthy man. The Green no doubt a worthless ruffian. A baker's son perhaps. There's justice in all her beauty. A rich man and a baker's son hanging side by side."

"Nevertheless, I would expect a magistrate to inquire into a man's name before condemning him."

"I acted as magistrate. Should I beat a man's name out of him if he won't cooperate? I admit the hearing was conducted in haste. There's been no time to waste lately and the emperor's orders were plain. The executions were meant to serve as an example to the populace. To show that the emperor sides with neither faction. He allies himself only with the law. Even handed justice is what was wanted."

"Everyone is trying to be even handed lately," John remarked, thinking of Porphyrius' recent demonstration at the Hippodrome. "When did you find out about Hippolytus?"

"Shortly after those meddling monks carted him off to Saint Laurentius several miscreants showed up here to petition for his release."

"You sent them away?"

"Justinian's orders were to execute the criminals. It wasn't for me to contradict the emperor."

"How politically active was Hippolytus?"

"Active enough to get himself hung."

"What were his crimes, exactly?"

Eudaemon pursed his lips thoughtfully. "Exactly? Well… that's hard to say. I'm sure a lawyer could find the appropriate offenses, given more time than was available. Hippolytus instigated a riot against the emperor the night before the execution. He and his friends went on a rampage, all the while calling for the emperor's head. To be precise, they broke into a butcher's, stole the carcass of a swine, dressed it in a purple robe, and decapitated it in front of the Praetorium. Do you doubt there's a law against that?"

"I'm not a lawyer."

"And, you are…what? I'm not sure you mentioned your position."

"I'm a chamberlain to the emperor."

The prefect's face reddened slightly. "Yes, I see. My apologies. I am trying to be helpful. It's just that I've been rushed off my feet."

"I understand the gallows had to be constructed in a hurry."

"It's true I had short notice."

"Could that account for the failure of the ropes?"

"I can't see how. We keep our equipment in the storerooms next to the prison. There's quite a collection of devices. The empress in particular often has whims. The ropes were simply not up to the task. It happens. Whoever sold them to us will suffer for it, when I have time to go over my accounts and determine who that was."

"I was thinking that someone could have tampered with the ropes. There must have been a lot of confusion in the rush."

"It was the usual crew. Of course, these Blues and Greens insinuate themselves everywhere. There's always bribery. But that would mean the ropes had been cut and they weren't. Not according the reports I received."

"Your executioner, Kosmas, doesn't think they were cut. You met Hippolytus. Do you have any opinions? Is it possible who he was had anything to do with his escape or his murder?"

"In what way? I can't think of anything."

John had held off questioning Eudaemon about the guards who had been dispatched to the Church of Saint Laurentius and had failed so miserably in their task. Since it seemed he could learn nothing more about the executions, he mentioned their failure.

The prefect turned even redder. "Are you questioning my integrity?"

"I'm only trying to make sense of things. From what I've been told, a stranger bearing an imperial seal was allowed past the guards. However, the guards had already failed in their duty. The prisoners were already gone. As it happens they had been murdered. Whether they were killed in the church and dragged off to the cistern, or taken outside and killed near the church, isn't clear. Nor is it clear who killed them. It was military men, apparently, who disposed of them. But it was a blind man who told me that. Were your guards responsible? Can you account for them all?"

"No. Several have gone missing. You see, I am being honest. But then again, I've lost a large portion of my force in the past few days. Not that my men are cowards, but they don't necessarily want their families in the city if it goes up in flames. And others, I regret to say, are probably wearing the colors of the factions right now. As for the men sent to Saint Laurentius…if a few have vanished, can you blame them? If you were given the task of guarding prisoners in whom the emperor took a special interest and failed in your duties, you might decide to look for other work far from the capital. A reasonable man might conclude that before long an imperial official would be asking questions and looking for someone's head."

He gave John a pointed look.

"I'm not looking for anyone's head," John said. "Just for information. Those guards might have left Constantinople with hefty bribes. What can you tell me about Sebastian? He struck me as old and incapable for such an important command."

"That depends on what capabilities might be required. It did occur to me that in this case we had more to fear from treachery than from direct, physical force. I assigned Sebastian the task precisely because he has served so long and with absolute, unquestioned loyalty." Eudaemon's gaze flickered in the direction of the bust of Justinian. "And see where his loyalty has got him."

The prefect appeared genuinely distressed at the thought of his elderly commander imprisoned in the imperial dungeons. "I will put a word in for him," John said.

"May I ask why you so interested in these two ruffians?" Eudaemon asked. "They should've been executed straight away. What difference does it make if their deaths were delayed by a few hours? Why should anyone care who was responsible? Justice is done."

John's reply was interrupted by a clerk who burst into the office, gasping for breath as if he'd sprinted down the corridor. John could tell he was a clerk because he still held his reed pen, although the agitated man didn't seem to realize it. He waved his hands frantically, sending droplets of ink flying. "Prefect! Come quickly! There's trouble at the prison. The mob is demanding the prisoners be released."

"Is that so? If that's what they want, that's what they'll get. We'll hang every one of the prisoners from the portico in the front of the Praetorium. That will end the demands!" Eudaemon turned to John. "Excuse me, excellency. I will return as soon as I've given the orders." Now Eudaemon did move fast, striding out of the office and following the clerk down the corridor.

John glanced around. The abruptness of Eudaemon's departure had taken him by surprise. He walked over to the desk and studied the codices scattered across its marble top. City regulations and imperial proclamations. An account book lay against a partially opened scroll displaying what appeared to be classical poetry.

Eudaemon did not return.

John had intended to ask the prefect for an escort back to the palace. He waited for what felt like a long time, then decided further waiting was not a good idea. He stepped into the corridor. As soon as he did he could hear raised voices and smell smoke.

He started toward the vestibule.

A figure leapt from a doorway and slammed John into the wall. He had an impression of a blue cloak, an unnaturally high forehead where the hair had been shaved away in front, yellow teeth in a snarling mouth. Then something smashed into his side. He fell sideways and slid down the wall.

Another Blue, holding a splintered length of wood, loomed over him. Others emerged from the room opposite. Clouds of smoke followed. One of the men held a torch.

John tried to blink back the dark fog swirling at the edges of his vision.

"Who's that?" asked the man with the torch.

"He came out of the prefect's office," someone answered.

The Blue standing over John raised his irregular club. "It's time you're introduced to justice."

Before John could react, the club dropped from the assailant's hands and clattered onto the floor. A gurgling shriek came out of the Blue's mouth, followed by a gush of scarlet.

The man's companions turned and fled.

Felix pulled his sword out of the man's back. It took several hard tugs, while the Blue convulsed like a speared fish and blood bubbled from between his lips. The burly excubitor kicked the body away and leaned over to help John to his feet. "I appreciated your saving me from my own folly in the gardens last night. I didn't expect to repay the favor so soon."

John stood up. Aside from a pain in his shoulder where he'd hit the wall, he seemed to be uninjured. "I thought you intended to go straight from the kathisma back to my house?"

"I did. But I thought I'd scout out the situation in the streets first. I didn't like what I saw. People were pouring straight out of the Hippodrome and down the Mese. The factions weren't fighting each other, either. They were setting fire to shops. I knew you were coming here to talk to the prefect."

"I'm glad you came after me, my friend." Belatedly John pulled from his robes the short blade he always kept concealed there.

Felix looked at the weapon dubiously. "Now we have to get back to the palace," he said. "We'd better get moving. As soon as the rioters realize the prefect's men are all battling at the prison this part of the building will be swarming."

"Unless it burns down first," John remarked as they ran into a roiling mist. He pushed part of his cloak over his mouth. The acrid fog burned his throat.

A confusion of shadows surged through the haze in the vestibule. No one challenged John and Felix. In the chaos they appeared to be just two more rioters.

They emerged onto the portico and stopped abruptly. The view of the Mese was partly obscured by a macabre curtain, a line of hanged men dangling from the front of the portico. Some inventive person had managed to loop ropes over the ornamental work and decorative statuary above.

John pushed one of the dead men aside to reach the steps leading to the street. The boot that swung round and nudged him in the back as he ducked past was military footwear. The guards had ended up being hung, not the prisoners.

He scanned the row of dead-eyed men. He did not see Eudaemon's bovine form.

Felix bent over a body crumpled on the steps. He straightened up and held out a short spear. "John, take this. I don't see any swords. At least it's a better weapon than that little onion chopper of yours."

John grasped the spear. He hoped it would serve him better than it had served its previous owner. He faced the street.

The palace wasn't far away, not much more than the length of the Hippodrome, less than a single circuit of the racetrack. But a clamorous multitude blocked the way, clogging the thoroughfare and the colonnaded walkways on either side. Smoke poured out from beneath the colonnades.

He and Felix went down the stairs. An unarmed man in a cuirass stood at the bottom, gazing around vacantly. Half his face was blackened. John couldn't tell whether it was soot or if the flesh had been burned off.

"You're one of the urban watch, aren't you?" Felix barked. "What's going on?"

"We were sent on patrol." The man rasped. "When I got back...the prisoners were gone...and...." He looked toward the line of hanged men and looked away.

"What's it like elsewhere in the city?" John demanded.

"Just like it is here. The Blues and Greens are fighting together. I saw three churches on fire. They hung our patrol leader from the neck of the bronze bull in the Forum Bovis. I must report to the Urban Prefect."

The man started to mount the low stairs and staggered.

"Forget that. Save yourself," John told him.

The man gaped at John, one white eye staring unblinkingly out of the blackened ruins of his face.

"You are relieved of your duties by order of the emperor's chamberlain," John went on.

The man tottered away.

Felix grunted. "If only you could relieve the two of us—"

A deafening roar cut short his words. Pieces of masonry and glass rattled across the pavement around them. Glancing back at the Praetorium, John saw that a section of the wall had collapsed inward. Flames licked out of a jagged gap. Figures flooded from the main entranceway to the building. Some were on fire. Many ran straight into the dangling corpses. One unfortunate dislodged a dead man and became entangled in the rope. The two rolled down the steps in a gruesome embrace.

John stepped aside to avoid being knocked over. He glanced down the crowded, chaotic street in front of them again. "I'd prefer not to fight my way along the Mese," he said. "I know a better way."

He broke into a run, leading Felix to what was little more than a crevice between the walls of the Praetorium and a neighboring church. He squeezed through the gap. He might have entered an inferno. The heat was unbearable. He touched the rough bricks and yanked his hand away as if from a glowing brazier.

"Careful," he yelled to Felix. "There's fire behind the wall."

Felix cursed. "Are you trying to cook us?"

John squirmed forward as fast as possible. The burning building might collapse completely at any moment. Sweat poured down his face, blurred his vision. The heat radiating from the wall felt intense enough to blister his skin.

The crevasse between the buildings narrowed further. John forced his way sideways and stuck.

No, it was only his cloak caught on a nail.

He yanked the fabric loose, kept moving.

Then he was in an alleyway that ran behind the Mese. There was nothing here but the backs of buildings. No inviting targets for arson or looting.

Felix emerged, grunting and cursing.

The two men ran.

Here and there the alley turned to accommodate a larger building. Mostly they passed behind shops. More than a few were ablaze. Although the shops presented marble facades to the Mese, by imperial decree, the structures themselves were wood.

In one place the exotic scents of a perfumer's mingled with the smell of burning. In another, they skirted rivulets of wax from a candle shop. A fine rain of ash continually fell from the sky, greying John's dark, cropped hair and his short blue cloak and Felix's beard.

Suddenly fire blocked their way. Flames leapt into the alley as if from the open door of a furnace. The air was alive with a deep, almost palpable rumble. The thick clouds of smoke accompanying the flames made it impossible to judge the extent of the inferno.

Without pausing, John flung himself into the flames.

Almost instantly he found himself in a semi-circular plaza where the Mese's roofed colonnade curved inward. Felix was beside him, brushing sparks from his beard. John slapped out a glowing patch on his sleeve.

An obelisk, the height of two men, bore carving identifying the place as a sculptor's workshop. Emperors and gods and goddesses, surrounded them—the artist's wares, mostly copies of classical works.

On any normal day wealthy patrons would be strolling around, making their selections. Today a man had been hung up by his foot from the raised arm of a bronze Julius Caesar. The man had been set alight, a still living torch. He screamed as a several ruffians prodded him with lances. Concentrated on their amusement, the victim's tormentors did not notice the two new arrivals.

John raised his own short spear.

Felix put his hand on John's shoulder. "No," he said in a whisper. "It's impossible. There are only two of us. The poor man is beyond saving anyway. If those thugs spot us we won't be able to save ourselves. I have an idea."

They were standing next to a marble depiction of a stern, bearded old man on a throne, a much reduced copy of the mighty Olympian Zeus.

Felix stepped up on Zeus' foot, pulled himself into the pagan god's lap, then onto his shoulder. From there he was able to climb to the back of the throne, grab the edge of the colonnade's tiled roof, and haul himself up.

John followed. He could see they had nearly reached the Chalke. The roof on which they stood led straight toward it, an elevated walkway. They soon would be back inside the palace walls.

Evening had fallen. The lurid glows of raging fires could be seen in all directions. Their yellowish red glare twinkled through the darkness of a city where decent people cowered behind locked doors and shuttered windows. Underneath the frantic screams of the burning man, John could hear a low, rhythmic roar like the beating of waves. The crackling of countless fires, perhaps, mixed with the shouted rage of thousands of rioters.

Movement caught his eye. Was the huge cross on the nearby roof toppling over?

No. There was a hunched figure perched on an arm of the cross, gesturing wildly, a silhouette against distant fires, ragged and demoniac.

"A fire fit to warm the demon emperor's haunches!" cried the figure. Then it dropped and scuttled away.

The two men watched the strange creature vanish into the night. Then Felix started along the colonnade roof in the direction of the palace. John went after him.

Now he could pick words out from the roar of the city. The same words repeated again and again.

"Nika! Nika! Victory! Victory!"

Chapter Sixteen

From a distance the four figures gathered in the latticed pavilion in the middle of the dark palace gardens suggested conspirators meeting to plot harm to the empire. On the contrary, the meeting had been arranged by Justinian in a location where the discussion could not be overheard except by the chubby, gilded Eros perched on the edge of the pavilion roof.

Felix considered it an unnecessary precaution. Weren't the private meeting rooms and reception areas deep within the Daphne Palace secure enough? Justinian had been unnerved by the growing anarchy outside the palace walls. He was starting to sense enemies lurking around every corner and he was a man given to whims.

This particular whim was chilling Felix to the bone. He stood in the arched doorway to the summer retreat and shivered. Captain Gallio had spotted him as soon as he and John had reached the safety of the Chalke after their flight from the burning Praetorium.

"You've been out in the streets," Gallio said. "Good. The emperor wants a report on conditions."

Felix wondered why Gallio hadn't sent patrols out. Perhaps the patrols had been sent but had not returned.

He was still sweating as he described the chaos to the emperor. He supposed he smelled of smoke but by now there was no place in the city that didn't smell of it. Justinian made no comment. Nor did he order Felix to return to his post at John's house. So Felix waited. The sweat had long since dried. Now he was cold and uncomfortably aware of the Eros squatting just above his head and glittering in the torchlight.

Justinian paced back and forth across the circular space, staring at the pavilion's tessellated flooring, while Narses and Belisarius looked on. The three men made an odd picture, the common-looking man who was nevertheless emperor, the handsome Belisarius, the dwarfish Narses.

Felix switched his gaze back and forth between the emperor and the general. Of the two he was more interested in Belisarius. How young he was for a general! Despite his youth he seemed unperturbed by the crisis. His sharp, patrician features betrayed no anxiety. Felix wondered if he should trim his own unruly beard. The closely clipped black beard Belisarius wore gave him a more disciplined look. More suited to a military man. The great general had offered a curt nod in his direction after Felix concluded reporting. Felix took the gesture as a compliment but pleasure died when he saw the dark expression that briefly flowered on Narses' face.

Had he said something he should not? The thought was cut short when Justinian turned on his heel and addressed Belisarius. "What do you know about the situation in the city?"

"The city is passing beyond mere restlessness. It is much as the excubitor said. The Blues and Greens have been torching buildings together."

"Anger may cause disputants to move in the same direction when they are in a mob," Justinian remarked.

"Very true, Caesar. Yet early this morning, before the races, a more telling incident occurred. A Green tried to rob a senator in front of the Church of the Holy Apostles. Four men passing by— laborers for the most part—set about the Green. He would have been beaten to death had not four Blues suddenly appeared and rescued him. They also stabbed the senator, but he will live."

Justinian's brow furrowed almost imperceptibly. "Blues coming to the aid of the Greens. Shall we now see fiery stars falling through the air and hear of unnatural births? How do you interpret these strange events?"

"Considering the chants in the Hippodrome it appears that the factions have truly joined together."

"And not with any good intentions," the emperor muttered.

Narses coughed in a meaningful fashion and Justinian glanced at him.

The treasurer took it as permission to speak. "If that is the case and the hordes cooperated in storming the palace, Hypatius or Pompeius might find themselves wearing the purple. They are after all the nephews of Emperor Anastasius. I am told there are those who still whisper in dark corners of their desire to place one or the other on the throne. There is always ingratitude."

Justinian smiled ruefully. "Whoever is not in power always has supporters who consider him a better wager. The weak and traitorous can be easily persuaded they have the right to rule. I would not be surprised if the brothers worked to that end."

"And perhaps, being in an excellent position to do so, they are engaged in spying as well?" Narses suggested.

"He's right," Belisarius put in. "As long as they remain within the palace as your guests they are better able to see what unfolds. Even though you have wisely put the pair under guard, we all know that servants, and even guards and courtiers, hear more than they should, and most have loose tongues."

"And it is not unlikely they have contacts within the palace," added Narses. "People who are working for them. Reporting to them."

"But if they were not inside the palace they might be inciting the malcontents," Justinian said. "Besides, we cannot risk an accident to Anastasius' relatives. That is why they and the girl have been invited to live on the grounds for the present."

"I should think an accident would not be the worst event that could befall the empire," Narses told him.

Felix heard Justinian's voice grow uncharacteristically sharp. "Do you then believe it would be wisest to execute Hypatius and Pompeius immediately, thus ensuring neither of them will wear the purple? I will not hear of such a thing. I have promised them my protection."

"I only meant that if the Lord saw fit to intervene in his own mysterious fashion, we could not complain," Narses said quickly, his reedy voice rising a pitch.

"Caesar, if I may…?" Belisarius interrupted.

"Speak."

"From a soldier's point of view and as a matter of strategy the pair mentioned may well prove useful at some point. If the factions unite to attempt to put one or the other on the throne, given they are already in your power, showing mercy toward them may curb the mob's temper."

"Excellent advice," Justinian replied after a lengthy pause.

"We all agree, then," Narses said. "But if I might sound a note of caution…I am uneasy about their reluctant host." He glanced at Felix as if to make certain he was listening.

"Do you not trust my chamberlain John?"

"Are you sure you can count on the loyalty of the Greek eunuch? While I do not endorse the calumny that paints all such as treacherous creatures, for I have served faithfully and—"

Justinian raised his hand, ordering Narses to be silent. "You are telling me that while I can trust the eunuch I know, the eunuch I don't know is a different matter? However, I believe I know John well enough to trust him."

Felix noted that Belisarius could not suppress the flicker of a smile. Nor could he miss the look of fury directed by Narses at the young general.

A flutter of purple glimpsed through the lattice work caught his attention a heartbeat before the three other men turned their heads.

"You are dismissed," Justinian said as Theodora appeared.

The empress addressed Belisarius. "A word with you."

Felix and Narses bowed and retreated. Narses pushed past Felix and headed off into the gardens at a rapid pace. Felix took a last glimpse back in the direction of Belisarius. When he heard what Theodora was saying he suddenly forgot he was cold. His face flushed.

"General, I have arranged a private supper in my apartments this evening. Do not fail to present yourself. Our friend Antonina wishes to meet you."

Chapter Seventeen

John wiped flecks of ash from the short, wide leaf-shaped blade that was always at his side.

"You need to get yourself a better defensive weapon," said Felix. "That's nothing more than a cheese chopper."

"I thought you called it an onion chopper. I got used to it—or rather one just like it—years ago."

"Yes. It looks like an antique. Seeing it reminds me that Narses is still sharpening his blade on your spine. And his blade is deadlier than that turnip sticker." He helped himself to more wine. "I expect he'll blame you if anything happens to your house guests and he's had Justinian's ear longer than you have. My advice is avoid the worst shadows, know who cooked your swordfish, and—"

"—get a better weapon." John had listened in silence, his wine cup untouched, as Felix recounted the conversation in the pavilion.

The two men were sitting in the private chapel of John's house, safely away from the ears and ministrations of the servants.

Felix took another gulp of wine and coughed. "This is foul. Have the imperial cellars run out of a drink a man can offer friends without apologizing?"

"You won't get an apology from me. That's Egyptian. I ordered it specially. It reminds me of happier times. Like my blade." He turned the dagger over in his hand, inspecting it, then slipped it back into the sheath concealed inside his tunic. "Besides, it's an acquired taste so Pompeius has left it alone. Not that he hasn't found sufficient drink that's more to his liking."

"He does seem to enjoy the grape." Felix gazed dolefully into his cup. "So do I...usually. Perhaps you could direct me to the stores Pompeius is drinking."

John looked at him thoughtfully. "It isn't just my wine that's making you morose, is it?"

Felix's jaw clenched and his cheeks reddened. He told John what he had overheard Theodora saying.

"You sound jealous," John said. "Why should you be concerned if Theodora has arranged for Antonina to meet Belisarius? You've only met Antonina once and after last night I would have thought you'd be happy to never set eyes on her again."

Felix set his cup down. "My friend, it is as if I have been enchanted. I wish I knew what sort of wine we drank together last night." He stared up in the direction of the cross on the ceiling. Since Felix was a fellow Mithran, John doubted he was appealing to the Christian god for guidance.

"You don't want anything to do with any friend of Theodora's." John spoke sharply. "Antonina is every bit as dangerous as Narses. You said he was sharpening his blade on my spine. Well, you can be sure Antonina is sharpening her blade as well, although not perhaps on your spine."

John looked around suddenly, stood up, and pulled open the door. Pompeius stood in the corridor. Corpulent, rumpled, and surprised.

"I...I...was just about to knock...."

"You were taking your time about it. You've been there for quite a while, breathing rather more heavily than most. Loud enough to be heard."

"It's all that exercise Pompeius gets lifting heavy jugs of good wine," Felix put in.

"Sit down," John ordered his visitor, and almost immediately regretted it. Although there was a stool available, the tiny chapel was barely large enough to contain two men let alone a third who was practically a crowd all by himself. John sighed as the legs of the seat creaked and threatened to give way under Pompeius' weight. "Why did you wish to see me?"

"To…to…ask if….you know when my brother and I will be permitted to return home."

"Immediately. I will have my servants escort you to the gates."

Pompeius' eyes opened wide within their nests of folded flesh. He drew in a wheezing, whistling breath. "Oh? Do you think that's wise? I mean—"

John smiled thinly. "That's not what you wanted to ask me, is it? Don't worry. I won't throw you out on the street. Now why were you lurking outside the door?"

The fat man squirmed on the inadequate stool. He seemed to be exuding a vinous miasma from his pores. The cramped space was filled with the smell of wine and sweat.

"Ah. Well…." Pompeius paused. "I happened to be going by and I couldn't help overhearing…um…the conversation about Antonina…"

"You have very acute hearing, Pompeius."

"Yes. Thank you, excellency. I…uh…I thought it prudent to hear what was being said. I agree with your advice. It is widely known that Antonina dabbles in magick and I would not be surprised if she were merely trying out a new potion on your excubitor friend. They say magicians will sometimes poison a cat, as a test…and…well…"

Felix looked murderous but remained silent.

John glared at Pompeius. "And you were about to knock on the door and impart this information to us?"

Pompeius waggled his multiple chins in a nod. "If that woman has decided on Belisarius he does not have much chance of escape. Besides her ability to gain assistance by means of strange potions and such, he is young and naive."

"He may be young but he is a great general!" Felix declared. "I am sure he can beat back the wiles of a woman." He frowned suddenly. "If he wants to, that is."

"You call him a great general," Pompeius said, "but he was nothing but a common commander making forays into Persarmenia five years ago. And not for military purposes either. No, your general was there to capture slaves for the empire."

John's expression darkened. "Is that so?"

"Anyway, bored courtiers make up all sorts of nonsense," Felix said. "A lady of the court wouldn't be practicing magick."

Pompeius waved a chubby finger and shook his head. "I would not be so certain, young man. I happen to know Antonina once wanted to assist a certain charioteer to win his race, not to mention her favors. After all, to the winner goes the spoils, do they not? And so to ensure he triumphed she boiled up several gulls and a couple of crows and gave the resulting gruel to his horses after they exercised in that field near the lighthouse."

Felix glared. "Do you think I'm a fool?"

Pompeius ignored the interruption. "Now, I know a crow from a crowbar and I'd have wagered the only possible result was the horses would be sickened and useless, but the horses immediately tried to fly off the sea wall!"

"It does not sound likely to me," Felix replied. "But supposing it is true—"

"Oh, there's no doubt about it. I heard it from a most reliable person, who had the story from a man whose brother cleans out the stables at the palace, who saw it happen with his own eyes! His own eyes, mind you! But that's not the most interesting story about Antonina and her magick. No. There was the time when—"

John stood abruptly, squeezed past Pompeius, and looked down the corridor toward the semi-darkness of the atrium where a lone wall torch flickered.

Yes, he had heard footsteps. A man trotted through the shadows, his face bone white with fear.

It was Pompeius' brother, Hypatius.

"The rabble are attacking the palace," he shouted in panic. "The barracks are on fire and the senate house. We have to get out before the blaze reaches us!"

Pompeius wobbled to his feet and banged into the table.

John strode to Hypatius' side. He could see the man was trembling. The square jaw worked, as if he were trying to speak and couldn't.

"I went for some air," he finally managed to blurt. "At first I thought the glow was merely part of the city burning. Just some more of those wretched wooden tenements. Then I realized it was closer. I could see the flames and sparks in the sky."

"Does Julianna know?" John asked.

"Julianna? Oh, yes, yes. Julianna. Of course! Someone save my daughter!"

Felix and Pompeius joined them. Felix cursed softly. Pompeius carried the cup of wine John had left unfinished.

There was a hiss and a pop. A bright speck arced briefly through the dimness.

"We're on fire already!" Hypatius cried.

"It's just a torch," John said. "I'll see what's happening."

There was no need. Before he could move the house door flew open, revealing Haik. "The Chalke's on fire," he reported.

"Where's Julianna?" John demanded of the two brothers. Pompeius gaped at him and Hypatius began to stammer something.

"I'll find her," Felix said. "I'll send some of my men to help with the blaze." He pivoted and went pounding along the corridor toward the back of the house.

John glared at his aristocratic guests with ill-concealed contempt. "We'd better get out in case the place catches fire." Neither Hypatius nor Pompeius protested.

Haik gave John a grim smile.

Several servants had appeared in the atrium, looking apprehensive. John ordered them to find their colleagues and leave the house, then he left himself.

As soon as he was outside he could see flames leaping skyward above the roof tops. He made his way through the knots of people who had emerged from nearby residences to stare toward the approaching conflagration. Once he passed the stables he felt heat beating against his face.

He saw immediately that the Chalke was lost.

Men carrying buckets and ladders raced out of the massive, blocky structure in which the bronze gate was set, pursued by roiling clouds of smoke. Anyone caught inside would be dead.

A man perched atop a ladder just outside the gateway hacked at a burning roof spar that threatened to fall across the entrance, apparently oblivious to the fact that his dangerous task was now pointless.

The roof of the barracks next to the Chalke was already ablaze, sending cascades of sparks into the air.

Grooms were leading horses from the stables.

John wiped his smarting, watering eyes. He instructed his servants to help dowse the fires springing up all over the open courtyard, thanks to the steady rain of sparks and burning debris borne by a gusty, scorching breeze. His nose and throat burned painfully.

Then he grabbed a shovel and joined those engaged in filling leather buckets with earth, which others carted off to smother the flames that ran along the dried grass in front of the stables in scarlet and gold lines.

It wasn't work a chamberlain to the emperor should be doing, and a single pair of hands could make little real difference but it wasn't in his nature to simply stand by and give orders.

John saw that Haik shared his feelings. His old military colleague had joined a chain of water carriers running back and forth between the palace gate and a watering trough.

It was not unlike being on a battlefield again with the clamor, the confusion, the crush of men working frantically, half hidden in smoke and darkness, shouting, cursing. Horses whickered and snorted, terrified by the fire and noise.

John's shovel might have been a sword. He wielded it until his muscles were on fire and his breath came in searing gasps.

At last, despite all efforts, the roof of the Chalke caved in, sending a fountain of embers swirling upwards.

As a pillar of smoke rose into the sky, John could hear the roar of mob outside, exulting in the destruction. Above the shouts of the fire fighters and the crackling and popping of flames he could make out words.

"Nika! Burn them all! Heaven's will shall be done!"

He shivered. The moment his shovel was still he was cold. Sweat poured down his sides. He realized the wind had shifted. Now it carried the chill from the sea rather than the heat from the burning city.

The multitude continued to chant but the rising wind blew their anger back at them and blew the fire away from the palace.

John leaned, exhausted, on his shovel. "Thank Mithra," he muttered to himself.

Chapter Eighteen

"The Lord sent a miracle, changing the wind like that," Haik told John. "Then again, my aching muscles insist on taking some of the credit for saving the palace."

He grimaced as he turned his chair to better see out the doorway which opened onto the portico surrounding John's overgrown garden. The room John's guest had been given was near the back of the house, across the interior courtyard from the suite being used by the Anastasius family.

Haik sat at the small bedside table and poured the obligatory wine. Wine, John thought, was as much a prerequisite to conversation as opening one's mouth. The first cup did little to wash away the taste of ashes.

"Maybe you should leave the city before it burns down around you," Haik said. "Start afresh. Come back to Antioch with me. You know the area. It doesn't get so chilly."

John could feel a draught from the open door eddying around his boots. The air smelled of smoke, but not so strongly as his clothing did. "I'm not fond of the cold. I've suffered worse. Constantinople isn't Bretania."

John could see that Haik was studying him. The light from the oil lamp beside the wine jug threw unnatural shadows up around his old colleague's face, accentuated the great beak-like nose, made him more than ever resemble a bird of prey.

"I'm not shocked to find you in such a high position, John. When we served together, you always struck me as a deep thinker."

"Back then? I ran away from Plato's Academy to fight."

"There was definitely a stoic air about you."

"Just as well, as it turned out."

Haik shook his head. "I'm sorry. I didn't meant to bring up—"

"You didn't. Some things are never far from one's mind. I try not to dwell on. It is only the thinking about it that is distressing now."

"See, you are a philosopher."

"So my old tutor Philo used to say. In truth, when I was younger I thought philosophy was only good for amusing children who hadn't gone out into the world and consoling old men who were done with it."

"Now you know better."

"I know it is very dangerous to be a philosopher at the emperor's court."

"More dangerous than being an emperor's advisor? What if Justinian doesn't survive this uprising? What would your future be like then?"

"Very short, no doubt."

"Doesn't that bother you?"

"Every morning that we pulled on our boots to march to battle we knew we might be face down in the dirt by the time the sun set."

Something moved in the garden. A night bird, or the wind swirling around the courtyard, swaying a branch.

"You're right," said Haik. "That seems a very long time ago. I guess I was braver then. Maybe we only have so much courage and I've used all mine up."

"I doubt that. You were as good a fighter as any of us. It is hard for me to see you as an estate owner rather than a soldier."

"It suits me, John. I took enough orders when I was a fighter. And I like having my fate in my own hands. Isn't it vexing to have your fate tied to one man? Even if Justinian survives this crisis, there's sure to be another. And suppose he dies in his bed? What happens to his advisors when the new emperor takes control?"

"Nothing drastic necessarily. Look at Hypatius. He's served both Justin and Justinian. Not only was he a favorite of Emperor Anastasius, he was a family member. If Hypatius hadn't been in charge of the armies in the east, far away from the capital, when his uncle died, he would have been proclaimed emperor rather than Justin."

"And then Justin couldn't have made his own nephew, Justinian, his successor. Does the throne descend through nephews now?"

John smiled slightly. "You see my point, though. Emperors need experienced men."

"Even if they are experienced at failure? Everyone says his military record was dismal. Justinian removed him as eastern commander and replaced him with Belisarius hardly three years ago, you'll recall. He might bear a grudge. Doesn't that make him a threat to Justinian now?"

"Justinian might think so. But I can assure you, Hypatius wants no part of being emperor. I suspect he has made a realistic assessment of his own abilities."

"As opposed to just being a coward." Haik turned away from John to peer into the garden. John heard what had caught his attention, a rustling sound, like a rodent scurrying through dead leaves. The wind had grown even stronger. A gust of frigid air blew into the room.

Haik got up stiffly and shut the door.

"What about your own profession?" John said. "It would worry me if my life depended on pistachios."

"They're more reliable than an unpopular emperor. Need barely any water. Live practically forever. On a quiet night, if you stand under a tree which has reached perfect maturity, you can hear the sound of the shells bursting open. That's said to bring the listener good fortune."

"There was a time when I dreamed of simply owning a farm."

"Why not now?"

"My life has changed." He did not add that he had dreamt of sharing his life with Cornelia. Where was she? Still touring with the troupe? Was she alive? Even if he had some way to find her they could no longer share a life together, given what had happened. The city was preferable for the solitary creature he had become. The crowds, the noise and danger, kept him from slipping away completely from the rest of mankind.

"And you must have resources, considering the position you hold," Haik was saying. "Buy a small estate. You can grow anything you want. Breed horses. Or we could be partners."

"There are days when I might almost consider what you suggest."

"Such as the day Justinian flees the city? If you were to purchase some land, now, then you'd have a place to go. It might be too late for that, but you could at least make sure you have enough of your assets in gold, ready for transport."

"Are you preparing to replace Justinian yourself, Haik? You sound convinced that his days—and mine—are numbered."

"I'm just going by what I've seen since I arrived. Riots, fires, the factions rising up together. It's not like this in the city all the time is it?"

John laughed, without humor. "It is usually much more restful, although hardly bucolic." He put his wine cup down. "I need to get some sleep, my friend. As far as I know Justinian is still the emperor and I am still under orders to investigate the murders of those two faction members."

"Have you learned anything useful?"

"I may have, but if so, I haven't recognized it yet. Maybe Porphyrius will know something helpful. After that exhibition of his at the races, I want to talk to him."

Haik frowned. "Talk to Porphyrius? Surely you don't suspect him of anything? He was just trying to be even-handed, or so I've heard."

"Is that all? I hope so. Nevertheless, I want to know if he's been approached by anyone from the factions. He's a highly respected man and very influential, when he wants to be."

Haik stared at the guttering flame of the lamp. "John, if you're going to be asking Porphyrius about his visitors, I know of one he will probably mention. Myself."

John looked at his friend in surprise.

"You traveled here to see Porphyrius?"

Haik shook his head. "No. Not at all. I have business in the city, as I said. But Porphyrius spent years racing in Antioch. I knew him in passing. I just wanted to pay my respects."

"Is that all?"

"Well, I hardly spoke to him. We were interrupted by a visitor."

"You did speak, however."

"Yes. I'm thinking of expanding my business. I won't bore you with the details. Nothing was settled anyway. I didn't think to visit him until the day before those botched executions. You know the state the city's been in since then. He hasn't been able to see me again."

"You say the meeting was about business."

"It's a new venture. And, Porphyrius is respected in Antioch too. I thought he might put in a good word for me. I see you disapprove. You're thinking your old military friend has turned into just another conniving businessman. What can I say? Once a mercenary, always a mercenary."

Chapter Nineteen

The woman peered over the low brick parapet. From the tenement roof she could see into the Augustaion. Tongues of fire outlined the Great Church. The leaping, flickering red light revealed dozens of men and women howling and dancing in obscene drunken delight. Shrill screams resounded across the square, littered with broken and spoilt goods from nearby shops which had been forced open and pillaged.

She had seen thieves dart into the burning church and emerge, coughing and retching, clutching treasures which flashed in the firelight. They vanished into the warren of alleys beyond, to whatever life gold and silver would buy in a world that seemed to be coming to an end.

The woman behind the parapet was more interested in the group of men clustered in the alley below. They had pursued her. She had managed to escape their forceful attentions, but for how much longer?

As if in reply came a hoarse shout from above. She looked up toward the roof of the adjoining building which leaned crazily over her temporary sanctuary, nearly touching the timbers she stood on. She saw the dark outline of a figure against the night sky.

"They will not harm any green thing!" cried the figure.

The woman wept with fear and crouched lower, shrinking into the shadow of the parapet.

The hoarse-voiced man continued to shout over the background noise—screams of pain, and the dull roar of men drunk on stolen wine and violence.

"I tell you they won't harm any of them! Success is assured! Why are not the armies of the righteous storming the gates of the palace?"

There was a brief pause and then a lower pitched voice, still strong enough to carry to the woman, replied. "Greens, Blues, what does it matter who they are? They just need a strong leader. Someone not afraid to confront the demon emperor!"

She could not see the other man.

"I am here to do that! And I see—" The first speaker moved suddenly. The woman flinched. She thought he was leaping down toward her. Instead he lurched sideways, landed at the very corner of the building and tottered on the edge. "I see necklaces of fire cleansing the city of its filth! Hear the sinners scream!"

"Is it as foretold?" asked the other.

The reply was uttered in a weary tone. "No. The horsemen, the four horsemen are overdue. Ah, but did you ever see Porphyrius race? Now there's a man who's won me many a wager. How the women love him! I've often wished I were a charioteer."

Fearful as she was, the woman continued to stare upwards, intrigued. Who were these men, conversing as if they were at a social gathering while the city burnt round them?

Now they appeared to be discussing horses.

"The Greens raced several chestnut horses last week," one observed. "Red horses…it was an omen of peace departing. I said so at the time. Porphyrius just laughed, the great fool. There's always strife, he said, and especially when we Greens are winning. Why, he even said I should contribute a bag of silver coins toward his expenses, as if I hadn't contributed more than most of the faction to ensure the team's victory!"

A quieter voice answered, pointing out that a greater victory hung in the balance.

"The horsemen are late! Where is the black horse carrying the man with the scales?" The speaker's voice rose into a shriek. "Where is death, riding a pale horse with hell following? Hell is here already! Where—"

A hand fastened on the woman's shoulder. She screamed.

One of the men in the alley must have guessed where she had gone and made his way up the tenement's staircase while her attention was diverted.

She jerked away with the strength of desperation, raking the leering face with her nails. She jumped to her feet, ran across the timbers, and clambered up onto the overhanging roof where the two men had been talking.

She had no way of knowing if they were different than the men who pursued her. They couldn't be worse.

The ragged figure perched at the corner of the building took no notice of her. She stumbled and scrambled over to him on her hands and knees. She saw her assailant pulling himself up onto the roof.

She clutched the ragged man's leg and begged him for protection.

"A scarlet woman! An abomination!" the invisible speaker proclaimed.

"Away with her!" shouted the man whose leg she was holding.

The woman had time to realize there had been but one person on the roof before the bloody, ragged man grasped her by the waist and threw her over the edge.

Chapter Twenty

The dull red ember of the mid-morning sun glowed through the smoky haze as John hurried through the gardens to meet the emperor. A light snow of ash fell continuously out of the thick overcast. It had been falling all night. Ash partially covered the marble walkway. Bands of men ran back and forth hauling buckets of water from ornamental ponds and fountain basins, dousing small fires smoldering in the bushes.

A grim faced silentiary ushered John through a series of antechambers leading into a private meeting room above the Augusteus. John tried to brush ashes from his cloak. His fingers made grey streaks across the dark blue fabric. The imperial couple stood at a high narrow window, the shutters of which had been partially opened despite the cold. Seeing Theodora, John prostrated himself in accordance with court protocol, as enforced by the empress.

Justinian ordered him to stand, sounding irritated by the necessity of doing so. "Report on my guests."

"All three are under guard at my house, Caesar."

"We are glad to hear it," Theodora put in. "Your personal safety depends upon keeping them unharmed."

"They have had no visitors?" Justinian asked.

"No. Do you wish me to bar visitors?"

"It would be more useful if you reported any immediately," Justinian said. "We need to find out who, exactly, is behind all this."

John followed the direction of the emperor's gaze. What he saw through the window shocked him. Of the Baths of Zeuxippus, only a single charred wall remained. Where the Chalke gate should have been were mountainous piles of rubble. Chunks of masonry lay scattered like enormous boulders. In places smoke and flames issued from the bleak landscape. Beyond the remains of the Chalke, across the open space of the Augustaion, the timber roof of the Great Church blazed. The walls of the long rectangular building remained standing, but John realized this was a temporary condition. One of the portico's supporting columns already lay shattered across the square.

He had glimpsed the destruction earlier when he had set out to continue his investigations. His way had been blocked where a roof had collapsed into a corridor leading toward the Chalke. He had not realized the extent of the damage.

"A sorry sight indeed," Justinian remarked, turning to John. Despite the chill in the room, he made no attempt to close the shutters or order them closed. "The Great Church built by Constantius was burnt during a riot at the beginning of the last century. Then the masses were not agitating over a couple of rogues. They wanted the exiled Patriarch to be returned. The result was the same. Strange how the past repeats itself. Do you suppose that is God's way of teaching us a lesson, or is he punishing us for refusing to learn the lesson the first time? But more pressing matters engage our attention. Have your investigations revealed anything further?"

"I regret that they have not. I will inform you as soon as—"

Theodora interrupted him. "It is already too late. Do you propose to wait until the cabal expose themselves by placing the crown on the head of a new ruler? If so, you are going to have a long wait. Before then, you will be executed for failing in your duty."

"We are taking steps to quell the riots," Justinian said quickly. "At his own suggestion, Narses has gone out into the city with a large sum of money in an attempt to persuade the ringleaders to see reason."

"It might work, Caesar," John said. "We still have no proof that these riots were planned. I think we can be sure that someone has by now tried to take control of them. Can Narses find the ringleaders?"

"He says they will rise to the surface to take a few coins like fish in a pond coming up for bread crumbs."

Theodora gave a cawing laugh. "Narses is a good judge of men. All are attracted to gold."

"Does that not include Narses himself?" John asked.

Theodora curled her lips unpleasantly. "Are you often tempted, John? I mean in the handling of imperial property rather than women?"

John's cheekbones reddened but he kept his voice steady. "I have never placed my own interests above those of the empire."

"There are many who would praise you for that," Theodora observed, "and in particular those with strong religious convictions."

"We are also attempting to appeal to men's better natures," Justinian said. "I have suggested to the Patriarch that a procession of holy men carrying icons might serve to calm the mood of the factions."

"Whereas I am inclined to send Belisarius and Mundus out to teach the rabble a lesson it will not forget." Theodora spoke as lightly as if considering whether she wanted a dessert of fruit or sweet cakes.

John felt a chill which had nothing to do with the cold air coming in through the open window.

Was Haik right? Would a prudent man leave Constantinople?

Perhaps Narses wouldn't return. At this very moment he might be riding through the Golden Gate, out of the city, the bribe money jingling merrily in the pouch at his belt, more than enough to set him up for life on an estate in his far off homeland of Persarmenia.

He wished it were so. Narses' leaving would make John's staying considerably more tenable.

Justinian had turned his attention back to the scene outside. From John's vantage point, the emperor's face displayed no sign of emotion. Whereas Theodora's eyes now burned with a demoniac fire, her husband's visage might have been an expressionless mask concealing some inhuman creature beneath.

"John," the emperor said, his lips barely moving, his voice toneless, "it appears that the situation in the city is changing, and not for the better. I have been forced by circumstances to take another step which you should know about."

◇◇◇

"Captain Gallio, as soon as I heard I decided to report back. You'll need all the fighters you can get."

Felix's urgent words caused the portly excubitor captain to look up from his meal, annoyance obvious in his florid features. Gallio swallowed, stuffed another piece of cheese into his mouth, chewed and swallowed again before speaking. "What are you talking about?" He stuck his knife into one of the boiled eggs on his plate.

"The rebellion, sir. I've been told the emperor is facing a full scale rebellion. No longer just disorganized rioting."

Gallio sat and blinked up at the younger soldier. His watery eyed gaze seemed to stray to the egg impaled on the knife then back to Felix.

"Who told you this?"

"I...I heard it...on good authority."

Felix found his captain's unconcern somehow ominous. He thought he had better not mention that John had arrived back at his house and recounted a private conversation with

Justinian. A conversation which both John and Felix had found disturbing.

Gallio nibbled at the boiled egg. He wasn't wearing his armor, Felix noticed, nor was any weapon in evidence, unless Gallio planned to fight the mobs with his table knife.

The long barracks room beyond the door to Gallio's private quarters was noisy and crowded, due to the fact that one of the barracks had burnt to the ground during the night. The excubitors appeared to be mostly arguing over how to share the limited space. No preparations for battle were evident.

Gallio waved his knife. "Why have you deserted your post, Felix? What is it you've heard?"

"At some point early this morning the factions stopped demanding the release of the two prisoners. They wanted the heads of Justinian's closest advisors instead."

"Yes. And he obliged them. Figuratively. He removed his legal advisor Tribonian and the tax man, John the Cappadocian, as well as the Urban Prefect Eudaemon. He's also sacrificed some underlings. Why should that be of concern to you?"

"It's everyone's concern when the mob starts calling for the emperor's head as well. They're openly agitating to return the family of Anastasius to power. They went looking for his nephew Probus, and when they discovered he'd fled the city, they burned his house down."

"This has all been communicated to me."

"Yet you sit there eating."

"Of course. Why else do you think I'm having breakfast so late? I was delayed listening to reports. If the factions are looking for the nephews of Anastasius that's all the more reason you should be at your post guarding them."

"You expect me and a handful of men to defend a house against a mob? The rioters must be dispersed. If they manage to become organized and break into the palace it will be too late."

"That's enough, Felix. Return to your post immediately."

"Sir, as a military man who has fought on the frontiers, I know that trained men can easily attack and defeat a—"

Gallio banged his knife down on his plate. "You think I'm not a military man? How do you suppose I got this post? I've fought in Scythia and Thrace. I was defending the borders against Cabades while you were still learning to get your tunic over your head."

"I'm sure that years ago—"

"Besides, I would think that a military man would not be so eager to come to the defense of one who capitulates to the rabble the same hour he hears their demands. Who do you suppose is in charge in this city? Outside the palace walls there is a badly armed but very angry army, led by…who? Disgruntled senators, some wealthy patrician? An unknown palace official? And inside are two renowned generals with their personal troops. And, of course, an emperor who takes orders from a mob."

"It isn't for us to question Justinian's decisions," Felix knew his words lacked conviction. Gallio was right. The emperor was not a fighter. Felix would have preferred to take orders from Belisarius or Mundus.

"I am not questioning our emperor's wisdom or his authority, so long as he possesses any authority," Gallio said. "In fact, the excubitors will continue to carry out their assigned task faithfully. I have already sent word to Justinian that we will staunchly defend the palace grounds, which has always been our mission. Nothing will move us from our entrenched position. Nothing!" He glanced out into the tumult in the barracks. "You see, our forces are settling in for the siege right now."

Felix realized what Gallio was saying. "You told the emperor you weren't moving from this barracks."

"Not all of us are stationed in this barracks."

"You won't fight."

"We'll fight when we know who is in charge."

"You're a traitor!"

Gallio sprang to his feet. "I'm your commander! And I am ordering you to resume your duties. Were you a less capable man, one I could replace easily, I would have you executed on the spot. Under the circumstances, I will give you the chance to save your thick German skull by resuming your watch over the imperial guests."

Felix stared at the captain, nearly blind with fury. It was all he could do to keep from drawing his sword.

To Felix's surprise Gallio smiled grimly. "I know you fancy yourself a fighter. You'd rather be taking orders from Belisarius than from me or Justinian. If you won't take my orders, then take my advice. Do your job. Have patience. Before long you might find yourself serving an emperor more to your liking."

"Belisarius isn't a traitor!"

"He isn't a traitor to the empire. Sometimes serving the empire entails making difficult choices." Gallio sat down and pulled his plate toward himself. "As for me, I choose to wait."

Chapter Twenty-One

His meeting with the emperor convinced John that he needed to talk with Hypatius and Pompeius. He could not drive from his thoughts Theodora's remark that his personal safety depended on him keeping his guests safe. It reminded him of a bit of history he had read once. In the days when Rome was still the capital of the empire, Juno's shrine was graced with a bronze of a hound licking at a wound. The figure was considered priceless and such was its worth that those into whose custody it was given insured it under the threat of losing their lives should it come to harm.

John feared he was in a similar position to the custodians of that remarkable statue, except that a bronze hound would not be likely to get itself into any trouble. The same could not be said for a pair of aristocratic brothers and a headstrong young girl.

He found the brothers in his dining room. Pompeius lay on a couch, drinking. His flaccid bulk reminded John of half decayed remains he had seen washed up on the shore. Hypatius was trying to string a bow. His hand shook too badly to manage the task.

John wondered if Justinian would still consider the pair a threat if he could see them.

A brazier warmed the air. The screens were closed but enough light fell through the windows overlooking the garden to dispel the gloom. Assorted strings and arrows littered the marble tabletop.

"If you're afraid the palace will be stormed, I'll ask Felix to provide you with more suitable weaponry," John said.

Pompeius emitted a sound somewhere between a burp and a laugh. "Aren't you afraid my brother will fight his way out of the house?"

Hypatius slapped the bow down on the table. He half turned in his chair, eyes wide with alarm. "I wasn't thinking of fighting. Can the rioters overwhelm the guards at the walls? Wouldn't Justinian leave the city first? Certainly there are enough ships available to transport the whole court."

"The palace isn't in danger," John replied. "If you weren't thinking of fighting why were you stringing the bow?"

"I love to hunt. I'd planned to spend the week at one of my estates. There's nothing like stalking partridge, pheasant, and hares when the weather's crisp."

"I keep telling him he should keep a few wild boars in his preserve," Pompeius put in. "But he wants nothing to do with boars."

"There's no sport in boar hunting," Hypatius said. "The hounds corner the beast and you spear it. Now flushing out a pheasant and hitting it with an arrow in mid-flight, there's a challenge for you."

"Also, pheasants do not have long, sharp...tuss...tuss...tusks." Pompeius struggled to get the words out.

"You must excuse my brother," Hypatius told John. "It's the wine talking. He used to hunt himself, before he became too fat to climb onto a horse."

Pompeius made a rude noise.

"It's much more pleasant to be riding around a forest than cooped up in the city like this," John observed.

"You understand. The ancients said that hunting and hounds were invented by the gods Artemis and Apollo, and yet a Christian may pursue the sport, don't you think? Many fine warriors have honed their skills during the hunt."

John had done a lot of hunting during his mercenary days, simply out of the necessity to eat. However, knowing how to spear a deer properly was not very useful when it came to hand to hand fighting on a battlefield.

"It's been a favorite sport of many emperors," he said. "There are those in the city who want you to take up more than an emperor's pastimes. I just came from the Augusteus. As I passed by the walls near the Hippodrome I could hear the populace chanting your name."

Hypatius' face turned the color of the ash that littered the palace grounds. "Surely not!"

"You are the nearest relative to Anastasius left in the city." John pointed out. "The old emperor is recalled fondly by many, especially those who share his religious beliefs or feel they have been wronged in one way or another by Justinian and Theodora."

"The whole city, in other words," put in Pompeius.

Hypatius ignored the remark. "The reign of Anastasius is long past. It's been fourteen years since he died."

"Dead emperors are always wiser and more benevolent than living ones. You are the nearest embodiment of him. You have his face."

"So I've been told. A strong family resemblance. Does Justinian think I want my face on the empire's coinage? That I would incite the throngs? Is that why he's locked us in here?"

"He questions your loyalty."

"But Pompeius and I came to the palace for safety's sake as soon as this unrest began! We were afraid the ruffians would drag us out of our houses and demand we betray the emperor. That must be clear to Justinian?"

"Being inside the palace would also serve a traitor well."

"But what could we possibly do, confined to your house like this?"

John studied Hypatius' face with its noble, overly long nose, the square, small chin. The man appeared to be terrified. Perhaps too terrified for someone who had commanded of the armies in the east, however poorly. "Have you had any visitors?"

"Of course not. Who would dare to visit? The emperor suspects we're spies. Isn't that so?"

"You could have followed Probus when he fled to the country-side. You would be hunting right now."

"We considered it more loyal to stay by the emperor's side!"

"Is that true? Or did you want to insure you were giving an appearance of loyalty by remaining in the capital?"

Hypatius looked away from John, toward the hunting equipment spread out on the table. "Do you think I wanted to place myself under arrest at the palace? And make no mistake, we all realize that is exactly what it is. I may have sought sanctuary but it is in a prison. Do you recall Vitalian?"

"I was fighting in Bretania two decades ago. I am aware, though, that Vitalian challenged Emperor Anastasius. He claimed that he wanted to force the emperor to accept orthodoxy."

"So he claimed. But everyone knew that although Anastasius was a monophysite he was not averse to listening to those whose beliefs differed slightly from his own. In that case I led the fight against the traitor. By ill fortune I fell into his hands. I spent a year in captivity before the emperor paid my ransom."

"Our uncle was always parsimonious," put in Pompeius.

Hypatius glared at his brother but continued. "Can you imagine how difficult it was for me to allow myself to become a captive once again? When I discovered you don't use your dining room I decided to spend more time here. It feels less confining than our rooms."

Was Hypatius' telling the truth? John had spent time as a captive of the Persians. He had been left with permanent physical wounds, though he preferred to believe that his spirit had not been wounded. "I can see that this must be very distressing to you," he told Hypatius. "Justinian is a prudent man. He is ever alert for possible danger. He means you no harm."

"Are you certain?" Hypatius' tone was almost pleading.

"Knowing the emperor as I do, I am as certain as I can possibly be." John omitted to add those who knew the emperor well understood better than others that his thoughts were utterly unreadable. "Are you certain you didn't have a specific reason for taking refuge here? Were you approached by opponents of the emperor? Disgruntled faction members, perhaps?"

"No. I swear it. We came here practically as soon as the rumblings began."

"That is supposing the unrest started spontaneously. There are those who believe it was planned. That the fire was intentionally set."

"If we had assisted we would surely have remained outside of Justinian's reach, in order to take advantage."

"Perhaps you didn't expect things to get so far out of control. You might have had second thoughts. Or you may be here to hide your complicity."

Hypatius stared at John in distress. "How can we prove our innocence if the emperor has set his mind against us?"

"Justinian hasn't set his mind against anyone. He's trying to find out who is responsible. He would be grateful to anyone who helped lead him to the culprits."

"If I had any information I would have shared it with you already. Do I strike you as a man who would try to withhold information from the emperor?" He held up a hand. It trembled like a leaf on an aspen tree. "Just the idea I might be under suspicion is torture to me, let alone...."

"The emperor has no intention of moving you to the dungeons." As John uttered the assurance he couldn't help think of the unfortunate old commander Sebastian, the commander who had failed in his duty at Saint Laurentius, being led away to a terrible fate.

Pompeius let out a gurgling laugh. "All of us at court know the dungeons are right beneath our feet."

John shot a glare at him but the man had already buried his face in his wine cup again. "Did you know any of the faction members who were executed?"

Hypatius shook his head. "Why would we? A gang of low ruffians, weren't they?"

John thought he saw an indication of surprise cross the man's face. Was it because the question made no sense to him or because it did make sense but he had never expected John to ask? "Were they all low ruffians?"

"I...I'm sorry," Hypatius said. "I don't know why you would be questioning me about some criminals. I admit, it is most puzzling why Justinian didn't just release those two from the church. Yet he removed three of his closest advisors. Are some anonymous Blue and Green more valuable to him than them?"

"Well of course," interjected Pompeius, "since they were pulled safely off the gallows by the hand of God."

It did not seem wise to John to reveal too much. And to question Hypatius further on the matter would be to stress the emperor's interest in it. That was the sort of information a spy would find valuable. Not that he could imagine the two brothers as spies. "Where is Julianna?" he asked instead. "I wish to speak to her."

"Justinian doesn't suspect her too, does he? She's just a girl!" Hypatius looked horrified.

Pompeius snorted. "She's better off here, Hypatius. Except she should be kept under lock and key to keep her away from that slut with the evil eye, not to mention—"

Hypatius leapt out of his seat and flung his arm in a wide arc. Pompeius' silver cup flew into the screen with a bang and clattered to the floor. Pompeius stared dumbly at his empty hand. "That's enough of that! You're disgusting!" Suddenly Hypatius did not sound like a frightened man.

Hypatius sat back down. "My apologies. It is true Julianna frequently visited Antonina. She is a friend of the empress, hardly a slut. Nevertheless, for a girl Julianna's age to befriend a woman such as...that is to say...a woman so much older..."

"The excubitors will prevent her from leaving the house," John pointed out.

Hypatius shook his head. "She's probably in the garden. She's spent all her time out there. Reading. She found several codices in her room. Or it could be she's merely sulking. Being confined is even more vexing to Julianna than it is to me."

John looked toward Pompeius. He seemed to have fallen asleep. He was motionless. One swollen hand hung limply over the side of the cushioned couch. A ragged snore offered the only evidence of life.

"My brother intends to spend this crisis in the company of Bacchus," Hypatius said with a feeble smile. "He told me so and advised me to follow his example."

"Bacchus makes for a most untrustworthy friend in times of trouble. Not that most of us haven't sought him out at one time or another."

"I hope you will assure Justinian that Pompeius offers no threat. In his present state he couldn't find his way to the throne, or sit upright on it if he did."

That appeared to be true, but John had been at court long enough not to trust appearances. The nephews of Anastasius had survived and apparently thrived for years. Perhaps it was because they were, in fact, too inept and lacking in ambition to threaten anyone. On the other hand, they might find it useful to give such an impression.

He exchanged a few more words with Hypatius, then went out into the garden, shutting the screens behind him. He glanced around at the unkempt vegetation, the yew trees growing up into the blue rectangle of sky in one corner, statuary peeking out from shaggy bushes. Not surprisingly he didn't see Julianna right away.

He took a few steps down a partly overgrown path. On a bench at the end of the path lay a leather bound codex. He picked it up. Xenophon's treatise on horsemanship. The house's previous owner had been fond of horses.

There was a rustling in the bushes. Julianna pushed branches aside and stepped onto the path. Her face was flushed and she was breathing hard. "I've been clearing weeds away from a few of the little horse statues. The garden is full of them."

She did not appear to be dressed for such work. Her robes were green silk, dyed in a hue so brilliant as to be almost iridescent.

Again John was struck by her resemblance to Cornelia. He remembered with a pang how she had come to him, after a performance, flushed and nearly breathless. He had been able to feel the heat radiating from her slim, muscular body. It was not something he should be recalling under the circumstances. Wherever Cornelia might be, she was no longer a girl and John was....

He forced the memories away and realized Julianna was giving him a puzzled look.

"I have been to see the emperor," he heard himself saying stiffly. "He is concerned with your safety. You must inform me immediately if anyone seeks to contact you."

"Certainly, not that anyone is likely to get past the guards." She wiped perspiration from her forehead with her sleeve. "Let me show you what I've found. Some of the sculptures are marvelous."

"I regret I have some urgent business. Tomorrow perhaps you can show me. Please take care."

He turned and went back down the path. "Take care," he muttered to himself, as memories swirled around him insistently. "Take care."

Chapter Twenty-Two

So far as those inside the palace could ascertain the violence of the previous night had tapered off. Now, as the Great Church, the senate house, and the baths smoldered, the angry masses congregated behind the ruins of the Chalke chanted slogans and shouted out demands. John left the palace grounds by an obscure southern gate.

Not everyone had taken to the streets. At the stables beneath the Hippodrome the regular business of the factions continued. John sought Porphyrius and had no trouble finding him. He was in a stall where a knot of young men had gathered, easily identifiable as charioteers by the leather wrappings around their legs. The great man was partly hidden by the flicking tail of a powerful bay whose hoof he had stooped down to examine. He straightened up and spoke to a worried groom. "He'll be fine. He's got hard hoofs, like me."

The onlookers nodded and murmured to each other at this revelation.

Porphyrius had the arms of a dock laborer. His receding hairline made him look older than his fifty odd years. He had a broad, flattened nose, perhaps the result of a racetrack accident. His square-cut unbleached tunic would have been more suitable for a slave than a man of wealth and fame.

"A good looking animal," John remarked. "One of your funales."

Porphyrius' gaze located the speaker. "You know something about racing then. You can tell an outside horse from an inside one." The charioteer's half mocking smile indicated that he wasn't impressed. A few of the young charioteers chuckled appreciatively.

"It's easy enough to see he is bred for speed more than strength," John said.

Porphyrius ran his hand over the horse's back. "Zephyrius has served me well for many years." He directed his words toward his admirers as well as John. "I've lost track of the palms he's won. He's an African, as I am. We both plan to retire to some place where the sun is hot all year, if our opponents ever convince us it is time to retire."

"Never!" shouted several of the charioteers.

"I must speak to you in private," John said.

Porphyrius gave his insolent visitor an appraising look. "Half the population of the empire wants to speak with me. I can probably see you later in the week, if the Hippodrome hasn't burned to the ground by then."

John handed him his orders. Porphyrius glanced at the scroll bearing an imperial seal. "So it's the emperor wishes my assistance," he said loudly. "That's different."

The charioteers buzzed excitedly as Porphyrius led John away, along a corridor and then up a wide ramp. They emerged into sunlight at the far end of the deserted race track.

"We won't be overheard here. There are many ears but only stone and metal ones." Porphyrius nodded toward the statuary lining the spina, a motley collection including ancient gods and goddesses, emperors and heroes, animals real and imagined.

"You have a large following," John remarked.

"It makes it difficult to work sometimes. Wherever I go, someone passes the word. The great Porphyrius walks among us. He is visiting the stables. He is inspecting the starting gates. He is using the latrine. Then they swarm and I am knocking people over with my elbows just to relieve myself. A man arrives home and orders his wife never to clean his boots again for the famous Porphyrius has pissed on them."

"You are both admired and influential. The crowds pay attention to your every word and even to the colors painted on your palms."

"I hope Justinian appreciates that my intended message at the Hippodrome was one of reconciliation between the factions. Since I have raced for both, they both respect me."

"But they have united to oppose the emperor."

"An unfortunate event and totally unexpected. Usually it is the clashes between the more unruly faction members which develop into riots. That is what I sought to prevent. This constant animosity between the supporters of our teams is burdensome to those of us who only wish to race."

"The Blues and the Greens seem to be bred to hate one another."

"It is because there are really only two teams these days. When the Reds and the Whites were equally prominent all four teams competed against each other. It wasn't simply the same rivalry, endlessly repeated, every race, year after year. One didn't see rioters at the Circus Maximus in Rome."

Porphyrius began walking down the sandy track and John followed.

"I race for the Blues, the emperor's favorites," Porphyrius said. "He can't suspect me of trying to undermine him."

"You used to represent the Greens."

"When Anastasius ruled. In fact, I may have headed the Green team when our empress was born to a bear keeper who belonged to the Greens. Anastasius actually preferred the Reds."

"Who were allied with the Greens and have now joined them, as everyone knows. However, it seems now that all the factions want the family of Anastasius returned to the throne. It's well remembered how you helped rally the people against Vitalian when he staged his revolt against Anastasius. They may be look-ing to you for leadership, to aid the family again."

"That was an eternity ago."

"Seventeen years. Have Christian or heretical beliefs changed since then? Vitalian was a defender of orthodoxy, like Justinian. You were a supporter of a monophysite emperor then. Am I supposed to believe you truly support an orthodox emperor now?"

The cries of gulls echoed around the stadium. Its tiers of wooden seats were empty except for gulls searching for scraps that had been left behind.

"I am a Blue," Porphyrius said.

"Do you change religious beliefs as easily as racing colors?"

"Matters are hardly that simple. Remember that one of the old emperor's nephews—Pompeius, I believe—shares Justinian's faith. And the populace would happily elevate him if Hypatius wasn't willing. Or so I've heard. You don't think this unrest is due to religious differences do you?"

"I am just wondering how you are connected with it, Porphyrius."

"As I explained, I was hoping to stave off the usual bloodletting between the factions. I thought it might help if I suggested impartiality."

"Not unlike the emperor's decision to execute an equal number of Blue and Green troublemakers earlier this week. Did you know any of the condemned men?"

"I don't mingle with common criminals."

"My understanding is these were faction members who went on a rampage. Racing supporters."

Porphyrius came to a halt. He scanned the empty seats reflectively then looked upwards. Over the rim of the Hippodrome smoke rose in ghostly columns. "We're preparing to race. Some say we should be preparing for the end of the world. What do you think?"

"If the world is going to end then preparations will come to nothing. However, like you, I intend to pursue my work. It usually happens that the world doesn't end after all."

"A good answer. I'll ask if anyone can tell me the name of the condemned men. More than likely they are the sort who only hang around the fringes but like to call themselves Blues or Greens when it suits them. Which is mostly when they're looking for a fight."

"Justinian will appreciate your cooperation. I am told, by the way, that you were visited recently by a man from Syria. An estate owner named Haik."

If the question surprised Porphyrius his expression didn't show it. "That's so. Normally I would tell you it was a private matter, but since the emperor has ordered you to speak to me I will reveal that Haik wanted assistance in some business ventures. To be specific, he asked me to put in a good word with several petty officials who have been blocking his acquisition of a bit of prime orchard land. As you mentioned, I am a man of some influence, even in places where I haven't raced for years."

John wondered whether the request might have been accompanied by gold then reminded himself that a couple of local officials could no doubt be bribed far more cheaply than a famous charioteer. "Did you discuss anything else?"

"Do you suspect this Haik of wrongdoing?"

"Not in the least. He's a friend of mine. He mentioned in passing that he'd spoken to you. He told me you were interrupted by a visitor. Do you remember who?"

"It's rare that I don't have a visitor. Let's see. Hippolytus, I believe. Yes. Hippolytus. A wealthy young fellow. A Green. I am telling you because I know very well that you will find out anyway and then you will become suspicious of me, as if you aren't already."

John concealed his surprise. It seemed hardly credible that Porphyrius hadn't learned that a man who had so recently visited him was one of the two who had escaped execution. But what did he have to gain by such a transparent lie? Perhaps he really hadn't heard. How well known had Hippolytus been among the charioteers? Prefect Eudaemon was not likely to have been spreading around details of the execution. On the other hand, it might be that Porphyrius was depending on the audacity of his lie to make it more believable.

Porphyrius did not appear perturbed. "You are wondering what Haik might have been up to aren't you?" he continued. "You want to compare our stories."

Perhaps the charioteer feared that Haik knew, or had found out, who Hippolytus was and had already told John. It might be better, John decided, not to challenge Porphyrius on the matter yet. Let him think John was missing that piece of information. "Why would a Green be visiting the head of the Blue team?" John asked instead.

"The Greens think they can coax me to return to them. There's another statue in the works, I'm told. Or was it Glabrio who was here when your friend came by? Another young man, Glabrio. Extremely tiresome but his father is a generous patron. No, I'm sure it was Hippolytus. I don't expect I'll be seeing either of them until this trouble dies down."

John noticed they were standing in front of one of the monuments erected to honor the man with whom he spoke. The bronze figure astride the decorative plinth depicted a classically handsome youth, a paragon of Greek beauty. Nothing like the pugnacious, middle-aged man beside him. Perhaps the idealized statue was how the masses actually saw their hero, particularly those who never glimpsed him up close but only from the stands, if at all. Perhaps the statue was, literally, all they ever saw of him. Why strain to see the tiny figure in the chariot when an enormous gleaming image towered above the swirling dust of the track?

Was it Porphyrius who was rallying the factions against Justinian?

John's gaze fell on the epigram inscribed on the base of the monument. "...Selene loved Endymion and now Victory loves with Porphyrius...."

Victory. Nika. The word the rioters chanted.

John thanked Porphyrius and took his leave. He did not believe in messages from gods, ancient or Christian, let alone from an anonymous poet.

◇◇◇

"Haik!" John pounded on the door to his friend's room.
As he walked back from his interview with Porphyrius he had
become increasingly annoyed. Not only the charioteer, but Haik
also, had seemed reluctant to speak about their meeting. John
got the impression that both had tried to see how little they
could get away with saying, offering just enough to allay his
suspicion. Revealing only what they felt was necessary to avoid
being caught out in a lie.

John pounded harder. Was Haik there? According to the
servants he'd been in his room most of the day.

He gave the door a shove and it moved, then stopped, as if
impeded. He gave the door another push.

It opened further, enough for him to see what was in the way.
A body lying on the floor.

"Haik! What happened?" John managed to squeeze into the
room and knelt beside the supine form. Haik was still alive, but
his face was a ghastly red mask. His pupils were hugely dilated.
He looked as if he'd been all but scared to death. He stared word-
lessly at John. His bloodless lips trembled but no sound emerged.

John glanced down over the rumpled garments. No blood
that he could see. A convulsion ran through Haik's body.

"Were you attacked? Did you fall ill?" John raised his friend's
head. It didn't seem to help his shallow breathing.

Haik managed a strangled wheeze. "The document...
Chosroes...missing...ask Hypatius...."

The final word trailed away in a fading hiss of breath.

Chapter Twenty-Three

"Poisoned!" Rusticus gave a grunt of pain as he straightened up slowly from the bed to which Haik had been moved. The elderly physician's tunic bore the marks of a day's calls on patients. He pushed a spray of white hair away from his watery eyes and turned to face John.

"Are you certain?" John demanded.

Felix, stationed in the doorway, shook his head vehemently. "Impossible. No one's been in the house who doesn't belong here."

"There's no doubt about it," Rusticus insisted in grave tones. "Considering the convulsions you described and the dilated eyes, it was belladonna. Ladies of the court use it to make their eyes look larger. Some call it Atropos' plant. Enough taken and she cuts the thread of a man's life. Not that it matters what it was at this point. If only I'd arrived earlier."

"You might have saved him?"

"I can't see how. But I would have been able to identify the poison more positively. As it is I have to go on what you tell me. I should have liked to be sure. Poisonings are most interesting. Tending to the court as I do, I could tell you about more than one poisoning. Oh, yes. Not as many as you'd think. Especially lately. Back in Emperor Zeno's day things were handled more subtly. Now it's just a knife in the back. And often enough, not in the back. All brute force and no guile."

Felix gave an audible grunt. "Easier to guard against."

John was almost relieved to hear that Haik could not have been saved. Although he had acted quickly it felt like a long time before the physician arrived. As soon as John shouted for a servant the whole household came on the run, along with Felix and a couple of his excubitors.

It was Hypatius who suggested sending for Rusticus. The physician had long treated the family. Once Haik was placed on the bed John ordered everyone but Felix out of the room.

He knelt by the bed speaking to Haik, listening to his breathing become shallower. The man did speak again before giving a few stentorian gasps and lapsing into utter stillness.

John looked down at Haik. The man's great beak of a nose jutted up like a small peak from the dead face. He bent over and pulled the sheet over the corpse. "You can treat a knife wound more easily than a poisoning?"

"That depends on the kind of poison and which rib you put the knife between and at what angle. Now if—"

"Who would use belladonna?"

"An aristocrat, I'd say. It's a very refined poison. Or else a gutter bred scoundrel who wanted to make it look like an aristocrat's work. On the other hand, it's easily derived from nightshade, so it might be used by someone from the countryside, or by a city dweller who purchased it at a shop, or from—"

"I see. Just about anyone might have decided to use belladonna."

"Anyone who wanted to kill someone." Rusticus wiped at his watering eyes. "These days I'm seeing more of the dead than the living. If it's not the result of beatings and stab wounds from the riots, it's certifying condemned men are definitely dead after their executions. Some of the deaths I've seen, no one would want to see. Oh, I could tell you things you wouldn't want to hear."

"I'm glad you can restrain yourself."

Rusticus shuffled over to the room's table, picked up the jug there, saw it was empty. He made a noise of disgust. "If the wine was poisoned there's none left to tell the tale. Was there any food left lying about?"

"No. Not even an empty plate," said Felix. "John and I searched the room while we waited for you."

"That's too bad. Years ago a senator was found dead in his garden. There was half a sausage left on a plate on the bench beside his body. I mixed it with chicken liver and fed it to a cat. When the beast promptly died we knew there was no doubt that the senator had been poisoned."

"Did that enable you to identify the poison?" John wondered.

"Hardly, but the beast's reaction was fascinating. One would never guess that muscles could spasm to that extent. By the time I see poisoning victims, they're usually dead or nearly so."

"What a shame," Felix remarked.

"Yes, confirming that a man's dead isn't physician's work. Not usually. Now, just the other day, there were those two faction members who survived hanging. You wouldn't think a physician would be needed to certify that a man who's been hung is dead, would you? But when you've lived as long as me you see a lot of strange things."

"Are you referring to the Blue and the Green who were rescued and taken to Saint Laurentius?"

"That's right. Now there was something I had never seen before although I have a large charioteering clientele who are always injuring themselves, keeping me busy setting dislocated shoulders and limbs broken in collisions or when the men are dragged by their horses halfway round the track before they can cut the reins, spectators crushed in the stands, that sort of injury."

"You mean the condemned men were charioteers?"

"One of them was a team patron. And the strangest aspect of the affair is that I knew him."

"Which one?" John asked quickly.

"The Green. Fellow named Hippolytus. He consulted me about a little problem he had with his waterworks. He had a lot bigger problem with the other end once the hangman got hold of him! I'm surprised Pompeius didn't tell you all about it. I went straight from the execution to his house. Pompeius is a regular patient mostly because he keeps half the wine merchants in the city solvent single-handed. He had over-indulged the night before and there I was, trying to tell him about the executions, and all he could do was groan and order his servants to bring him more wine. Why, the tale I was telling would have gathered me invitations to dine for weeks!"

John thought again of how Porphyrius had denied knowing the identities of either of the men who had survived their hangings. If even Rusticus knew—especially if the loose lipped physician knew—what were the chances Porphyrius didn't? "Did you know Hippolytus well?" John asked.

"Not at all. I only saw him once, recently, which is why I remembered. I think one of the charioteers I treat sent him to me. He seemed well acquainted with racing. We didn't talk for long. I gave him a remedy and sent him away. I had no remedy for what ailed him the next time I saw him. There's no cure for the condemnation of the emperor."

"Perhaps the botched hanging was intended as a cure," put in Felix.

"It's true he was not properly hung. But things were getting chaotic. The spectators were pressing in and making threats. Even the guards were frightened. The hangman was in a panic so far as I could tell. He probably wasn't thinking clearly and didn't adjust the ropes properly. There's no excuse for that. It could have resulted in a very cruel death."

It wasn't surprising that Kosmas had not mentioned making such an error, John thought. If, indeed, he had been responsible. The Urban Prefect Eudaemon hadn't mentioned any unruliness amongst the spectators either. It was possible his guards had tried to protect themselves by not reporting their failure to keep the crowd in check. Or Eudaemon had said nothing in order to protect himself. His men had already failed to protect the two at Saint Laurentius. It would have been understandable if he had not wanted to admit to yet another fiasco.

John turned his thoughts back to Haik. "But as for my friend, is there anything else you can tell me, that might be helpful in finding out who did this?"

The physician glanced at the covered form on the bed. "I fear not. And nothing to be done for him. Considering the horses are out of the barn, and jumped the fences, and vanished into the woods, and died of old age, there's no point in locking the stable door, is there? Whoever is responsible is long gone."

"My guards were stationed at every door," Felix said, his voice rising. "I was at the front entrance myself. No one could have got by us."

"Guards can fall sleep, or neglect their duties," John said.

"I picked these men myself, John. I know them. I trust them. Can you say the same of all the servants living in this house?"

"You have a point, my friend. But I see no reason why any of my servants would want to kill a complete stranger."

"Maybe he made unwanted advances to one of the women. Who knows. I only know that your house has been well guarded."

Felix was speaking too loudly. John thought he probably realized it could as easily been one of his aristocratic charges who was killed. And, besides, if someone could get into the house to murder Haik, he could return.

It was possible one of Hypatius' family had been the real target. It was too obvious to need saying.

Chapter Twenty-Four

"**H**ow are we going to endure staying here, knowing a man's been murdered down the hall?" Pompeius selected an olive from the plate on the dining room table and popped it into his mouth. The corpulent man was as sober as John had seen him. Possibly the shock of Haik's death had temporarily cleared his mind.

Hypatius sat across the table, warily eyeing the assortment of snacks but not sampling any. "You're a fool to eat any of that, brother. How do you know it isn't poisoned?"

Pompeius spat an olive pit onto the floor. "I'll find out soon enough. If it's poisoned my troubles will finally be over."

"Someone must be after us." Hypatius' voice quavered with alarm. "Why would anyone creep into this house to murder a business traveler from Syria? We need more guards. Different guards. I don't trust that big, bearded German."

"I can vouch for him," John said. "He told me he chose the guards himself. Men he knows and trusts. He's questioned them all separately and compared their stories. There's no indication any of them left their posts or have any secret connections with anyone who might have wished to do Haik, or your family, harm."

"Silentiaries are what we need. Men better known to the emperor," Hypatius insisted.

"Maybe it's Justinian who wants the relatives of Anastasius out of his way," muttered Pompeius.

"Haik showed signs of poisoning but there's no evidence of the poison," John said. "The wine jug in his room was empty and there was no food. It could have been administered anywhere."

"It's true not all poisons take effect immediately." Hypatius directed a meaningful look toward Pompeius. "How well do you know your servants? Have you questioned them?"

John's mouth narrowed into a thin line before he spoke. "If I could find them I would. They've left."

"Left? Every one of them?"

"They all came in a rush when Haik was dying," John said. "They must have talked it over and realized they would all be under suspicion."

"That's clear evidence of guilt," said Hypatius.

"Not necessarily. How could they all be guilty? With the city in chaos it's a perfect time for slaves to slip away to freedom. I can't say I blame them."

"They must be apprehended. Brought back and questioned."

"And who is available to do that? I doubt the servants were involved. The fact remains that no one was allowed in or out of the house."

"Until the servants fled," pointed out Hypatius.

"Yes," John admitted. "They got out while the guards were searching the house for a possible assailant. But that's done with. I have to base my inquiries on the resources I have available. Which, at present, is the two of you. Did either of you know Haik previously?"

"Not at all. Why would we?" Hypatius replied.

"You spent time in the Antioch area, didn't you? Haik was a mercenary there. Now he owns an estate."

"I was commanding the forces in the east! I didn't mingle with common fighters and petty landowners!"

"Yet the last word Haik uttered was your name. Dying men do not usually mention people they've never met with their final breath."

"My brother is a very popular fellow," put in Pompeius. "Emperors seek out his services. Mobs revere him. Dying men call out his name."

Hypatius looked horrified.

"Not all of his words were intelligible, but at the very end, he said, '…the document…Chosroes…missing…ask Hypatius….' The words were clear. The meaning is not clear. Explain."

"Document? Chosroes? I…I have no idea. When I was fighting the Persians, Cabades was still the king. I had nothing to do with his son…except…." All the color left Hypatius' face. He resembled an unpainted marble bust of Anastasius John often passed by in a corridor deep within the administrative warrens of the palace. "He might have meant the adoption documents."

"Continue."

Hypatius closed his eyes for a heartbeat and exhaled, calming himself. "You remember, several years ago, Justin almost adopted Chosroes?"

John nodded. He had been in a lowly position, serving the Keeper of the Plate, but everyone at the palace heard the rumors. For Justin the adoption meant peace with the Persians. For Cabades it meant strengthening the claim of his youngest son to succeed him. "How would I forget? Everyone at court was convinced Justin was turning the empire over to the Persians and they would have to prostrate themselves before the rising sun every morning. Then a two headed dog—or was it a cat?—was spotted in the Forum Bovis and the Persians were immediately forgotten."

"Unfortunately Cabades and Chosroes weren't so quick to forget the break down in negotiations."

"Indeed, the war might have ended years ago, but at what price? Were documents actually drawn up? I understood that the adoption was to be by arms and armor only?"

"That's right. Justin's legal counselor cautioned against an adoption by Roman law. Proclus feared it might give Chosroes a claim to the empire. Ridiculous, really. We've been trying to make peace with the Persians one way or another for centuries. Look at this Eternal Peace Justinian has decided on. It was a diplomatic gesture. It has nothing to do with succession."

"Proclus was known as a prudent man," John observed.

"Overly prudent," put in Pompeius. "If you wanted to wager him on whether the sun would rise tomorrow he'd insist you define 'rise' and 'tomorrow' and stipulate to how it would be proved the sun was actually up if it was obscured by clouds."

Hypatius' eyes narrowed. "In this case I agree with my brother. Proclus' prudence nearly cost me my head."

"Why was that?" John asked.

"The Persians took our offer as an insult. Adoption by arms and armor was the barbarian way. They weren't impressed that it had been good enough for Theodoric who was after all king of Italy." Hypatius paused, took another deep breath.

"I remember every detail of those negotiations. An enormous tent had been set up near the Persian border. An assortment of second-rate statuary was supposed to make the place look official. Most of it Greek warriors and eastern gods resembling demons. It looked like the courtyard of some dealer in dubious antiquities at the far end of the Mese. It was sweltering inside. I could hardly breath between the stifling heat and the overpowering perfumes the Persians soak everything with. I find myself wandering through the place in my nightmares."

"He is such a dainty person," his brother put in.

Hypatius ignored him. "It wasn't my fault. I don't think the negotiators were serious to begin with. I suspect the second son, Zames, had influenced them."

"He was the son most of the Persians wanted to see on the throne, wasn't he? A warrior."

"Yes. If he hadn't had an eye put out he wouldn't have been disqualified under Persian law and we'd never have heard of Chosroes. At any rate they brought up Lazica, as if the area were still in dispute. Finally they stalked off. Chosroes had camped on the other side of the Tigris, prepared to return to Constantinople with us. He was humiliated and angry."

"If he had come here, he would have been a hostage, in effect," John said.

"But he would have been present when Justin died and, according to Proclus, the legal heir to the empire."

"If my brother had been in the city when Anastasius died he would have been emperor rather than Justin," Pompeius pointed out. "In fact he'd be emperor right now. He's always in the wrong place at the wrong time, but has had the good fortune to escape with his life nevertheless. Why do you think I've attached myself to him like a limpet during these riots? He even came away from that diplomatic fiasco unscathed."

"Don't remind me. It was a close call. There were those who sought to blame me for the failure. It was claimed I had purposefully betrayed the empire. I was an heir of Anastasius, after all, so obviously I was seeking to take my rightful place. The emperor was suspicious. He had several of my friends tortured. Nothing happened to me, luckily." Hypatius' voice shook.

"Lucky indeed," John remarked. He did not believe a pair as cowardly and ineffectual as the brothers appeared to be could have survived so long, let alone maintained their positions at court. More than luck was involved. One might make a lucky throw of the knucklebones on a given day, but not day after day for years on end. "What about this document Haik referred to? If you were not instructed to offer an adoption by Roman law you would not have needed documents."

"I wasn't given any documents. But Justin—and Justinian— were enthused when they first heard the offer, before Proclus talked them out of it. They could have had documents drawn up and sent on ahead to be ready for the negotiations they were expecting. Any legal papers should have been destroyed when the plan changed."

"But perhaps someone simply took the document instead, as a curiosity, or with an eye toward monetary gain."

"Or a cup of wine," suggested Pompeius. "Some illiterate servant poking at the embers where he was burning the trash noticed the fancy lettering, took it down to the nearest tavern and exchanged it for a cup of wine."

"That's possible," John said. "And now it appears to have been stolen again. Haik said it was missing, ask Hypatius. Do you know anything about it?"

Hypatius met John's steady gaze with surprising calm. "Don't be ridiculous. Why would I kill a man over such a document? And obviously nothing more than a draft, since the adoption never came about."

Pompeius noisily spit out another olive pit. It clicked off the wall and ticked down onto the tiles. "Who cares, anyway? Justin couldn't have left the throne to a son, adopted or otherwise. Any fool knows the emperorship doesn't pass by blood."

"Proclus reasoned that it is a universal law, among all peoples, that the son is master of the father's estate," Hypatius said. "The empire might be considered Justin's estate."

"More importantly, such a document could be used to discredit Justinian," John pointed out. "It is commonly thought that he was really running the empire during Justin's last years. Justin's signature on a document giving the empire to the Persians, as some would characterize it, would be as damning as Justinian's own."

Hypatius licked his lips nervously. "If it were signed. And you think Haik brought this document with him?"

"It seems so. Are you sure you aren't a thief, and a murderer too?"

"I can see you're just trying to make me angry," Pompeius said mildly. "You're hoping I might forget myself and blurt out something incriminating. But the last thing in the world I want is to see Justinian deposed, or to give the rabble any hope that they might put me on the throne. I value my head too much."

"Do you know Porphyrius?" John asked.

"The charioteer? Not personally. Do you think he's involved?"

John was silent. He preferred not to reveal his suspicions to the brothers. On the other hand he needed information, if they had any. He looked away from Hypatius, toward the screen. It was the middle of the night. Beyond the screen lay the dark tangle of the garden, and on the other side of the garden the door to the room where Haik's lifeless body lay, submerged forever in a darkness beyond that of any night.

Pompeius reached for the glass wine decanter.

"Can't you at least try to stop drinking?" Hypatius shouted. "The city's going up in flames. Justinian thinks we're spies. Someone's quite possibly trying to murder us. It might help if you could think straight."

Pompeius shrugged and filled his cup. "I don't see how." He took a long gulp and then turned to John. "But it seems a strange coincidence you should mention Porphyrius. He spent years in the east, in Antioch, and not just racing chariots either. Twenty-five years ago he led an attack on the synagogue there. Plundered and set fire to it, massacred every Jew he could lay hands on. Then in a final insult he set up a cross on the ruins. A fine man, is Porphyrius. Just the man to stir up trouble, too."

Chapter Twenty-Five

January 15, 532

Felix picked Eros up by his gilded wings and shook him.
"Don't kill me," screeched the costumed boy. "I'll tell you how to get to Antonina's apartments."

Felix dropped the little godlet. One of the wings crunched against the tiled floor. A cloud of powder shaken off the boy's clothing and face hung in the corridor.

Felix struggled not to cough.

The boy scrambled to his knees, the broken wing dangling pathetically from his narrow back. He was one of the court pages who decorated certain inner sanctums at the great palace. Only now he was not so decorative. Tears ran down his face and the rosy makeup on his cheeks was blotched. "Just turn right at the next hallway." The boy snuffled. "Then right again. Not that you'll be admitted."

"I'm sure I'll be admitted." Felix felt for the sword at his belt.

The page got to his feet and wiped at his eyes. "You're not going to put your sword into her, are you?"

"Of course not. I'm a friend of hers."

"But not so good a friend as to put your sword into her?" The smeared lip coloring accentuated the boy's leer. He started to back away.

Felix reached out and grabbed a scrawny arm. "I'm not letting you run off and alert the guards. Show me the way."

He pushed the boy in front of him and drew his sword.

Suddenly the floor seemed to lurch beneath his boots, nearly throwing him backwards. He was almost overcome by dizziness. Why he could not say. He put his free hand out to the wall, steadying himself.

How had he managed to make his way so far inside the Daphne Palace? He couldn't quite recall. A fog kept swallowing up the immediate past, as it had two nights ago, when he had been running around the gardens attacking statuary. Apparently the trained excubitors who usually watched these precincts had been sent to secure the palace walls against the rioters. It might also be that the emperor didn't want the excubitors so close to him, given Captain Gallio's practically treasonous stance. Whatever the reason, the usual guards had been replaced with doddering old silentiaries used to posing ornamentally at doorways and scholarae who normally paraded on horseback when the emperor required spectacle.

So far they had all been willing to let Felix pass on the basis of the orders from Gallio—orders intended to allow him to move freely enough to carry out his duties toward the Anastasius family. They didn't give him the right to wander around the Daphne Palace, but Felix's blade and demeanor discouraged any of the hangers-on from daring to actually read what was on the parchment beyond identifying Gallio's official signature.

"Go on," Felix told the boy gruffly. "Don't try running away. My blade will move faster than you do."

The boy went slowly down the corridor and turned left.

"I thought you told me to turn right?" Felix said.

"I didn't, did I? You scared me so. I don't know what I was saying."

"No tricks, Eros. No one will care much about a dead page. They'll be more concerned about the bloodstains on the floor."

The boy emitted a faint whimper and continued on, his broken wing dragging on the floor.

Felix followed warily. It was all very strange. It occurred to him that he should be at his post at John's house, particularly since John's friend had been murdered a few hours ago. Possibly by an intruder. Poisoned? Had Felix been poisoned too? Had the intruder found his way into the kitchen? Was that why Felix felt so peculiar? What exactly had he eaten at John's house most recently? He couldn't recall. Oddly enough, it all seemed unimportant.

He may as well have been lying in bed, dreaming. How foolhardy could someone be, not only to abandon their post at a time of peril, but to do so to visit the imperial quarters to pay a surprise call on a woman friend of Theodora's? It must be a dream and since it was only a dream—and a most entertaining one—he did not want to wake himself. Besides, he felt a compulsion that overrode reason. Just as he had in the gardens the other night.

After all, Antonina had invited him to meet her in secret. Now it was he who was arranging the meeting. She would surely be delighted and it would be as it had been in the Hall of the Nineteen Couches. However it had been there. He could not remember anything about it, except that it had been very, very good, until he woke up hacking at Emperor Constantine. That hadn't been so good.

Another wave of dizziness hit him.

How odd. He had felt fine since John had hauled him out of the gardens after his tryst with Antonina. Until he woke up this morning. Then he had felt almost drunk, although he had not been drinking. It wasn't surprising that he felt peculiar, though, since clearly he hadn't really awakened yet.

The boy vanished around a corner and Felix lurched after him.

"Stop! Don't go any further!"

Felix blinked. He had fallen into a daze. He swung his sword. The figure blocking in his path leapt out of harm's way.

"You stupid man! Can't you see? It's me, Julianna."

Felix gaped in horror at the slight girl dressed in blue, dark hair coiled on either side of her face.

Julianna's eyes blazed with fury. "Not only did I just save myself, I saved you from a horrible death in the dungeons. What's the matter with you? What are you doing here?"

"I need to see Antonina," Felix stammered.

"Did she send for you?"

"Yes. Or, rather…not exactly."

"Look at me, Felix." Julianna stared into his eyes and gave a sniff of disgust. "I can see what the problem is. I should have guessed."

"I'm not drunk."

"No. You're not. You're…well…never mind."

The haze that kept closing in on Felix dissipated a bit. He could suddenly see his surroundings more clearly. "Where's the boy? He's run off. He'll fetch the guards."

"Don't worry," Julianna said. "I'm appointing you to be my bodyguard. In case anyone questions why you're here. Which means you use that sword on anyone who comes after me. Not on me. Put it away."

Felix slipped his blade back into its scabbard. "But what are you doing here?"

"I've been to see Antonina. She's a good friend."

"Then you can take me to her."

"I hardly think so. Belisarius' men are protecting her, as they are the imperial couple and a few others. They aren't traitors like the excubitors or incompetent cowards like the court fops who've taken their places."

"But…I'm your bodyguard."

"Believe me, Felix, Antonina doesn't want to see you right now."

Felix shook his head, trying to clear it. His ears buzzed. His surroundings were beginning to seem more solid, less dream-like. "But I am your bodyguard. I'm supposed to be guarding you, at John's house. You shouldn't be here. How did you get out?"

Julianna stepped past him and grabbed his sleeve. "Let's worry about getting you out safely."

"Have my guards been sleeping at their posts? Did you bribe them?"

She tugged his sleeve. "Follow me. It would be best if we weren't seen."

She hurried back in the direction from which Felix had come and pushed through some heavy purple draperies, which Felix had taken for wall hangings, revealing an arched doorway. Warm air issued from the narrow hallway beyond.

Felix followed. The hallway curved gradually. The air grew warmer and droplets appeared on the walls.

Abruptly they emerged into an enormous room whose high ceiling was obscured with mist. The air felt as hot and moist as that in the baths. Enormous potted plants with exotic-shaped and colorful leaves hid the walls. Shafts of light fell through the mists from windows far above. Felix could hear water gurgling and birds singing. As he gazed upwards there was a flash of yellow as two birds rose from the fronds of a tree unlike any Felix had ever seen.

The flash of yellow was followed immediately by a flash of red, the predominant color of the long tunic and loose trousers of the man who stepped from behind the tree. The man's black hair hung to his shoulders in glossy ringlets. A pointed beard accentuated the length and angularity of his face. Ear rings dangled from both ears.

The stranger regarded Felix and Julianna with the eyes of a hawk, then walked straight past them and went out into the corridor without a word.

Felix stared after him in amazement.

"It's the Persian emissary," Julianna said. "Antonina told me he traveled here with Belisarius. Something to do with the peace treaty Justinian is negotiating. He's staying somewhere at the Daphne and is always wandering about. I keep running into him. Gives me chills every time."

"I'm not surprised," Felix said. What other wonders might they encounter in this strange and secret place?

"Come on," Julianna told him. "There isn't any time to waste." Her voice echoed in the huge space.

Then they plunged into another, colder, hallway. A door of intricately carved wood opened on a long room illuminated by a single lamp. The meager light glimmered on busts arrayed on pedestals all around the walls. An enormous central table receded into the darkness, more like the highway outside the Golden Gate than a mere piece of furniture.

Purple silk billowed from the walls and ceiling of the passageway beyond. The silk rippled constantly, like the windblown sea. Felix felt his giddiness returning.

He stumbled. Closed his eyes for an instant trying to regain his equilibrium. When he opened his eyes again he saw he was standing in a gilded alcove, in front of an archway guarded by a shining metal statue. Neptune, he supposed, judging from the trident the stern, bearded figure held upright. Beyond the archway a wide marble staircase curved upwards. Curious, Felix took a step toward the stairway.

There was a click, followed by a loud squeak and the trident came crashing down into a horizontal position, blocking his path. He recoiled in surprise and the trident sprang back into its original position.

Julianna giggled. "That stairway leads to the emperor's private chambers." She put her foot out and lightly tapped the floor in front of the archway. The trident came down again and then went back up. "It amuses him to have a pagan god guarding his door. Or maybe it was Theodora's idea. The armed men at the top of the stairs are not mechanical."

Felix shook his head in amazement. He knew that no one was admitted to Justinian's private quarters, apart from a clergyman or physician. Not even high officials were allowed inside. No doubt a common excubitor should not even venture this close.

Without any urging, he followed Julianna away down another corridor. Before long vivid wall mosaics depicting classical myths gave way to painted scenes of the countryside and finally to plain, whitewashed walls on which hung the occasional silver cross.

Then they emerged into the crisp sunlit air beneath the portico in front of the Daphne Palace.

Felix took a deep breath. His head felt clear. He could hardly believe he had actually tried to see Antonina in her private rooms. His memory of it all seemed less substantial than the memory of a dream.

"You're lucky you didn't get any further," Julianna said. "Do you feel yourself now? Can you get back to the house without deciding you want to drop in on Theodora?"

Felix grunted. He felt his cheeks reddening. "I don't know what I was thinking."

Julianna's eyes narrowed. "Only what you were told to think, I suspect."

"What do you mean?"

"Just that Antonina can be very persuasive. I will have to leave you now." She started toward the steps of the portico.

Felix took hold of her arm. "Wait. You're not supposed to leave John's house. I'll forget I saw you here, since you assisted me, but I can't let you roam around. You'll have to come back with me."

She tried to pull her arm away but Felix held tight. She glared and pursed her lips. He was afraid she was going to spit at him, but she didn't. "Do you really want to see Antonina again?" she asked him. "I can arrange it."

"No. I have orders to guard you and your family. Besides, it's for your own safety."

"All right. You're hurting my arm. Please let go. Or do you think a girl can outrun you?"

Felix released his grip.

Instantly Julianna grabbed at his sword. He placed his hand on the hilt, to block her. But her hand never arrived. Instead she spun around and raced back into the Daphne Palace.

Felix cursed under his breath and went after her. She had already vanished down one of the hallways opening off the bare, marble atrium. He heard receding footsteps. From what direction?

He headed down what he thought was the right hallway.

A scholare wearing a ridiculous plumed helmet and holding a nasty looking curved sword stepped in front of him.

"Excubitor!" Felix barked. "Emergency. Here on orders of Captain Gallio." He reached for the order tucked in his belt.

It was gone. Julianna hadn't been trying to grab his sword. She'd stolen his orders, and with them his access to the Daphne!

Chapter Twenty-Six

"Porphyrius isn't at the Hippodrome today." The young charioteer eyed John suspiciously. The tall stranger in the dirty tunic and threadbare cloak did not look the sort of visitor Porphyrius would deign to see.

"He is at his home?"

"So they say. Packing up his gold and silver in case the fires come any closer. Not that it's any of your business."

John returned to the Mese. He had dressed in plain clothing before setting out for the Hippodrome and taken the precaution of dirtying it and his face and hands. Any person caught on the streets even suspected to be from the palace was not likely to survive the fury of the mob. Already several courtiers who had attempted to flee the capital had been killed in sight of the guards at the Golden Gate. Under orders not to interfere, they had watched the slaughter. It would have been a better plan, John thought, to depart by sea but for the fact the only two vessels lying in the palace harbor were already loaded with furniture, silk, gold and silver plate, and other valuable items on the order of the emperor.

Most of the shops he passed were charred ruins. Rubble blocked the colonnades in places, forcing him to move out into the street. The fires had jumped some buildings, however, particularly those not constructed primarily of wood.

The air smelled as if it were itself singed. In one spot there hung an unpleasant odor of charred meat. John could not recall whether a butcher's shop had occupied the gutted shell.

He thought not.

As he walked he couldn't help thinking about Haik. What had been on his friend's mind as he hurried to his meeting with Porphyrius?

After speaking with Hypatius and Pompeius John had returned to the room where his friend's body lay, decently covered with a linen sheet. He and Felix had searched every bit of the room, seeking a clue to the murder but had found nothing. They would have found the adoption documents Hypatius had spoken of, had they been there.

They had not, however, searched the body.

John had done so.

Haik had not been carrying the documents. Or, at least they had not been anywhere on the corpse.

John did not like to think about it. He was relieved to reach Porphyrius' mansion, so he could turn his mind to something else.

The building could barely be glimpsed through the nondescript barred gate in the archway under the colonnade. Only when John had satisfied the guards that he was truly on business from the emperor, had walked down the alley between the brick walls of several surviving shops and stepped into the graveled courtyard, did he see what hundreds of racing victories could buy.

The facade of the house reproduced almost exactly that of the emperor's box in the Hippodrome, right down to the carved images of Pegasus on the capitals of the towering columns supporting the portico. Inside, frescoes in the entrance hall depicted Hercules cleaning the Augean Stables. A waterfall poured down the far wall of the atrium beyond. Heroic sized statuary occupied massive pedestals strewn around the enormous space. John waited in front of a gilded quadriga which would have accommodated a cyclops.

Porphyrius came to meet him. At home, in contrast to the peasant's tunic he wore at the stables, he had outfitted himself in a jeweled blue dalmatic. The straps wrapped around his muscular calves in charioteer style appeared to be woven with golden threads.

"You have an impressive house," John remarked. "The four bronze horses in front are particularly fine. You might have spirited them out of the Hippodrome. They look identical."

Porphyrius smiled. "Mine of course are copies, whereas the emperor's are the originals, cast by Lysippos himself, or so it is claimed. The old Greek created beautiful equine portraits, even if he didn't get the ears quite right."

"Some of the many equine ears in the stables must have heard things I would like to know. If only horses could speak. They might be more forthcoming than the people I talk to."

"I hope you aren't implying that I wasn't honest with you. A horse will obey the whip. I'm not a horse."

"A man will look out for his own welfare. A few days ago you spoke to the Syrian traveler Haik. Your patron Hippolytus was present. Now both are dead."

John studied the charioteer's homely features as he told him how Hippolytus had been hung, rescued, and subsequently killed and how Haik had been poisoned. Did the nostrils in the squashed nose flare slightly? Did the lips tighten all but imperceptibly? Was Porphyrius trying to remain impassive?

"When you've been around the track as many times as I have, nothing surprises you. One instant you're headed to the finish line. The next, you're being dragged to death, tangled up in your own reins."

"Under the circumstances, are you sure you aren't tangled up in your own reins, or something equally deadly, right now?"

Porphyrius reached into his dalmatic, pulled out a vicious-looking curved knife, and waved it in John's direction.

John stepped back quickly.

Porphyrius chuckled. "I've found myself caught in the reins more than once and used this to cut myself loose every time. I admit on one occasion I owed as much to my physician as to my blade." He put the knife back in its sheath. "I carry it even when I'm not racing. It makes me feel safer."

"Whoever killed Hippolytus and Haik might not be afraid of a charioteer's knife. And whoever it is may be exceptionally adept at getting into places where one would feel safe."

"But there is no connection between Hippolytus and Haik. Haik simply happened to be present when Hippolytus arrived, unexpectedly. I never saw your friend in my life. I'm positive Hippolytus never met him before. Haik had just come from Syria."

"And you insist that you didn't know Hippolytus was among the condemned faction members or any of what followed?"

"Not until you told me just now. If I'd known I would have said so the first time we spoke."

"It is hard to believe no one thought to inform you that one of your wealthy patrons had been murdered."

Porphyrius shrugged. "I have more wealthy patrons than I can count. Hippolytus wasn't a major supporter. He was trying to convince me to return to the Greens. I belong to the Blues. If the Greens knew he was dead they'd have no reason to give the news to a Blue."

"My impression is that both the factions respect you."

"I'm the enemy of the Greens."

"We can respect our enemies."

Porphyrius crossed his arms. He didn't raise his voice when he spoke but John could see the sinews in his huge forearms tighten. "What else can I say? The city's in turmoil. Many people have died already. I'm sorry to hear about Hippolytus and your friend Haik. But the deaths have nothing to do with me. Do you think I spend my time collecting gossip? I've been exceptionally busy the past few days preparing for the races. And thanks to the commotion in the streets, I've had no new callers, aside from yourself."

"I might be able to accept that you did not withhold from me knowledge of Hippolytus' death. However, my friend informed me that he came to see you about a document. You never mentioned that."

"He wanted me to put in a good word for him respecting a business venture. There weren't any documents involved."

"This was not a commercial document. It was a written undertaking by which Emperor Justin agreed to adopt the Persian Chosroes."

Porphyrius was silent. John felt the charioteer staring at him, as if trying to gauge how much he knew. He was deciding what course to take. Did he dare drive his horses toward the inside of the track? Would his opponent give him room or precipitate a collision? Or should he cut between the chariots ahead? If they continued to draw apart there might be room. "Yes, I admit," he said after no more than an instant. "Haik did mention such a document. It was idle gossip. Small talk. He thought the foolish rumor he'd heard back in Antioch would interest me, since I spent so many years in the area. I didn't think it worth mentioning. As I explained just now I am not one for gossip."

"I cannot believe a man would spout idle gossip with his dying words."

Porphyrius shook his head. "Men say strange things in their last breaths, when their senses are deserting them. Long ago I knelt in the sand of a racetrack cradling the head of a colleague who had been crushed by his horses. I could feel his blood pooling around my knees. He told me to look at the waves, how they sparkled, and to observe the whale. The whale was coming. What a magnificent sight. Now what do you suppose that meant except that the poor fellow's skull had been cracked wide open?"

"I hope you are right, Porphyrius, that it was just a rumor. But if so, why was Haik murdered?"

Porphyrius uncrossed his arms and sighed. "Life is full of mysteries, isn't it?"

◇◇◇

John walked slowly back down the Mese.

As far as he could see, the problem before him was growing more complicated rather than less.

Haik had been found dead in John's well-guarded house, inside the palace grounds. The Blue and the Green had been found murdered in a guarded room in the Church of Saint Laurentius. Had the same person managed to find a way to the victims? A person who could go wherever he wanted, at will, gaining access to guarded rooms? A person seemingly adept at magick?

On the other hand, there was no proof Haik had been poisoned at John's house. It was more likely he had been poisoned elsewhere simply because it was so unlikely that a murderer could have managed to get into both the palace grounds and a guarded house within. Haik had died in his room, but he could have been poisoned anywhere in the city, or the palace. John had no idea where his friend had gone, aside from the Hippodrome.

And what about the mysterious visitor who had discovered the murders at Saint Laurentius? The old commander, Sebastian, claimed the man had an official seal. He could have been mistaken. Documents can be forged. Or Sebastian might have lied to cover his incompetence.

Then again, the visitor might have been sent by Justinian for purposes the emperor did not care to reveal. It was impossible to be certain what the emperor thought, or what his aims really were.

As John neared the palace he saw a sullen crowd gathered at the end of the Mese in front of the ruins of the Chalke gate. He stopped and surveyed the remaining length of the street. It was difficult to determine if the bodies slumped here and there in ruined porticoes were rioters who had quarrelled, intoxicated looters, or merchants killed defending their wares. Wisps of smoke rose from the shells of destroyed shops, swirling around a group of men breaking open amphorae of wine beside a blazing pile of broken furniture. Several women danced around the fire, yelling obscene songs and offering their services without cost to passersby. A small church that had escaped the general conflagration was now burning briskly, its door missing.

It would be better for him to take to the alleyways to reach the unobtrusive door by which he had left the palace.

Scattered shouts caught his attention. And another sound. Rising and falling in a measured cadence. Chanting.

A procession of priests entered the Mese from the direction of the Augustaion. They wore rich vestments and carried painted icons. Some of the flat, wooden panels had been attached to long poles, others were simply held, by one or two priests, depending on the size. The haloed, gaunt holy men in the icons stared out at the sinful world through enormous, dark eyes like those of the starving children only too common in the streets.

The procession moved slowly, picking its way around the debris strewn along the thoroughfare. As the priests shook the poles or thrust the panels at the people in the street the golden details in the icons flashed.

Evidently the priests hoped the display would bring calm to the streets. A foolhardy gesture, John thought, but a brave one.

The procession reached the burning church and mounted the few steps to its narrow portico. Tongues of flame ran along the building's roofline.

One of the priests brandished his icon above his head and began to admonish the throng in booming tones. "Brothers and sisters! Go home and repent your sins!"

John recognized the short, stout figure silhouetted in front of the red glow emanating from the doorway as Leonardis, the man he had spoken to at the Church of Saint Laurentius, who had appeared so fascinated by the fiery torment of his church's martyr.

Many of the crowd, their attention drawn to the spectacle of the icons, moved toward the church.

"Return to your homes!" Leonardis thundered. "I command you, in the name of our Lord!" He moved the icon from side to side. The stern gaze of the Christian saint swept over the entire assembly. "Pray for the emperor's mercy and justice!"

"What justice is there on earth, much less heaven?" A man who looked like a beggar pushed his way to the front of the rabble. He emphasized his words with flourishes of a splintered piece of wood stained in sinister fashion. "What justice was there for the Blues and Greens?"

A full throated roar of approval drowned the priest's attempt at a reply. A dark object came flying out of the crowd. Leonardis raised his icon like a shield. The clot of dung splattered across the holy image.

The priest's outraged words were drowned out by a roar of laughter.

The ragged man who had addressed Leonardis lurched forward with shocking suddenness, knocked the soiled icon from his hands, and spat on it. "Saints! Relics! Prayers! Do they fill our bellies or keep us warm?"

"No!" came the crowd's response.

The man's laugh sounded more like the wild cry of a gull than any sound formed in a human throat. "They'd keep us warm if we burnt them!" He grabbed the icon and tossed it through the open doorway. Flames spurted out.

John tried to move closer to the church but his way was blocked by the packed bodies. The priests on the portico huddled closer together, muttering terrified prayers as children began to throw stones and broken bricks at them. A filthy-faced girl dressed in an obviously stolen, lavishly embroidered tunic too large for her, approached the holy men and lifted up her garment to expose her dirty nakedness. "I'll keep the lot of you warm!" she shouted. "Who's going to be first?"

More laughter echoed across the broken buildings as the priests shrank back, their prayers growing louder. The girl grabbed the arm of one priest and willing helpers dragged him forward and threw him to the ground.

"Don't be shy, dearie," the girl said, "we're all friends here."

A woman suggested since her victim was insulting the girl by not showing interest, someone should make certain he would never insult a woman again. "And I've got a nice sharp knife!" She stepped forward to bend over the priest.

The man on the ground gave a shrill scream and fell silent.

It all happened quickly, before John could fight his way forward, before Leonardis could react. The stout priest was shaking. "What have you done? Are you animals? You will burn! Sinners! Murderers! You will writhe in eternal torment!"

The ragged man sprang at Leonardis, grabbed him by his vestments, and shook him. "You! I know you! You Judas! Betrayer! Your threats are worth as much as your lying promises of salvation! Oh yes, my friends are dead but I, I have conquered death! Now let's see you do the same!"

With that he picked Leonardis up and flung him into the blazing church.

Then he swung around, let out a piercing howl of laughter and scuttled off the portico. A path opened in the now terrified crowd and almost instantly he was gone.

The way he moved sparked John's memory.

Was it the madman he and Felix had seen perched on the rooftop cross on their way back from the Praetorium?

He had vanished now.

An angry knot of rioters pressed in toward the remaining priests. Some of the priests were on their knees, praying and crying. A couple of braver souls jabbed out with the poles bearing their icons. The hard reality of the painted panels did not deter the attackers any more than their symbolic power had.

There was nothing John could do. The crush was too thick. He was jostled, practically lifted off his feet. An inadvertent elbow jabbed him in the ribs. He was shoved from behind. It was all he could do to remain standing. Anyone who fell would be trampled to death.

Usually, in the streets, he could command respect with a glance, but not now. These were no longer human beings but rather a single, monstrous beast intent on mayhem.

"To the Augustaion," someone cried. "Nika! Nika!" Other voices echoed the words and then John was borne along with the surging mob, as helpless as if he had fallen into the dark currents of the Bosporos.

Chapter Twenty-Seven

"Your chamberlain friend hasn't passed this way, Felix. Not while I've been on guard." The excubitor, Bato, leaned back against an irregular chunk of masonry which had once been part of an interior wall or the ceiling of the palace entrance, to judge from the bright mosaic patterns. He was one of several men stationed amidst the ruins of the Chalke. The rest remained inside a nearby barracks, close at hand in case of trouble, but under their captain Gallio's orders not to venture outside the palace. "What are you doing out here anyway? Weren't you assigned to look after the chamberlain's guests?"

"I've been taking a walk. I needed to get some air."

The cold had cleared Felix's head. Julianna had eluded him. He had circled the imperial residence for a while, in case she emerged, but he had not seen her again.

"Maybe you'd like to take my place out here?" Bato said. "I wish you'd chosen me to assist with that relaxing job you've been handed."

"You know Gallio refused to make you available. Perhaps he thought we knew each other too well. Bad for discipline. Anyway, I prefer fighting."

"Out of sorts, are you? A bit too much wine last night I'd say."

Felix looked along the Mese. Smoke and heaped rubble obscured the people gathered there. A continuous murmur of voices drifted toward the ruined Chalke. Flames flared through the drifting haze. "I hope John isn't out in that," he finally said. He hoped Julianna wasn't out in it either. At least John could take care of himself.

"It's quiet now," Bato said. "A lot of the troublemakers left a short time ago. Shouting about victory, whatever they mean by that. At least if your friend was out there near that fire he'd be warmer." Bato shifted his lance from one hand to other. He blew on his free hand and flexed his fingers.

"You'd be warmer too if you were busy driving that rabble from the streets."

"I'm carrying out Captain Gallio's order."

"To do nothing!" Felix snorted.

"Our captain is being prudent. Waiting until the enemy presents an opening."

"More likely waiting in order to drive up the price of his services."

Bato smiled. "You think he's already been bribed to sit inside the palace?"

"It's possible."

"I suspect Narses. He's the treasurer. He went by here a few hours ago. I could practically hear him jingling. He was creeping along like an overburdened mule."

"Justinian wants him to buy off the factions."

"Eunuchs are a sly lot. You need to watch your step, my friend."

"I thought you said Gallio was being prudent," Felix grumbled.

"We need to consider every angle don't we?"

"Consider then, how could it be prudent to disobey Justinian's orders?"

"That's easy. Gallio must have decided that the emperor is not going to be driving the winning chariot. What else? But he doesn't know yet who will cross the finish line first. So he waits and I stand here in the ruins and freeze my feet." He stamped his boots.

"What do you think, Bato? If you aren't willing to side with the emperor, what chariot would you place your wager on?"

"I'd put my money on whatever team Porphyrius was on. Wouldn't you?"

Felix nodded. "I imagine a lot of people would."

Bato poked his lance at the debris scattered on the ground. He flipped over a few small pieces of what resembled charred rock, revealing a fragment of brilliant blue mosaic the color of part of a peacock's tail. "Impossible to say what's going to turn up, isn't it? I don't blame Gallio for waiting. I only wish he'd ordered me to wait inside."

Felix decided to return to John's house. He'd had no legitimate reason to come out here. He hated sitting behind walls when there was fighting to do. He peered down the street again. "No one's threatened the palace?"

"No," Bato said. "I think they're tired from burning and looting. They're just enjoying themselves."

"That won't last long."

He had hardly finished speaking when shouts echoed down the fire-gutted colonnades, followed by the clatter of hoofs. Through a gap in the rubble, Felix saw mounted soldiers. He recognized among them Belisarius.

Jeers and insults showered on the soldiers. A few people flung bricks and stones. An obviously intoxicated man staggered into view, brandishing what looked like the burnt remains of a wooden cross. It was hard to tell, through the smoke. Belisarius leaned over casually in his saddle and swung his sword. The attacker's head flopped forward unto his chest and tumbled to the ground.

Then the cavalrymen lowered their lances and spurred their horses.

"This way!" someone shouted.

Bato stiffened, lowered his own lance and stepped forward, ready to call for assistance. Then he laughed. "I see they have enough sense not to head this way. They're taking to the alley across from the church."

Felix could see that Belisarius' company was pursuing the mob. He realized he had his sword in his hand. Then he realized something else. "That alley…." he muttered, "Mithra!"

He sprinted away from Bato without pausing to explain.

By the time Felix passed the rubble partially blocking the Mese, pursuers and pursued had vanished. He saw a blazing church spewing a fog of smoke. He felt the heat on the opposite side of the street. He could see bodies crumpled on the portico.

He raced into the alley.

It narrowed almost immediately. Enclosed balconies jutting out from the second floors of the surrounding tenements almost met overhead, creating a virtual ceiling through which only a crack of sky remained visible.

The sounds of battle reverberated along the brick-walled ravine—oaths, the clash of swords, cries of wounded men and horses.

From the corner of his eye, Felix glimpsed a dark shape hurtling toward his head. He leapt aside and the pot of night soil exploded at his feet. A face leered down from an open window.

He ran on. Now there was barely space for two horses abreast. The passage veered abruptly and as Felix rounded the corner he saw what he feared.

Belisarius had been trapped.

As was common in the city, the alley turned into a stairway to descend a steep hill. The stairs were too precipitous to be navigated easily on horseback. Perhaps the first rider had been unable to slow up in time, or his horse had panicked. Whatever the exact cause, several horses and riders had fallen, clogging the alley. Part of Belisarius' company had spilled down the stairs, the rest remained at the top. Sticks of wood, bricks, and flaming torches rained from windows.

A few of the rabble may have taken the chance to escape but many had chosen to fight. Armed with clubs, lengths of chain, cleavers, hammers, and other makeshift weapons they ducked nimbly in and out between the packed cavalry, slashing at legs and bellies, both human and equine.

There was no room for trained fighters to maneuver. Lances were all but useless in the crush, as likely to impale a comrade as an attacker. Horses wheeled about, only to collide with each other. One reared up, throwing its rider, as an oil lamp trailing flames smashed into the side of the terrified creature's head.

Felix moved forward swiftly. How many years had it been since he had fought in such a melee? It didn't matter. The deafening clamor, the stink of blood and death, brought back all his skills.

He was confronted by a big red-faced man. The assailant raised an axe. Before he could bring it down, Felix was pulling his sword out of the fellow's chest.

Then a ruffian, too intent on eviscerating a wounded soldier, was surprised to suddenly find himself dying from a gaping wound in his side.

Felix felt his boot slip, staggered sideways, tripped over a body. He managed to reach out to break his fall. He pushed himself up off the ground with a crimson hand.

Someone backed into him. Before he could react he was shoved from the other side.

He swung his sword at a ragged form, not sure even if the man was armed. Anyone who wasn't a soldier was an enemy.

Felix forced his way forward, pushing, stabbing, swinging his blade when he found space.

He stayed next to the wall, freeing himself from fending off any attacks from that side.

Suddenly he was looking down the stairway. Dismounted soldiers at the top of the stairs had begun to form a defensive hedge of lances. Too late perhaps.

A helmeted head emerged from the tenement doorway Felix was standing beside. The man carried a sword. Behind him, in the dimness, Felix glimpsed other armored men bearing weapons.

Had the excubitors finally decided to fight? Or were they from the urban watch?

"You're just in time," shouted one of Belisarius' beleaguered soldiers.

The newcomer lunged forward and split the speaker's skull open with his blade.

Was someone arming the troublemakers, or had they stolen the weapons? It made no difference. Felix threw himself in front of the doorway.

The man who had killed Belisarius' soldier took a sword in the throat. Felix yanked his blade free in a gush of blood at the same time kicking the body backwards into the man behind, who went down in a heap.

Another attacker tried to climb over the two bodies in the doorway. Felix blocked his way. For what felt like eternity he fought alone, refusing to allow the newcomers into the fray. He could feel his heart pounding, the ache in his sword arm, and the fire in his chest every time he drew a breath. He did not experience these sensations as pain or discomfort but rather as useful information, the way a bowman might note the dwindling number of arrows in his quiver.

By the time he was forced backwards, the ambushers had lost the element of surprise. Soldiers had joined him. He fought shoulder to shoulder with Belisarius' men.

By now the dismounted cavalrymen had time to form an impenetrable wall of lances and began to push the crowd back. Felix and his companions moved forward, stepping over bodies.

Abruptly the mob was gone, fleeing down the alley, and the stairs, and into doorways, dispersing as quickly as water down a drain.

Felix was aware of the weight of his sword, and how sticky the hilt felt. There was a roaring in his ears.

"I've rarely seen such a fighter," came a voice beside him.

He turned wearily and saw the patrician features of Belisarius.

"Tell me your name, man, or I shall have to say I was rescued in the city streets by a bear."

"Felix, excellency."

"Felix! Not one of my men, are you? I shall speak to Justinian about that."

Chapter Twenty-Eight

The rioters in the Augustaion knew nothing of the battle in the alley a few streets distant. They had left the Mese before Belisarius' arrival, crying out for victory. But the deserted square was not worth conquering. The Great Church had already been burnt as well as the nearby baths. Had there been anything to incite them they might have taken torches to Samsun's Hospice or the Church of Saint Irene. But there was only desolation and the inhuman moaning of a bitter wind.

Some fell to quarreling with each other, others drifted off in search of taverns which had not yet been ransacked. A few simply went home. A pack of young charioteers had found a girl.

There were ten of them. They surrounded her at the base of the five wide stairs which had once led to the portico of the Great Church but now led to a blackened pit filled with smoldering debris. She had been scanning the ruins so intently, as if searching for something amidst the jagged remnants of walls and upthrust timbers, that she had not noticed them approaching until too late.

They closed in around her. They were outfitted in the leather leggings and helmets they wore for races, as useful in street fights as chariot spills.

Julianna made a dash toward a gap in the tightening circle.

A stocky dark-haired man smacked her across the face and knocked her to the ground. She tried to get to her knees and someone else kicked her back down.

Julianna felt blood running from her nose. "If you harm me Porphyrius is sure to find out," she said. "And when he does—"

A boot thudded into her side, taking her breath away.

"Why would you know Porphyrius, little girl?" asked the stocky man.

"She's a new charioteer, can't you see?"

A boot pushed her tunic up to her waist.

"She's got a boy's legs. No meat on her."

"Stop complaining," said the stocky charioteer who seemed to be the ringleader. "You want meat, you know where you can pay for it. This one's free."

"Let's get on with it," came another voice.

"Wipe your face, girl. I hate the sight of blood." The ringleader bent toward Julianna, then stopped at the sound of a keening voice.

"Halt! The Lord commands you!" A bent figure crouched at the top of the stairs. Its eyes shone like sparks from an ash blackened face. The strange creature waved a golden cross.

The ringleader looked from the wild-eyed creature to the prone girl and back again. "You'd better be off, whoever you are. We have business to attend to here."

The creature scuttled part way down the stairs. "Business? You call the blackest of sins business? Woe unto you, I say! The beast walks among us! You will have no time to repent!"

Several of the charioteers drew their knives.

The hunched creature laughed, spread its arms wide and thrust its chest forward. "Strike! Strike if you dare. My father will send a bolt from heaven."

The ringleader sneered. "You claim your father's Zeus?"

"Greater than Zeus. Far greater! Strike me. In three days I will rise and dance on your graves."

"I've seen this fellow," one of the others put in. "He preaches from the roof tops. People say he's a holy man. A prophet. I'm not sure we should…."

"I saw him yesterday," said another. "Leaping from building to building as if he was flying. He's not natural. Not a prophet. A demon!"

"A madman more likely," said the ringleader.

"They say a madman has the strength of ten."

The creature on the stairs danced from side to side. "The strength of twelve," it cackled. "The strength of twelve Apostles." He brandished his cross threateningly. "Which do you want to have your brains dashed out by? Matthew, Mark, Luke?"

"He's mad," someone muttered. "I don't want any part of a madman. You can't tell what they'll do."

"What if he really is a holy man though?"

The ringleader sheathed his knife. "Madman, holy man, demon…It's not worth it." He spit at Julianna. "We can do better than this one. She looks more like a boy than a woman, anyway."

The charioteers sauntered off slowly, glancing back over their shoulders but trying not to reveal their wish to be gone.

Julianna got to her feet, pushing her tunic back down.

The creature came down off the stairs, straightened up, and wiped ashes from his face.

Julianna snuffled and dabbed at the blood running down past her mouth and onto her chin. She looked up at her tall rescuer. "I suppose I must thank you, chamberlain."

"You should thank whatever deity made sure I happened to be here just now," John replied. "You're not supposed to leave the palace. What were you doing out here?"

"I needed to take a walk. I don't like being cooped up."

They turned back toward the palace. John stayed a pace behind, in case she decided to run. "It seemed to me you were looking for something, the way you were peering into the ruins of the church."

"I thought I saw something moving in there. I was curious. Is that why you were there? Looking for someone? Or was it you I saw?"

"As I was crossing the square I thought I glimpsed that strange creature who's been seen here and there since the riots began."

They were approaching an obscure entrance to the palace which had remained untouched by the riots. Realizing that they would not encounter any of Gallio's guards until they had reached the interior side of the short corridor into the grounds, John was startled to be accosted. "Excellency! Please, excellency! Take mercy on a poor soul who is living in hell though not dead."

A ragged man sat just inside the arched entrance, his skeletal hand extended. John started to reach for his coin pouch, then remembered he was still holding the cross he'd found in the ruins of the Great Church. He thrust it into the hands of the astonished beggar.

From behind them came a high-pitched titter. He swung around to see Narses.

"John. How good to see you. And your pretty young charge." He made a slight bow to Julianna then looked at the beggar who was staring at the cross with amazement and sniffed disdainfully. "There are more effective ways to spend gold, believe me." He jiggled the pouch at his belt. It made no sound. "You really do have some things to learn, young man. But considering how you have failed the emperor so far I fear you're not going to have enough time."

He passed under the archway. John waited before following. He didn't want the eunuch's company.

When they reached John's house, John asked "How is it you know Porphyrius?"

"I don't."

"I heard you telling your attackers otherwise."

"I saw they were charioteers and I thought of saying it."

"You think quickly."

"Like you." She gave him a faint smile and went inside.

Chapter Twenty-Nine

"It appears you've had an eventful time," John observed as Felix peered into his office from the doorway to the atrium. "Come in. Sit down. Never mind the blood!"

Felix noticed that the long cut running across the knuckles of his right hand still bled.

"You're going to have quite a scar there," John said. "Don't worry about the furniture. I can get more."

"You could use more than two chairs and a desk in here," Felix grunted. "I looked for you first in that private chapel of yours."

"I've had enough religion for the day. I decided to sit here instead."

"We're not likely to be interrupted now that your servants have gone."

"It suits me. I can find a bit of bread and cheese to eat without assistance."

Felix passed a weary hand over his face and sank onto the uncushioned wooden seat. "Things are very bad out there. Very bad. Pass the wine. I'm parched. Not to mention it feels as if I've got a demon inside my head trying to chew its way out." He took a long drink directly from the jug and wiped his mouth with the back of his hand. "Not surprising. Half the city seems to have turned into demons!"

"I can agree with you there, my friend."

Felix took another gulp of wine. "It's obvious we're losing control of the city. After I helped Belisarius—"

"You helped Belisarius?"

Felix related what had happened. "It was poor strategy, getting caught in a spot like that," he concluded. "But then he's a stranger to the city. He couldn't have known about that particular alley."

"All the more reason not to have ventured blindly down it."

"He's a warrior, John. He's been criticized for being too cautious, always on the defensive, unwilling to spill blood. A bit of recklessness is good in a fighting man."

"Up until it gets him killed."

"He took time afterwards to speak to me!"

"Most flattering, and doubtless well-deserved."

Felix gave a proud smile which turned quickly to a frown. "Yes, he said he would mention me to Justinian. From what I've seen Justinian might not have much time left to bestow favors. The city has gone mad. I've seen a naked woman with her hair on fire running, screaming, falling to the ground. A baby left crying in an alley. Two women fighting over a pile of clothes as a crippled beggar stole the lot while they spat and cursed and struck each other. It's not the sort of fighting I trained for, not real warfare, it's…it's…I'm not sure…."

John pushed the wine jug toward him. "It's mob rule. Once the mob finds a leader it will be worse."

"And Gallio refuses to order the excubitors into the streets. I don't know whether he's had a direct order from Justinian or not. If so he won't obey."

"Justinian and Theodora have a ship ready to sail. I'm surprised they haven't already left." A sudden rising crescendo of noise interrupted him. It vibrated through the screen between the office and the garden, loud as a distant rumble of thunder.

John got up, pulled the screen open a crack to listen, shut it. Rather than sitting down again he paced back and forth. The baying of the multitude waxed and waned as the wind shifted. "They must be close to the walls for us to hear that clearly."

"They're working up to storming the palace. Then the excubitors will have to fight!"

"Perhaps. Perhaps not. Are you still an excubitor?"

Felix frowned. "Probably not, if Gallio discovers I left the palace to fight with Belisarius' men against orders. I certainly won't be one when this is over."

"Sign on with the general. That would be your safest course."

"What's your safest course, John? I'd rather have Gallio for an enemy than Narses. He thinks you're ambitious, that you want to take his post at court."

"It's understandable. After all, are we not both those most untrustworthy creatures, imperial eunuchs? Why, we'd kill our own parents if we thought we could achieve further advancement by it."

Felix looked uncomfortable. "So they say. What about your investigation? Does it make any difference at this point who's responsible for killing those two faction members at the church?"

"It might be more important than ever, if whoever was behind their deaths is behind the riots."

"Find the culprit and bring him to justice and you cut off the insurrection at the head. If, in fact, there is any particular person behind the riots and it isn't simply a general uprising. Don't you think it's too complicated to work out in time?"

John smiled bleakly. "I have to keep trying. There's always hope. Even men hanging by the neck from the end of a rope sometimes have reason to hope. And Haik's death must be related."

"What makes you think so?"

"For one thing the fact that Haik and Hippolytus both ended up murdered after visiting Porphyrius strikes me as too much to be a coincidence."

He felt too tired to go into details. Or was it that John himself was unsure there was any connection? Did he imagine there was one, simply to justify his search for his friend's killer?

Felix didn't press him on the question. "I'd say you'd do better to be thinking about your own life rather than someone else's death, John. Are there any arrangements to get the court to safety if necessary? I'd wager Narses has an escape route planned and paid for!"

John shrugged. "Just as well. There won't be room on the ships for everyone."

"Do you suppose your reluctant house guests will be taken with Justinian? No, probably not. More likely they'll be disposed of should he abandon the city to devour itself. I wonder if I could find Antonina and escort her to safety?"

"I see you still have your mind on Antonina. I strongly advise you to turn your thoughts elsewhere. Antonina will be safe. You don't think Theodora would abandon her close friend do you? What we have to worry about in this house is protecting Hypatius and his family. They are in my charge and I don't want to give Justinian an excuse to remove my head if they get away or are killed in the riots. I have come to an agreement with a certain fishing boat owner."

Felix stared at him.

John offered his friend a thin smile. "Have you noticed that ship that's been lying off the northern end of the palace grounds this past day or so? Its owner is a brother in Mithra and we have come to an arrangement. If it sees smoke at a certain point on the shore it will sail in to pick up our reluctant guests."

"But how will it know it's your signal, with half the city in flames?"

"They're waiting to see white smoke billowing at a specific place on the shore."

"And how do you propose to produce white smoke? Magick?"

John shook his head. "No. By burning wet leaves and branches. There are plenty in the palace gardens. The city fires produce darker smoke, and are nowhere near the pick-up point. Or at least not yet. Provided it doesn't rain, this particular column of smoke will stand out."

"And then they'll be taken where?"

"Across the Golden Horn to the monastery of Saint Conon. They can be hidden for now. I don't think they will try to escape, given they'll be almost within sight of the scaffold where the

Blues and Greens were executed. It'll serve as a reminder that it is not safe to venture abroad just now."

"It's well thought out, John. But I can see one problem. What if, when their escape becomes necessary, you've been summoned elsewhere and cannot escort them to the meeting place?"

"I suspect a certain excubitor might act as guide. They won't be in gaudy clothing, Felix. Just ordinary servants as far as anyone else is concerned. And Julianna has the right build to pass for a boy in appropriate clothes and her face dirtied. Or that was my opinion and it has recently been seconded."

Felix nodded. "Couldn't say that for Antonina. Not that I've seen her recently. Although I did go—" He broke off and hid his face in his wine cup.

"You went where?"

"Oh, nothing. My mind's wandering." He looked thoughtful. "Have you met the Persian emissary, John? I was told he traveled to Constantinople with Belisarius. Didn't your friend Haik come here with Belisarius? Do you think he knew the emissary?"

"If so he never mentioned it. But then there seems to have been a lot left unsaid."

Chapter Thirty

January 16, 532

John ran through the palace gardens. The covered walkway he followed veered wildly, first one direction then another. When he looked back he couldn't see his pursuers. He could hear the thud of boots. Or was it hooves? Rhythmic, relentless.

He needed to reach the safety of the ship but he had somehow lost his way. He didn't recognize this part of the palace grounds. He could see nothing but thick, dark vegetation, like a forest. How had he got here?

Who or what was chasing him?

The walkway emerged from the forest onto a vast plain. John peered around, hoping to spot a familiar landmark. Red twilight spilled across a rock strewn landscape. Where was the sea? Where was the Great Palace?

John saw only a charred ruin. Did nothing else remain? Had the fires spread so far?

The clamor of pursuit grew louder.

John ducked under a crumbling archway.

And found himself in a windowless room. The wooden door was shut, although he didn't recall closing it. A familiar figure confronted him.

"You shouldn't be here," Haik said.

"Haik! Thanks to Mithra! I thought you were dead."

"Hardly. I must have stayed too long at the baths. We were detained by the Persians, you see."

"The Persians? You mean the Persian emissary?"

There was an explosive pounding at the door.

"They're here!" Haik cried. "They're here!" His voice rose to an inhuman howl.

His eyes turned red and his flesh began to melt.

The knocking at the door continued, accompanied now by shouts. "Chamberlain! Chamberlain!"

John was suddenly aware that he was lying in his own bed. For an instant he was paralyzed, suspended between nightmare and reality. Then he forced himself awake.

What hour was it? The oil lamp beside the bed guttered as he threw off his blanket.

The pounding continued. "Chamberlain! Can you hear me?"

He recognized the voice of Pompeius. His suspicion was conferred by the gust of stale wine breath that hit him in the face when he yanked open the door. The fat man was frantic as well as drunk. "Dead! I was afraid of it! Hurry! It's Julianna!"

"Julianna? Dead?"

"No. You. I thought you were dead. I kept knocking. You wouldn't answer. Julianna's ill. Poisoned, like that house guest of yours. Must be poison. She's in her room. Come quickly." Pompeius lumbered off, unsteadily.

John glanced around for his clothes, half expecting to see Haik, but the phantom had gone back to wherever dreams go. It was said the gods spoke to men in dreams. Had some kindly deity sent him the solution to the murders of Haik and the faction members? If so, he couldn't remember. As he pulled his dalmatic on over a light tunic he tried to hold onto the vision. It was like trying to grasp sea mists at sunrise.

He rushed after Pompeius and caught him at the entrance to the suite of rooms the guests were occupied. "Have you summoned a physician?"

"Yes. Of course. Rusticus is staying at the palace. One of the excubitors agreed to go for him. I think, at first, he thought it was some sort of ruse. But I...I...well....it's your house...I thought you should— "

"Where is she?"

"In her room."

"But I'm not a physician or a clergyman. It wouldn't be appropriate." John well knew that in aristocratic circles the women's quarters were strictly off-limits to men. In this case, those quarters were the single room Julianna was staying in. Even if Pompeius were too intoxicated to take offense, others might.

Pompeius stared at John glassy eyed. "What? Not appropriate? Oh...Oh...I see. No. It's fine. As Hypatius agreed. Because of your....um....your status."

John felt a sudden rush of heat to his face. He managed to control his voice. "I see. Very well. I have no antidotes for poison though."

By the time he reached Julianna's bedside his anger was under control.

Hypatius, hovering nearby, snapped at his brother. "It's about time. I was afraid Bacchus had detained you or you'd fallen asleep under a table."

John leaned over the girl. Her face was shockingly pale and her breathing shallow but her eyes were open and alert. "I'm fine." Her voice was barely a whisper. "I just felt dizzy. It's nothing to worry about. Please reassure my father and my uncle."

"She collapsed," Hypatius said. "The crash woke me up. When I got her she was crumpled up on the floor. You can imagine what I was thinking, after what...just happened."

John wondered if she had been injured during her confrontation with the street thugs, or had inhaled smoke while out in the city. Probably the exertion and worry of recent days had finally caught up. He knew he should alert Hypatius to his daughter's secretive comings and goings. Julianna knew it too. The gaze she fixed on him clearly demanded that he say nothing.

He was reminded again of Cornelia. She had been strong-willed too.

"I'm not a physician," he said. "but it doesn't look to me as if she's been poisoned. The past few days have been too exciting for her. That's all it is."

"Exciting? It's not very exciting here, is it?" Pompeius shook his head. "More likely she's taken a chill from spending all her time out in your garden."

"Quite possibly." As John straightened up the white haired physician Rusticus entered in his usual flurry of words.

"Apologies, sirs. Your guard had to drag me out the barracks. Been there half the night. Belisarius got into a tussle in the streets. I've been treating wounds that would made Galen weep to see them." He pulled a stool up to Julianna's bedside. "Fainted, you say?"

"That's right," Hypatius confirmed. "Fell down as if she were poisoned."

Rusticus took hold of the girl's chin and turned her face to him. "Look this way, child. Show me your tongue. The lips aren't blue."

"I'm fine," Julianna protested weakly. "I just feel a bit sick."

"You think you're sick, do you?" Rusticus rambled on. "Be glad both your leg bones aren't protruding from your skin. You'd be sick then. And that wasn't the worst." He placed a hand on her abdomen. "Breath now. There, you can breath. If you'd been hit with a brick, it might be a different story. Home-made weapons are the worst. Some untrained ruffian with a splintered board in his hands or a jagged shard of pottery isn't as likely to inflict a wound as a trained soldier with a proper sword or spear. Oh, but when he does he makes a nasty wound indeed. At least a well honed blade, precisely placed, will kill you on the spot. A plank full of rusty nails just rips your guts open. Tortures you for days before putting you out of your misery."

"Are you sure she's all right, Rusticus?" demanded Hypatius.

"Fine. Fine. A touch of woman's complaint most likely." The physician struggled up off the stool. "I can give her something for it."

"I don't need anything." Julianna's voice sounded slightly stronger.

"You'll take what Rusticus thinks best," said Hypatius. "I don't want you visiting Antonina for any of her evil concoctions."

Rusticus shuffled to the door, followed by Hypatius and Pompeius. John took a last glance around the room. The family had not had time to bring much from their homes. He noticed a wooden chest, probably filled with clothes. On a marble topped table a tiny, painted horse sat surrounded by perfume bottles and fancy enamelled containers of the sort that might hold unguents and make-up.

He was alone in the room with Julianna, who was looking at him.

"Thank you for being discreet," she said in a whisper.

"Please try to be more discreet yourself. No more excitement."

He went out into the corridor where Hypatius was gesticulating at Rusticus. "You're sure it isn't poison? Haik could have been poisoned outside the palace. Everyone agreed. It might have been slow acting."

"There would be signs," Rusticus said. "Why I recall, back when Senator—"

"But what if there's a poisoner among us?" interrupted Hypatius. "Or a murderer with access to this house? I could be next. Or my brother."

Pompeius put a hand on Hypatius' shoulder. "Come away now. Have some wine with me. For all you know you might be poisoned already. The pain might start any moment."

Hypatius looked stricken. Pompeius chuckled, then began to sway on his feet. His hand tightened on his brother's shoulder. Hypatius grabbed Pompeius' arm to steady him.

"You'll be nearby if my brother should need you, Rusticus?" Hypatius asked. "Or if I should?"

Rusticus gave a curt nod. "Yes. The last thing either of you need is wine. I will send a concoction for Julianna, and a sleeping potion for the two of you."

"I'll accompany you out," John told the physician after the brothers had departed. "Perhaps you should just stay at my house. You seem to visit the family constantly."

"Mostly Pompeius. Julianna is healthy as a horse."

"I suspect she would appreciate your saying so."

"The last time I saw her was when I treated her uncle, right after the executions. It was Pompeius who was on his sick bed that afternoon. Julianna had come over to tend to him until I arrived. The two houses are practically next to each other. She's a strong girl. Not squeamish. Demanded to hear every detail of what I'd witnessed. Did I describe the executions to you?"

"As a matter of fact, you did and it was most interesting," John said quickly, as they walked into the atrium. "Please excuse me. I have something to attend to."

He left the elderly physician beside the statue of Aphrodite.

An image of Haik floated through his mind. The dream was already dissipating from his memory. Haik had said something about Persians, hadn't he? Felix said that the Persian emissary traveled with Belisarius. Haik had also accompanied the general's troops to the city. Then too, Julianna had been with Pompeius when Rusticus had treated him. These were connections John had not known about. They formed new possibilities.

◇◇◇

It took only a few inquiries before John was being ushered into the Persian emissary's rooms at the Daphne Palace. No one sought to deny him entrance. It was perfectly natural that the chamberlain in charge of the imperial banquet might wish to confer with the honoree. The only puzzle was why preparations were still ongoing, given the state of the city, but then the emperor was known as a man of strange whims.

The quarters had been decorated in wall hangings with Persian motifs. The emissary was sitting at a table, poring over something there. When he rose, John saw he was a tall man, not much older than John, with a black spike of a beard and hair that hung to his broad shoulders in glossy ringlets.

John's breath caught in his throat before he could speak. He recognized the man, from his time in captivity.

For an instant he was back in the Persian encampment. A military officer with a sharply pointed beard walked down the line of chained men. "This one, and this one," he said, and the men were dragged away to the waiting executioner. Only a handful had been spared, John among them. Spared to be led into a tent, where they were tied to a table and a man with a razor-sharp knife relegated them to a worse future than the condemned whose heads already had been piled up in blood soaked baskets.

No, John realized. That commander would have been much older today. The emissary was the same age that other Persian had been when John's life had been so drastically changed, more than ten years ago, an eternity.

The commander had worn the same style of beard, and was Persian. There was no other similarity.

Nevertheless it was only with difficulty that John managed keep his voice from shaking as he returned the emissary's greeting.

"Please tell your emperor that I appreciate his hospitality all the more in light of the crisis with which he is dealing," the emissary said. "You speak Persian well. You have spent time in Persia, perhaps? One hopes your stay was pleasurable."

John made no reply. His heart was still racing from his initial, mistaken impression. What had the man said his name was? Bozorgmehr? How peculiar. That translated as Great Mithra. So the Christian emperor was negotiating an Eternal Peace with Mithra, John's god. "I wanted to insure the banquet arrangements are suitable," John said. He showed him a proposed menu he had written out on a sheet of parchment.

John had no clear idea of what he might learn from his visit. He hardly dared question the Persian official directly. Particularly if his reasons for being in the city were other than diplomacy. Bozorgmehr's crimson tunic bore a decorative pearl-outlined roundel of a boar's head. The boar stared at John while the emissary studied the parchment. Over the Persian's shoulder John saw what the man had been looking at so intently on the table.

It was a rectangular board of light, polished wood inlaid with long triangles of darker wood. Several rows of flat, enameled disks had been laid out in lines along some of the triangles.

Bozorgmehr must have noticed the direction of John's gaze. "That is the ancient game known as Nard." He handed the menu back. "Your choice of courses is excellent, Chamberlain."

"Thank you. I imagine a game like that would be a good way to pass the time during a tedious journey."

"True enough. That is why I brought it with me, in part. But in addition, I have been refining the rules. Rather as your emperor has been organizing the welter of your old Roman laws. I find games to be exquisite miniatures of life."

"Assembling a guest list and arranging seating for a banquet is not unlike placing pieces on a board," John remarked.

"Exactly. Men are fascinated by games, even if their outcomes change nothing. The wealthy and the poor are passionate over the races, though the wealthy have no need to win more than they already possess and the poor are not made wealthy by cheering for the winner."

"Charioteers have a financial stake in racing, however. Their game is their life. Perhaps it would please you if I seated Porphyrius within speaking distance. Or have you had the chance to speak to him already since you arrived?"

Bozorgmehr displayed no reaction that John could see beyond genuine perplexity. "Why would I have spoken to Porphyrius? I know him only by reputation."

"My apologies. He is one of the city's most famous residents and I am certain would have been highly honored if you had granted him an audience. I fear that in my eagerness to provide suitable entertainment for you the thought was father to the assumption."

"Certainly I have heard of this Porphyrius," the other admitted.

"In Constantinople," continued John, "who has not? And his name is known even further afield. If you happened to speak to Haik, a fellow traveler on your journey here, you would have heard a great deal about Porphyrius."

Still, John could see nothing but puzzlement in the Persian's long, angular face.

"I do not recall speaking with anyone named Haik."

"He accompanied Belisarius, as you did. I know him from my time in that part of the world. A hearty, hawk nosed fellow. A pistachio grower."

Bozorgmehr betrayed no awareness that Haik had ever lived, let alone that he was dead. "General Belisarius escorted a large number of people to Constantinople. I stayed with my own retinue."

"Ah. Then I should strike Haik off the guest list. I wondered how he would know such a high official as yourself. No doubt he was playing his own game —to win an invitation to an imperial banquet. It is a good thing I came to speak to you."

The emissary laughed. "I see. That would explain it. Why don't you invite him anyway? Allow him to win."

John wondered whether he could risk questioning Bozorgmehr further. He gave no evidence of knowing either Haik or Porphyrius, but then Chosroes would doubtless have sent as his representative a man highly skilled in diplomacy, which invariably required more than a little expertise in duplicity.

Their conversation was ended, however, before he could decide which way to turn it.

Narses walked into the room.

Was it possible the treasurer was having John followed and had decided to purposely break up his talk with the emissary?

"John," said Narses. "I am surprised to find you here. I am sure you will excuse us."

Narse's expression made it clear that he was ordering John to leave.

"I hope you have come to take me up on my offer to teach you this game of mine," said Bozorgmehr. He thanked John for his efforts.

John went out. It was hard for him to imagine Narses taking any interest in a game played on a wooden board with inanimate pieces, considering the games to be played at court with real people. There was one advantage such games had over the great game of life, however. You knew in a short while who had won or lost, and then could play again. You had only a single chance to win or lose at life, and you could not be certain what the outcome was until the very end, which could be a knife to your back.

Chapter Thirty-One

Deep in thought, John walked toward the southern end of the Hippodrome. Was it possible that the Persians supported the insurrection? He had no proof of it. But there was the coincidence of Haik having traveled to Constantinople with Bozorgmehr. Perhaps they were working together. Was it the Persian emissary who had brought the potentially dangerous imperial adoption papers Haik had revealed with his last breath?

Why would the Persians wish to see Justinian removed? They had arranged for an Eternal Peace with him, hadn't they? Realistically, whatever the peace was called, Chosroes could hardly depend on eternity in this case to extend beyond Justinian's death or exile.

Did the Persians want to see a weak emperor on the throne? A man less shrewd than Justinian? A bungler like Hypatius?

Or were they looking to place the empire into the hands of a man who had, perhaps, agreed to be an ally, or even a vassal, of the heir under the document, Chosroes? General Belisarius?

The millennium-long thread that lead back to the beginnings of Rome would then be cut. The Roman Empire would become nothing more than a part of the Persian empire.

There was no evidence for that. Should he question Porphyrius about the document again? He would certainly not betray a plot of such magnitude, but he might reveal a bit more, to see if it might satisfy John, provided he knew more. And then there was the new path of inquiry he had glimpsed during Rusticus' most recent visit to treat Julianna.

There was one solution to it all, he was sure, no matter from what direction he finally reached it.

By the time John reached the stables beneath the Hippodrome he was blinking and wiping his stinging eyes. Smoke filled the air. New conflagrations had broken out somewhere to the north. From the street he had been able to make out gray plumes in the distance but there was no way to tell what exactly was burning. The winds driving the fires south swirled around the Hippodrome and carried the smoke deep into the stadium corridors. Trapped in the huge vaults under the track, it hung like a thick fog against the high ceilings.

Panicked horses plunged back and forth in their stalls.

He spotted a familiar face. Junius, the young charioteer he had encountered inspecting the quadriga, ran out of the haze.

John put out a hand to detain him.

Junius came to a halt. He was breathing hard. "You're back? I don't have time to talk."

"Whatever errand you're on is less important than the emperor's business."

Junius ran a hand across his sweaty forehead leaving a streak of grime. He looked ready to bolt.

"I wish to speak to you," John said. "Do I have to show you my imperial orders?"

Several men rushed past to join others trying to control a horse rearing up in its stall. A hoof crashed into the side and sent shattered boards flying.

"Let's get out of the way." Junius led John through the chaotic stables into an enormous curved passage. Through a stone archway wider than four chariots abreast John could see the concrete ramp which ran up to the far end of the racetrack.

"I'm surprised the teams haven't transported the horses out of the city."

"Porphyrius still thinks we might race. Besides, trying to move all the horses through the streets under the circumstances...." Junius shrugged. "If we'd realized in advance what was going to happen...but no one expected the whole city to go up in flames. When the factions fight it's usually blood in the gutters and an extra body or two to fish out the sea. Rats don't set fire to their own holes."

John thought that what was true for rats might not apply to humans. He coughed as thicker smoke eddied through the passage. Conditions were less than ideal for an interview. He decided to get to the point immediately. "There are women who take a special interest in charioteers, aren't there?"

"You mean the whores who hang around the entrances to the Hippodrome?"

"No, I mean women who don't call themselves whores."

"Ah, well, charioteers do have their admirers, if that's what you're asking about."

"Despite the fact they are not allowed to view the races?"

"Everyone in the city knows the names of the winning drivers, whether they sit in the stands or not. Brothers and husbands and fathers talk about the exploits of their favorite teams over dinner." Junius ran a hand through his dark hair. "Not that women don't ever get into the Hippodrome. It's not a monastery."

"You mean they come to watch the races?"

"To see the races and...to see those they admire."

"Do you have admirers?"

Junius grinned. "Oh, yes. Even the stable lads. Anyone with any connection with racing can have their pick of women." The charioteer's expression darkened suddenly. "You didn't risk coming here to ask about women. Unless you're looking for a woman for yourself."

"No. I'm looking for information. How about Porphyrius, does he have women callers?"

"Naturally. He's the most popular, old as he is. The most successful always have the best choice. Why, even the youngest girls want to explore the ancient ruins. I suppose they can picture they're lying with one of the statues of him along the spina."

John smiled. "Even as a youth Porphyrius could never have matched the idealized bronze and marble images of himself."

Junius laughed. "Porphyrius rarely takes advantage of the girls anyway. His taste runs to high born women. There was one senator's wife, Fortuna smiled on her all right! I brought a friend down here one night, to show her what goes into putting on a race, you see, and the racket coming from Zephyrius' stall was enough to frighten the rest of the horses. Frightened my friend off too."

"You suspect it was Porphyrius?"

"I suspected nothing. Next day Porphyrius bragged about it to me. He said it amused him to think of her husband orating about the glory of the Blues in the Senate House while he—"

"What about the wealthy patrons like that senator? Does their support buy them access to the charioteers?"

Junius sniffed. "I've known a few drivers who weren't averse to being driven by men."

"I was referring to the fact that patrons come and go as they please."

"That's true. They're always under foot. But without them… well…bowing and scraping to rich fools and weaklings is part of the job, like shovelling manure."

"Are you bowing and scraping now?"

"Oh, I didn't mean—"

Their conversation was interrupted by the clatter of hooves. Stable hands led a procession of horses past. The animals tossed their heads and whickered in distress.

When the passage was quiet again John asked, "One of the faction members who was murdered at Saint Laurentius—the Green—he visited Porphyrius, didn't he?"

Junius looked genuinely puzzled. "I can't say. Why would a Green visit Porphyrius?"

John paused. He was afraid he had already said too much, without eliciting any useful information either. No doubt everything he'd asked would soon get back to Porphyrius. "I take it that it isn't difficult to sneak women in here when the races aren't going on?"

"Couldn't be easier. It's a huge place, with all sorts of back doors, and deserted most of the time."

"What if a woman wanted to watch the races?"

"It's still not that hard to get in, if you know where the merchants bring their wares in or the entrances the laborers use. With thousands of people packed into the stands, intent on the chariots, no one's paying much attention to whether there's a woman on the next bench. Especially if she's wearing men's clothing."

"Have you seen a girl disguised like that recently?"

Junius stiffened. "Some aristocrat's daughter's run off. Is that what this is about? You don't suspect me, do you? I only wish I had some sweet, wealthy creatures like that thronging to me. Maybe when I've won enough races. I'm happy with a baker's daughter right now."

John refrained from asking him how he could be certain a baker's daughter who'd disguised herself as a man to creep into the Hippodrome wasn't really a female cousin to Justinian, pretending to be a baker's daughter pretending to be a man. "You're free to go now, Junius. Where can I find Porphyrius?"

"He's out on the track." Junius waved a hand toward the ramp ascending from the archway. "He's convinced all the trouble in the city is due to curse tablets, so he's out there digging for them."

"Junius!" someone shouted. "The weapons are here!" The rattle of cart wheels echoed in the passage.

John saw a donkey cart piled high with sacks and a variety of lances, swords, and armor. It might have trundled straight from the imperial armory.

Junius must have noticed John questioning gaze. "We're not joining the insurrection," he blurted. "Some of our supporters—senators—have arranged to send weapons to guard the horses.

The Greens might decide to cripple them....though there's also the fact that horse meat makes a good meal, and there's little food in the city. And, well...Porphyrius thinks they're needed. It's not for me to question him."

"No, it isn't," John agreed. "It's up to me. You had best attend to your business."

◇◇◇

"Those weapons will allow us to protect the horses and equipment, not to mention ourselves and the Hippodrome." Porphyrius stood, muscular arms crossed, beside the wall of the spina at the far turn of the sandy track, overseeing several men who were up to their waists in the holes they were digging. "You can't fault people for trying to preserve their livelihood. We're taking every precaution, not only against the rioters, but against supernatural threats like curse tablets and natural dangers as well." He nodded toward the stands.

John saw workers with buckets moving along the tiers damping down the wooden seats to prevent the structure from catching fire. The scattered flakes of ash that swirled down into the arena were black and cold, but they might be replaced by sparks at any moment.

"Don't you trust the urban watch?"

"They didn't manage to protect the Great Church did they? Or their own Praetorium, or those two poor wretches at Saint Laurentius. I hope we never have to use those weapons. I'm a charioteer, not a soldier."

"You led an attack in Antioch many years ago, and you rallied the populace to Emperor Anastasius during the insurrection by Vitalian."

"Once a man becomes famous they say all sorts of things about him. A man is skilled at one thing and suddenly he is considered skilled at everything."

"You deny your role in those events?"

"My role has been exaggerated."

"So you plan to hang back and wait for an attack? Then defend yourself? That isn't your racing style."

"I am a great charioteer, not a great general. This is the third day in a row you've visited me," he added with obvious annoyance. "Am I under surveillance?"

John made no reply.

Porphyrius strode over to the nearest excavation. One of the workers stopped and leaned on his spade. "You see we've gone right through the lime and crushed brick," the digger said in querulous tones. "Shall we try somewhere else or do you expect us to continue on to Hades?"

Porphyrius planted a boot in the complainer's back and shoved his face into the hole he had dug. "Keep going until Cerberus bites off your nose, you fool! How many times do I have to explain? The riots are getting worse, but they began here and that means curse tablets are buried here somewhere! And the turn is one of the favorite spots for them."

One of the spade wielders working further along the track called out to them. "Found one!" He waved a grayish cylinder hardly as big as a finger.

Porphyrius trotted over, took the rolled lead artifact, and pulled it open. He began reading the words inscribed on the tablet aloud. "Demons of night and wandering untimely dead, you who go by the powerful names of Hecate of the crossroads and Resheph, bringer of plague, bind the horse Servitor, steed of the Blue, Gentius. Hobble his feet and make him fall at the turn with his driver—"

Porphyrius broke off, grunted, and balled the tablet up in his fist.

"It isn't what you're looking for?"

Porphyrius gave a snort of disgust. "This must've been lurking under the track since Anastasius ruled. Gentius was killed in an accident years ago."

"On the turn?"

"Fell out the third floor window of a whore house."

He instructed the worker to keep digging and made a circuit of the rest of the excavations, none of which revealed anything of interest.

After squatting down beside the final hole Porphyrius straightened up, moving with the fluidity of a man decades younger, and smiled at John. "You believe it's all superstition, don't you? You're bemused that I would take such nonsense seriously."

"I wouldn't say that."

"Of course you wouldn't. You're a diplomat. But I can see that's what you think. Charioteers have a different way of looking at things. Every time I step into my chariot I'm putting one foot in the Styx. We are all aware of how close the other world is to this one. Close enough that we are never more than a step, or a shove, from leaving this world. But what did you come here to ask me this time?"

"I've been pondering your meeting with my friend Haik. You admitted he hinted at the existence of a document by which Justin agreed to adopt Chosroes."

"It was a rumor he thought I would find interesting."

"Didn't you think he might have been judging your interest in such a document? He couldn't be sure how loyal you are to Justinian. There was no way of telling how you might react. Had he made it plain that he had actually brought such a document to the city, you might have reported him to the emperor for fomenting an insurrection."

Porphyrius turned his attention to the track, tested the surface with the toe of his boot. Finally he said, "Haik did say that a document like that would be worth an enormous sum...to a collector of historic documents. If there were such a document."

"Did he offer to sell it to you?"

"There wasn't any document, so far as I know. It was simply speculation. I suspect he was trying to make conversation, to get me on his side, so I would endorse his business plans."

John thought Porphyrius might be telling the truth. It would have been prudent to approach potential buyers cautiously. For all John knew Haik might have tried to to sell it to others—senators or wealthy aristocrats—or might have intended to do so. He preferrred to think that Haik was not involved in any plot but had simply been looking for monetary gain from an artefact he'd stumbled across. He'd admitted he was still a mercenary. Is that what he'd meant by the remark? Had Haik even believed that the document could be employed to any great effect? John hoped not.

He decided there was little more to learn from that line of inquiry. But there remained another question. "You told me Hippolytus visited when Haik was meeting with you," he said.

"Hippolytus again? You think I have something to do with his death? Or with that botched hanging you told me about?"

John ignored the question. "Was anyone else present at that meeting?"

"No."

"Did Hippolytus ever bring anyone else with him to the Hippodrome? A woman?"

"Women are not allowed at the races."

"I'm not talking about the races. He may have brought a friend to meet you. There are racing fans who would rather touch your sleeve than dine with the emperor."

Porphyrius smiled. "You flatter me. But no, I didn't see Hippolytus very often. He never brought anyone to gawk at me or tug my sleeve. I appreciated his discretion. I did catch a glimpse of him across the stables one day, showing off Zephyrius to a callow looking fellow. When I mentioned it later he told me it was his younger brother. I invited him to bring the lad in to see me one day, but he never did."

The charioteer bent down and ran a hand over the sand on the track. Then he stood, gave the track a few kicks with the heel of his boot, and shook his head. "The surface is too loose. Not surprising. Most of the workers who ought to be taking care of the track are nowhere to be found. Speaking of which, I can tell you where to find Hippolytus' family. Your curiosity about him had me worried. I asked around, to make sure there wasn't something he had neglected to tell me. I can't be responsible for investigating the motivations and background of every would-be patron."

He described to John a mansion located at the top of the ridge overlooking the northern harbors. "At least I've been told that's where he lived," he concluded. "No one seemed to know him well. Maybe you can learn what you want from his family."

Porphyrius did not add that then John might also leave him alone, but his meaning was clear from his tone.

They were startled by a shout. The worker who had been kicked into the hole by Porphyrius yelled again and pointed up toward the spina. "Demons take you, Porphyrius! There's that croaking harbinger of doom! He's the one brought evil to the city, not these ridiculous scrawls on scraps of lead! They say he's returned from the dead!"

With that the man threw down his spade, leapt out of the excavation and fled, swiftly followed by his fellow diggers.

John peered up at the confusion of monuments running down the length of the spina. There, in a golden bowl supported on a column formed by three entwined serpents, stood the same ragged, grotesque creature he had seen running across the roof tops. It scrambled over the side of the bowl, slid down the snake column, embraced one of the statues of Porphyrius which stood nearby and began singing an obscene song to its bronze visage.

"What's that demon doing here?" roared Porphyrius.

John suddenly wanted to know that too. He pulled himself up onto the spina and sprinted toward the creature, dodging several marble emperors who obstructed his path.

The creature saw him, cackled, ducked beneath a replica of the she-wolf suckling Romulus and Remus, and was away. Cursing, John clambered over the top of the wolf.

John's prey vanished behind a monstrous wild boar and reappeared swinging from its tusk. For an instant he hung from the tusk by one arm, let his head loll to one side, rolled his eyes back, and stuck his tongue out. Then laughing hysterically, he dropped and raced on.

The chase covered the length of the spina. John passed a brazen eagle with a snake in its claws and the monumental Hercules.

Though the demon gave the appearance of scuttling along like a monstrous crab, John couldn't catch up. The creature was well ahead when it vanished behind the Egyptian obelisk at the end of the spina. In an instant it reappeared on the track.

John leaned wearily against a massive bronze leg, part of a monumental bull.

"Mithra!" He cursed softly as he watched the demon scramble across the track, feet sending up gouts of sand, before it reached the starting boxes and vaulted over a gate into the darkness beyond.

◌ ◌ ◌

The ragged man skittered across the concrete, leaping, falling, sometimes upright, sometimes crawling on all fours. Shadows melted out of his path. The poor souls who inhabited this benighted place did not care to confront him.

At last he emerged into a cold wind. He could no longer hear the demon, could no longer smell the evil. The terrible creature had come swooping out of the sky and pursued him along the narrow precipice where the old gods stood, frozen forever in stone and gold. A feast for the eyes of idolaters.

But he had escaped with the Lord's help.

He crouched down, hugging his knees to his chest, listening. He clutched the sacred shard of wood in his hand more tightly, felt hot pain as a splinter pierced his skin. Blood blossomed on his palm. He remembered the crosses reared up against the sky. He had been brought down from the cross.

To what purpose?

He turned the wood over, examining it. He knew what it was—a fragment of the True Cross. But the ribbon wrapped around it puzzled him.

His past was nothing but the fog of a dream, grasped at futilely as it slips away, unremembered.

He had traversed hell. Surely it was hell, where a man sat in a corner pulling his intestines away from a black dog. Where a child emerged from a fiery pit, face hanging in charred strips from a blackened skull in which eyes still glistened with life.

How long he had been in hell, he could not say. Forever perhaps.

And where was he now?

He scrambled around and stared upwards. A high, brick wall rose above his head.

Why did he feel he wanted to be here, in the freezing shadow of a wall?

He crept forward, keeping to the shadow. It wasn't safe to stay long in one spot. The demons were always searching.

Even as he shivered at the thought of the demons, a cold hand grasped his.

No. Not a demon's hand, after all, he realized. He felt the hard fingers of a statue.

Or, rather, a corpse.

The dead man's arm extended from the alcove where the rest of his body lay crumpled in a heap of costly robes. What good was that gold thread now?

It was the new leather boots that caught the ragged man's gaze.

Looking down at his own feet, he saw he had lost a sandal. When?

It didn't matter. The Lord saw everything. The Lord provided.

The ragged man recognized the wall. He was outside the Great Palace. This was the place he had crossed hell to reach.

Because he had to speak to the emperor.

He remembered now. Because he could hardly meet the emperor while wearing a single filthy sandal. So the Lord had sent him this fine pair of boots.

Chapter Thirty-Two

John stood in front of the Hippodrome and surveyed the Mese while he caught his breath. There was no sign of the demon he had pursued across the spina. The creature might be right around a nearby corner, or halfway to the city walls. Even if the demon were still lurking around a corner, John would be unlikely to find it. Constantinople with its crooked alleys, slanting streets, and unexpected squares boasted as many corners as there were stars in the sky.

There wasn't time to waste. In not too many hours, it would be a week since the two faction members were killed at Saint Laurentius. John felt he had barely begun his investigations. Who had he spoken to, after all? Only a handful of people had told him anything useful.

As he looked up and down the street with its fire-gutted shops and ruined colonnades, he reminded himself there were reasons for his lack of progress. It was dangerous and difficult to traverse the chaotic city, and harder yet to locate anyone. Many had fled, or were missing. It was impossible to say who, amongst them—people John did not even know—might have been able to lead him to the killers.

Then too, he had to deal with the Anastasius family. Justinian should never have asked him to host three troublesome aristocrats while undertaking a vital investigation. But he couldn't say that to the emperor.

He considered the information Porphyrius had given him, the location of Hippolytus' house. It wasn't too far away. The charioteer thought the young aristocrat kept apartments in the family mansion. Perhaps the family would be able to tell John what their son had been involved in, and who his associates were.

The streets were relatively quiet. John cut through the Copper Market. The metal working shops which predominated there offered little to attract the wrath of the mob. He could still see the plumes of smoke to the north which he had noted on his way to the Hippodrome. At any time his way might be blocked by a wall of fire.

What he feared more was finding himself suddenly surrounded by fires, or in the path of a blaze driven by the gusty wind.

After awhile the streets ran steeply uphill. The wind hit him in the face, numbing his skin. He blinked, trying to drive away the sharp, icy pain just behind his eyes.

He paused to look behind him. From his elevated position he could see through a gap in the buildings all the way to the Augustaion. Samsun's Hospice and the Church of Saint Irene were on fire. Whether they had been specially targeted or were victims of fires set elsewhere, it was impossible to say.

When the crest of the ridge he was climbing came into view he was greeted by another dismal sight. The riots had cut off John's newest line of inquiry. The house where Hippolytus lived had been reduced to a fire-gutted shell.

The front of the house had toppled into the street. If there had been a courtyard it was buried in rubble. Parts of the colonnade along both sides of the street were crushed. However, a short distance away a couch with red upholstery sat on an undamaged portion for the colonnade roof. John wondered whether it had fallen there, incongruously, when the house collapsed or if someone had moved it there. For what reason? To have a good seat from which to view whatever had been taking place in the street?

Although the place was obviously deserted, John picked his way through the ruins. There wasn't much to see. One interior wall, still standing, bore bright frescoes of chariot races. Water glinted from beneath a pile of bricks, marking the remains of a fountain. An enormous rat crawled from the bricks, and skittered away.

In one spot John's gaze was caught by bits of charred parchment protruding from the ashes, waving in the wind like dead leaves on a winter tree. Scuffing with the toe of his boot turned up burnt scrolls and codices, little more than charcoal. He saw what he guessed, from what could still be seen of the elaborate binding, was a gospel. Had its teachings prepared the family for the senseless loss of both their home and their son?

The stables had also been destroyed. Whether the family had escaped, John could not say, but the overpowering stench behind the house told him that the horses had not. One breath sent him back rapidly through the ruins. He had just exhaled when a dark shape came hurtling off the top of a wall at him.

He caught a glimpse of its moving shadow first, from the corner of his eye, and spun out of the way. All he could think of was the demon. Had it followed him here?

Then he saw a large, black cat, stirring up a cloud of ash. The cat whirled and slashed with its claws, a blur of motion. There was a high pitched shriek. The cat's prey, a rat, burst free.

The rat turned back toward the shelter of the ruined fountain from which John had seen it emerge earlier. It was not just any rat but a truly imperial-sized rat. But before it could reach safety a mottled brown and white shape darted from the rubble. The small cat clamped its jaws on the rat's back. It looked hardly bigger than the rat. The captured rodent squealed and writhed but the small cat's hold remained firm.

The much larger black cat trotted forward. The two cats looked at each other. Their differing colors made John think of the racing factions. Then the small cat ran off, carrying its huge, struggling meal away. The black cat followed.

Would they share the bounty or fight over it?

John didn't wait to see. He picked his way back through the ruins.

Once on the street he paused. He had wasted another hour learning nothing.

From the top of the ridge he could see out over the northern harbors and across the waters of the Golden Horn. The molten orange globe of the sun hung in a coppery mist of smoke. John imagined he could almost see the disk moving as time raced past.

He feared that time was running out for his investigation and for the emperor and the empire itself. Already, in the half-light created by the haze, the panorama before him looked unreal, like an aged wall painting. The haze lent its coppery tint to everything, not just the water but the buildings and streets and the ships in the harbor.

Across the harbor lay the monastery of Saint Conon whose monks had rescued, temporarily, the two condemned faction members. Almost from the outset of his investigations, John had dismissed the idea that the monks might be involved in any plot. Yet the directions in which he had chosen to take his inquires had mostly turned out to be dead ends.

Rather than turning back to the palace, John began to walk down the hill toward the docks.

◇◇◇

At the docks commerce had come to a halt. Crates, amphorae, and sacks lay neglected in haphazard piles in front of the warehouses at the base of the sea wall. The crowds ignored them. They had not come to loot but to escape. John could barely see the water for sailing vessels of every shape and size, from merchant ship to wooden planks.

Here and there those desperate to flee the burning city haggled with ship masters desperate to earn as much as they could while the opportunity lasted.

"How could I pay a fare like that?" John overheard one man shouting. "I'm a baker. Do I look like the emperor to you?"

Elsewhere he saw several husky men dressed in the plain tunics of laborers lashing together a collection of charred beams to make a raft.

John had little difficulty hiring a boat. When on the emperor's business he went well prepared to offer bribes, though he rarely did so. The amount requested in this case amounted to a bribe.

Once he was out on the Golden Horn, John wished he had searched out a larger boat. The water looked perilously close to him where he sat. He didn't dare stand. The boat's owner, mindful of the coins to be made with each passage, rowed as if he were being chased by demons. As he toiled at the oars he stared at his passenger appraisingly.

"Take me as near as possible to Saint Conon's monastery," John instructed him.

"I'd never have guessed you for one to join a monastery, sir. I've already taken two there but they were such as had to haggle over my price. They said there was no use going further. No one could outrun the four horsemen."

"I'll be returning to the city shortly," John said. "Wait for me. Don't worry, I will compensate you."

He didn't bother displaying the imperial orders. In this case, Justinian's money spoke loudly enough.

He came ashore on a stretch of waste ground littered with debris and the remains of chariots. The scaffolds hurriedly erected to execute the faction members were still standing. He gave them a wide berth. Shoddily constructed, they leaned into each other like drunken men in front of a tavern. The ropes had been removed.

The Blue and the Green twice lay crumpled on the ground under those scaffolds. Hours later the men floated in the cistern from which John had pulled the Blue.

Had dying three times sufficiently punished them for their transgressions?

The strange coppery light gave the scene the same appearance of unreality John had noticed earlier as he stared across the water from the ridge by Hippolytus' burnt house. It lacked only suffering figures to turn it into a painting of Christian martyrs.

Beyond the scaffolds a stony path led through tall, brown weeds and squat thorn bushes. The path ended behind the monastery, a long, box-like structure, that might have housed government bureaucrats rather than holy men.

Between John and the monastery lay a patch of flat ground which served as a garden in warmer seasons, to judge from the wooden frames, sagging trellises, and tilted stakes festooned with blackened vines. A man in a brown tunic knelt beside a rosemary bush, one of several green highlights in the otherwise drab expanse of earth.

He looked up at the sound of John's boots crunching across dried, discarded stalks. He might have been a sailor from whose gaunt face the sea had weathered all signs of age.

"I must speak to the head of the monastery," John said.

"You are. I am the abbot of Saint Conon's." He put a few sprigs of greenery into the basket at his side. "The way the wind howls across us here we're fortunate to have plenty of hardy herbs. Every plant has its seasons, though."

John almost expected him to add that there was a lesson in that, but he didn't. Instead he got to his feet and brushed the dirt off the front of his clothing. "If you seek refuge, we would not turn you away. But we are far too crowded to offer any degree of comfort. To the body at any rate."

"I am here on the emperor's business," John told him.

"What could the monks of Saint Conon's possibly have to do with the emperor's business?"

"A few days ago you interfered with it."

"Ah. You are speaking of those hanged men."

"There are grumblings at court. Some accuse you of involvement with the emperor's opponents."

The abbot's leathery face showed no reaction. "A serious accusation. Totally untrue. But what proof could I offer? Should

I invite you to search the monastery to see that none of Justinian's enemies are hiding there?"

"Proof of any entanglement will come out eventually, when the insurrection is defeated and the plotters are arrested and questioned. I am giving you the chance to make the emperor's task easier. As you know, he is a devout man. If you are willing to give him useful information, I am sure he will not look so harshly on your past transgressions."

"So I should confess to you and expect forgiveness from the emperor?" The abbot smiled faintly. "Alas, I have nothing to confess."

"Why did you rescue the hanged men? Are you so concerned with earthly matters?"

"You don't know the story of Saint Conon, do you? He was an Isaurian. When the Christians there were persecuted he was tortured for refusing to sacrifice to pagan gods. They say he was stabbed with knives. When the population heard, they took up arms and rescued him from his tormentors. He wished to suffer martyrdom but instead he lived for two more years. Given the history of our saint how could we stand by and watch the terrible spectacle down there?" The abbot nodded in the direction of the gallows clearly visible from where he and John stood.

"You are telling me you were acting in the tradition of your order," John said.

"And out of human compassion. The palace is only a short boat ride from where we are standing, but it might as well be another world. Don't suppose all people are villains and cynics just because those who reside at the palace are. The monks of Saint Conon's serve the Lord. Believe me, there is not a constant undercurrent of intrigue between us and our Lord. We are simple people." He pushed a stray green sprig back into his basket. "I admit too, that a few of us thought we were witnessing a miracle. Only the hand of God could grasp the hangman's rope, twice, to save two men. We were being called upon to reenact Saint Conon's story."

"Did God's hand clear a path to the gallows for the rescuers? Did it brush aside the imperial guards, lift your monks, and the condemned men into a boat and push it safely out into the water?"

"I believe so. His hand was the crowd which greatly outnumbered the guards and felt the same compassion and awe that we did. They made it plain that we were to be left untouched."

John remembered that Kosmas, the executioner, had said much the same thing, that the restive spectators had assisted in the rescue.

"But what was the point in saving the lives of those men?" John asked. "Wasn't it merely putting off the Lord's judgment?"

A gust of wind made the dead vines clinging to stakes and trellises wave like pennants and brought tears to John's eyes. The abbot did not invite John inside. Instead, he turned his face into the wind.

"You aren't a Christian," the abbot said.

John could not conceal his surprise.

"I can tell by the way the name of the Lord passes your lips," the abbot explained. "Don't worry, it does not distress me. Before I found my calling I traveled. I've been everywhere from Egypt to Bretania. Even Isauria. I stood on the spot where Saint Conon's blessed blood was spilled. The Lord is everywhere, but people see Him in accordance with their own natures. Or so I believe. I would not confide that to the Patriarch."

They were looking across the Golden Horn toward the city. Even from a distance they could make out huge swathes of burned out buildings. Pillars of smoke climbed into the sky.

"You can't believe the Lord is over there?" John said. "Surely the city is more like the pits of hell."

"Perhaps. If that is the way you are inclined to see it. People concoct their beliefs to cure what ails them. A pinch of earth from subterranean Hades. A few drops of fiery torment from the gospels. And why not mix in some demons, since pagans and Christians both believe in them?"

"You don't believe in hell?"

"Hell is not a place. When we die we enter into the presence of the Lord. Those who love the Lord are joyful to be eternally in His presence. For those who hate the Lord, His presence is an eternal torment. But it doesn't really matter how people picture these things. They are beyond human understanding anyway."

"People can understand fire and demons easily enough."

"Can they? Did you know that Saint Conon could command demons? Demons are part of creation too. They are perfectly able to serve the Lord. In fact—"

John cut the abbot off. "I don't have time to discuss theology."

"No. Of course not. You might want to return when you do have time."

"You have nothing to tell me?"

The abbot met John's steady gaze. "Rest assured, the monks of Saint Conon's are not involved in any plot against the emperor."

As the two men spoke a crow dropped out of the wind and alighted on one of the garden trellises. Several companions flapped down to join it. The black glass beads of their eyes seemed to stare at John and the abbot. It wasn't hard to imagine they had been dispatched as spies by some demonic master.

"Eight crows," John said. "When I was in Bretania the peasants had a fortune-telling rhyme. One crow meant sorrow. Two was for joy. But it only went up to seven—for a secret. Perhaps eight crows foretell nothing. That many are devoid of sense, like a mob."

The abbot laughed softly. "Superstitious beliefs are even more varied than religious ones. During my own stay in that dreary land I learned a different rhyme from an old village woman who performed auguries. She said that seven was for heaven and eight for hell."

"So those eight black harbingers are foretelling hell." John looked away from the crows and toward the burning city. "That is more an observation than a prognostication."

"Not to mention inaccurate. I tried to explain to the old woman, about heaven or hell not being places but simply the ways we experience the everlasting presence of the Lord, according to our natures. Seven and eight should both mean eternity. I could not convert her to such belief. It would have ruined her rhyme."

"A bad rhyme, but better augury. Eight crows will always be right, in some sense."

"Yes, we all face eternity. We are all a part of it, living and dead."

"But perhaps we don't always want to be reminded." John clapped his hands. The crows rose in a flurry, circled once, and flew away from the city.

Chapter Thirty-Three

"Hypatius told me he was going to the kitchen." Felix sat on a stool at the entrance to the corridor leading to the quarters John had lent to his aristocratic guests.

"Is Julianna in her room?" John asked.

"You can be certain of it. That's why I'm here. So there's no doubt she's safe."

"Is she sleeping?"

"I couldn't say." He turned his head to look down the hallway. "Her door's stayed shut. I'd notice if she tried to leave. Do you want to speak with her?"

"No. It's her father I need to see."

Felix shifted uncomfortably on the stool. His legs stretched across the corridor. "Being on watch for wayward girls doesn't suit me. I can't risk any further mistakes."

"If anyone made a mistake."

"I have no reason to mistrust any of my excubitors. But with the state the city's in, for some it's every man for himself."

"Understandable if not commendable. Perhaps Belisarius will ask Justinian for your services and rescue you from my household," John remarked with a smile.

He made his way to the kitchen at the back of his house, an area somewhat less familiar to him than Alexandria but currently as hot. Hypatius was bent over a steaming, copper pot set on one of the long braziers. "Eggs," he explained. "I decided to cook myself some eggs."

"I realize my servants have deserted but the storerooms are full of—"

Hypatius waved his hand. "No. No. Eggs are exactly what I want." His face was red from the heat. Sweat beaded on his upper lip.

John peered into the bubbling water. There were at least a dozen eggs sitting on the bottom.

"That isn't much a meal."

Hypatius licked his lips. "Yes, well, but…I found the eggs… and…the shells weren't cracked…so…."

"Ah. I understand. It's difficult to poison an egg inside the shell. A good choice, Hypatius. Now if the shells were poisoned—"

"The poison would be boiled off and….oh…well…that is to say…." He wiped the sweat off his face. "You think I'm a coward. I can see that. Men in my position need to be cautious."

John could see the eggs bobbing slightly beneath the bubbling surface of the boiling water. One of them had cracked and emitted a thin rope of white. "There is a thin line between cowardice and caution. We all have our fears."

"I'm glad you understand." Hypatius fished the broken egg out of the pot with a pair of tongs and tossed it aside. He studied his remaining charges carefully.

"Young people are often not as cautious as they should be," John said.

"Very true." Hypatius looked away from the pot and toward John. "You're talking about Julianna, aren't you?"

"Apparently you have reason to suspect her of being incautious to jump to that conclusion."

"How many other young people are there in this house? You're not a man who seeks others out in order to speak in generalities." He lifted the pot off the brazier and sat it on the long wooden table behind him. "Julianna is the same as any other girl her age. A bit of a dreamer. Careless at times. We all had our heads in the clouds at that age."

"I take it she loves horses."

"Don't all girls?" Hypatius transferred the cooked eggs to a plate and tapped one delicately with a long spoon to break the shell.

"All girls may indeed love horses, I'm not an authority on the matter. Some, however get into the Hippodrome to watch races, or so I hear."

Hypatius looked startled. "Not Julianna. She's a well bred young lady. Related to an emperor, remember. You're not accusing her of any such thing, are you?"

"Yesterday I saved her from being raped in the Augustaion, Hypatius. Do you have any idea what your daughter was doing out there? An assignation perhaps? You don't have to worry about her reputation. Anything you tell me will remain private."

Hypatius' face was no longer red. He looked as pale as his eggs. "I have no idea why she left this house. I will speak to her severely. She's a dreamer. An innocent though. Just a child."

"You don't trust me, do you? Maybe I am treacherous. Your daughter's life is at stake, Hypatius. Are you going to cook eggs for Julianna too, or risk having my staff preparing her meals?"

"I...I...No one's trying to kill Julianna...are they? If she's in danger it's because of because of me and Pompeius. We're the targets. Julianna would be safer back in our house with her mother. Then anyone trying to...to...kill me wouldn't...."

"If you want to protect Julianna you must tell me what you know."

Hypatius looked away from John. He pushed the eggs around on his plate, then brought his spoon down on each, too hard, sending pieces of shell flying. "There's nothing I can tell you. Nothing. I wish there were."

Chapter Thirty-Four

January 17, 532

Felix opened his eyes a slit but remained otherwise motionless on the stool where he'd spent most of the night. He was sure he had heard a sound.

A footstep?

Grey, pre-dawn darkness filled the hallway leading back to the rooms where Hypatius and his family were staying. Why wasn't the wall torch burning?

He slid his hand stealthily toward the hilt of his sword. He hadn't been sleeping, only dozing, he assured himself. It would have been impossible to fall asleep sitting on the three-legged wooden stool.

He remained with his back to the wall, legs extended into the hallway, and strained to see into the darkness. A hazy phantom floated into view and moved slowly down the corridor.

He blinked, trying to clear his vision. Then the figure suddenly darted in his direction.

Felix sprang forward. His arm shot out and his hand fastened around a slender wrist.

Julianna uttered a string of oaths an aristocratic girl should never have had the opportunity to hear, let alone commit to memory.

"At least you have the sense to curse quietly enough not to wake the household," Felix muttered.

She tried to pull away with more strength than he would have expected for such a slight thing. Felix refused to release his grip. "I'm glad I insisted on taking most of the watches here. I had a feeling you'd try to creep off again."

"I didn't intend to do that, Felix. I need to see Antonina. I was about to ask you to accompany me, but you decided to try and break my wrist before I had the chance."

"That explains why you put the torch out, and that dark cloak you're wearing."

"Don't you want to come with me? You seemed very keen to visit my friend the other day, when I saved you from making a grave mistake."

Felix took his hand off her arm. "You claim you saved me. I'm trying to return the favor by saving you. Which is to say by making sure you stay safely inside."

Julianna made a show of rubbing her arm. "Safe? With rioters baying at the palace walls? Nowhere's safe. Besides, you can guard me as easily walking to the Daphne as here. You do want to see Antonina...."

She was right. Felix had to admit it to himself, although not to the girl. He hadn't been able to banish Antonina from his thoughts except for when he'd been fighting. She'd been whispering in his ear all night long while he guarded the corridor. "I'm sure Antonina wonders why I haven't paid my respects." Felix got to his feet. "You did go out of your way to help me. I'll come with you, it's the least I can do."

He sent the guard in the atrium to take his post. The man gave him and Julianna a curious look as they went out but Felix offered no explanation.

The cold outside made him catch his breath. The rising sun turned ice-filled ruts in the muddy yard outside the stables into an orange embroidery. Ice-glazed marble walkways and frost glistened on grass and shrubbery.

Felix was happy to enter the Daphne Palace, which wasn't much warmer. The silentiaries hardly glanced at Julianna. They didn't seem concerned that she'd brought a companion.

"You're a frequent visitor," Felix observed.

Julianna nodded and led him along a bewildering series of hallways. He half expected to see the Eros he'd treated so cruelly during his previous visit but no one else was about at this early hour.

By the time they reached the tall double doors at the entrance to Antonina's quarters, Felix was breathing hard, not the result of exertion but rather in anticipation of seeing Antonina again.

A servant answered their knock.

"Eugenius," said Julianna, "I have brought a visitor to see Antonina."

The servant ushered the two into a cramped vestibule where more silentiaries stood shoulder to shoulder with life-sized Greek sculptures. Another set of doors opened onto a warm, humid atrium graced by potted plants.

Felix felt his heart pounding. He glanced around, expecting Antonina to appear. How would she receive him?

He followed Julianna past low hanging palm fronds and into a room filled with cushion-strewn furniture. Frescoed seascapes covered the walls. Three golden cherubs flew above painted waves in an ascending line. Tables and alcoves displayed a welter of enameled boxes, ivory figurines, and elaborate glass vessels.

"Don't look so surprised, Felix. A lady of the court is bound to accumulate expensive gifts and it's only polite to display them."

Felix realized he must have looked as awestruck as a peasant on his first visit to the capital.

The air felt warmer than in the atrium and heavy with unidentifiable scents, a mingling of perfumes, spices, and strange herbs. His breath caught at the sight of Antonina. No, only a small marble statue. He spotted at least two larger than life bronze busts.

Julianna tugged at his hand, leading him deeper into Antonina's abode, down a short hallway, and then into a room lined with shelves crammed with bottles and stoppered clay pots. A pan steamed on a brazier and dried herbs hung from the ceiling.

Finally, he saw her. She stood at a marble table, working a mortar and pestle. She looked up, pushing a loose strand of hair away from her eyes. Beads of perspiration glistened on her forehead.

"Felix," she said.

Was she surprised to see him? Happy? Annoyed? To his dismay, her tone conveyed absolutely nothing.

She wore a plain silk tunica, almost immodest. Her pale hair dangled to her shoulders in disarray. He could make out faint wrinkles at the corners of her eyes.

"I needed to see you," Julianna said. "Felix agreed to accompany me, for safety."

Antonina put down the pestle. "Very wise. I've nearly finished the charm I promised you. Everyone at court wants my services. I've already supplied Theodora with the magickal devices she requested, along with several philters."

"It wouldn't be necessary if the excubitor's would fight like men," Felix said. "Sharp blades are all the charms the emperor needs."

"Spoken like a soldier," Antonina replied, without looking at him. "Now, Julianna, if you will go and wait in my reception room, I can complete your charm."

"Maybe a potion to make the excubitor's fight is what's wanted," Julianna said.

"I'm not sure that's within my power."

"I thought we might visit for a time," Julianna told her.

"Yes. Surely. But you must allow me to finish first." She looked directly at Julianna.

Clearly she was avoiding looking at Felix.

"Antonina," he blurted. "Did I somehow offend you the other night? If so...I...I apologize. I had to see you again."

Felix realized she was staring straight past him, over his shoulder.

He turned his head.

In the doorway stood a rumpled and sleepy-eyed Belisarius.

Chapter Thirty-Five

At dawn John was walking through the palace gardens. He had been walking for a long time. He had lain in his bed thinking, unable to sleep, and finally decided he would think better on his feet whatever the hour. All the time he walked, a false ruby dawn illuminated the western sky, the glow from countless fires. Now the light from the rising sun had begun to drown out the lurid firelight.

The sun—John's god, Lord Mithra.

Did Mithra care about the empire upon which he looked? An empire which had chosen a different god?

Shadows lingered beneath covered walkways amidst the trees and shrubbery and on the western sides of the buildings. John saw movement in the shadows. Something red passed through a patch of light then vanished into another shadow.

He narrowed his eyes. The red shape resolved itself into the red robed Persian emissary Bozorgmehr.

Why would he be out on the grounds so early, so far from the Daphne Palace?

Had he also been unable to sleep?

John followed him at a distance. To his surprise Bozorgmehr headed to the remains of the Chalke. Laborers had cleared a path through the rubble, at the same time piling debris so as to form a more or less unbroken wall where the gate had stood. The emissary nodded to the excubitors guarding the way out. They waved him past.

John waited until the man was out on the street before approaching the guards. "Do you know the man who just went by?"

"That was the Persian emissary, Chamberlain. I'm sorry, I can't remember his name."

"You have seen him before this morning?"

"Several times. Early mornings and evenings too."

"He goes out by himself?"

"Always alone, yes."

The guard's partner looked down the street after the dwindling red figure. "Peculiar isn't it? But the Persians are so fierce, I reckon they have no fear of anything they might find in our streets."

John went after Bozorgmehr. He wondered what the guards said about his own solitary peregrinations.

The emissary walked straight down the Mese, necessarily keeping to the middle of the street since most of the structures had collapsed. John suspected he was going to the Hippodrome. Would Porphyrius be waiting there?

But he moved briskly by the high, arched entrance.

A short distance further on he abruptly swerved to the far side of the street.

John saw he was merely avoiding a group of men in front of a half destroyed tavern. By the look of them, they had managed to save much of the wine. Some staggered about, others sprawled on the street or leaned groggily against a column or a wall. They would be in no shape to engage in whatever kind of mayhem they had planned in their state of grandiose inebriation the night before.

Knots of people loitered quietly. No murderous crowds had formed yet. Even rioters needed to sleep. Later, it would be different. Perhaps that was why the emissary had left the palace so early. Or perhaps it was to avoid detection by anyone except the lowly guards at the gate.

By now the morning sun found its way down the Mese but with rubble and overturned carts everywhere it was a simple task for John to stay out of sight. His quarry did glance back over his shoulder from time to time but John thought that was probably more to insure that none of the ruffians milling around were approaching than any apprehension of being followed.

They came to the Praetorium and John saw that it was still burning. Flames licked above the remaining walls. The first fire must have been brought under control, but now the building was being consumed again. At least the macabre curtain of bodies had been removed from the portico.

Was Bozorgmehr going to the Forum Constantine?

No. Abruptly he veered down a side street.

They had come some distance from the palace, but it made sense for conspirators to meet as far away from the gaze of the emperor as possible.

By some chance the colonnades here remained mostly intact but they edged a continuous line of blackened debris from which charred and jagged beams thrust up like the shattered bones of giants.

Bozorgmehr turned and went under a miraculously preserved archway. It might have been the entrance to the grounds of a patrician's mansion. In reality it was courtyard ringed by mundane commercial establishments, a candle maker and a perfumer among them.

A nondescript door across the courtyard opened and admitted the red robed figure. There was no sign or plaque to identify what lay beyond.

There was no time to debate what to do. John strode across the courtyard and rapped on the door.

It opened a crack, emitting a gust of almost overpowering perfume. A girl no older than Julianna looked up at John. She wore a gauzey blue garment which might have been sea mist, except that a heavy mist would have hidden her body to some extent. Her lips were stained bright red. Behind her John saw other similarly attired girls moving about a room filled with plush furniture.

He had followed the Persian emissary to a brothel.

◇◇◇

The enormous silence in the palace reception hall swallowed up the dull thump of John's boots. He noted that the room was deserted, except for Justinian and Narses huddled in conversation near the raised dais with its double thrones, and Theodora, who stared down from one of them.

Justinian broke off his conversation and turned to face John. "As you can see, this isn't a public audience. I threw them all out." His reedy voice sounded too loud. Or was it only that the vast empty space made it seem so? The emperor rarely raised his voice.

"Everyone needed a favor," the emperor went on. "Lend me a ship, an armed guard, a bag of gold. Two bags of gold. As if I could insure their safety. Find a church, I told them. Pray to the Lord. That's what your emperor is doing." Justinian glanced upwards, toward the cross painted on the ceiling.

It was a giant version of the one decorating the chapel at John's house. He supposed it might bring comfort to a Christian. Though it was nothing but insubstantial gilt, to John it felt more like a sword of Damocles that might come crashing down on his head at any time.

Justinian took a few nervous steps to one side, as if he had the same idea, although he still remained underneath the looming image. The emperor's gaze darted around the hall.

Theodora's voice ripped through the silence. "The whole court is nothing but a gang of begging sycophants. No different from the mob outside except they don't smell as bad." Even from a short distance John could see her eyes glittering, her pupils hugely dilated.

She was largely correct in her evaluation of Justinian's courtiers, he thought. Now the air was harsh with smoke from hanging lamps, but there remained a faint memory of perfume, a ghost of the almost choking miasma of scent that filled the place when it was crowded.

"Courtiers and aristocrats carry more concealed blades than any street rabble," Narses remarked. The bald eunuch looked toward John and pursed his lips as if he dared to spit.

"Narses assures me that this uprising has been carefully planned," Justinian said, fixing John in his gaze. "Whoever had the faction members at Saint Laurentius killed is behind the unrest. That being so, your investigation is critical. Haven't you made any further progress?" The emperor's countenance was bland. Which, John knew, meant nothing, particularly since he detected an uncharacteristic edge to the voice? Anger? Fear?

"I learned nothing new this morning, Caesar. It is nearly impossible to move around the city. There are fires up and down the Mese all the way to the Forum Constantine. I hear the rioters have occupied imperial offices around the city."

It had been difficult returning to the palace. The people in the streets had become more restless. After following Bozorgmehr to the brothel, he had spent considerable time making certain that the establishment was not, in fact, being used for illicit meetings of a more sinister purpose than it might have appeared. In the process of interviewing the inhabitants of the establishment, he had learned much more than he wished to know about the sexual proclivities of Persian men.

Narses issued a high pitched cackle. "If you are afraid to go out on the streets, John, why don't you stay inside? I'm sure you can serve the emperor just as well. Like Plato's cave dwellers you can observe the shadows of the real conspirators outside, cast upon the palace walls by the flames of the burning city. You are clever like that, having been schooled at Plato's pagan academy."

"I see you have concerned yourself with my past, Narses."

"It is prudent to know what beliefs are held by those the emperor chooses to hold close."

"Quite true," put in Theodora. "Do you know, I once saw a performer who created shadow plays with puppets. Highly amusing." She spoke much too quickly, sounding tense.

"There's plenty of work to do in the palace," John said. "If there is a plot, it probably reaches into the palace."

"Straight to those two vipers under your guard," Justinian replied. "They haven't said or done anything to rouse suspicion? They've had no visitors? Haven't gone out?"

"No. They have made no attempt to see anyone or to leave. The last thing they want is to leave."

"How can you be certain what they've been up to? You've spent most of the past few days out, looking into the murders," Narses put in.

"Felix and his excubitors report to me."

"Can you trust them?"

"Indeed, I can. I know Felix personally and can vouch for him."

Justinian offered a forced smile. "But how observant are they? That foreign visitor of yours was murdered under their noses."

"Caesar, Haik was poisoned. The physician said it might have happened anywhere."

"Do you think his murder has anything to do with the riots? Were the plotters involved? How could it be a coincidence?"

"I can't say, Caesar."

"There's much you can't say, John. I am disappointed in you. How do the brothers pass their time? Can you say?"

"Pompeius drinks and Hypatius broods."

"Don't assume those two are what they appear to be," Narses said. "They've been at court since long before you arrived."

Justinian paced nearer to the throne where Theodora sat. When agitated he never stood still. Most men's features moved in revealing fashion. In Justinian's case it was his feet that moved and they were impossible to read. The habit made him hard to talk to but no one dared tell the emperor that. Perhaps it was his version of the long walks John took when he needed to think. "Narses tells me you spoke to Porphyrius. Is the charioteer involved? He's meddled in politics in the past."

"I have suspicions but no proof."

"Some say that display at the Hippodrome was clearly a signal for the factions to join together in revolt."

"There are other explanations."

Narses glanced in Theodora's direction. "Do you wait until the bee stings before you crush it?"

"An excellent point," Theodora said.

Justinian turned and walked back toward John, his footsteps echoing around the hall. "Porphyrius dead would give us all a nastier sting than Porphyrius alive. He might be helping incite unrest. His death certainly would do so."

"And if he is involved in a plot," John added, "you would alert the other conspirators by moving against him."

Justinian stopped in front of John, at enough distance that John's advantage in height was not especially obvious. The emperor's face remained emotionless as a mask. His eyes peered out from behind it. Whereas Theodora's eyes were huge and glassy, Justinian's gave the impression of being apertures into a strange, dark world. "Surely you have learned something of value. What is your theory?"

"It is plausible that the murders of the faction members were planned, since the riots on their behalf have been transformed so swiftly into an insurrection."

"Was it part of the plan for the hangings to fail?"

"I don't think so, Caesar. The executions may have been rushed because the spectators had become restive. The executioner and the guards feared for their lives."

"Perhaps that is what the plotters wished us to think."

"Planning for the hangings to fail would have been too complicated, left too much to chance, involved too many people. Unless the monks of Saint Conon were involved, the condemned men would simply have been hung again, and I have no reason to believe the monks were involved. As it was, the ropes failed twice. And—"

Narses cut him off. "Have you pursued this matter of the monks?"

"I visited the monastery once."

"Is that all? Is that enough to uncover any sort of wrong doing?"

"It's plain that the emperor needs a solution quickly. I have confined myself to the lines of inquiry most likely to be fruitful."

Narses leered at him. "And have you learned anything? Something more useful to yourself than the emperor? Have you perhaps discovered that monasteries can be very wealthy? Not to mention successful charioteers and aristocratic families! Are you sure you haven't been paid not to make inquires or reach conclusions?"

Theodora let out a harsh caw of laughter. "You do amuse me, Narses." She rose from the throne in a swift, jerky motion like a huge bird, in a flurry of swinging robes, heavy fabric rustling and jewels clicking against the throne. She descended from the dais and clapped a hand onto Justinian's arm. John thought the emperor stiffened. "Why waste your time talking with these creatures? Belisarius will give you better advice."

"I have already solicited Belisarius' opinion," Justinian replied.

"It's time to heed it."

"He's young. Reckless."

"But also brilliant. And experienced in military matters."

"The emperor does not take orders from his generals. Or anyone else." Justinian's voice rose. The familiar thin timbre vanished. Then he was speaking softly and soothingly again, as he added, "Sometimes caution is best." He turned his attention to John. "I have come to a decision. I don't trust those two scoundrels in your charge. I am convinced they are spies. I am ordering the family out of the palace. I will send an escort for them. They can return to their houses, if they haven't burned yet."

"Are you certain that's wise, Caesar?" John realized immediately that he had allowed himself to speak too quickly.

"It is assuredly not wise to contradict the emperor," snapped Narses.

"I only meant to point out that so long as Hypatius and Pompeius are within the palace they are under your gaze and under your control," John replied.

Something flashed in the darkness behind the emperor's eyes. "And possibly undermining my authority practically from within my household, or opening the palace gates at the arranged time."

"I understand, Caesar. The daughter though—a mere girl—Julianna. Allow her to stay under my protection."

Justinian paused before replying. His frozen face looked lifeless, as if whatever lurked behind the mask had momentarily forgotten to operate it. His voice was icy. "I'm not sure I need to be taking advice from one who seems to believe that a girl cannot commit treachery."

Theodora spoke before John could reply. "In this case, he is right." Her huge pupils fixed a gaze of pure hatred on John. "Julianna is a good friend of Antonina. I would not want to see her come to harm. Let her stay with Antonina."

Chapter Thirty-Six

As John entered his atrium he startled Hypatius who looked away from the marble Aphrodite in the fountain. "Ah, it's only you, Chamberlain. I thought they had come for us."

His voice sounded calmer. When informed earlier of Justinian's decision to remove the brothers from the palace he had accepted it much better than John had expected.

"The rioting will be over in a few days," John said. "Everything will soon be back to normal."

Hypatius nodded absently in acknowledgment of the comment rather than agreement. Baskets and crates holding his family's personal belongings sat around his feet. A small arsenal of hunting bows leaned against the fountain's basin. His embroidered robes looked more suitable for an imperial banquet than expulsion from the emperor's palace and good graces. "I must not forget to thank you for the hospitality you have shown us. I would put in a good word with the emperor…but…alas…." He smiled wanly and gave a small shrug. "At least I shall see my wife once more."

"You know Justinian's moods. You have been out of favor with him in the past. I'm sure you'll be speaking with him on friendly terms again before long."

"If these were normal times, perhaps that might be so."

"The worst of the violence has probably passed. Anger burns itself out. People begin to feel the tug of their everyday lives."

"Many of us will not have lives to return to. I am happy, though, that whatever my fate, Julianna will not be anywhere near me to suffer because of it."

"You can be sure Julianna will be safe with Antonina, living practically next door to the emperor."

"If only I could be certain she was actually with Antonina and not…well…who knows where." He paused, obviously turning something over in his mind. The water spilling into the fountain from the seashell Aphrodite held made a melancholy sound. The day John had moved into the house, he had found the sound to be cheerful.

Hypatius expelled a long breath and resumed speaking. "There's something you should know. About Julianna. I didn't think it necessary to say anything before. But now, since I will no longer be here, it may help you to protect her."

"I will do everything I can to help. What do you have to tell me?"

Hypatius turned his face back toward Aphrodite before speaking, less to study the statue than to avoid looking at John. "When we were talking in the kitchen, you were wondering whether Julianna had been going to the Hippodrome. I denied it. I wasn't being entirely truthful."

"You believe she might be one of the girls I was told about, who follow the racing factions?"

"Yes. It is possible. But as to any assignation…you remember you accused her of being out in the city to meet someone…no, that is impossible. I am positive of it."

"Why are you so certain?"

"Because the man she would have met is dead. His name was Hippolytus. One of the men murdered at Saint Laurentius. That's why I said nothing, you see. I was afraid to get her involved in… well…who knows what. Hippolytus was a rascal. For all I know he might have been part of a plot against the emperor. Julianna is years younger. An innocent. The murderer did our family a favor, God forgive me for saying so." Hypatius turned his face back to John. "Is that of any assistance to you?"

"A great deal of assistance. My thoughts ran in that direction, but our thoughts can lead us astray. How did you find out about the man's death?"

"From Pompeius. Rusticus visited him right after attending the executions and relayed the whole dreadful story. The old man has treated my family forever. A fine physician but he always leaves you with a pain in the ear."

Hypatius' words confirmed what John had already deduced. He had spent days and risked his life out in the dangerous streets while so much of the story he sought could have been found within his own house. "Was Julianna told about Hippolytus?"

"She didn't need to be. She'd gone to assist Pompeius when Rusticus showed up. She's looked after her uncle more than once. She's young. She hasn't had time to become disgusted by his drinking."

"She must be terribly upset. Have you spoken with her about Hippolytus?"

"I've tried to. She just flies into a rage." He glanced toward the water bubbling in the basin beside him. "It's better for her to rage against the world than throw herself off the sea wall."

"She doesn't strike me as the sort to kill herself. Too headstrong."

"I worry that she may have been taking advice from Antonina rather than from her mother and me."

"Do you think Antonina is offering more than advice?"

"You mean her potions? I'd rather Julianna took a sleeping draught once in a while than follow her uncle's example and turn to Bacchus. Besides, I doubt they do more harm than some of Rusticus' foul smelling concoctions."

"Julianna mentioned that Antonina has an interest in the races, naturally enough since she comes from a family of charioteers. Did Julianna meet Hippolytus through her?"

"Not at all. She met him at the palace. Riding at the polo field. He was a scholare. Used to dressing up and parading around at official functions."

"An aristocrat?"

"Of course. But a ruffian nonetheless. He was wealthy, from a good family. He might have passed his time studying the philosophers or writing poetry or hunting. He preferred to go out to the taverns with low-born charioteers. And they only humored him because he paid."

"Putting on a show at ceremonies is hardly the same as racing a chariot."

"Exactly. You and I and any charioteer knows it. But all Julianna saw was horsemanship. And he was a racing patron. Belonged to the Greens but he supported Porphyrius as well. Many of the Greens do. They think they can convince him to race for them again. I suspect Hippolytus helped her get into the Hippodrome from time to time."

John remembered the brilliant green robes she had been wearing when he found her in the garden, supposedly clearing brush away from the sculpted horses. He supposed the outfit was her own version of the green tunics worn by the faction, yet the hue differed from any common green as purple differed from blue.

"Did she ever meet Porphyrius?"

"If so she would not tell me."

Hypatius bent to pick up one of his hunting bows. He pivoted, raised his weapon, and aimed an imaginary arrow at a Greek vase in the corner of the room. He pulled the string back and released it, making a loud twang.

"I never liked that vase," John remarked. "Ostentatious. I'll wager it would be in pieces now if you had an arrow on your string. Do you want to take the vase back to your house as a trophy?"

Hypatius shook his head and lowered the bow. "I would not have long to enjoy it. In fact, I may have taken my last shot. Julianna hunted with me all the time. She enjoyed riding mostly. She always missed the shot, no matter how easy. Couldn't hit a rabbit if her horse had a hoof on its tail. Yet, when we practiced at the estate she hit the target every time."

"She got her love of horses from you."

"I'm afraid so. It always pleased me that I had given her a love of something that gave her so much pleasure. But you see how it turned out…."

In response to further questions, Hypatius told John where Hippolytus' family could be found. John feared he would not have time to speak to them. Of any friends Hippolytus might have had, beyond anonymous charioteers, Hypatius knew nothing.

"Is there anything else you can tell me?"

Hypatius shook his head. "I wish there were, if it would help keep Julianna safe. I thought her…her…infatuation with Hippolytus would be a revelation but you don't seem surprised. Then again, you work with Justinian so there isn't much that would surprise you."

"You have been closer to emperors for much longer than I have, Hypatius. Are you sure you aren't ambitious? Can't you see yourself wearing the purple, as your uncle did?"

Hypatius stiffened visibly. For a moment the weakness in his aristocratic features was not apparent. He looked every inch a member of an imperial family. "I spent my whole life avoiding that fate. One might as well wear a noose as a crown. The emperor may look down on the rest of us but he never knows when the trapdoor is going to open up under those red boots of his."

"Yet, you seem remarkably composed this evening."

"Do I? Yes, I suppose I probably do. Cowardice can make a fine shield, you know. That and mediocrity. But the best defenses eventually fail. At least there's an end to it now. It is very tiresome, being afraid all the time."

Before John could reply, Felix's voice rumbled out of the corridor. "Must be more difficult than staying inebriated every hour of the day."

Two excubitors followed Felix into the atrium, dragging Pompeius between them. The excubitors were husky young men but John could see the strain in their faces as they struggled to support the bulky and seemingly boneless man who flopped listlessly in their grasp.

They got him to the fountain and lowered him into a sitting position on the edge of the basin, holding his arms to prevent him from falling into the water.

Pompeius managed to turn his head toward Aphrodite. "We have met before," he said thickly. "I fear we shall not meet again."

John could smell the stale wine on the man's breath from an arms-length away.

Felix eyed Pompeius with disgust. "I'll wager it's been a long time since a man in your condition has had anything to do with the goddess of love," he growled. Then his face darkened. "Count yourself lucky. Aphrodite doesn't seem to get along with Fortuna."

Hypatius walked over to Pompeius and hunkered down so their faces were level. "Can't you muster up a scrap of dignity, even at the end? Don't look away from me, brother. Is this how you want to be remembered? What would our Uncle Anastasius have thought?"

It was hard for John to believe that Hypatius, the very image of a ruler, could be the brother of the bleary-eyed man to whom he was speaking.

Pompeius mumbled unintelligibly.

"You suppose the mob doesn't want a drunk as emperor, don't you?" Hypatius said. "Who would seek to raise up a flaccid sack of humanity like you? But perhaps you have miscalculated. Justinian is abstemious, isn't he? And the mob hates him. Perhaps they are ready for a stumbling sot. They might decide one such as yourself would denude every vineyard from here to Egypt but leave the rest of the empire alone."

Pompeius' mouth moved like that of a fish hauled out of the water, but no sound emerged. He looked ready to cry.

From the vestibule came the sound of voices.

Hypatius stood up. "Good. The sooner it is over the better."

Enough armed excubitors to subdue a contingent of Persians flooded into the room followed by Gallio and Narses.

Hypatius addressed Gallio. "We are ready to go. Although my brother may need some assistance to return to his house, if any of you are brave enough to venture beyond the palace walls."

"I'll be happy to accompany him," Felix put in before Gallio had a chance to respond. "With your permission, Captain Gallio."

"Let those two who have hold of him carry him home," Gallio said. "You are relieved of your duty at the chamberlain's house, Felix. You are no longer an excubitor. I am sparing your head because you are as brave as you are stupid."

Felix's mouth tightened into a grim line. He said nothing. John could see it was a struggle for him to remain silent.

Narses threaded his way through the excubitors. Compared to the big, mostly youthful, military men, he more than ever resembled a performing dwarf. He peered around with ill-concealed glee.

"Why are you here?" John snapped. "Don't you trust the captain to carry out orders? Or do you just want to gloat?"

"You are most inhospitable, John. I would think you should be pleased to have these serpents out of your home. Your life depends on Justinian's safety, as much as mine does. Do you think the rioters will hang the emperor and let his chamberlains go free? Unless you have come to an understanding...."

The excubitors gathered the brothers' belongings. One of them picked up an intricately carved hunting bow. "A fine piece of work," he remarked.

"Keep it," Hypatius told him. "I won't be using it."

The men began to file out. John noticed that Narses watched the proceedings intently. It occurred to him that the emperor's treasurer had come to make certain that Gallio carried out Justinian's orders. The excubitor captain refused to venture into the streets to battle the rioters. How could the emperor be certain he wouldn't deliver Hypatius and Pompeius to them? Why hadn't Justinian sent some silentiaries? Perhaps he had reason to mistrust them as well.

"Thank you again, Chamberlain," Hypatius said. "Please do what you can for Julianna." He turned and went out. Pompeius, head lolling to the side, was carted out behind him.

Felix and John were left alone in a silence broken only by the bubbling fountain until John spoke. "I wouldn't worry about

Gallio, Felix. When this insurrection is over he will no longer be in command. Anyway, from what you've told me, you can always depend on General Belisarius for employment."

Felix looked at the marble Aphrodite and said nothing.

Chapter Thirty-Seven

After Felix left to retrieve his belongings from the barracks, John went to Julianna's room. The door was open and the room empty. The chest which had sat beside the bed had been taken away. He wasn't aware that she had already made arrangements to move to Antonina's as Theodora had decreed. He would have preferred for the girl to stay under his watch.

He made his way to the garden and sat on a bench near the closed screen to his office, partly concealed by an untrimmed shrub. A chilly breeze swirled around the peristyle, sending dry leaves rattling around its columns. The last of the daylight gradually faded from the rectangle of sky, revealing cold sparks of stars.

After what seemed like a long time there was a scuffling noise from above. A figure appeared on the roof, just visible against the dark sky. It climbed nimbly onto the limb of a yew tree. John was standing at the base of the tree by the time Julianna reached the ground.

"Chamberlain! How did you guess?"

"I once knew a woman who performed with a traveling troupe."

"She climbed out of a garden and went over the roof to meet you?"

"No. She had more sense. But she was as athletic as you are."

John could see Julianna looking at him curiously. "I remind you of her, don't I?"

"I'll escort you to Antonina's apartments right away. Your room's already been emptied. There are some questions first, though. It's warmer inside."

"If you don't mind, I'd rather talk here."

"I want you to tell me the truth about Hippolytus."

Julianna bit her lip. "He's dead."

"I realize that. Your father told me as much as he knew. Out of concern for you."

"Father's only concern was that I stop seeing Hippolytus. I'm sure he's glad Hippolytus is dead. He's no longer a danger to me."

"That's not true. If Hippolytus was involved with a conspiracy against the emperor then you might be in grave danger. Whoever killed him, for whatever reason, might want to kill his associates. Hippolytus might have told you something you would be better off not knowing."

"We only talked about the races and…what people talk about."

"You must have known he was causing trouble. He fomented a minor riot after all. It isn't everyone who manages to catch the emperor's attention so as to be hung by imperial decree."

If Julianna was shaken by John's words she didn't show it. "We weren't able to meet often. What he did with his time, outside of following the races, he never said."

"Do you really think there is someone in this city who wanted to kill Haik, a stranger who had never set foot in Constantinople before?"

"You're trying to scare me. You want me to believe I was the target. I don't see how anyone could have mistakenly poisoned Haik rather than me. It doesn't make sense. Besides, he must have been poisoned outside the palace. How would anyone get in?"

"You've had no trouble coming and going. Why should Haik's murderer?"

"I think your friend was here on some dangerous business. It had nothing to do with me, or Hippolytus. He should have stayed in Syria."

"Possibly. But even if you won't accept the fact that you're in danger, surely you want me to find Hippolytus' murderer?"

"Will that bring him back?"

She walked away. John saw her hand go to her face. He followed and when she stopped and turned she was blinking glistening eyes. She had come to the carved horse with the cross on its stone blanket. She ran her hand over the equine back. "I used to dream about racing at the Hippodrome when I was a child," she said. "Mother came into my room one night and found me on the floor, tangled up in blankets. She wanted to know what happened. She heard me fall out of bed. I told her it was just a nightmare I couldn't remember. Actually my chariot had tipped over and I had to cut myself loose from the reins. It didn't stop me from dreaming again. Usually I crossed the finish line first. How I wished to be a charioteer!"

"You may not think so highly of them after that incident in the Augustaion."

"I shouldn't have been there by myself. Charioteers are used to taking what they want. It's their nature. I can never be a charioteer. Can you imagine, Chamberlain, what it is like, to know that you are barred from ever being what you wish to be, no matter how diligent your efforts?"

"Perhaps I do. But people are never free to do anything they wish. Not even the emperor."

"Antonina does whatever she wants. She takes what she wants."

"You may not know her as well as you think, Julianna." John shivered. The night wind was rising. "It's time I took you to her. On the way you might think of something you haven't told me. Whenever you do—if you want Hippolytus to be avenged—tell me."

They left the garden and went through the atrium out into the dark grounds of the palace. John wondered if Julianna appreciated that she might never see her father or mother again. He thought she did not understand the seriousness of the situation. At her age one never does. At least she did not appear to be in despair over the death of her friend.

They were out of sight of the house when Julianna suddenly stopped and spoke. "There's one thing you should know."

"Yes?"

"About Hippolytus. He's nothing like father says. He's not a ruffian."

"I see."

"You do believe me?"

"I do."

She hurried on and said nothing more.

As they approached the Daphne Palace several figures emerged from the darkness and came racing in their direction. The men brandished spears.

"What's happening?" John demanded.

"Intruder!" one of the guards yelled, hardly slowing down.

A knot of people had gathered in front of the building. They talked excitedly. One pointed in the direction of the ornate portico, the entrance to the kathisma. Lights from the imperial complex flickered across the massive rampart of the Hippodrome which loomed over the much lower palace walls.

Antonina was suddenly beside Julianna. Her face was flushed. "You've arrived just in time for all the excitement."

"I hear there's an intruder," John said.

Antonina regarded John without curiosity. He was a familiar figure at the court. "Some claim the rioters are infiltrating the palace grounds," she told him. "Others claim it's a phantom. An inhuman creature. It was seen leaping along the top of the walls. And someone else said they saw it on the roof of a house."

"On a house? Near the stables perhaps?" John glanced down at Julianna. Her expression was opaque. "Just someone's imagination, I'm sure."

"I hope you're right. Everyone's terrified."

John left Julianna in Antonina's charge and walked slowly back to his house, pausing now and then to look up at the distant stars, so far removed from the turmoil below. How strange people could be. The city was going up in flames. The angry multitudes were plotting to storm the palace. Yet they were terrified of a phantom.

As he crossed his dimly lit atrium his attention was caught by a flash of color beneath one of the benches against the wall. He bent down and pulled out a slipper.

The yellow slipper Pompeius had lost what seemed like an eternity ago.

Chapter Thirty-Eight

January 18, 532

As Justinian moved slowly through the ashen morning light slanting into the imperial box in the Hippodrome, John remarked to Felix that the emperor resembled a shade more than he did a living man.

Felix grunted. "What's put that in your mind is the uproar over that phantom in the gardens last night."

"You may be right. That and the demons who pursued me through my dreams."

From where they stood near the door to the kathisma there was no denying the pallor in the emperor's face and the white silk robes falling from his bent shoulders accentuated the deathly effect. He was bare-headed, the imperial diadem left at his residence. He meant to approach his subjects as a humble supplicant. Yet, when he stepped up onto the rostrum at the front of the box, John saw a flash of blood red, the color of the boots reserved to the emperor, concealed from the view of the masses.

The mob had taken over the stadium. A murmuring sea of humanity filled the racetrack and such tiers of wooden benches as remained, much of the seating having been consumed by fire during the fighting. They had congregated here to vent their anger, to spread rumors and plot mayhem, to await the orders of anyone brave enough to give them, or simply to sleep because they did not care to go home or because their homes had been destroyed. A few were even now sitting up or climbing groggily to their feet, startled to be awakened by the emperor.

"Romans, hear me." Justinian's voice sounded thin and tired, nothing like the resounding tones of his herald. It barely carried back to John and Felix. Eventually several in assembled masses below noticed the man addressing them, then a few recognized the emperor and as word spread so did silence until the only sounds were the sharp calls of gulls gliding overhead.

"I have come to confess to you my errors," Justinian continued. "I confess that I have been blind to the evil doers within my own house. Just as demons will assume a human shape to deceive, so did my advisors, the treacherous Tribonian, Eudaemon and the Cappadocian, pretend to a humanity they had no right to claim."

"You're a demon too," came a shout. "You're all demons!"

"The demons walk among us!" cried another. "I've seen one myself!"

Justinian picked up the codex that lay on the marble stand in front of him. He held it above his head. "What I say, I swear by the holy gospels."

The jeweled covers had fallen open. John wondered if the emperor had chosen the page, a verse meaningful to him, or of particular power? He could only see that the text was written in gold on purple-dyed vellum.

The throng quieted and Justinian set the gospel down again. "Even as I labored for the good of the empire and its citizens, my advisors betrayed me," he said. "I confess further that when you brought their villainy to my attention, I at first refused to believe."

John's gaze wandered from the emperor. He looked upwards. From the ceiling the painted images of four renowned charioteers stared down—Julian, Faustinus, Constantine, the son of Faustinus, and Porphyrius. Even as Justinian attempted to salvage his emperorship, the great charioteer was lurking nearby.

"Then last night," Justinian was saying, "I gazed from my window and prayed to the Lord—He who I represent on this earth. And the Lord appeared to me in a vision. In the dark pit of the burnt Augustaion, where the Great Church once stood, there suddenly arose a fabulous edifice. A new church, glowing as if made of light, surmounted by a vast dome to rival the very dome of the heavens. And the voice of the Lord thundered from the dome. He instructed me to exile the traitors, confess my errors, and begin anew."

Justinian's voice was far from thunderous and easily drowned out in a fresh outburst of shouts.

"Where are their heads?"

"Show us the Cappadocian's head!"

"Bring Tribonian out and throw him down to us!"

Justinian raised the gospels again. John noticed that although the emperor's face was deathly pale, his expression was as emotionless as ever. "Hear the rest of the Lord's message! He told me that as you forgive my oversights, so too shall I accept your repentance for the violence you have done. Therefore I grant a general amnesty. No man shall suffer at the hand of law no matter what crimes he may have committed. Now go in peace and pray for forgiveness."

Before the emperor had finished speaking raucous screams echoed around the Hippodrome.

"Liar!"

"Betrayer!"

"Fool!"

"You murdered the Blue and the Green!"

Then a voice cried out, "Long live Hypatius!"

Almost instantly the mob erupted, "Long live Hypatius! Long live the heir of Anastasius!"

A wave of people surged up the seating tiers directly below the kathisma. Justinian turned and walked toward its door. As he passed John caught his eye.

"You are, of course, relieved of your duties here," Justinian told him. "I will need you at the palace in a short while." He was holding the jeweled gospel. He glanced down at it and then back over his shoulder. "The Lord may speak in a vision. Perhaps he speaks in the voice of the mob as well."

Then he went out, closely accompanied by a handful of silentiaries and scholarae.

Felix spat on the floor. "What a useless crew! Gallio won't let the real guards do their duty. Those carpet soldiers won't be of any use in a fight. All they know about active duty is surrendering their pay to Justinian to avoid it."

The shouts from the multitudes had become almost deafening. The imperial box overhung the seats in such a way as to make entry from below difficult. Before retreating back down the stairs to the palace, John strode to the balustrade, to risk assessing the situation. He was surprised to see that the incipient attack on the kathisma had been abandoned. The crowd had started to flow toward the Hippodrome's main gate.

"Off to burn something else," remarked Felix from his side. "Soon there'll be nothing left."

"I don't think that's it. Listen."

Clearly the babble of shouts had now coalesced into a booming chant. "Long live Hypatius! Long live Hypatius!"

Felix cursed. "They're off to seize their new emperor, aren't they? Do you think Hypatius has had the sense to flee the city?"

"I have no idea what his plans were. If he's still here we might be able to get to his house before the mob arrives and warn him." John turned and left the box.

Felix was at his heels. "Does he want to be warned?"

"Do you mean would he prefer to be crowned? He told me he's been avoiding the possibility his whole life."

"Was he telling the truth? He's been a soldier. A general. He personally commanded the army of the east, however poorly, which is more than Justinian can say."

There was no reply to that. It was impossible to be certain what Hypatius really thought.

Rather than taking the stairs back to the palace, John veered into a narrow, descending corridor. "There is an entrance on the western side of the Hippodrome, mostly used to bring in supplies. It comes out near the Mese."

The two men broke into a run. The corridor ended in a hallway just off the concourse at the front of the stadium. The noise of the throng moving toward the entrance was the roar of a flooded river. They found themselves behind the curved line of the starting boxes. Over the top of the stalls and their double gates they could see the spina. He was surprised to see that horses occupied most of the boxes. They snorted and whinnied as John and Felix rushed past.

Then a group of men armed with lances stepped out of a stall into their path. Felix drew his sword, but he and John were surrounded and outnumbered.

"Lower your weapons," came the order. "They aren't horse thieves."

John recognized the young charioteer who strode forward. "Junius. I'm surprised anyone's here. I expected you would all want to join in the coronation of the new emperor."

"We race for the Blues. Why would we favor a member of Anastasius' family? He supported the Reds. We'd be persecuted again."

"Most of the Blues in the city don't seem to agree."

"No. They're deranged with hatred for Justinian. All they can think of is ridding themselves of the imperial demon. They'll come to their senses soon enough."

"What about Porphyrius? What does he think?"

"Ask him yourself." Junius nodded toward a storeroom, from which Porphyrius was emerging.

The charioteer immediately spotted John. "Chamberlain! What are you doing here?"

"I'm being detained from urgent business." He gestured at the armed men who still blocked his path.

"It's far too dangerous to be out."

"You're here," John observed.

"We started to lead the horses to the gates, in case the track could be cleared."

"You're not leading the factions into the streets? And it was you who united them?"

"You overestimate my influence."

John began to reply but was cut off by a high pitched voice. "And you, Porphyrius, are much too modest."

Narses stepped out of the storeroom Porphyrius had come from, carrying with him a miasma of perfume, weirdly out of place in the earthy atmosphere inside the Hippodrome.

"What business do you have here?" John snapped, realizing immediately that he had no authority to question Narses.

"The emperor's business, obviously. Preserving the empire. Avoiding violence."

John shot a questioning look at Porphyrius.

"I don't have time to talk," he said.

John felt Felix's hand on his shoulder. "Neither do we, John."

"You're right," John muttered. "You'll allow us to pass, Porphyrius."

The charioteer silently gestured to the armed men who stepped aside.

Outside the Hippodrome, the Mese was eerily lifeless without even a beggar or stray dog to disrupt the stillness.

"We're too late," Felix growled.

The mangled iron gate swinging open in the archway leading to Hypatius' courtyard confirmed his words.

The two men ran across the gravel to the mansion's portico.

A woman dressed in dark blue silks sat on the steps, head in her hands, shaking with sobs. John guessed it was Hypatius' wife, Mary. Two of her attendants tried to comfort her.

John spoke without preamble. "Has Hypatius gone?"

Mary looked up at him with reddened eyes. Grey, disheveled hair hung around her face. She looked older than her husband. "They came for him. Dragged him away. I begged him not to go, to barricade himself inside the house. He was afraid they'd hurt me, or burn the house or seek out that drunken fool of a brother instead."

She ran a silken sleeve across her tear streaked face.

"Do you have any idea where they went?"

"To Forum Constantine. He's to be crowned emperor." She pushed stray hairs out of her face."

"Where is Pompeius? Is he here?"

Mary shook her head. "No. When they had carried Hypatius off he went rushing after them. What did he suppose he was going to do? He'd had so much wine he could barely stay upright. Hypatius should have let them take Pompeius. He sacrificed himself for nothing."

"Not for nothing. You're still safe, and your daughter Julianna is safe as well. Hypatius must have told you she's with Antonina."

The woman nodded and loose hair fell across her face. She pushed it away. "One of the rogues stole the gold chain from my hair. He said they had no diadem so a gold circlet would have to do. Perhaps already I am the wife of an emperor. Is this what it feels like? I do not envy Theodora." She began to weep again.

Chapter Thirty-Nine

The Mese had been empty when John and Felix made their way to Hypatius' house. By the time they returned to the street it was jammed with humanity. The whole population of Constantinople seemed to be funneled into the main thoroughfare.

"Like sausage meat into a length of pig's gut," Felix remarked.

"What's happening?" John called out to a youth who trotted along at the edge of the throng.

When the young man ignored the question Felix grabbed him by the arm. The youth gaped in terror at the big, bearded soldier who held him. "It's the new emperor, sirs," he stammered. "Hypatius. We're taking him to the Hippodrome. He's going to vanquish the tyrant."

Felix pushed the youth away. "More likely the poor man is going to end up dead, as his wife knows only too well."

"If the populace considers Hypatius to be emperor, it should be ready to take orders from him," John pointed out. "He can order them to abandon the revolt. Or at least put off attacking the palace. I might be able to convince him that he could save his head."

"I suppose anything is worth a try. If you can get to him to talk." Felix surveyed the crowd which continued to stream past. "We'll never get to the kathisma through the Hippodrome."

"We'll go in by the entrance inside the palace."

"And we can use the back alleys to get to the palace, once we cross the street." Felix smiled grimly, unsheathed his sword, and began displaying it to the passersby blocking the way.

It didn't take long to re-enter the palace. The would-be rioters were eager to see the great mass of their companions but much less enthusiastic about facing a sharp blade themselves. The torrent rushing along the Mese had sucked the alleys dry of humanity. The excubitors at the obscure southern entrance to the palace allowed the two familiar men in without hesitation, but those blocking the passageway to the kathisma from the Daphne Palace were under orders that no one should pass.

John demanded to speak to the commander. He and Felix waited by one of the monumental columns supporting the towering arch at the head of the passageway. Finally Captain Gallio strolled out and sneered at Felix's request to enter. "You expect to be allowed to join the rioters? Deserting wasn't enough? Well, I suppose you can only hang once, or so I would have imagined until recently. The excubitors have their duty and we intend to carry it out."

"You want to be close at hand to serve Hypatius," Felix snarled.

John stepped between Felix and the captain. "Felix is under my command right now, Gallio. And I am serving Emperor Justinian. As you can see from my official orders."

He stuck them under the captain's face. Days of use had wrinkled the parchment, frayed the cord around it and flattened the embossing on the lead seal. The condition of the orders did not render them less impressive, although Justinian's precarious situation did.

Gallio brushed the orders aside. "From what I hear Justinian will be halfway across the Marmara by the time you get to the top of the stairs. And Emperor Hypatius will not appreciate being disturbed."

John tucked the parchment back into his tunic. "It may be that Justinian and Hypatius can come to an agreement. A great deal of blood might be spared. Emperor Hypatius will not look

kindly on the man who stopped the former emperor's emissary
from saving him trouble."

Gallio's lips tightened. "I would not want to cause any
emperor trouble." He glared at Felix. "I cannot allow an armed
soldier into the imperial box. You, Chamberlain, may go."

"Very well. Felix, please wait here for me."

Felix obeyed, scowling ferociously.

John followed Gallio down a short passageway lined with
armed men, through a double set of barred doorways, to the
base of a white marble stairway. Since he had risen to the position of chamberlain, John had climbed these stairs every time
Justinian presided over a race or ceremony in the Hippodrome,
more times than he could count. Unlike most of the palace
architecture, they were less than aesthetically pleasing, and far
from grand. They were steep and narrow and dimly lit. A few
armed men could defend them from an army.

At the top of the stairs a number of rooms, including a small
dining hall, opened off the corridor leading to the imperial box
itself. The place was crowded with a noisy conglomeration of
citizens—faction members clothed in their colors, wealthy aristocrats wearing rich robes, other men whose ripped and stained
clothing made it clear they had been fighting in the streets.
There was even a beggar with a cup. Whether he'd come in for
the warmth, or with the idea of earning extra coins, or simply
found himself swept up there by accident, John couldn't say.
The man had, however, sat down beside a doorway, as was his
custom outside.

More men milled around the cold imperial box, but here
John recognized several senators and palace officials. They looked
startled and quickly turned their backs to him.

Hypatius sat on the elevated throne, looking out over the
packed Hippodrome. It was peculiar, seeing him there rather
than Justinian. He looked much more an emperor.

From far below the masses they would see the noble profile,
the square chin and aquiline nose, the very image of his uncle
Anastasius. They would see the purple drapery around his

shoulders and be able to make out the sparkle of sunlight off the gold encircling his head. They would not be able to make out the pouches under his eyes, or the way his lips trembled. They would not see that the sparkling diadem was a woman's gold hair chain and the purple drapery a torn piece of a silk gown.

John made his way to the throne and spoke quietly. "Hypatius."

The would-be emperor looked down. "Chamberlain, if you have come to save me, you are too late."

The crowd roared his name and Hypatius raised his hand tentatively and the roar grew louder. "Long live Hypatius! Long live Hypatius!"

The trembling of his lips subsided and he waved his hand again, more confidently.

"There's still time, Hypatius. I am told you were taken from your house against your will. You can hardly be blamed for that. Advise the rioters to return to their homes."

"I doubt they would love me so well if I did."

"Then simply leave with me."

"I am afraid I am outnumbered." He gestured at the ranks below who broke into cheers again.

"You don't have to fight your way through them. The stairs to the palace aren't far away, and I spotted more than a few men who would be happy to let you go in return for my forgetting to tell Justinian that they were here."

"Does anyone still fear Justinian? I heard he had already sailed." Hypatius caught the eye of a nearby man dressed in a green tunic. "Isn't that right?"

"Yes," said the Green. "Justinian fled to Trebizond this morning."

"Porphyrius said so," confirmed his companion.

"No, it came straight from Narses," someone else said.

A dissenting voice chimed in. "Narses only saw the ship in the harbor. It was one of Justinian's officials said it had sailed. A chamberlain I think."

"You see," Hypatius said. "If Justinian has ceded his position to me than I have nothing to fear except the wrath of the crowd.

It would be foolish to betray them. Besides, it is my duty. The empire should not go rudderless because the coward who was at the helm has chosen to flee." He raised both hands and smiled as the tumult rolled across the stadium and crashed in waves across those in the imperial box.

John realized there was no point in arguing. He swept the box with his gaze and saw Pompeius. He had wedged his bulky figure into a far corner from where he stared dolefully at the back of the throne.

"Shouldn't you be at your brother's side?" John asked.

Pompeius looked at him in surprise. "Chamberlain! What are….what do you mean?"

"I would have expected you to be basking in his glory."

"What glory? He's up on the scaffold. True, a scaffold higher and more elaborate then most." Although he stank of wine and his robes were stained and rumpled, he wasn't slurring his words. He sounded completely sober.

"Then you might try to talk him out of this folly. If you really believe it's folly."

"Oh, I do believe it." He shook his head and gave a mournful laugh. "Thousands of ambitious men do everything in their power to advance and yet nearly every one fails, and often at a high price. You would think it would be easy enough to avoid advancement if you turned your efforts to it. And yet…as you see…."

"Fortuna has a strange sense of humor. There's still time, however."

"No. I'm afraid there isn't. Events have gone too far."

"Why are you here?" John demanded.

"I…I'm not sure…when I saw them drag Hypatius off…he's my brother…I thought I could talk him out of it as you said… not that they would have let him go…and they won't let him go now either…I wish I hadn't followed. I wish I were at home…." Suddenly tears ran down his fat cheeks and his billowing robes shook with sobs.

◇◇◇

"You think Julianna can make her father see sense?" Felix stepped out of the way of two servants hauling a litter piled with crates from the Daphne Palace.

"It may be the sight of his daughter will bring him back to reality," John said.

"But the reality is that he has the whole population of Constantinople on his side."

"Do you believe that?"

"Do you believe Justinian doesn't intend to flee? Like the rest of the court?" Felix swerved to avoid a pile of sacks beside a door. "We haven't seen a single guard. Just a steady stream of valuables being carted off. I wonder how many of these servants we've passed are actually thieves?"

"Or, more likely, both. And they might well slink away and enjoy what they've stolen when order is restored, but then they're anonymous, they aren't sitting on a throne in the Hippodrome and they're taking a few trinkets, not the whole empire. How long do you suppose a man like Hypatius could manage to hold the throne? Besides, I want to make sure Julianna is safe. She was placed in my charge by Justinian. She's my responsibility, despite Theodora's meddling."

A man's raised voice issued from the open doors leading into Antonina's quarters.

"Belisarius," Felix growled.

John motioned for him to stop. They stood in the vestibule in front of a statue of Plato, not hiding but not revealing themselves either. He could make out Antonina and the young general in the atrium beyond, partly concealed by a potted palm.

Belisarius sounded agitated. "Fight? I wish he would let us fight!"

Antonina made an inaudible comment.

"How do I know why he's so timid?" Belisarius replied. "I tried to explain to him, we need to strike while the mob's in the Hippodrome. In the streets they elude us, but in that open space, and packed together so tightly they can barely move, we can cut them down like a scythe through a field of wheat. Yet he hesitates."

"You must speak to him again." Antonina's voice had grown louder.

"He dismissed me, warned me about insubordination. He seemed angry, and frightened. And he is still the emperor."

"You'll come to no harm. I'll have a word with Theodora."

"Yes. Of course."

"Consult Mundus. Make your plans and present them to Justinian as a necessity."

"If Justinian hasn't fled already."

Belisarius turned to leave. Antonina put a hand on his arm. "By tonight it will be over. You will be victorious, and you will be in my bed."

John and Felix entered the atrium as Belisarius left, casting a scornful glance toward Felix.

John spoke before Antonina could protest the intrusion. "I wish to talk to Julianna."

"She's not here. She went to retrieve her belongings from your house." Her gaze went over John's shoulder to Felix. The look in her brilliant blue eyes was not inviting.

"I'll check the house, John," Felix said. He departed with alacrity.

"You sent servants with her?" John asked.

"No. She said she only had a few trifles to carry back."

"How could you be so irresponsible? She was given into your care!"

"Does this look like the imperial dungeons? Do you expect me to chain her to the wall?"

Had Antonina been too harried to attend to her make-up? She looked much older today. Her cheeks were not rosy and there were lines in her forehead.

"She's just a girl. You're old enough to be her mother. You're old enough to be Belisarius' mother. You ought to realize how dangerous it is for her to be wandering about."

Antonina pursed her lips into a pout that emphasized the fine wrinkles at the corners of her mouth. "You are most unkind, Chamberlain."

John controlled his anger. "How did you snare Belisarius, Antonina? One of your magickal potions? You are an ambitious woman. Do you see yourself as the wife of a general? Is that why you wanted to meet Felix at the Hall of Nineteen Couches? To test out your potion on him?"

"A man, or a woman, will succumb to a potion only if it is their wish!"

"A convenient philosophy. Do you by any chance have a potion that will impart courage to an emperor?"

"Even the strongest magick cannot bring forth what is not there."

"I see. Then I will have to try reason instead."

Chapter Forty

The silentiaries leaning on their lances just beyond the double doors of Justinian's reception hall allowed John to approach with hardly a glance. He paused as a sound resembling a rising wind filled the air.

"That's from the Hippodrome," one of the guards remarked. "It's swarming with rioters. Thousands of them. When the wind changes you can hear them baying for blood."

"It's a wasp's nest," another silentiary put in. "Before long they'll come flying out. What will we do then?"

"What you need to do is set fire to the nest while the wasps are still in it," commented his companion.

"Or run before they come out."

Justinian may have made up his mind to flee, but he had not gone yet. Narses and Theodora stood at the base of the double throne, while Justinian paced back and forth like a terrified horse trapped in its stall. His red boots flashed against the tiled floor. He still wore the plain white garments he had appeared in when addressing the assembly in the Hippodrome, but he was now wearing his diadem.

Around the group sat an assemblage of crates, sacks and chests, mimicking on a larger scale the previous evening's scene in John's atrium. Justinian had ordered Hypatius and Pompeius to leave, and he was apparently preparing to do the same. A pair of husky servants arrived, shouldered sacks, and departed.

Courtiers were scattered in knots here and there. More than one glanced nervously over his shoulder, perhaps expecting a howling mob to break down the doors. One man made his way to the imperial couple and prostrated himself.

"Highness, I humbly petition for permission to leave the city."

"Who is stopping you?" Justinian replied. He looked around and scowled. "I am not to be disturbed by petty details. Is there anyone left to obey my commands?"

Reluctantly John approached the emperor. "Caesar, I must report that Hypatius has been taken from his home. He has been crowned and installed in the kathisma."

Justinian nodded and smiled faintly. "Thank you, John. I have a few loyal advisors left at least." His gaze flickered to Narses for an instant, then he turned away, paced a few steps, and returned. "So, it is finished."

The emperor stared down at the supplicant still prostrated before him and nudged the quivering man with the red toe of his boot. "And what do you advise, Narses? Shall we all grow wings and flee through the heavens from the rats creeping from their foul nests?"

Narses bowed. "It is imperative that yourself and our dear empress be kept safe, and therefore it would be prudent—"

Theodora's face flushed with anger. Her enormous eyes had the demoniacal glow of fiery pits. "We will have nothing of such cowardice! Eunuchs may scream and scuttle and hide, but our beloved emperor has an iron will and refuses to be intimated by the cries of a horde of fools."

Several servants were picking up chests from behind the throne. The emperor's waiting ship must be well packed by now, John thought. One of the servants, bowing repeatedly, took a step toward Justinian. "Caesar, if I may ask, is it your wish that we take these thrones—"

"Traitor!" shrieked Theodora. "Guards! Execute this man! Guards! Guards!"

John noticed the silentiaries were no longer in sight. The servant retreated hastily. The unfortunate courtier, still lying on his face, moaned in terror.

Theodora gave him a vicious kick to the ear. A droplet of blood spattered onto the hem of Justinian's tunic. "Who dares to suggest our brave ruler would run away, frightened by a crew of unwashed beggars! Traitors! Ingrates! Vipers!" With each exclamation she administered a kick to the prone man's ribs.

Then she whirled, sending a gust of exotic perfume and sweat in John's direction, and stabbed a bejeweled finger at Narses. "And you! Have you been bribed that you would even contemplate advising such a retreat? The imperial torturers will find out the truth of that!"

Narses paled. Before he could reply, one of the few onlookers left in the room—one who was at a safe distance—called out in a quavering voice. "We will stay and defend our ruler to the last man if that is his wish."

Theodora emitted a cawing laugh. "And who would say nay to the emperor? But I say this is not a time to flee, never to be safe, always looking over our shoulders, afraid of being hunted down like common criminals. We are of the purple and all bow down before us."

Narses managed to speak. "You will not be abandoning the right to rule if you leave the city, highness. I suggest we sail to Heraclea. You will be able to summon the army of the west. They and the eastern army will be on the march as soon as orders reach them."

Theodora's eyes widened, her nostrils flared. Her beringed hand shot out and grasped the front of Narses' garment, ripping halfway down his sunken chest. The reception hall was silent. The rumble from the Hippodrome could be heard clearly.

Theodora looked Narses up and down. "It seems I was wrong, Narses." Her voice was a hiss. "I thought you would have breasts, for you speak like a woman." Her gaze swept past

John and settled on Justinian. "Are these the only advisors you have left, this pair of poor unmanly creatures?"

"It would appear so," Justinian replied. "What do think, John? Is it worth standing and fighting if losing is a certainty?"

John bowed slightly. "Nothing is a certainty. However, even if it were, what one may lose by fighting is not necessarily the same as what one may lose by fleeing. The question is what you most fear to lose."

Theodora laughed. "This one speaks some sense, if doubtless only to further his scheming ends. You should have listened to Belisarius. Crush the traitors immediately. "

Even now Justinian's features betrayed nothing. John had always considered the emperor a marvel of self control. Was he in fact a demon, as was whispered across the city, or did he suffer from some ailment which rendered him incapable of displaying normal human emotions?

"I prefer to believe John is playing the oracle," Justinian said. "He wants me to decide that he means what I want to hear. Prudence is always the best course. We will not be without resources once we leave the capital."

"You don't expect the armies to rally to a coward who takes flight, do you?" Theodora's voice shook with fury. "My father was a bear keeper. I come from the dung in the stables and the filth in the streets. No one can imagine what I have suffered to reach this place. I will die before I am dragged away from it. Haven't you poured out gold for the masses? Provided for the poor and weak? Why should you fly from those who should love you? We are of the purple. That is all that is necessary to know."

"Stay here, highness, and I fear you'll be buried in purple," Narses observed.

"Purple makes the best shroud." Theodora put her hand on Justinian's arm. "If the empire's existence depends upon the safety of our beloved ruler, then by all means let him leave, and leave now. But I wish to remain."

"I cannot allow that," Justinian replied. "Let us go. We can discuss our next actions once we are safely at sea."

◇◇◇

A covered walkway connecting a series of stairways between the terraces on which the palace gardens were built led to the imperial docks. John accompanied the emperor and empress, along with several silentiaries recruited in the halls. As the small party started down the first stairway Justinian gave John instructions. "Once we're safely on board, return and assist Narses. I want as many ships as possible loaded with our belongings. Don't forget the imperial plate."

John noted that neither he nor Narses, ordered to remain in the Daphne Palace to make final arrangements, were invited to flee with them. "And Belisarius and Mundus?" he asked.

"They are to leave for Heraclea as soon as possible. The contingents they brought with them are not large enough to subdue the city. In Heraclea the generals will be able to take control of both armies and return to put down the riots. Once on board, I will issue written orders for you to take to them."

"I am not a soldier," said Theodora. "I am barred by my sex from that profession. Yet it seems to this woman that a thousand trained men should be able to crush any number of rabble, if they are ordered to do so."

"And how can you be certain my generals wouldn't be as likely to cut my throat as follow my order?" Justinian replied mildly.

Were Justinian's fears well founded, John wondered.

As he descended the stairs he felt he was once again in the strange dream garden where he had met Haik's shade. The stairways felt unfamiliar now that they were leading not just to the docks, but to another world. A world where Justinian no longer occupied the palace. Where would that leave John?

The thought occurred to him that his investigation was finished. He would never discover what had happened to the mysterious adoption document Haik brought to the city. It was hardly worth mulling over at this point, but John couldn't help thinking about the document. Was it the reason he was helping usher Justinian into exile? Had it, in some manner, sealed the emperor's fate? Had it convinced Porphyrius to rally the populace to Hypatius? Why not? Porphyrius once rallied the crowds to Hypatius' uncle, Emperor Anastasius. It might not have taken much to convince the charioteer to side with the family again. He changed racing colors like rich men changed tunics.

Had the document also, perhaps, convinced Belisarius to abandon Justinian, or given him a pretext to do so? How much pretext would an ambitious man need? Who could argue that conspiring to make a Persian heir to the Empire was not traitorous? Porphyrius might have approached Belisarius with the damning agreement and offered his own support at the same time.

It was all speculation and would remain so now.

The party reached the next terrace, another step down toward exile. Behind them loomed a high masonry wall, overhung with greenery and lined at its base with trees and shrubbery. The gardens narrowed here and before long they could see the waist high parapet marking the edge of the terrace.

The path to the stairway led through an arbor surrounded by ornamental bushes and shrouded by thick ropes of leafless vines.

As they passed into the semi-shadow John thought he heard a rustling sound. He turned his head. There was no one following them aside from the trailing guard.

He heard a sort of crunch nearby. John peered over the shoulders of the imperial couple. The path ahead was as clear as that behind.

A tiny bit of bark drifted down onto his sleeve. John looked up. The thickly entwined vines overhead were trembling almost imperceptibly.

Someone was moving stealthily along the top of the arbor.

Justinian and Theodora had reached the end of the arbor.

There was no time for a warning. John sprang forward, past the imperial couple, and as he did so, the toe of a boot appeared at the edge of roof. John leapt, caught the intruder's foot, and brought him crashing to the ground.

The intruder rolled and sprang to his feet. John saw a dark, hunched creature in rags. The demon he had pursued along the spina in the Hippodrome.

"I crave an audience!" cried the demon.

John drew his blade. Justinian laughed and waved him and the guards back. "How could I refuse such an ingenious petitioner?" He smiled at his unexpected visitor. "Speak before you are put to death."

The demon took a few lurching steps. The rags it wore appeared to be half burnt and ashes speckled its wild hair. It carried with it the sharp odor of smoke. "I have already conquered death and I shall do so again, and therefore I have no fear of dying! But you, my emperor, I see have a great fear of death. Surely you realize that wherever you go, no matter how far across the seas, you will find death waiting."

"True enough, but your death is much closer at hand. Why do you desire an audience?"

"To tell you how you may be saved."

An expression of interest crossed Justinian's face. "Are you here on behalf of your fellow rioters?"

"I bring a message from heaven."

Theodora laughed contemptuously. "From heaven? You're the first angel I've ever encountered who smells like he's been smoldering in hell!"

"Not so!" responded the visitor. "For I have seen demons roaming the streets of Constantinople! They are leading loyal subjects astray, whispering lies about our rulers! Encouraging them to kill the old and crown the new!"

John thought it strange that such a demonic creature should be speaking against demons. Yet, peering closely, he could almost make out the features of the young man the thing had once been.

The creature turned its bloodshot gaze to Justinian. "Peace will return, excellency, but to achieve that you must banish the demons."

"Do you mean by magick?" Theodora asked with obvious interest.

"Not just common magick. Magick far more powerful!" The creature reached into the tattered fabric at its chest and drew out a length of splintered wood with a ribbon dangling from it. "This is a piece of the True Cross! What miracles can be wrought with such a relic! It will banish evil and heal the sick and raise the dead! Am I not a living example?"

Justinian regarded him with an even gaze. "You say you've been dead?"

"Oh yes. I was foully murdered. But in heaven we forgive our enemies, so I bring you this…." The creature bent, laid the splintered piece of wood at Justinian's red boots, and backed slowly away.

Justinian gestured to John to pick up the object. It was cylindrical, with a piece of shredded ribbon from which hung an embossed lead disk.

"A broken spoke from a wheel, probably a chariot wheel," John said, turning the object around. "And there's an imperial seal attached to it."

Theodora leaned over to examine the seal. "Anastasius!" she cried. "It's one of Anastasius' seals!" She glared at the ragged creature now slowly creeping backwards. "You're from the conspirators! You're one of the traitors!"

Justinian had taken the peculiar talisman from John and was regarding it pensively. "The Lord is free to send whatever sort of messenger he wants. What could be more persuasive than a message authenticated with an imperial seal? In simpler times a burning bush might have sufficed. It may be this is what a miracle looks like in our present age. A spoke from a wheel… or perhaps a piece of the True Cross? Is not our empire being crucified on a cross made by the racing factions? Clearly, the Lord has spoken. We shall stay. Victory will not be given to the mob. It will be ours!"

A hoarse cry drew John's attention back to the tattered messenger. "His will is done," the creature shouted.

He scuttled to the parapet at the edge of the terrace. "Now I may fly back whence I came."

He spread his arms wide and flung himself into space.

◇◇◇

Rusticus lifted his head to look up from the crumpled body half buried in the thorn bush at the base of the terrace wall. "He's dead," he announced, remarking to John in an undertone "but then that's obvious, isn't it?"

Justinian had ordered John to send for Rusticus. Was it simply one of the emperor's strange humors? Did he expect the dead man to rise again? Or was it more a case of wanting reassurance he would not?

Now Justinian's face was as unreadable as his image stamped into the gold face of a coin. Was he reconsidering his decision to remain in the city, John wondered?

"Apparently our sooty angel was deluded," Theodora remarked. "He didn't have wings after all."

Rusticus turned his attention back to the corpse and pointed out two grooves in the neck. "It looks as if he was half strangled, doesn't it? In a way he was as I happen to know he was hung."

"It's Hippolytus, isn't it?" John asked.

Rusticus got to his feet with a grunt. "Yes. The Green I saw who was supposed to be executed. He's finished the job himself."

"Caesar," John addressed the emperor. "The fact that this man was alive all the time we considered him dead solves the mystery. Hippolytus was the murderer. He strangled the other condemned man from the rival faction, while they were imprisoned at Saint Laurentius. There was never any plot to kill those two. The opposition is not as organized as—"

Justinian interrupted. "Yes. I see that. Explain later. There isn't time now. We will return to the palace at once."

Chapter Forty-One

The noise from the Hippodrome was different this time. Before, heard from the palace grounds, it had been a roar, the voice of the city, inarticulate and monstrous. Now it was a wail, the death cry of some incredible beast.

When John reached his house Felix was standing outside and it was clear from his grim expression that he also was listening to the dreadful sound.

"I've just come from Justinian," John said. "He's ordered Belisarius and Mundus to the Hippodrome to confront the mob."

"I wish I were out in that battle. They were fools to assemble in one place. So much easier to kill the lot."

"It isn't a battle. That's the sound of a slaughter," John said. "Have you seen Julianna? She was supposed to come here for her belongings."

"She isn't here." Felix did not have to add what he feared, that she had gone out into the city again and been caught in the bloodshed.

"It occurred to me that Julianna might be able to talk her father into ordering the rioters to make peace with Justinian. Perhaps she had the same thought."

"It's as good a guess as any, John."

They set off without further discussion. John explained how he had been detained, described Hippolytus' interview with Justinian on the terrace and his own conclusions about the murder of the Blue. The murder no longer seemed important.

"At least Justinian can't accuse you of having failed in your investigation, even if it turned out to be of little consequence," Felix remarked. "We're fortunate he finally allowed Belisarius and Mundus to fight. But for such a strange reason. Only a Christian would ignore generals and heed a madman."

They picked their way around the huge boulders of masonry where the Chalke had stood. Ribbons of smoke rose from the rubble. A scrawny dog worried what might have been an arm protruding from a pile of scorched bricks.

By the time they reached the Mese the terrible wailing had begun to die away and up and down the thoroughfare individual voices could be made out. The loud words of a dispute. Laughter.

Knots of people clustered under part of a colonnade that had survived the fires. The Hunnish hair-styles many sported marked them as Blues. A man with a long braid wandered in circles in the middle of the street. Seeing him, John could feel the wet rope of the braid by which he had pulled the drowned man from the cistern. A chill ran down his back.

"Dancing with Bacchus," Felix muttered.

A burst of raucous merriment drifted from a nearby tavern which was apparently still in business, if somewhat smoke stained. A figure lurched out, staggered over to them, and put a hand on John's shoulder to steady himself. Felix drew his sword.

John removed the hand from his shoulder. "Don't worry, Felix. I know this man. What is it, Junius?"

The young charioteer swayed but managed to remain upright. "Good thing I saw you. Need to warn you. Stay away from the Hippodrome. Too dangerous."

He exhaled a fog of wine along with his slurred words.

"You are telling us this because...?"

"So you'll put in a good word for me with Porphyrius, for saving your life," the other replied with what probably struck him as impeccable logic in his inebriated state. "Just been celebrating the triumph of Justinian, thanks to a benefactor of the Blues."

Felix grabbed Junius by the arm and yanked him around so he could glare into the charioteer's suddenly panic-stricken face. "Better to ask what all these Blues are doing out here drinking themselves into the gutter when people are being killed in the Hippodrome."

"All of us were ordered to get out," Junius stammered. "By Porphyrius. And I heard Narses was making money available out in the street, or at any rate the taverns would be serving free wine. I had to leave. All the Blues were leaving."

Felix pushed Junius away. "So the Blues were paid to leave the Greens to their fate."

He and John finished their journey to the Hippodrome at a run. The clatter of hooves greeted them on the concourse. A bleeding man stumbled across the open space. His mounted pursuer overtook him, ran a spear through his neck, yanked it free in a gout of blood, and rode back into the stadium. From its depths echoed isolated shouts, screams, and hoof beats.

"It's over," John said. "They're hunting down survivors."

He and Felix continued on toward the racetrack.

Bodies filled the stalls behind the starting gates—those who had tried to flee. John stepped over and around the dead until he emerged onto the track.

"Mithra!" he heard Felix mutter. Was it a curse or an invocation?

Both men had seen battlefields, but nothing like this. The Hippodrome was a well-filled abattoir. The dead covered the entire length of the track. They were heaped along the spina like debris drifted against the sea walls. John walked forward a few paces. It was difficult to find footing and where there was a space to place a boot, the sand was slippery. It had absorbed blood until it became saturated.

He accidentally stepped on a hand, cursed, and moved backwards, reflexively. The lifeless fingers appeared to have been clawing at the ground when they stopped moving for the last time.

The scene should have been still but the carrion birds lent to it a horrible animation. The birds hopped from corpse to corpse, stabbed with their beaks, and flapped away. The far end of the track might have been a refuse heap crawling with flies. The birds cawed and squawked as they fought over their banquet. Amidst the harsh screeching John could make out scattered moans. A single shrill, thin scream emanated from a distant point he could not locate. It went on and on. Already, he saw, several beggars had arrived to pick over the bodies.

A suffocating stench of blood and death hung in the vast enclosure.

"It was nothing more than a slaughter," John said. "A crowd this size, packed in here. No need for strategy. They could scarcely move let alone fight. And there was nowhere to take shelter, even if they could have run. No proper weapons to speak of, either."

He kicked at a sharpened stick in his path. "To think that I have been searching for the murderer of two men, and now this. Half the city dead and no doubt at all who killed them."

"What choice was there, John?"

"There's never any choice, is there?"

He was having trouble breathing. His chest suddenly felt constricted. The shock of seeing the carnage had driven everything else from his mind, but now he recalled why they had come here. To find Julianna.

Suddenly he did not want to continue the search.

Not here, where there was nothing left alive.

He walked amidst the dead, hardly seeing them. Afraid that his gaze would be caught by a lithe, familiar figure.

For some inexplicable reason he kept seeing Cornelia in his mind. But it wasn't Cornelia he was looking for. She had been lost to him long ago, vanished into the countless masses of humanity, alive and dead, of whom John would know nothing until the day he died.

For the dead were all knowing.

No, he was searching for Julianna, a young girl who meant nothing to him at all.

Felix caught at John's sleeve. "We can't look everywhere. If she were here...." He let his voice trail off.

They were halfway down the track, approaching the huge box of the kathisma. There was no emperor to gesture imperiously at his audience of two far below. A hawk rose up from inside the enclosure, bearing away whatever dangled from its talons.

John narrowed his eyes as he scanned the tiers of seating "There," he finally said. "Up there."

It took an eternity to climb the tiers.

Julianna lay at the base of the kathisma wall. She wore the iridescent green robes she had worn in John's garden. The wall was high, designed to keep the masses safely away from the emperor. An athletic young woman might have been able to climb it, using the ornate carvings for hand-holds—or she might have thought she could.

There was no blood. Her head rested on her hands as if she had laid down to go to sleep, except that her eyes were still open and staring.

"She fell, trying to get up to where her father was crowned." John spoke quietly, though there was no one to overhear their conversation.

"Better that than her being trapped down there," Felix said, "or sent to the gallows with the rest of her family."

John bent down and pulled a wisp of green silk over the still face.

Epilogue

January 22, 532

John's house was empty. All the furniture had been carted away. There remained only whispers and shadows.

John and Felix passed through the atrium, conducting a final inspection.

"If I were you I would miss this place," said Felix. "Usually when people are promoted they request a larger house, not a smaller one."

"It will be more convenient. I will only need a couple of servants, and neither of them will be slaves either."

"It's fortunate you were able to give the emperor an explanation of the matter of the missing Blue and Green, otherwise you would be residing in a very small house indeed."

"A tomb, you mean?"

"Indeed. As for myself, I'm happy just to be back in the excubitors' barracks. Though I am sorry Gallio was relieved of his head as well as his command. He was nothing worse than a coward, in my opinion."

"Most of the court is grumbling Justinian didn't carry out more executions alongside those of Hypatius and Pompeius." John's gaze was caught by a shaft of light falling from the compluvium, past the marble Aphrodite in the atrium's fountain. The light sparkled on the water in the basin. "It's rumored their bodies were thrown into the sea. The first time I saw Pompeius he was sitting in the basin there, soaking wet, and now...."

He broke off, scanned the atrium a last time, and turned away. It made him shudder to think of the dead men who had been his guests floating in the lightless depths.

Felix followed him into the corridor. "I hear Narses took great delight in pointing out how much time you had spent investigating the death of your friend Haik instead of carrying out Justinian's orders. I suppose he was angry enough to spit lamp oil when you were elevated to Lord Chamberlain."

"Narses had a right to be angry. His efforts bribing the factions probably influenced events more than anything I did."

"The emperor is as unpredictable as Fortuna. But at least the city is returning to normal. It wasn't just poor Hippolytus who went mad. The whole capital did. A colleague was telling me about the strange sights he saw during the riots. There was one fellow who was gathering up tesserae. Scrabbling around in the street after bits of glass with all the gold and silver there was for the taking!"

"Bits of glass can be turned into mosaics depicting stories more precious than any silver goblet. The bits and pieces gathered during an investigation may not seem valuable, but when assembled into a solution, that's a different matter."

"Your mind is still on your investigations, isn't it?"

John peered through the open door of a deserted room as they passed. It was as bare as the rest of the house. "When you mentioned Haik I couldn't help thinking that although I was obligated to look into his murder since he was an old comrade in arms and brother in Mithra, as it turned out he posed the most serious threat to the emperor."

"Because of the document he brought with him, by which Justin was to adopt Chosroes?"

"Exactly."

"Do you suppose he was entrusted with the document to help overthrow Justinian? If so, by whom? Was he working with the Persian emissary, Bozorgmehr? Or did he come by it some other way?"

"I'd like to think that Haik came by it quite by accident and decided it might be sold for a good sum in the capital. When he told me he was here on business, he was telling me the truth."

"But even if that's the case, why would anyone buy it, except for political reasons? He must have seen the implications."

"Again, I am pleading on behalf of a friend, but it may be he thought he could sell it to someone who would buy the document to make sure it was destroyed. We'll never know that or establish where it's gone. My belief is someone had a good reason to destroy it and did. But before that, talk of the document, by its very existence, probably helped set off the riots."

"That's a startling assertion."

"And like almost everything else about this whole affair, one that can't be proved now that most of those involved are dead. But my speculation is Hippolytus started the trouble for which he was hung after he overheard Haik talking to Porphyrius about the attempted adoption. He might have decided the time was ripe to depose Justinian, having realized that Julianna's father would be the most likely successor to the throne."

"Being married to the emperor's daughter would be a good job and Julianna was certainly interested in him," Felix said.

"Haik and Porphyrius gave me conflicting accounts of why Haik went to the Hippodrome to see him, but Haik said they were interrupted by a visitor whom Porphyrius identified as Hippolytus. I am guessing Hippolytus lingered outside Porphyrius' office long enough to learn what was going on before making his presence known."

"Then do you think the hangings were deliberately botched?"

"No. The preparations were rushed, the executioner was nervous because of the mood of the spectators."

"You told me Hippolytus killed the Blue after they were taken to Saint Laurentius, and then escaped. Was that, at least, part of a plot?"

"Not one against the emperor. Hippolytus was deranged from having been nearly strangled to death during his hanging. I imagine he hardly knew what he was doing. He wasn't capable of reasoning. He saw a Blue. An enemy. So he killed him."

"But if he was so impaired how did he escape?"

"Julianna freed him."

They had come to the dining room where Hypatius and Pompeius had spent most of their time. Sunlight poured in from the garden through the gap left by the half opened screen.

Felix shook his head. "You amaze me, John. I can't see how it's possible."

"Sebastian couldn't see either. When I arrived at the church, he ran his fingers over the seal on my orders instead of actually reading them. He told me of a young man who had arrived earlier with orders the prisoners were to be taken to the palace. He too had an imperial seal."

John paused to collect his thoughts. "Now what if this young man was Julianna? Let us suppose it was. Then it seems likely the alleged order she brought with her was in fact a piece of parchment carrying one of Anastasius' seals. Being relatives of his, the family doubtless have seals on a number of such documents, one of which would seem genuine enough."

Felix looked dubious. "That's a big leap, John."

"Not when you consider I myself saw Hippolytus possessed one of Anastasius' seals when he died. Julianna is the only person who could have given it to him. He was in a dangerous predicament. Perhaps she thought it might be of use."

"Even so, I can't see how you connect Julianna with this mysterious young man," Felix replied.

"Hypatius told me he suspected that she left the house in secret to visit Hippolytus or to see the races at the Hippodrome." John stepped into the garden and gestured toward the opposite side. "I caught her coming in across the roof over there. Probably she had been out searching for Hippolytus. Porphyrius mentioned Hippolytus showing one of the faction's horses to a callow-faced fellow, whom Hippolytus claimed was his younger brother. Yet despite an invitation from the great Porphyrius to meet him and his evident interest in racing, the boy did not reappear. Then one of the other charioteers remarked women were known to see the races disguised in male clothing, and some would visit the Hippodrome's substructure to see charioteers they admired."

"So you think Julianna was both the alleged younger brother and the young man with the seal? I suppose it's possible." Felix frowned. "But it's a distinct possibility Sebastian will be in complete darkness now after the torturers' needles have done their work, and that's assuming he's still breathing."

"Sebastian's been released."

"Released?"

"The emperor told me he was demonstrating Christian mercy. Besides, he reasoned that it was Prefect Eudaemon who was at fault for giving a practically blind commander such an important task. What's more startling is that Sebastian's got his eyesight back. According to that loose-tongued physician Rusticus, the old commander suffered from cataracts. Purely by accident Justinian's torturers treated them to the traditional cure when they inserted needles into his eyes."

"Remarkable! That will give Rusticus another story with which to entertain his patients. But when I said I was puzzled I wasn't thinking about the seal, but about Julianna's involvement. The escape took place not long after the hanging. How could she possibly have known she would find Hippolytus at Saint Laurentius?"

"After Rusticus examined Haik he told me he'd called on her uncle Pompeius immediately after serving in his official capacity at the executions. He mentioned Julianna was at the house, tending her uncle. Naturally Rusticus regaled them with an account of the executions. He had recognized Hippolytus as one of two men who were saved, having treated him as a patient not long before, meaning Julianna realized he was still alive."

"She had a quick intelligence. When she got to Hippolytus only to discover he'd killed his fellow prisoner, it must have been a shock."

John nodded. "And the two guards posted at the door to keep the prisoners safe were even more shocked, I'll wager. It wouldn't have taken a very large bribe to convince them to carry off the evidence of their utter failure and flee the city to find work elsewhere. I am sure Julianna came prepared to offer bribes if necessary."

"Plenty of people decide to find work elsewhere whenever riots threaten to break out," Felix observed.

"When panic broke out in the church, it wasn't hard for them to get out without being seen," John continued. "There was doubtless more than one exit from the vault. The blind beggar who heard something being carted past was perfectly willing to have heard as many men go by as I wished, and when I dragged the Blue with the marks of strangulation and rope tied round his wrist out of the cistern I leapt to the conclusion that whoever had killed one of the prisoners had killed both."

"You were thinking in terms of them being disposed of by those involved in a plot so Justinian could not produce them."

"Yes. But it's no excuse. I erred badly."

"Then after Julianna had to return home Hippolytus was free in the city although I don't suppose he fully understood what was happening. Yet he did retain enough cunning to kill Haik. Obviously he could get onto the palace grounds, since he confronted Justinian. But as to remembering the significance of the document…and surely that is why Haik was murdered?"

"I don't doubt it."

Felix scowled in perplexity. The two men had walked out into the garden. John stopped beside the stone horse Julianna had found half hidden by brambles. On the day he had first seen the horse a cold breeze was rattling dead leaves. Today thin, bright sunlight illuminated the small statue, making the lichens partly covering it look more gray than blue. Then Julianna had been alive. Today she was dead.

"Most people would kill to be emperor," John said. "Some might kill to avoid the throne. Hypatius was not ambitious." He ran a hand lightly across the back of the horse. "Julianna told me her father didn't want to be emperor. She was afraid the mob would crown him and both she and her father realized what the outcome was likely to be, even if Hippolytus did not."

Felix pointed out that except for Fortuna intervening Hippolytus would have died before the population took to the streets.

"The Hippolytus Julianna knew did die before that happened. She was right, though, in thinking she could have saved him, had he not been so badly hurt by the failed hanging," John replied. "Justinian had ordered the execution of several troublesome faction members as an example. He can be surprisingly forgiving, if Theodora does not interfere. If he had found out one of the condemned was, say, to marry into an aristocratic family—for Julianna surely hoped it would be so, despite her father's opposition to her friendship with Hippolytus—a family which had remained loyal during the riots, he almost certainly would have pardoned the man."

"That's true, John. I strongly suspect Theodora must have persuaded Justinian to have Hypatius and Pompeius executed immediately, before he had a chance to change his mind."

John was silent for a time, looking reflectively at Julianna's horse. Should he remove it to his new house? No, perhaps not. It would remind him of Julianna, and she had reminded him of someone else.

"We mourn people and places time has stolen from us," he said. "But sometimes it is better that past things remain lost. I wish I had never seen my old friend Haik again, for it was that cursed document that caused all the trouble, as I've said. It isn't surprising that Julianna knew about the document. She was meeting Hippolytus all the time. He would surely have told her about overhearing Haik and Porphyrius. Or maybe he told her when she arrived at the church.

"He was deranged but not to the point of having lost all his senses. And when she heard about it, Julianna certainly would have known how dangerous the document was. It would have fueled the mob's anger. And whether by enticing Porphyrius or some other prominent person to enter the fray or simply by providing another rallying point for the rioters, it increased the likelihood that her father would not be able to retain any appearance of loyalty, but would instead be dragged to his doom. Or even go to it willingly. What if Haik, who was staying in the same house, had decided to forget about Porphyrius and present the adoption document directly to Hypatius?"

Felix tugged his beard. "You just said you thought Hippolytus wanted Hypatius to become emperor." He paused, then his face brightened. "Wait. Now I see. Hippolytus was unhinged. He didn't know what he was doing. He intended to steal the document to ensure it was given to Hypatius, but in his terrible state he forgot what he was doing and murdered Haik instead. Why else should Haik have been killed? The document was the important thing."

"But what if Haik had possessed other documents, or was prepared to reveal that something of value had been stolen and demand its return? The murderer waited for the chance, slipped into Haik's room and stole the document. Why take more risk than necessary? Why not insure Haik couldn't meddle any further by slipping poison into his wine?"

"So Hippolytus planned the murder."

John offered Felix a thin smile. "Planned a murder using belladonna? A man who had, by all appearances, strangled another man with his bare hands at Saint Laurentius? And where would Hippolytus obtain such a poison? Was he a friend of Antonina, whose apartments are filled with all sorts of concoctions for magick and aids to beauty, including making eyes more attractive? No, it was Julianna who poisoned Haik to save both her father and her lover. But she saved no one. Not even herself."

Again in memory John pulled a wisp of green silk over Julianna's still face.

It was not the last time he would do so.

Afterword

Eight for Eternity is based on historical events and many of the characters who appear in the novel were real people.

Justinian I is generally acknowledged as one of the greatest of the Roman emperors. He reconquered Africa and Italy, his codification of the laws served as the basis for western jurisprudence, and we still marvel at the architectural wonders he commissioned, such as Istanbul's Hagia Sophia. However, his long reign (527 to 565) was nearly cut short by a series of street riots in 532.

Many of the rioters belonged to the Blue and Green factions, who took their names from the colors of the chariot racing teams they supported. The factions were notorious for engaging in agitation, hooliganism, and murder. On January 10, 532, the City Prefect Eudaemon ordered the execution of seven of them. Something went wrong and two—a Blue and a Green—survived their hangings, were rescued, and taken to sanctuary at the Church of Saint Laurentius.

Calls for the release of the survivors soon escalated into a general political uprising. Justinian attempted to placate the citizenry by removing from office three unpopular officials: Prefect Eudaemon, the tax collector John the Cappadocian, and

the legal advisor Tribonian. However, rioting and arson continued in Constantinople. Neither armed force nor bribery by the
emperor's treasurer, the eunuch Narses, seemed sufficient to put
down the insurrection. The emperor and his court took refuge
in the Great Palace. It has been said that Justiian intended to
flee but was persuaded to stay and fight by Empress Theodora.

The mobs looked to the family of former emperor Anastasius
for leadership. When Justinian expelled Anastasius' nephews,
Pompeius and Hypatius, from the palace, the crowd quickly
dragged Hypatius from his house and crowned him emperor.
Fortunately for Justinan, the generals Belisarius and Mundus
happened to be in the capital with their troops. When the rioters
congregated in the Hippodrome, the generals descended upon
them and the ensuing slaughter left at least thirty thousand
dead and Justinian still in power. Hypatius and Pompeius were
executed on January 19.

There are contemporary accounts of the riots from Procopius,
John Malalas, John Lydus, and Marcellinus. They differ in
their emphasis and their explanations of the causes, although
none seems to have pointed to the near adoption of the Persian
Chosroes by Emperor Justin some years earlier. The adoption
negotiations described in Eight For Eternity actually occurred,
according to Procopius in his History of the Wars. As personal
secretary to Belisarius he was in a good position to know.

The charioteer Porphyrius was also a real person, famed both
for his racing prowess and his excursions into politics, as we
mention. Much of what we know about him comes from the
epigrams on the monuments erected in his honor.

Belisarius married Antonina. According to Procopius' *Secret
History* she kept the great general at her beck and call by means
of magick.

Glossary

All dates are CE unless otherwise indicated

ADOPTION BY ARMS AND ARMOR

Ceremony apparently involving the gift of these items, which when carried out between individuals of similar power but different ages created a father/son relationship. It was looked upon as appropriate only for barbarians.

ANASTASIUS I (c 430-518; r 491-518)

Minor functionary who became emperor upon the death of Emperor Zeno (d 491; r 474-491), whose widow, Ariadne, Anastasius married after his elevation to the purple. Anastasius was a MONOPHYSITE, which put him at odds with the orthodox church and caused an unsuccessful rebellion led by VITALIAN, who was defeated in 515. Anastasius was a supporter of the REDS racing FACTION.

ATRIUM

Central area of a Roman house.

ATROPOS

Oldest of the three Fates. The other two were Clotho, the spinner, who formed the thread of life, and Lachesis, the allotter or dispenser of time, who measured its length. Atropos, the inexorable, cut it with her shears at the moment of death.

AUGUSTAION

Public square on the south side of the GREAT CHURCH, accessible from the MESE.

BATHS OF ZEUXIPPOS

Public baths in Constantinople. Situated northeast of the HIPPODROME, they were generally considered the most luxurious of the city's public baths.

BELISARIUS (c 505-565)
General whose exploits included retaking northern Africa and successful campaigns against the Vandals and the Persians. He also assisted in putting put down the NIKA RIOTS in Constantinople. He is said to have relied heavily upon advice from his wife Antonina.

BLUES
See FACTIONS.

CABADES I (b 449; r 488-531)
King of Persia and father of CHOSROES I. Also known as Kavadh.

CERBERUS
Three-headed dog guarding the entrance to Hades.

CHALKE
Main entrance to the GREAT PALACE. One of many structures destroyed during the NIKA RIOTS and rebuilt by JUSTINIAN I.

CHOSROES I (b 501; r 531-579)
King of Persia whose rule spanned most of JUSTINIAN'S reign, he was the third son and favorite of CABADES I. Although Chosroes concluded an Eternal Peace with the Romans shortly after assuming power, hostilities resumed in 540.

CODEX
Book with manuscript pages.

COMPLUVIUM
Opening in the center of the ATRIUM roof admitting light and air and allowing rain to fall into a sunken pool for subsequent household use.

CONCRETE
Roman concrete, consisting of lime, volcanic ash, and pieces of rock, was used in a wide range of structures from cisterns to the Pantheon in Rome, which has survived for nearly 2,000 years without the steel reinforcing rods commonly used in modern concrete buildings.

CONSTANTINE I (c 272-337; r 306-337)
A Christian convert although not baptized until he was dying, he made Constantinople the capital of the empire.

CONSTANTIUS II (c 317-361 r 337-361)
Son of CONSTANTINE I.

DALMATIC
Long, wide-sleeved tunic.

ETERNAL PEACE
See CHOSROES I.

DAPHNE PALACE
Complex of buildings, said to be the oldest on the grounds of the GREAT PALACE. Located on their western side.

EUNUCH
Eunuchs played an important part in the army, church, and civil administration of the Byzantine Empire. Many high offices in the palace administration were typically held by eunuchs.

EXCUBITORS
Imperial guard. JUSTIN, uncle of JUSTINIAN I, became emperor after rising through the ranks to become commander of the excubitors.

FACTIONS
Supporters of the BLUES or the GREENS, taking their names from the racing colors of the chariot team they favored. Great rivalry existed between them, and they had their own seating sections at the HIPPODROME. Brawls between the factions were not uncommon, and occasionally escalated into city-wide riots. Originally the factions also included REDS and Whites. Although these still existed, by the sixth century they had become secondary and were absorbed into the two more prominent factions.

FUNALES
Outer pair of horses pulling a four-horse chariot.

GALEN (c 130–c 201)
Celebrated physician whose writings on medical topics greatly influenced the profession for centuries. Eighty or so are known, and he also wrote numerous philosophical treatises.

GREAT CHURCH
Also known as the Hagia Sophia (Church of the Holy Wisdom). The first Great Church was inaugurated in 360 and burnt down in 404. The second was erected in 415, but destroyed during the NIKA RIOTS. It was replaced by the existing Hagia Sophia, constructed by order of JUSTINIAN I and consecrated in December 537.

GREAT PALACE
Located in southeastern Constantinople, it was not one building but many, set amid trees and gardens. The grounds included barracks for the EXCUBITORS, ceremonial rooms, meeting halls, the imperial family's living quarters, churches, and housing for court officials, ambassadors, and various other dignitaries.

GREENS
See FACTIONS

HALL OF THE NINETEEN COUCHES
Located on the grounds of the GREAT PALACE, the hall was used for ceremonial banquets.

HECATE

Goddess associated with the underworld, darkness, and sorcery. Crossroads, particularly where three roads met, were sacred to her. She was often evoked in magick rituals and on curse tablets.

HERACLEA

City lying on the coast of the Sea of Marmara. Its modern name is Eregli.

HERULI

Germanic people thought to have originated in Scandinavia. Large numbers of Heruli served in the Roman army.

HIPPODROME

U-shaped race track near the GREAT PALACE. The Hippodrome had tiered seating accommodating up thousands of spectators and was also used for public celebrations and other civic events.

ISAURIA

Province in Asia Minor, occupied by a notoriously rebellious people. ANASTASIUS I quelled a revolt, but although the Isaurians were soundly defeated at the battle of Cotyaeum (491) it took several years to finally subdue them.

JUSTIN I (c 450-527; r 518-527)

Born in the province of Dardania in present day Macedonia, Justin and two friends journeyed to Constantinople to seek their fortunes. All three joined the EXCUBITORS. Justin eventually rose to hold the rank of commander and was declared emperor upon the death of ANASTASIUS I. Justin's nephew JUSTINIAN I was crowned co-emperor in April 527, four months before Justin died.

JUSTINIAN I (483-565; r 527-565)

Nephew of JUSTIN I and his successor to the throne. Justinian's greatest ambition was to restore the Roman empire to its former glory. He succeeded in temporarily regaining North Africa, Italy, and southeastern Spain. He ordered the codification of Roman law and after the NIKA RIOTS rebuilt the GREAT CHURCH as well as many other buildings in Constantinople. He married THEODORA in 525.

KATHISMA

Imperial box at the HIPPODROME.

KEEPER OF THE PLATE

Court official responsible for the care of palace plate, which included ceremonial items as well as imperial platters, ewers, goblets, and various types of dishes, often made of precious metals.

KNUCKLEBONRS

Popular pastime resembling a game of dice.

LAZICA

Lying along the Black Sea, the territory was claimed by both Romans and Persians and was the scene of a number of conflicts between the two empires.

LYSIPPOS (4th century BCE)
Greek sculptor notable for his bronze works, said to number over a thousand.

MESE
Main thoroughfare of Constantinople. Enriched with columns, arches, statuary depicting secular, military, imperial, and religious subjects, fountains, religious establishments, monuments, emporiums, public baths, and private dwellings, it was a perfect mirror of the heavily populated and densely built city it traversed.

MITHRA
Sun god. It was said Mithra was born in a cave or from a rock, and that as soon as he emerged into the world he clothed himself with leaves from a fig tree and ate of its fruit. Mithra is usually shown in the act of slaying the Great (or Cosmic) Bull, from which all animal and vegetable life sprang. A depiction of this scene was in every MITHRAEUM. Mithra was also known as Mithras.

MITHRAEUM
Place of worship dedicated to MITHRA. They have been found on sites as far apart as northern England and what is now the Holy Land.

MONOPHYSITE
Adherent to the belief that Christ had only a single divine nature, as opposed to the orthodox church's position that Christ had both a divine and a human nature. Monophysitism had many adherents during the sixth century including ANASTASIUS I and, reportedly, THEODORA.

MUNDUS (d 536)
General serving JUSTINIAN I. He was in Constantinople when the NIKA RIOTS broke out and assisted BELISARIUS in defeating the rioters.

NARD
Persian name for backgammon.

NARSES (c 478-573)
Served JUSTINIAN I both as chamberlain and general. A EUNUCH, he held administrative roles at court and was among those responsible for subduing the NIKA RIOTS. In 552 he was commander of the Roman forces which temporarily reconquered Italy.

NIKA RIOTS
Much of Constantinople was burnt down in 532 during these riots. They took their name from the mobs' cry of Nika! (Victory!) and almost led to the downfall of JUSTINIAN I.

NOMISMA (Plural: NOMISMATA)
Standard gold coin at the time of JUSTINIAN I.

NUMMI (Singular: NUMMUS)
Smallest copper coin in the early Byzantine period.

ON HORSEMANSHIP
See XENOPHON.

PATRIARCH
Bishop of the see of an eastern orthodox church.

PERISTYLE
Colonnade around a building or the four sides of a courtyard or similar enclosed space.

PLATO'S ACADEMY
Greek philosopher Plato (?428 BCE-347 BCE) founded his academy in 387 BCE. It was among pagan schools closed in 529 by order of JUSTINIAN I.

PORPHYRIUS (6th century)
Born in Libya, Porphyrius had a long and successful chariot-racing career, originally with the BLUES and then the GREENS, subsequently switching back and forth between them. Both teams erected statues honoring him on the SPINA of the HIPPODROME. He is said to have continued racing until into his sixties.

PRAETORIUM
Housed the administrative offices of the Prefect of the URBAN WATCH, courts, and a prison.

QUADRIGA
Chariot drawn by four horses harnessed abreast.

REDS
See FACTIONS.

RESHEPH
Ancient near-eastern god of pestilence.

SAMSUN'S HOSPICE
Founded by Samsun (d 530), a physician and priest. Also known as Sampson or Samson the Hospitable, he is referred to as the Father of the Poor because of his work among the destitute. His hospice was near the GREAT CHURCH.

SAUSAGES
Popular Roman dish. Spicy Lucanian sausages, said to have been brought to Rome by soldiers returning from service in Lucania in southern Italy, were considered the best type.

SCHOLARE (Plural: Scholarae)
Member of a ceremonial mounted military unit, composed largely of wealthy young courtiers.

SILENTIARY
Court official whose duties were similar to those of an usher.

STYX
River crossed by the souls of the dead in order to reach the underworld.

TESSERAE (Singular: tessera)
Small cubes, usually of stone or glass, utilized in the creation of mosaics.

THEODORA (c 497-548)
Influential wife of JUSTINIAN I, whom she married in 525. The contemporary writer Procopius alleges she had been an actress and a prostitute. Her father was said to have been a bear-keeper for the GREENS, a faction she subsequently supported.

THEODORIC (454-526; r Ostrogoths 471-526; r Italy 493-526)
Known as Theodoric the Great, he was educated in Constantinople, having been taken there as a diplomatic hostage at the age of eight. During his reign he favored Roman methods of government and law.

TREBIZOND
Important center of commerce located on the Asia Minor side of the Black Sea.

TUNICA
Under-garment.

URBAN WATCH
Responsible for maintaining public order and equivalent to a modern day city police force.

VITALIAN (d 520)
Defeated after leading a rebellion in Thrace against the MONOPHYSITE beliefs of ANASTASIUS I, Vitalian went into hiding in 515. When JUSTIN I became emperor in 518 Vitalian returned to Constantinople. Appointed consul in 520, he was murdered several months later at an imperial banquet. Popular rumor maintained JUSTINIAN I was responsible for his assassination.

XENOPHON (c 430 BCE-c 355 BCE)
Athenian soldier, historian, and author, his treatise ON HORSEMANSHIP is an outstanding work on equine training and care. Having fought on the side of the Spartans in their war with Athens, he was exiled and lived for some time in Sparta. Although his banishment was lifted, it is not known when or if he returned to Athens. The location and date of his death is uncertain.

To receive a free catalog of Poisoned Pen Press titles, please contact us in one of the following ways:

Phone: 1-800-421-3976
Facsimile: 1-480-949-1707
Email: info@poisonedpenpress.com
Website: www.poisonedpenpress.com

Poisoned Pen Press
6962 E. First Ave. Ste. 103
Scottsdale, AZ 85251

3 1115 00587 2048

NO LONGER THE PROPERTY OF
BALDWIN PUBLIC LIBRARY

BALDWIN PUBLIC LIBRARY
2385 GRAND AVENUE
BALDWIN, N.Y. 11510-3289
(516) 223-6228

DEMCO